I0823850

The HEIR *of* WHITESTONE

The HEIR of WHITESTONE

CATHERINE COULTER

KENSINGTON PUBLISHING CORP.
kensingtonbooks.com

JOHN SCOGNAGMIGLIO BOOKS are published by

Kensington Publishing Corp.
900 Third Avenue
New York, NY 10022

All Kensington titles, imprints, and distributed lines are available at special quantity discounts for bulk purchases for sales promotion, premiums, fund-raising, educational, or institutional use. Special book excerpts or customized printings can also be created to fit specific needs. For details, write or phone the office of the Kensington Special Sales Manager: Attn. Special Sales Department, Kensington Publishing Corp., 900 Third Avenue, New York, NY 10022. Phone: 1-800-221-2647.

The JS and John Scognamiglio Books logo is a trademark of Kensington Publishing Corp.

Library of Congress Control Number: On file

ISBN: 978-1-4967-6089-0
First Kensington Hardcover Edition: March 2026

ISBN: 978-1-4967-6091-3 (e-book)

10 9 8 7 6 5 4 3 2

Printed in the United States of America

The authorized representative in the EU for product safety and compliance
is eucomply OU, Parnu mnt 139b-14, Apt 123
Tallinn, Berlin 11317, hello@eucompliancepartner.com

Dear Reader,

It's 1842 in England. Queen Victoria has given birth to her first two children Victoria and Edward, and there are rats in Buckingham Palace and a horrible sewage system, projects for Prince Albert.

Alex Ivanov is a young innovator, improving train engines, born in Ukraine, only he really wasn't. When he was a boy he was dragged from the Thames, declared drowned. But Ryder Sherbrooke (the twelve-book Sherbrooke series) saves him, realizes this was no accident when he sees the boy was struck on the head, which means someone tried to kill him. The young boy has no memory of who he is, but Ryder knows he's a gentleman's son. Ryder makes him his ward, invents the Ukrainian background for him to make him "socially" accepted, educates him, loves him.

But who is he?

Enter Lady Camilla Rohman (Cam), the youngest daughter of the Earl of Whitsonby. She is smart, funny and desperate. She has a wicked stepmother, many years younger than her father, who is superb at using her "assets" to get her way. Cam also has a sister who gives her endless grief. Not to mention Lady Deveraux, her father's much older sister, who lives in the Royal Crescent in Bath, is deaf as a post and shouts everything. She tells Cam in detail about her former lovers, e.g., how Napoleon put his hand under her skirt. She, like all the characters, is smart and fun and won't stop talking.

Of course Cam and Alex, whose real name is Graham Hepburn, marry, and both are nearly killed on their honeymoon. You may believe you know who the killer is after the third attempt. But, hey, you're not there yet. Not quite.

There's humor and conflict, a heartwarming reunion between father (Vereker, Earl St. Lucy) and son (Viscount Whitestone) at King's Head, the family estate—near the Dover Coast.

There are characters you'll root for, characters you'll want to punch out, maybe even shoot, and then there's Ryder Sherbrooke, a major minor character, and an amazing man.

And don't forget—trains and theorems.

Enjoy, Catherine Coulter

CHAPTER 1

Graham lay very still in twilight darkness until the nausea lessened, a blessing, he didn't want to puke. He swallowed the horrible bile, felt his innards settle. At least his head didn't pound quite as much. When he'd awakened, he'd cried because his head had hurt so badly he thought he'd die. And what good had it done? None at all except make his cheeks itch with dried tears and now there was nothing he could do about it. His hands were tied behind his back.

He had to calm, he knew that, but it was so hard. He forced himself to breathe deeply, slowly, slowly, and a bit of the awful fear lessened. He realized he was in the hold of a boat, had to be small because it rocked gently side to side. He was probably in the hold of a skiff. How long had he been here slumped against rough boards, his wrists and ankles tied with stout hemp? Where was he?

Someone had hit him on the head, tied him up, brought him here.

How much time had passed?

Where was his brother? "Simon?"

He called out his brother's name again, and another time, but there was only the creaking of the boards beneath him.

He didn't want to, but he had to believe either Simon wasn't here with him or he couldn't answer him. *Or he was dead.* Graham felt shock, awful fear, no, no, maybe they'd gagged Simon after they'd struck him down like Graham. But wouldn't he have awakened by now? He knew he'd have heard his younger brother breathing, even gagged.

He called his name again, then again.

Simon's dead, Simon's dead.

He leaned back against the wooden hold wall, closed his eyes. In his gut he knew he could shout for help forever and no one would come and if someone did hear him, he wouldn't care.

Graham had to accept he was in deep trouble. Someone had done this to him. But why?

He was hungry and really thirsty now. Wait. He heard voices from above him on the deck of the skiff, then a louder man's voice, but he still couldn't understand the man's words. Were there two men? And they were arguing?

Calm, calm, he had to be calm and think. It only made sense he and Simon had been taken for ransom. Their father was wealthy. He would also be mad with fear, willing to pay any ransom to get his sons back. He knew to his soul his father would offer up his own life to save him and Simon. He felt tears choke his throat. Simon. No, he didn't have to be dead, maybe Simon was bound as he was and unconscious behind those wooden crates stacked opposite him, secured to the wall with stout rope on the other side of the hold.

He tried again to pull on the rope tying his wrists behind his back. Maybe he could roll over and over and open one of those crates, maybe find a knife, anything he could use to get himself free. He tugged and pulled forward and realized soon enough he couldn't roll anywhere. He could only move a foot from the wall because there was a rope securing his tied hands to the boards behind him. He pulled and pulled, but it was no good. He felt blood on his hands, felt wrenching pain in his shoulders and arms.

He couldn't give up, just couldn't. There had to be something, some way to get free—his thoughts turned back upon themselves, repeating over and over in a loop, and he finally felt frozen in place. Over and over he tried to think of who could have struck him down and brought him to this boat. And Simon? Of course he'd been struck down too. Had they been separated? But why? Why wouldn't the men have put them together?

Think, Graham.

It's not for ransom.

The men who'd struck him down and brought him here wanted something else, but what? He was fourteen years old, Simon thirteen. What could two boys give them if they weren't taken for ransom?

Simon is dead, they hit him too hard and he died. No, Graham couldn't, wouldn't accept that. How many hours had passed since he and Simon had been in the home wood arguing about the best position to hold a bow before letting an arrow fly, arguing as only two brothers could, calling each other names even as they ran back toward the shed where their bows and arrows were stored. Because Graham was fourteen months older than his brother, he was ahead of him. Then Simon had called out to him, and now Graham realized there'd been something strange in his voice. Did he want him to slow down? No, Simon would never say that, he'd only run his feet off to catch Graham. He'd stopped, ready to taunt Simon when suddenly, he'd been struck on the head and the world was gone.

Had Simon seen their attackers? And he'd called out to Graham, to warn him? How many men were there? There had to be at least two, one to bring down each brother. Without warning Graham felt his belly twist in on itself, not from nausea but from raw fear, for himself and his brother. He leaned over and vomited, dry heaves since he hadn't eaten since breakfast. When was breakfast? How long ago? One day, two? How long had he been tied here in the hold of this skiff?

Graham pictured his father's face, frantic with fear, searching everywhere, shouting their names, tearing up the countryside to find him and his brother, all their people, all St. Lucy Head's townspeople searching with him. But who would ever look on a small skiff? And where was the skiff? Bobbing in the waves near the cliffs in the Channel?

No, the skiff wasn't in the Channel. He'd sailed many times in and out of Sally's Cove. He knew how the waves flowed and rippled or soared high and deadly, and this wasn't it. This was slow, gentle rolling. But then where was he? Where was the skiff? How long had he been here?

Yet again Graham worked the ropes on his wrists, but there was still no give at all. If he stopped pulling and jerking on the knots, would the blood on his hands dry? He fell back against the wood-planked wall, and felt hope leach out of him.

Get yourself together, Graham, don't just sit there and give up. You use your magnificent brain. Come on, you're my son, you never give up.

Not his father's voice this time—it was his mother's, loud, insistent, right in his face. But his mother was dead, dead when he was only five years old, but he remembered her voice, the strength in her arms when she hugged him, her kisses on his cheek. And her laugh, full and happy and loud, and more kisses. He whispered, his voice thin and frightened, "Mother?"

Of course she wasn't there. He wanted to cry again, but wait—she'd told him to use his magnificent brain? He had a magnificent brain? If he hadn't felt so rotten, he would have laughed. No, no, be calm. Never panic. He felt new resolve, at least he believed it was resolve, one of his father's favorite words, or desperation, more like.

He gritted his teeth and pulled with all his strength. To his amazed surprise, he felt the board behind him split. He pulled away from the wall. He worked his bound wrists to the top of the board and off. He felt the rope dangle between his wrists. He managed to roll onto his side and began inching his way across the wooden floor, not more than eight feet away. The boards beneath him weren't even, jagged in places. The skiff was very old. He felt a nail rip into his shirt, and he yipped with pain, but kept inching. Slowly, awkwardly, he managed to push himself up and press his back against the boxes, breathing hard.

He said his brother's name. No answer. He whispered his brother's name, prayed. No answer.

He hadn't seen clearly from across the hold, but now he saw the stacked crates were tied with not one, but two ropes. One above his head. He felt his will crack. No, no, he had to somehow get the rope untied, he could do it, he had to, no choice, no choice. He was limber, skinny as a snake. He managed to scoot his tied hands under his butt and work out his legs until his hands were tied in front of him.

He felt elated. He began to work the knots with his teeth.

He heard footsteps, worked faster.

Light flooded the small hold.

A man's voice said, "Well now, aren't you a smart nit, got yourself free from the wall. Don't know how you managed to do that, but no matter. It's time to give it up." A stranger, an older man with a seamed, sun-weathered face, his tangled dark hair threaded with white, leaned over him. "Now, lad, you won't drown because you won't feel a thing. You'll just float away, forever."

"But why? Who are you—"

A heavy bar came down on his head.

CHAPTER 2

PRESENT

Outside Westminster Palace
London
March 1842
Tuesday

For someone who didn't know who he was, it didn't seem to bother Alex. He sat at his ease on an ancient wooden bench on the bank of the Thames outside Westminster Palace, his head tilted back to enjoy the precious sunshine, always a blessed event in England. Because he wasn't a dolt, an umbrella lay beside him on the bench next to his new hat and goat-leather gloves.

Alex smiled. He knew to his bones something was going to happen, something amazing. Although Ryder had said little, Alex knew he was excited too. It was hard, Ryder admitted, but Alex simply had to wait. He was vaguely aware of men's voices, none of them close enough to make out their words, all he knew for sure was none of the men were Ryder. He hated waiting, knowing he would bring him news, but what exactly the news would be, he didn't know. But he simply knew it was something grand. He clung to Ryder's words he'd overheard him saying to his wife, Sophie, before they'd come up to London. *If this happens, it will change his life.*

Change his life. Alex hummed with anticipation. He'd been Ryder's secretary for a year, and wasn't it strange he wasn't including him in his meetings with other members of Commons? He'd always sit in a corner taking notes, listening, to get the men's measure, to be discreet, charming and deferential. He was simply to watch these men and learn. And when he got bored, he could retreat into his brain and continue developing and cataloguing his ideas and design experiments for the train engine, and prepare prospectuses on costs to implement his ideas during the days and evenings when he wasn't otherwise engaged. But for now he was to observe. Alex had been mildly excited to be in the bowels of English government, but he quickly learned very little was ever accomplished. The gentlemen consumed gallons of tea since anything stronger was frowned upon in these august halls, and they spent most of their time gossiping about their peers, their hunting prowess and their mistresses. Ryder had only laughed at this observation, confided business that meant anything was done in small groups over port at White's. And Alex gave him his opinions of the various gentlemen, his estimate of the size of their brains and the thickness of their wallets and their level of willingness to side with Ryder on child labor laws.

It wasn't that the House of Commons met every day or so, which meant Alex spent most evenings at Ryder's club White's, again listening, observing, and he learned more than he'd ever imagined watching the gentlemen gamble.

But this trip was different. He thrummed with anticipation, with hope. Upon their arrival at Portman Square, the home of the Sherbrooke townhouse, Ryder had taken him to his tailor, Mr. Smythe-Jumper on Savile Row, to refresh his wardrobe, emphasis on evening garb. "An excellent tailor is a gentleman's best weapon," Ryder told him. "That and a brain." And he'd eyed Alex and nodded, buffeting his shoulder. "You are going to accomplish amazing things, Alex."

A precise, crisp girl's voice said from above him, smoothly and without pause, "You're going to turn red soon, maybe blister your too-handsome face, which means you're probably conceited, and would continue to be even though your face would be covered with nasty blisters. I will save you and hold my parasol over your face and thus you won't be taken for a herring and thrown into a cooking pot, though that probably wouldn't happen, not if ladies were around you, admiring you."

Too-handsome face? Alex had opened his eyes during this very smooth and pause-free monologue and looked up at a girl with rich chestnut hair plaited on top of her head in thick braids, an unusual style, one he hadn't seen before, but it suited her face. Her eyes were a clear hazel behind glasses that were sliding down her straight nose. She had a nice mouth currently grinning down at him like a sinner who'd filched the collection plate, and a stubborn chin, not at all dissimilar to his aunt Sophie's. She wore small gold earrings with a sapphire set in each.

He smiled, a devastating smile, she noted, and worked hard to be unmoved by that smile. He said, his voice all lazy and smooth, "Thank you, but a red face would be a small price to pay for the warmth and the sunshine. A herring isn't red, it's silver with a green back." He closed his eyes again just to see what she'd say next. He knew she wouldn't simply walk away, not this girl.

She said, "I believe you're quite wrong about herring, but I shall be magnanimous and let your incorrect observation float away, maybe swim away would be more apropos. My mother, who isn't here because she's in Heaven, always said it's important to enjoy the sun when it makes a surprise visit since it hates England and only comes out when Mother Nature forces it to.

"Since you look like a gentleman and speak like a gentleman, you should offer to hold the parasol over both of us."

Alex cracked open an eye again, patted the seat next to him. "Forgive me for not standing up as a gentleman should, but the lovely sun has melted my bones and I find I cannot move. So please sit down and we can sun-bask together, no parasol needed—just yet. Perhaps you can tell me why ladies aren't supposed to enjoy the sun on their faces."

"I don't understand it either, but it's something my companion and maid, well, my best friend for years upon years, always insists on, says she doesn't want me to look like a flower girl with a baked face, although I do love flowers."

Alex saw a footman, young, dressed in gold and dark blue, standing some six feet behind the young lady, his expression both agonized and stoic.

Well, it was true the chit wasn't behaving as a well-bred young lady should, speaking to him first, no introduction by an older very proper individual, and now she sat beside him, a perfect stranger in a rather plain day dress, arranging her dark gray skirts around her. Fortunately she wasn't wearing so many crinolines that her skirts would either cover his legs or push him off the bench. He saw a stout black leather walking shoe sticking out. She wore a darker finely stitched blue pelisse over her gown. He said, "Where is your chaperone? One usually doesn't see young ladies near the seat of government except for the queen and that's only once a year. Nor does one see ladies speaking to strange men without appropriate introductions, anywhere, for that matter."

Like him, she raised her face to the brilliant sun, gave a low hum of pleasure, and said without looking at him, "Since there is no one about to call me a floozy and Henry my footman would never say a word, I'm free to do what I wish, well, within bounds, naturally. Besides, you look like a well-mannered gentleman wearing very nice clothes and thus supposedly safe to a young lady's virtue. Since there is no one proper to give us an introduction, I will take matters into my own hands." She looked at him now, gave him a big grin showing straight white teeth. "I wanted to see the blue of your eyes up close. There are so many different blue shades, quite remarkable really, a startling blue, a vivid blue I've never seen before. Mayhap they're a wild blue like an animal might have in the wild. Actually, to be honest, your eyes highlight your too-handsome face. With those eyes, even with your dark hair, it's impossible not to think of a pirate on the high seas, looking for prey."

She finally stopped, took a breath. Alex was mesmerized. He had startling blue eyes? Wild? Well, all right, his eyes had been remarked upon before, frequently, actually, and always by girls who always seemed to be close. All he cared about was his eyes could see very nicely, thank you. A pirate? Too-handsome face?

"As to my virtue, if you annoy me, I will crook my finger and my footman Henry will rush over to trounce you—well, he would try, bless his heart. Although Henry would be fierce, I daresay I could take him down myself. Why are you here, all indolent like a lizard sitting on a rock? Shouldn't you be at one of the gentlemen's clubs drinking a lovely snifter of French brandy or perhaps reading Homer to improve your mind?"

CHAPTER 3

Alex eyed this mouthy young lady. "I'm waiting for my guardian. And you?"

She said readily, "I'm here to meet my father. Well, to be honest, I'm surprising him. He doesn't expect me since I'm supposed to be on my way to Bath to visit Aunt Deveraux, who is quite deaf and yells and all the neighborhood hears her and doubtless enjoys her endless tales of seduction back in the olden days when she was young. Her cook, Mrs. Tartle, makes the most marvelous loganberry scones, a miracle all agree. As I said, she is quite deaf and you have to shout in her ear, my aunt, not Mrs. Tartle, then back away quickly because she can't hear herself either so when she talks, she bellows. My ears are ringing within a day, close to deaf by the end of my visits." She paused, smiled. "Ah, her stories, yes, they really are quite naughty, perhaps I'd have to go as far as to say occasionally prurient, like the time she drank absinthe with Napoleon and he put his hand up her skirt. Everyone in the neighborhood enjoyed that story. Did I tell you she also keeps the windows open, even in the winter, so perhaps her stories reach the Roman Baths. But truthfully, she's repeated the same stories since I was twelve so now I could tell them to her, no detail left out." She paused, sighed.

Alex eyed her, fascinated. "Really? Napoleon put his hand up her skirt? Where was Josephine? Weren't there others about?"

"Well, certainly, but Aunt Deveraux said he had no shame and quite the roving eye and not a single brake on his lust, and then she giggles." Cam frowned. "Although she didn't say, perhaps Josephine was sitting on his other side and Napoleon had his other hand up her skirts as well.

"To be honest, I quite enjoy her, but you see there's Pilcher Gayson. I heard Pilcher say to his older brother that he, Sydney, could have London and the House of Lords once their father departed our earthly climes and he became Baron Riggs of Blythe Point, and isn't that a pretentious name for a property? As for Pilcher, all he wants is to marry me for my impressive dowry, save his father from financial difficulties, which I understand are soon to be very grave, and hunt. I must be honest here, Pilcher is appalling."

"Appalling? Wanting you to marry him for your money, yes, that's appalling, but you don't mean that. Tell me, why exactly?"

"Pilcher chews on his fingernails, smacks his lips while he's eating halibut, and the worst, the most unforgivable?" She leaned closer. "He waltzes like a lame ostrich. No, wait, I must rethink that. I'm wrong, the very worst is his appalling name—Pilcher—too close to pilchard, you know, that oily fish the Cornish make into stargazy pie. I see you're not familiar with stargazy pie. The pilchards' heads line the crust so they're staring up at you, supposedly at the sky, hence the stargazy name." She shuddered. "I ask you, would you name your son Pilcher?"

"No, I most certainly would not," Alex said, trying not to laugh. "You're right about his name, better Cod or Herring than Pilcher. I've never seen nor heard of stargazy pie."

She grinned at him, pleased to her toes, and found it nearly impossible not to stare at those amazing blue eyes of his. From his father? His mother? Maybe from Zeus? She said, "I've never seen one either and I don't want to. I'm told they originated in Mousehole, a small fishing village in Cornwall.

"Yes, Cod of Herring as a name is an improvement. His older brother, Sydney, has excellent manners, dances well, but alas, he has horrid breath because he eats garlic in his breakfast eggs, brags it keeps him slim."

She closed her eyes and turned her face up to the sun. She said without moving, "So because of Pilcher, I really don't want to go back to Bath and that's why I'm here to talk Papa around to my way of thinking. But Averil—she's my new stepmama—she wants me out of her house. She holds powerful sway over Papa. It is painful to watch, I mean Papa is old—not without-his-teeth old—but you know what I mean. He's my father, not a young buck. Averil believes Pilcher is the perfect answer to my problems since I'm rather in a social pickle at the moment because I clouted Teddy Jewel, the toad, for trying to kiss me and put his hand down—well, never mind that. She's hopeful no one in Bath has heard of my physical attack on poor Teddy The Toad and that's why I'm to be exiled. I'm an embarrassment, she says in addition to being violent, and just because a gentleman lost his head in a single moment of seeing only the barest hint of my bosom."

Alex stared at her and yet again admired her perfectly wonderful monologue to him, a perfect stranger. She was telling him things he really shouldn't be hearing, but then again, maybe she was an exception. He was riveted. She was tall, not at all the fashion since the new queen Victoria wasn't even five feet tall. But like the little queen, this girl was slender as a sapling. He said, "When your father sees you here, what will he do?"

"If he's with his cronies he'll behave as though he expected to see me and smile and be all jovial. And then when we're alone I daresay he'll try to burn my ears even though he'll want to laugh because he wouldn't want to spend time with Aunt Deveraux. She's his much older sister, at least fifteen years older, and this is amazing—she still has her own teeth. She is always giving him unwanted advice and I know he wants to throttle her, but of course he merely smiles and nods." She paused, sighed. "Then Papa will try to scold me because he knows he must since I'm a lady now and no longer a saucy little girl because Averil will make him."

Sadly, the sun went behind a dark cloud that surely hadn't been in the sky but a moment before and a raindrop hit the top of her parasol. Alex quickly opened his umbrella, held it over both of them.

"Thank you," she said, and folded her parasol. "I don't wish to destroy this lovely Christmas present I gave to my sister but she tossed it in the dust bin. Actually, Eliza would like to smack me most of the time, or ignore me. I've never understood why. My maid and companion, Cilly, thinks Eliza didn't want me to be born since she was the princess of the house, but I was born and I'm here and Papa loves me." She turned, called out, "Henry, take shelter and have no worries. This gentleman will stay on the righteous path." The footman, no older than Alex, gave her a pained look and dashed toward a building portico.

"Righteous path? You mean, unlike Napoleon, I won't put my hand under your skirt?"

CHAPTER 4

She cocked a perfectly arched brow at him, gave him a shameless grin. How odd to be sitting beside a strange girl holding an umbrella over the both of them and Alex didn't know her name nor she his. He had little experience with well-spoken, obviously aristocratic girls like this one, but—his mind skipped to the lovely Jayne, introduced to him by his uncle Ryder so she could teach him what was what and make him believe in heaven. When in London, he always visited Jayne, brought her presents and prodigious enthusiasm, knew enough now to give her a little slice of heaven as well. He blinked. "I apologize. My name is—he paused, grinned to himself, and said, "Alexi Alejandro Ivanov."

Her lovely arched eyebrow climbed up again, just above her glasses' frame. "Alexi? Are you Greek? Russian?"

Alex's voice was smooth as a creek stone as he smoothly recited his history he and Ryder had created for him before he'd gone to Oxford. *Money, title and mysterious beginnings, are what is needed,* Ryder had said, and rubbed his hands together. Alex said, "I am originally from Kiev. However, you can call me Alex, most do."

"Your middle name is Alejandro? Are you also Spanish? A

mongrel of sorts? Are you a heathen? Come now, is such a name really from the Ukraine?"

"Oh yes."

"Hmm, Ivanov sounds quite quixotic, not at all what one would expect, not one of our common herd of names. Ivanov, your name melts on the tongue like ice cream. I prefer Alexi as well, but since we are in England, sharing an umbrella under an English sky, I shall call you Alex. I'm Camilla, but most call me Cam, except my sister who never calls me anything unless she's forced to because she says I'm skinny, nothing but a bother, and homely, and my worst sin? I wear glasses in public, even at balls, and that is surely an affront to our father's name." She sighed. "My stepmama calls me Camilla and I know she agrees with my sister." She shoved her glasses back up her nose and tried to look indifferent, and failed.

Alex said slowly, studying her face, "I can say with perfect honesty you are not ugly. As for your glasses, they make you look distinctive, make your eyes look quite mysterious. I like them. Should you like me to smack your sister?"

She laughed. "My sister is strong, not as strong as I am, but still, she'd likely smack you back. Well, no she wouldn't, she would think you far too handsome, very possibly right proper husband material, depending of course on your financial situation and your bloodline. I've seen paintings of monarchs and their families. So many are married to this or that royal cousin and mix their bloodlines and produce ugly and quite revolting offspring. Have you noticed this?"

"I cannot disagree with your assessment. One thinks of pharaohs in ancient Egypt marrying their sisters. It makes the common man of the time seem quite intelligent."

She gave him an approving look. "That was rather elegantly stated. Even though no one cares, you still made yourself sound like a deep sort with unplumbed depths. I shall try to remember what you said, however, and try to cleverly insert it into a conversation. Imagine, marrying your sister." Cam sighed. "Alas, if you were my sister Eliza's brother I doubt not she would be sorrowful at the connection given you look like a god. Even now, engaged, I know she would look at you and sigh, but believe me, she would never leave poor Winstead Towbridge, her fiancé. Don't get me wrong, Winstead is really quite fine-looking and nice. It is a pity."

"I do not look like a god, that is absurd. Why is it a pity?"

"Because Winstead—she calls him Winnie—can you imagine how demeaning that is? Well, he's a very nice man and my sister isn't. My father wanted to present me to the queen, but Averil, my stepmother, argued I would embarrass him and my poor sister, not to mention Winstead and his very well-received family. She tells my father over and over I would fit in better if I went to live with Aunt Deveraux in Bath, forever, or on a small island in the South Seas, if she could manage it."

Amazing. She'd spit that all out in a single breath. He said, "Your stepmother's name is Averil? An odd name. Perhaps she's a heathen? Just as I am? Did she raise you? Were you an unpleasant child?"

"Oh, she didn't raise either me or my sister or my brother, Bryant, who thankfully is ten years my senior and lives in Boston of all places, and runs a shipping business. So Papa had scarce met her when they wed and she moved into the London house with her maid, Elvira, who is as nasty as her mistress. Averil is twenty-six and considers herself the most lovely and desirable woman in London, maybe in all of Southern England, Northern France as well. I think she made up the name to be special. Maybe her real name is Maude or Jezebel." She sighed, pushed up her glasses. "My father thinks she's perfect. I don't know what my brother thinks, he came for the wedding but returned to Boston as fast as he could."

"Well, perhaps she is perfect, to your father."

"I don't think it's her character he admires, it's something else entirely. Aunt Deveraux whispered to me at their wedding, at the top of her lungs, that Averil is a seductress and she undoubtedly stuck out her—goodness, I can't say that to a strange man, to any man for that matter, even my brother, Bryant—so I'll be circumspect and say she stuck her upper parts in his face and Papa was a goner. He never used to retire for the night as early as he does now.

"I do try to be nice to her since Papa is so happy, but it is difficult. Look, here comes my papa walking with another gentleman, but I can't really see who it is because of their umbrellas."

"Would you like to meet the gentleman with your father? He's my guardian."

"Oh dear, I've let my tongue run on greased wheels and I don't know why you're here in England and not in Kiev and have an ever-so-romantic name. And a guardian." As she spoke, she rose to stand beside him and he wasn't surprised she came to his nose. He wouldn't get a crick in his neck waltzing with her. Strange thought. He held the umbrella over both of them.

She cocked her head at him, shoved up her glasses again. He wasn't particularly surprised when Camilla—Cam—looked at him up and down and observed, "Since you appear to have no obvious nasty habits, I imagine you are very popular at all the balls and soirees. You really are remarkably handsome and blessedly tall, but then again, maybe you're the repellent sort who kicks his dog, or you have other nasty habits."

Alex smiled, nothing else to do. "No, my dogs always slept with me, pushed me to the edge of the bed. What is an obvious nasty habit? You mean like some of Pilcher's shortcomings?"

She shuddered. "Nothing could be as repulsive as Pilcher's bad habits. Let me see—there is smoking those nasty cigars that make your breath smell like soiled sheets. You have very nice breath so smoking isn't a bad habit."

He stared at her, mesmerized. "Very true. What else?"

"Belching at the dinner table."

"Don't ladies belch occasionally?"

"If a lady belched in company, she'd be exiled to America to cook whale blubber."

Alex spurted out a laugh. "That sounds very severe." He wanted her to keep listing nasty habits, but she said, "Even if you were a heathen and had nasty habits, I doubt it would matter."

"Why?"

"Because you're a treat to the eyes, that's why, as I already told you—as if you didn't know. If you're to be considered good husband material, however, you must have at least a smidgeon of blue blood and a goodly number of groats in your pockets." She paused a moment. "For ladies, I've learned it's what's on the outside that really counts. If a lady has both groats and a lovely face she can attach a duke, but he just might be doddering with no teeth. I'm also told a lady must make a gentleman feel like a god. Can you imagine?"

He slowly shook his head. "I can't imagine. Come along and let me introduce you to my guardian."

"That would be lovely. And you'll meet my father. Isn't he fine-looking? Tall and straight, no paunch for him. Is he more fine-looking than your guardian? I really can't tell yet."

"My guardian could charm the socks off a monkey."

She burst into laughter.

The sun sailed out from behind a cloud at that moment.

CHAPTER 5

Ryder Sherbrooke looked up to see Alex walking beside a tall young lady he'd never seen before. And here he'd left Alex sitting comfortably on a bench but an hour before, by himself. He shook his head, Sophie wouldn't be surprised. She'd told him most every young unmarried girl in Upper Slaughter was in love with Alex. When Ryder had laughed, she told him so far Alex had received twelve pairs of knitted socks and so many hand-embroidered handkerchiefs with his initials he'd had to pile them on the top of his clothes' chest at the foot of his bed. And all the children made great sport, teasing him mercilessly.

Ryder was only half listening to his friend, Harold Augustus Rohman, Lord Whitsonby, Whit to his friends, his blue blood mixing nicely with his business acumen. He was blissfully remarried to a remarkably pretty lady, so Ryder had heard, and much younger than he was. Whit stopped in his diatribe on the influence of Lord Melbourne over the young queen, sighed when he recognized the lady striding beside a strange man coming toward them, shook his head, said, his voice philosophical, "Ah, here comes my youngest daughter, Camilla. I must admit to you I'm not surprised she's here and not on her way to Bath." Whit sighed. "She's here to talk me around to her side, something she's quite good at. I tried to tell Averil she wouldn't go, but go she must, according to my wife, for her sister's sake, and why was that I wondered. Forgive me for airing personal matters. Ah, I wonder who that young man is. A tall chap, handsome I suppose, well dressed, looks like a young gentleman. I don't believe I've ever met him before. At least Henry is close, ready to attack if the young man becomes forward, not that my daughter would need his assistance. Cam smacked young Teddy Jewel's nose, giving him a nosebleed. He was newly down from Oxford and feeling his oats and the idiot tried to pull her behind a statue in the garden." He sighed again. "She is so very friendly, you see, and some gentlemen can easily form the wrong impression. Her mother—ah, stepmother—despairs of her, tells me Camilla will be lucky to attach a clerk in the city if she doesn't learn to shut her mouth and become more pleasant to look at, like her sister, Eliza. Myself, I think Cam looks like her mother, my glorious Tansia, a beauty to her bones, she was, but of course I can't very well say that to my bride. I can but hope my Averil will come to appreciate my remarkably smart daughter. But oil and water, that's what they are and I don't know which is which." And Whit shrugged elegant shoulders, laughed. "Not that it matters. Ladies are an enigma and will remain so, I doubt not, for the next millennia and beyond. Maybe forever."

Ryder said, "I'm pleased to inform you there is no need to worry about the young man with your daughter, Whit. He is my ward, Alex Ivanov, the young gentleman I mentioned to you who excels in improving existing mechanical technology, trains his main interest. You'll find him very well behaved and very smart."

Whit looked thoughtful. "You also said he has amazing financial intuition. What do you mean exactly?"

"Alex has the ability to determine if a proposed project is

viable and if it has a good chance to be profitable. He is able to calculate costs remarkably well. Like you, as I said, he is very interested in trains and improving the working parts, making them safer and more efficient. He recognized them as our future when he was only a lad and newly arrived on our shores." It was enough. Ryder had primed the pump, Whit was hooked.

Whit never took his eyes off his approaching daughter. "You said his parents sent him to you from Ukraine during their revolution. So many uprisings in that part of the world, one cannot keep up. Ah, too much heated blood, unlike the English, a steady bunch, hot-blooded only in the bedroom and on the battlefield. A pity his parents didn't survive. However did you meet them?"

Ryder said smoothly, "I met Nicola and Maria Ivanov in Paris after Waterloo. It was my pleasure to welcome their only son into my home. It was good for him to be around all my other children at Brandon House as he was grieving and lonely when he arrived in England." He knew Whit was too polite to ask if his parents had sent funds with him.

Whit said, "I'd forgotten your penchant for picking up st—er, abandoned children. An excellent thing, of course, albeit rather odd. Naturally, you are to be commended."

Of course Ryder was commended and not derided since he was, after all, the Honorable Ryder Sherbrooke, an earl's second son, brother of the current Earl of Northcliffe, a very powerful gentleman in the government and in Society. He imagined Whit wanted to know if Alex had picked up criminal bad habits from the orphans in his care, but he said only, "With his permission, we changed his name from Alexi Ivanov to Alex Ivanov. In any case, Alex gives me great pleasure as he does all the children. As I mentioned to you, he is not only an amiable young man, and his love of trains is, of course, one of your passions. He is also well on his way to becoming rich with his financial investments." Had he primed the pump too much?

"Hello, sir."

"Ah, Alex, I'd like you to meet the Earl of Whitsonby."

Alex gave him a crisp bow, perfectly executed since Sophie had taught him. "My lord."

Whit eyed him up and down and nodded slowly. He turned to his daughter. "And, Ryder, this is my youngest daughter, Lady Camilla Rohman. Camilla, Mr. Sherbrooke."

She gave Ryder a lovely curtsey. "Sir, it is a pleasure to meet you. Alex tells me you can charm the socks off a monkey."

Ryder laughed, couldn't help himself.

Cam liked his laugh, full and rich, an honest, robust laugh. Mr. Sherbrooke was tall, sapling slender and straight, blue eyes and lovely silver threading through his dark hair. He was handsome, but not as handsome as her papa. "Sir, have you ever wished you weren't the second son and thus the Earl of Northcliffe?"

"Cam!"

Ryder was charmed and amused. "No, never. Thankfully God spared me from that fate, Lady Camilla. My brother fills the role splendidly and I am free of all his endless string of complications and expectations. He works two secretaries to the bone."

She nodded in approval, the minx.

Whit hugged his daughter, set her back, gave her a little shake. "Well, my pet, not in Bath, are you? I should forbid you the library for a fortnight, but"—he sighed—"knowing you I cannot say this is a surprise. Fact is I didn't want you to leave. Even Averil can't rub my shoulders like you do, dig in deep to all those tight muscles, or sing to me after dinner while playing a Scottish ballad and make the world seem less repellent, not to mention your creative retelling of the Myth of Sisyphus. Ah, I can't understand why Averil doesn't enjoy it. All right, tell me how you managed to sneak out of the house before Averil could catch you."

Cam said matter-of-factly, "Papa, you know she wouldn't try to catch me, she'd push me out the door, lock it after me and say good riddance. Henry saw me and followed to keep me safe, so please do not berate him."

Whit looked pained. "I do wish you would try to get along with your stepmother, but that's neither here nor there—enough airing of our private family matters—and that's my second apology to Mr. Sherbrooke. Now, Cam, however do you come to be in the company of this young man?"

The young man, Alex, was charmed. The daughter spoke with the wit and depth of her father. One would likely know these two after only one meeting. Cam gave him a grin, turned to her father. "It began to rain and Mr. Ivanov very gallantly offered to shield me with his umbrella. It was quite impossible not to introduce ourselves, even chat a bit. Everything proceeded quite properly and Henry remained all attention at my elbow, on the alert, ready to pound Mr. Ivanov if he became improper."

Well used to his daughter's verbal agility since she'd inherited it from him, Whit didn't have much trouble keeping to the point.

"Now, Daughter, you came here to find me, your plan to convince me to take your side and allow you to remain in London."

"Well, if you must boil my motives down to the bleached bones of absolute truth, yes, sir." And she took a step closer to her father, her mother's beautiful eyes on his face. "Papa, you're my only hope."

CHAPTER 6

Whit knew he was no match for those eyes of hers, his beloved Tansia's witch eyes, and saved himself, at least for the moment. "We will speak of this later, in private." He immediately turned to Alex. "Your guardian and I are dining with Elijah, Lord Carberry, this evening. I think you would make a fine addition to the dinner table. Carberry is not only very rich, he is also always on the lookout for excellent investment opportunities, particularly being part of the amazing train transformation here in England. Perhaps you and your guardian and I could discuss appropriate matters before we adjourn to Carberry's and I can provide more details."

Ryder knew this was coming, nodded. "An excellent suggestion. We're staying at the Sherbrooke townhouse, Whit, on Portman Square."

Alex said, "Sir, I read of your plans to extend the Cumberland railroad line into Leeds, an ambitious undertaking given the topography."

Ryder, not surprised at Alex's knowledge, kept his mouth shut, watched Whit beam, take a step toward Alex. "Ah, yes, I am on the committee to plan the actual route now we have sufficient investors. But you know, some of the gentlemen have socks for brains and believe it quite simple—buy the land, lay tracks, build train cars, shave off the tops of those hillocks and off you go—but naturally it's not simple. As you said, the topography is challenging." He paused, thought a moment, said slowly, "I'm also considering forming a consortium of investors to build more efficient trains and incorporating more efficient designs and materials for the route. I look forward to speaking to you about your train part designs."

Alex was so excited it was hard to keep his voice smooth. He wanted to dance, mayhap sing one of the obscene ditties he'd learned at Oxford. He managed not to sound as excited as he felt. He gave Lord Whitsonby a short bow. "I look forward to it, sir."

Whit eyed the young man, wondered if Ryder might let him take over Alex's guardianship. Probably not. He said, "I must warn both of you. Lord Carberry's brother-in-law, James Piercebridge, is a vicar from St. Lucy Head in Kent, not two miles from the English Channel. He will be present at the dinner table. I'm told it is his twice-a-year visit to London, a city he considers full of sin and debauchery. To warn you bluntly, evidently Vicar Piercebridge believes a man who seeks to enrich himself through business is the devil's tool and bound for Hell's fires. Thus, whenever he visits his sister here in London he tries to whip poor Carberry into shape. We will simply leave him to his tea—he won't drink port, it is too wicked."

Ryder said, "So warned. As you know, the earl, my brother, is very much involved in investing and putting in use new farming machinery. His tenant farmers bless the ground he walks on. Douglas says idiots who proclaim a gentleman doesn't dirty his hands making money will rue the day since change is coming, fast, to England, and all those men clinging to outdated beliefs will be smashed."

Cam said, "But what about forcing ladies to cling to outmoded beliefs, Father? For instance couldn't ladies be involved in business dealings as well?"

Dead silence.

Although Whit scented danger, he said, "My dearest Averil believes ladies should not involve themselves in such things, it lessens their true worth." What was perfectly clear, but left unspoken because Whit didn't want a bloodbath in front of Westminster Palace, was *when they wed, it is their husbands who decide what is and isn't acceptable.*

Ryder said easily, eyeing Whit's daughter with approval, "My wife, Sophie, not only manages our household accounts, she also has a very sharp brain and also an eye for a promising venture."

Alex said, "That's very true. She's given me excellent advice when I receive a prospectus on improving tools for shearing sheep, for example."

Her voice admirably calm, Cam said, only a hint of a sneer, "Papa, this change you speak of, everything sounds the same to me, at least where ladies are concerned."

Whit wasn't stupid, he got his brain together and said, "My pet, I must get you home and smooth all the ruffled feathers. Ryder, Alex, I will see you both this evening."

Alex imagined the carriage ride home with Lord Whitsonby would be very interesting what with the father trying to convince his daughter to fall into line. But would he push all that hard? Alex had seen the pride of the father for his daughter, but would his lordship defend her to his new wife? He'd simply never considered a lady involving herself in business. Fact was, though, he'd always taken Sophie's counsel for granted, and Jayne's too of course, hadn't even thought to question it because of their sex. Both of them were highly intelligent and competent. Without them Brandon House would be vastly different, and not for the better. He remembered the virulent fever he'd caught that had swept through Upper Slaughter. Both Jayne and Sophie had nursed him, spent hours with him, saved him, not the ancient local doctor who'd wanted to bleed him. It made him wonder what Ryder would say to Camilla Rohman if he were her father.

He remembered clearly at Oxford it was never questioned that males were the superior sex, that their rules, their pronouncements, ran the world. Of course a man was expected to marry eventually to produce children and have as many mistresses as he could afford, with discretion, of course, since he was a gentleman. But if men did allow women to involve themselves in business, what would happen to children and to households without the wife to oversee them? It made his brain ache to think of it.

As Alex rode in a hackney beside Ryder to Portman Square and the Sherbrooke townhouse, he knew to his bones Camilla Rohman was a force to be reckoned with, like Sophie and Jayne. He wondered if her father would give her business lessons on the sly.

CHAPTER 7

Whitsonby Home
Ormond Square
Tuesday

Whit watched his wife, Averil, Lady Whitsonby, pace his study, a room unchanged since he'd assumed the title when he was twenty-five. Averil rarely visited his study because he knew she found it ridiculously old-fashioned, but of course she'd never say that aloud since she knew it was a product of his first wife's taste. He'd accidentally heard her true opinion when she'd showed the room to a friend not realizing he was seated by the fireplace in a high-backed chair facing the fireplace. "Just look, Imogene—Egyptian clawed feet on the sofa and scrolled arms on every chair, all ridiculous shapes and colors, so awfully foreign, ah, but what can I do? My dear husband claims to like it." She'd laughed. "But maybe not for much longer. After all, the past is the past."

He'd allowed her free rein in their bedchamber. He still found it disconcerting to walk into the room to see a series of gilded mirrors set like a line of soldiers at her eye level along two walls against silk wallpaper with endless scenes of shepherdesses and sheep, so many sheep. He always saw his neck, which he admitted, gave him the opportunity to adjust his neckcloth.

He and Cam had arrived home only ten minutes before. Averil had taken one look at Camilla, then ignored her and asked in a very sweet voice if his lordship would please accompany her to their bedchamber. Even if he'd been blind and deaf, Whit would have known she was angry. Her walk was stiff, her hands fists at her sides. Because he was a man, he couldn't simply allow his wife to dictate to him, particularly in the servants' hearing, and so he told his wife he would speak to her in ten minutes in his study. He then turned to Cam and tried to make his voice commanding. "Go to your bedchamber, we will speak later."

Cam smiled up at him and said low, "*Bonne chance*, Papa."

Of course he knew he needed all the good luck God would see fit to bestow on him. When he strolled—a slow stroll—into his study ten minutes later, it was to see Averil eyeing the rendering of the first train in England, the locomotion #1 built by George and Robert Stephenson in 1825. Ah, he clearly remembered his excitement. Next to it was a drawing of Euston Station built but four years before, with the line running from Birmingham to London. Next to that one, his favorite, the Deptford Train Station built in 1836, providing the first passenger service. He'd been a vital part of both projects and was justifiably proud. Then there was the portrait of his first wife, Tansia, painted after Camilla's birth centered over the fireplace. She'd been dead now for many years, dying in childbed with their small son. It didn't hurt to think about her anymore, or the babe. But still, whenever he walked into his study, he still automatically looked at her portrait, her beautiful laughing face, and even though he'd remarried, his memories remained strong. Magical Tansia.

Averil whirled to face him. "She's a disobedient bitch, Whit! You always give in to her, always. Look at this latest fiasco—

she disobeyed you, blatantly. The girl is a termagant, a disgrace. You must lock her in her room, for at least a week. You must teach her to do what she's told. And then you must send her to Bath. Of course she has to come back for her sister's wedding, but afterward, the next day, she will leave again."

Whit watched her take a single breath, a very deep breath, and knew to his bones she wasn't done, she was just winding up. A stray thought popped into his head—could he write a ditty about oil and water and which would win in a contest? He thought of how funny a song Cam would write—

His wife's furious voice brought him back. "She's an embarrassment to both me and her poor sister. My sweet Eliza, always admired for her lovely smile and lovely disposition, must always apologize to other ladies and gentlemen for her behavior." Averil gave a delicate shudder. "Her most recent embarrassment, as you very well know, was just last Tuesday at the Biddlefords' musicale when she struck poor young Teddy Jewel in the jaw. All the ladies were appalled."

He did indeed know since she'd reminded him at least three times. Whit couldn't help it, he grinned, said without thinking, "It was rather amusing, really. Cam has an excellent right hook. How I wish I'd seen her clip him and—" He stopped in his tracks because he wasn't stupid. He cleared his throat, hoping it was over, but alas, Averil burst out, "It was not amusing. I was mortified as was Eliza. Imagine, a supposed young lady creating such a scene and the young gentleman hadn't really done anything at all offensive and it was Camilla's fault in any case. She shouldn't have gone out with him onto the balcony to supposedly see the full moon—"

Whit said, "*Young* gentleman? Jewel isn't young, he's thirty years old if he's a day, and he tried to slide his ungloved hand down her gown. What should she have done? Unfasten her corset to give him better purchase? And he followed her outside, Averil. The incident would have gone unremarked if he hadn't spilled everything to his mother when she questioned him about his bruised jaw. Then he lied, told her how Camilla Rohman had punched him for no reason at all."

"Come, Whit, no one believes the absurd reason she claims made her strike him. It is patent nonsense. Camilla made that up to try to defend her actions, to excuse her hitting him. Teddy is a gentleman. If he was perhaps too enthusiastic, it is only because he expects to marry her, however unlikely that seems to me."

Of course Teddy Jewel wanted to marry her, her dowry was splendid and Teddy was in need of money, always. He said, "Teddy doesn't have a chin. A thirty-year-old man shouldn't be called Teddy. That name's for a spaniel or a four-year-old. It's as bad as Eliza calling her future husband Winnie rather than by his name, Winstead; Winnie sounds like a demned horse being called to come eat his oats."

Averil marched right up to him and stuck out her lovely sculpted, rounded chin. "Whit, listen to me, it makes no matter if Teddy's chin isn't exactly what one would prefer. Ah, not all gentlemen can be as handsome as you, my dear." She shrugged. "Come now, your daughter could close her eyes."

Whit wondered—did Averil close her eyes? No, he was a fine figure of a man, albeit not quite as spry as he'd been at Teddy Jewel's age, the idiot.

Another breath, this one deeper, longer, perhaps her tirade had run its course. She stepped even closer, smiled up into his eyes as she pressed in her arms to push up her breasts, made her offering.

And she had him.

He was staring at her beautiful plump breasts, so enticingly displayed, right there. He wanted to lick her breasts, press his face against the incredible white soft flesh. She wanted him; he could tell by her quickened breathing. Surely her diatribe was done.

He was wrong.

CHAPTER 8

Her breasts in full bloom, his attention firmly riveted, Averil lightly laid her hand on his shoulder, even managed to soften her voice. "My love, to be honest, until Teddy Jewel showed an interest in Camilla, I despaired of her wedding at all despite her very impressive dowry. She is off-putting. Teddy Jewel is a gift from God. Well, if not Teddy, of course there is Pilcher Gayson in Bath. He's a possibility. According to your sister, he is much taken with her. She could choose which gentleman she preferred once she understands from you what she is expected to do."

"She is only nineteen, Averil. She's had only one Season. I happen to agree with her that there are no gentlemen hanging about who are worthy of her. If they find her off-putting, as you say, then she finds them equally unacceptable. I believe she said of Lord Steven, Plaxen's son, that he was a dead bore whose only interest was in his waistcoat buttons." He paused. "She'll be presented to the queen next month."

The presentation to the queen—that burned hot because Averil herself hadn't been accorded that honor, despite her marriage to an important, well-regarded peer. She plowed on. "As I said, most appropriate young men are put off by her. She readily voices her opinions and they're usually contrary. She sharpens her wit on them, which I've told her over and over she must not do because no gentleman wants to be out-talked and out-argued by a female, particularly a young one who has no sense. If she doesn't marry, Whit, you know she'll be a millstone around our necks." Dramatic pause. "Forever."

But she's only nineteen. The words remained unspoken. His eyes riveted on her magnificent breasts, the sinking man finally managed to murmur, "Cam makes me laugh with her sharp wit. She is very funny and smart and when she offers an opinion, it is well thought-out."

"She may be smart, but not in the right way. It's a very big drawback. And her striking a gentleman for being a bit too affectionate! If she doesn't curb her tongue, I strongly doubt she can bring either Pilcher Gayson or Teddy Jewel to the mark, and that means you'll be forced to find a gentleman in great need of money to make living with her worth it or, as I said, she'll remain at home, a spinster, seated with other spinsters and companions lining the wall of ballrooms. She will be an object of ridicule and pity. And all will regard you in the same way. Think of poor Eliza and her future."

Inspiration struck. Whit said, "Listen, my love, not all young gentlemen are put off by her. Why she met a young man today at Westminster who seemed quite impressed with her wit."

Averil rolled right over him. "I knew it. She came to plead with you, didn't she? To let her stay in London? Of course she did. And she found a man? A clerk? A secretary? A perfect stranger of no account at all, yes, of course, and doesn't that just prove my point. She has no sense, Whit, taking up with a man with no chaperone. You must hold firm. We mustn't let Teddy escape, but if he does, we must make her encourage Pilcher Gayson in Bath. Both are proper gentlemen.

"And the queen? If Camilla doesn't keep her mouth shut, the queen will not approve of her, and just what would be the consequences to you politically? And me socially?" She saw some from his expression she needed more.

Breasts on full display. "Listen, my love, Teddy is the heir to Viscount Dawes and there is some old family money, I inquired. Pilcher is the second son of the current Baron Riggs. His brother will take the title of course, and I'm told there is also sufficient family money. I know one of them is her only means of salvation. She would eventually become Lady Dawes or Mrs. Gayson.

"I believe we could offer her a choice—invite dear Teddy to dinner and you will order Camilla to apologize for clouting him. She could claim she was overcome by emotion. Tell her she must keep her tongue in her mouth, smile and agree with whatever he says. If she refuses, she goes to Pilcher Gayson in Bath."

Whit would have said he'd rather have dinner with a drunk Whig, even the arrogant queen-favored Lord Melbourne, when Averil lightly laid her palm against his cheek, leaned up and kissed him, her lips parted, her tongue sliding into his mouth, her breasts pressed against his chest. It was enough, too much. Whit wanted her so badly his brain died a painless death. What had she said? Something about giving Cam a choice between that idiot Teddy Jewel and that other idiot Pilcher Gayson?

She kissed him again, rubbed against him. She used her soft, steel voice. "Promise me you'll speak to your daughter, tell her she must apologize to Teddy when he comes to dinner or she leaves for Bath on Saturday to Aunt Deveraux and to marry Pilcher Gayson. Don't you remember? Your sister wrote he's mad for her, why I can't imagine, but it's a blessing. But first, my love, there's Teddy and for whatever reason, he appears to still want her. So do you agree?"

Whit would have agreed to having his feet cut off he was in such bad shape. "As you will, my darling." And he took her arm and led her out of his study.

Cam eased out from behind a thick, long, golden drapery and stared at the closed door. She'd known there would be unpleasantness when she'd arrived home and whisked herself off to her father's study, not to her bedchamber, because the witch would find her too quickly. She had to figure out what to do without her stepmother yelling in her face. She knew she would have to be logical, give reasoned arguments. But then her stepmother was coming into her father's study and Cam had hidden herself behind the thick drapery.

Now, as she stood in the middle of her father's sanctum, she realized she'd just witnessed the power a woman had over a man using her upper works, her tongue, and a soft, iron voice. When she'd heard her father suck in his breath, she peeked out from the edge of the drapery, watched open-mouthed and learned. It was amazing, like seeing a tree felled without a single axe strike. Cam might not like Averil, but she was forced to recognize and admire a master strategist. From what she'd seen, what some part of her understood completely, her father hadn't stood a chance.

But now she had to do something, and fast, because she knew if she didn't, she was a goner.

As she paced her father's study, she didn't doubt for a moment that Osbourne, their butler with all-seeing eyes, the housekeeper Mrs. Willig who'd buried three husbands and could spot a dust mote from twenty feet, the footman Jeremy who was in love with Alice, the pert upstairs tweeny, the footman Henry, her champion, all of them knew what was going on upstairs in the viscount's bedchamber in the middle of the day. Not only that, they knew Cam was in big trouble and there was nothing they could do to help her.

What would her father do now? She knew to her feet if she didn't do something fast, it was either Teddy The Toad or stargazy pie Pilcher.

At least she'd seen how a lady could control a man if the need ever arose.

CHAPTER 9

Sherbrooke townhouse
Portman Square
Tuesday evening

Whit felt very fine, a man pleased with himself and his world. After a splendid afternoon spent with his enthusiastic wife, followed by a much-needed nap, he'd managed to escape from his house before his daughter could catch him. Nor did he see his eldest daughter, Eliza, doubtless in her room preparing for the evening with that sour-faced maid of hers, Claudine. His precious Averil, now pleased with him since she'd secured his promise to see his hoyden daughter off to Bath if she refused to apologize to Teddy Jewel Friday night, if, that is, poor Teddy accepted their invitation. If he refused, why then, she would chaperone Eliza to the Winter-Smiths ball. Whit profoundly hoped his presence wouldn't be required.

Soon Eliza would be out of his house. Whit wondered if Eliza's fiancé, Winstead Towbridge, who sported a good deal of blue blood in his veins, had ever witnessed his future wife's temper in full flight as her father had. Probably not. Eliza was too smart to let her tongue loose before she had him to the altar. Whit liked Winstead, a jovial young man, raised to privilege, of course. He loved the land and would doubtless prove to be a good master when his turn came, which Whit hoped would not be for a long time, but alas, he'd heard Jameson Towbridge was not in the best of health, melancholia, he'd heard Winstead tell Eliza.

Whit loved his daughter, recognized her dislike for her sister, he wasn't blind, but he didn't understand it. He had to admit too he'd witnessed Eliza's unkindness to the servants. Odd, but she and Averil appeared to get along splendidly.

All in all, Whit's life was very pleasant, well, except for the dislike between his precious Averil and Cam and the very real concern about what Cam would do if Teddy Jewel did indeed come to dinner. Sometimes he wished he'd had three sons. Daughters were the very devil. No, he wasn't going to worry about any of that until tomorrow. Just pesky little worries, nothing more. He thought of his wife, thought of their lovemaking just that afternoon and smiled, fatuously.

As he walked down the front steps and climbed into his carriage to travel the single mile to the Sherbrooke townhouse on Portman Square, it didn't surprise Whit when the English heavens split open and dumped rain. His coachman, John, flew off his perch to hold an umbrella over his master's precious head. As he settled against the lovely dark burgundy squabs in his grandfather's splendid old carriage that Averil believed should be in mothballs, he breathed in the lovely old smell of cracked leather, enjoyed every creak and groan, and felt contented to his boots. No mothballs for this splendid old conveyance.

Tonight he wasn't going to think about the minor problems at home. He was going to think about how he and Alex Ivanov, if Ryder was right about his ward, were going to make a good deal of money.

* * *

Whit had always been a bit intimidated by the Earl of Northcliffe's very impressive early Georgian townhouse, the largest on Portman Square, lovely pale weathered brick, perfectly maintained, the servants efficient and ever so obliging, the ancient butler Mr. Plume as impressive as a king.

Whit was seated in an exquisitely comfortable Spanish winged chair he imagined had been appropriated from Philip II's palace in Madrid after Elizabeth's drubbing of his armada in 1588. The drawing room was warm from the lovely fire in the exquisite Carrera fireplace, the dark blue and green Aubusson carpet soft and thick beneath his polished boots, the high shine achieved by his valet Slipper's special champagne recipe, a secret handed down from his grandfather.

In but a moment Mr. Plume gently placed a snifter of very fine brandy in his hand, informed him Mr. Sherbrooke would be with him shortly.

Whit admired Ryder Sherbrooke, a fine-looking man, a smile usually on his face, a jest on his lips. Mayhap before Averil he'd admired his wife a bit more, Sophie, a lovely name. She was charming, kind, attentive. And the stories he'd heard from others who'd visited Ryder's two grand houses in Upper Slaughter in the Cotswolds—one for all Ryder's rescued children. He'd been told how all Ryder's children clustered around him to vie for his attention, which he freely gave them. He loved them, took care of them, educated them so if some were criminals, as some believed, they at least spoke like gentlemen and ladies. He even educated the girls, something he couldn't imagine until, after Cam had begged him for a solid three months, he'd agreed to hire a tutor. Mr. Watts was short and thin nosed, with lovely white teeth and newly down from Cambridge. It had paid off, for Cam had found mistakes in Whit's own calculations for a new time-watch. Mr. Watts had informed his lordship that his sixteen-year-old daughter was smart, mayhap smarter than he, a difficult admission for a young scholar to admit. In odd moments Whit bemoaned the fact she wasn't a boy and off to Oxford like her much older brother, Bryant, his heir, but it wasn't to be. Cam was of marriageable age and what was he to do? In addition to a splendid dowry, she was blessed with her mother Tansia's beauty. Ah, and she made him laugh, singing him ditties made up on the spot about his cronies and the lords in Westminster. He flinched remembering how he'd heard Cam say to Mrs. Willig, "*No laughter now, Mrs. Willig, not after AA—*" *After Averil.* Whit knew he should remonstrate with her for that impertinence, but he hadn't. Oil and water, he thought again, and sighed.

Whit cursed under his breath remembering his promise to Averil wrung out of him after he'd collapsed from pleasure, sprawled on his back in the middle of his century-old feather tick: *If she doesn't apologize to Teddy, you know he won't offer for her and it*'s *off to Bath she goes, my lord. You promised.*

Ryder said from the doorway, "Whit, you look like one of my children, little Rory, ready to burst into tears whenever he's chewing over a difficult problem and he can't immediately figure it out."

Whit snapped back, managed a smile and rose. Was he so obvious? He regarded his longtime friend in his immaculate evening clothes. Always sought after, was Ryder, popular with men and women despite his peculiarity of housing children he'd rescued. They shook hands. Whit said, "Problems seem to multiply the older my children get. Does little Rory cry, or does he solve his problems after sufficient chewing?"

"Usually Rory figures out his problems on his own. The most recent problem he faced was how to coax a sparrow into eating from his hand." Ryder grinned. "He ended up using a long branch with a saucer tucked in on the end with grain in it. It worked. Every day the branch got shorter. It took a week, but the sparrow was eating out of Rory's hand. Come, Whit, you're looking on the constipated side."

"Ah, that's a lovely thought." He shrugged. "I'm no more concerned than usual. Homelife, you know, always there to make a man want to pull his hair out. Suffice it to say, children are the very devil." He pulled his grandfather's watch from his vest pocket. It was getting late. "Where is your ward, Ryder?"

"I believe I hear him now."

CHAPTER 10

Both gentlemen turned to see Alex Ivanov walk into the drawing room, dressed flawlessly, a shining young god with thick dark brown hair and eyes a vivid blue. Whit tried to remember if he looked like a god when he was young Ivanov's age. Had Tansia believed he did? An unexpected bolt of grief seared through him. Then he remembered clearly how he'd felt when they'd been newly married and looking to the future, hopeful life would be very fine indeed. And it had been, for a good while, at least.

Alex said, "Good evening, my lord."

Whit met the young man in the middle of the drawing room and shook his hand—a strong hand, and did he feel calluses? *Had this young man believed his daughter too forward, believed she exercised too much wit at his expense?*

Whit said as he searched the young man's face, drawn again to his striking blue eyes, "My daughter wished me to tell you she much enjoyed meeting you even though she shouldn't have gotten within ten feet of you without a chaperone."

Alex grinned. "It was the rain, sir, it came on all of a sudden and mine was the only umbrella in sight. I found your daughter quite—"*Delightful*—no, not the word for a father to hear. "I found her quite invigorating."

Was that a compliment? What did it really mean? Boxing and rounders were invigorating, but a young girl sitting with you on a bench under an umbrella? Imagine this young man was the son of a Ukrainian count and did that translate to an earl in England? Ryder believed him very smart indeed. Was he perhaps as verbally facile as his daughter and thus wasn't put off by her? He said, "Cam told me you were quite unexceptionable, and she smiled wicked as a bandit until—" *Averil had marched into the entrance hall, red-faced, ready to draw blood.*

Alex waited patiently.

"Well, until she was off again to read her newest book, *The Mysteries of Udolpho*." Pathetic, but his brain had stalled. Thankfully he'd seen the book lying on her shawl in the drawing room the day before.

"An exciting adventure story," Ryder said. "I read it to my children to the accompaniment of shrieks and moans and entreaties for just one more chapter before bed."

Whit waited until Ryder had given his ward a snifter of brandy, then said, "Let me tell you about Lord Carberry. He has six boys and thus he is always looking for new investments to increase his coffers. I know he would be perfect for this project," and Whit pulled a folded paper from his breast pocket, handed it to Alex. "Please read the major points I've written down on the current manufacture of such train components as the smokebox, the sand dome, and most important for me at the moment, the fire-tube boiler. Building railroad tracks is well and good, but you'll see my focus is on the trains themselves. As you know, we are in the middle of what I think of as the railroad mania—there are so many competing train expansion schemes, all vying for access into the heart of London. Lord Carberry has suggested a Royal Commission be formed to forbid further building in central

London. However, your guardian and I know that such a commission will take its good time to come to actual recommendations.

"In short, I have no wish to scramble to build more lines, here in London or throughout England. Ryder has told me this is your interest as well, Alex, better and more efficient parts for trains of the future."

Alex couldn't believe his ears, everything he wanted—would this really happen? He could only nod, so excited he could scarcely contain himself.

Whit smiled. He knew excitement when he saw it. "Review my points and give me your suggestions and recommendations."

Alex looked down at the page Lord Whitsonby had given him. It was written on both sides in a forceful hand. He moved to the branch of candles on a soft-as-satin mahogany marquetry table at least two centuries old and read points both concise and to the point. His heart began to thrum. After he'd read both sides of the page twice, he raised shining eyes to Whit's face. "Actually, sir, to build a plant in Manchester to manufacture train parts with emphasis on fire-tube boilers rather than water-tube—it is an excellent plan. There are far too many maintenance problems, even explosions with water-tube boilers in the current design. Actually, I've drawn designs on how to keep the supply of boiler water more regulated so the firebox metal doesn't become too hot. But like you, I believe fire-tube boilers are best because, as you know, they're smaller, more compact. I've done experiments and it appears the use of clean water is key, avoids contaminants that cause clogs and hot spots—ah, of course you know all of that already, forgive me for prosing on." And Alex closed his mouth. His embarrassment fell away when Lord Whitsonby gave him a big smile.

"Clean water, something I don't believe anyone's considered. Everyone has always simply piped in water from a canal believing water is water, after all. This is very clever, Alex."

Whit then handed the page to Ryder. After a moment, Ryder raised his head. "The cost will be steep, of course, finding an appropriate building, outfitting it properly, hiring and training men, bringing in the materials necessary—but of course you already know this. Let me say with Alex's improvements on the fire-tube boiler he's already designed and experiments already made, I believe if we move quickly we could begin production by the end of the year. I too, of course, will be investing in this project, Whit."

Whit said, "End of the year, huh? That's optimistic, Ryder, but possible"—he paused, grinned like a madman—"since I've already located a suitable building in Manchester." Whit rubbed his hands together. "We will assemble fire-tube boilers for the dozens of trains being planned and built. I imagine you have other ideas for improvements on existing parts just as I do." He paused, looked at each of their faces, and raised his brandy. "Gentlemen, I predict we will be wealthy men." The three men shook hands, toasted one another.

Ryder said, "I believe Lord Carberry will be eager to invest." He grinned. "Mayhap even offer up several of his sons to work in the factory."

Whit laughed. "We will mention it, see if he laughs or gives it serious consideration."

Ryder smiled complacently. He'd found the right man to partner with Alex, the right man to introduce him to other rich men eager to be part of an England soon to be crisscrossed with hundreds of miles of train lines. He couldn't wait to see how Alex dealt with Elijah Hallou, Lord Carberry, an interesting man, Ryder had always thought, whiskers all over his face, a wife who never said a word, and those half-dozen sons all eager to bankrupt him. Ryder remembered Carberry saying one night at White's, "If I can't keep adding to my groats, however will I be able to educate and civilize my boys so they can be loosed onto the world?"

On the carriage ride to Lord Carberry's townhouse on Mulberry Square, Ryder listened complacently to Alex and Whit discuss the benefits of using coal rather than wood and which would be as efficient and have the added benefit of saving the forests of England. Sophie had told him several years before she knew Alex would make his mark and not just a little barely noticeable mark, but a giant one. She was right.

The evening at Lord Carberry's cold, large tomb of a house went as hoped, and Ryder, Alex and Whit left the Carberry townhouse in fine spirits. They'd secured a major investor who'd pounded his fist on the table in his enthusiasm, knocking over his port.

As for Mr. Carberry's brother-in-law, the Reverend James Piercebridge of St. Lucy Head on the English Channel, he kept his opinions to himself, an unexpected blessing, Whit said later. But before they left, Vicar Piercebridge said to Alex in the Carberry entrance hall, "You look very familiar, young sir, but since you hail from the Ukraine, and are thus a foreigner, I must doubt myself since foreigners from places like Ukraine are not thick on the ground."

Still, Alex was aware the vicar continued to stare at him until he walked out the Carberry front door and into the rain.

As for the six sons, they were not seen. As for Lady Carberry, a placid lady swathed in purple, she was seen, but as Whit had said, she didn't say a word.

CHAPTER 11

It was well past midnight when Alex stretched out on his back in bed, a soft feather pillow beneath his head. The rain had turned to a light drizzle, dripped down the window. The skinny moon sent a weak shaft of light through the window, hitting Alex on the face. He was wide awake, so excited, so filled with plans, with hope, he couldn't calm his mind for sleep. He found himself listening to the rhythmic patter of the light rain. So much was happening so quickly and all because his guardian Ryder knew Lord Whitsonby who knew Lord Carberry with six hopeful, expensive sons. Both gentlemen were smart and experienced, rich and ready to invest and bring his ideas to reality. But what if his ideas, his designs, his experiment were somehow flawed? What if they wouldn't work? No, he knew to his bones each adjustment and change he'd make were right. Were there other rich men interested in investing? Of course there were. He thrummed with excitement.

Like Alex, most men believed trains would crisscross England and indeed most of the world in the next decade. He planned to be one of the men who improved those trains, made them more efficient and safer, made them more comfortable for passengers. He easily pictured the thousands upon thousands of passengers in the future.

He remembered when six months before he'd read about the American Henry Worthington's invention of the boiler feed water pump to replace the fire-tube boiler meant to generate steam in a series of tube walls running through heated water. It worked, but the heat produced could cause problems. Worthington's water pump was amazing and Alex had written to him. Worthington had actually written back to him and their written discussions concerned how to keep the water more regulated in the boilers to prevent one of the inevitable catastrophes—explosions. He'd suggested adding another copper tube or maybe changing to iron, wouldn't both smooth out the steam and make the boiler work more smoothly and efficiently? Worthington agreed. And there were the problems of clogs and heat spots caused by the actual water itself, and why was that? And how to avoid excessive heat? Yet another problem to be solved.

Alex remembered with a smile how the children at Brandon House had gathered around him when he'd told them about Heron of Alexandria who lived in the second century BC. "He put several tubes in a vessel of water, heated the water until steam came billowing out of the tubes and there you have it—the first steam engine invented. And this was even before there were huge white wigs and knee britches." And he'd given them a demonstration.

Then, suddenly, uninvited and shoving aside boiler improvements and Heron of Alexandria, was Camilla Rohman, real as life and grinning up at him, but not all that far up for she was tall, long-legged. When she walked her stride was long, easy, no mincing with tiny steps to make a man slow to a near crawl, and her neck was ever so graceful and—graceful? Alex blinked into the dark. He'd never thought of a girl's neck being graceful before in his life. All right, perhaps that was true, her long neck was graceful, like a flower stem and—he nearly gagged.

Alex fluffed his pillow, turned onto his side, but there she was with that wonderful white-toothed smile of hers, and her hazel eyes sparkling behind glasses once the sun made a brief appearance. She looked really quite fine in the glasses. If he took off her glasses, would he be a blur to her?

No, no, he couldn't think about her now, he needed to keep refining his improved boiler ideas—examine the excessive heated water problem, find a better material for the tubes, write Worthington, not have Camilla Rohman take over his brain, but it was not to be so he gave it up. For the past decade he'd had his share of female attention in Upper Slaughter. He was used to young ladies being charming to him, vying for his attention, it wasn't anything new, merely something he took in stride. When Ryder had first brought him to London after he'd come down from Oxford, he'd taken Alex to balls, soirees, excursions to Richmond, al fresco luncheons, even one masquerade ball where he'd been a masked highwayman, ever so dashing he'd overheard one young lady say. It seemed to Alex Ryder was invited everywhere, not only for his charming company but the fact he was the brother of the powerful Earl of Northcliffe, a gentleman who'd intimidated Alex until he'd smiled and buffeted his shoulder, complimented him on the improvement for the gardener's scythe, a simple matter really, shortening the shaft or snath for the short lad responsible for the south lawn of Northcliffe Hall, filing down the hook and whittling down the shaft for Benji's smaller hands. Ryder had grinned at Alex later when they were alone. "Well done. My brother will very likely back you, Alex, so consider you already have one investor in the pocket. Now it's off to London."

Alex had always loved London, but this time was different. He met gentlemen at the Royal Academy of Science, some smart, thoughtful men, others so old their beards dipped into their tea. He'd met wealthy peers at Ryder's club, White's, gentlemen who could change his life with their groats and commitment to his vision. And other venues, for amusement, surely, but again Alex met even more gentlemen with wealth and privilege.

Ah, and the ladies. He hadn't really thought about it, but he discovered the young ladies were just like the girls in Upper Slaughter. They sought him out, flirted with him and waltzed with him, their white hands soft in his. But none of the myriad quite pleasurable activities in London had ever diverted his busy brain and brought it to a standstill before Lady Camilla Rohman—Cam—a lovely name that suited her.

Graceful neck and vivid hazel eyes behind her glasses. He punched his pillow and gave it up. It wasn't like he'd never see her again except at balls since he'd be dealing with her father, Lord Whitsonby. Well, unless she was forced to go to Bath to Aunt Deveraux with her trumpet and tales of Napoleon's hand up her skirts.

Alex grinned into the darkness. Boilers and Cam—given the way his brain worked, they were both problems to be solved. He had to figure out why this one girl with her bright smile and clever mouth and long, graceful neck was invading his brain with no effort at all. Over the years when he had a problem that confounded him, he'd speak to Ryder, but what would he say to his guardian about a girl he'd just moved right into his brain with no effort at all?

CHAPTER 12

Whitsonby House
Ormond Square
Wednesday evening

Cam's brain squirreled around as she paced her bedchamber, up and down, up and down, not excessively tiring since her room wasn't all that big. She kept thinking of the nearly two hundred pounds she'd saved, more than most families lived on in a year. Better than the groats, she had a brain. She would make do. But make do at what? And then, uninvited, she saw Alex Ivanov clear as day, saw those brilliant blue eyes of his dance with amusement at something she said. No, no, he was a chimera, a fantasy, a single hour of amazing delight on a rainy afternoon, nothing more.

She stopped pacing and settled in on the soft-cushioned window seat. She banished the wild blue eyes. It was time to come up with possibilities—where she would go, what she would do, how she could get there, what story to make up for as yet unmet ears—but her brain didn't want to cooperate.

Not a minute later, her sister came into her bedchamber without knocking, as she'd done forever.

Cam raised her head, looked toward her sister to see the familiar impatience in her gray eyes, slanted slightly upward like their father's, the disapproval in her pursed lips when she looked at Cam, really pretty lips full and soft, many times pouting for effect. She was pretty, slender, glorious blond hair always perfectly arranged in a fat chignon.

"Why are you mooning about, just sitting there, your skirts all tangled, your hair a mess, and look, there's a tear in your stocking and one of your shoes has fallen to the floor?" Eliza shrugged. "I know, you're dreaming about all the charming gentlemen Aunt Deveraux will gather for you, line them right up for you to examine and then you can decide which one to hit in the nose, for no good reason, like poor Teddy Jewel."

Cam saw indeed there was a hole in her left stocking. Who cared? She said, "All she has to do is call them from her bed-chamber window, the entire city of Bath will hear her and send over possible candidates."

Was that a smile? If so, it was quickly gone. Eliza's voice became a bit conciliating, not much, but a bit, and that was a surprise. "Listen to me, Bath is perfect for you, Camilla, if you'd but accept it and leave. Even with an apology I doubt Teddy Jewel will be interested in you now. And there's Pilcher Gayson in Bath." She paused. "But if I know you, you're thinking about taking the money you've managed to squirrel away and traveling to Venice to live. But of course, the money wouldn't last that long, would it? And then what would you do? Starve or come home and do what you were supposed to do in the first place. So forget that. Time for you to be reasonable, time for you to behave and do as you're told.

"Since Teddy is very likely out of the question, you're going to Bath. You will be allowed to return in time for my wedding since I have no choice but to have you as my maid of honor, not Cecily Talmadge, as I wished." She frowned. "I will have to wear white since the queen did at her wedding and it's now the fashion. I would prefer a soft cerulean blue that makes my eyes sparkle and my skin glow. Averil believes yellow will be perfect for you, although she did allow it might make you look sallow." She tossed a *Tattler* magazine on Cam's desk. "Read it. You will learn how a proper lady behaves at a wedding."

Cam said without much interest, "I know how to behave, Eliza."

Eliza regarded her sister for a moment. "Given your recent performance, I doubt it very much. Listen to me. You will smile and keep your smart mouth shut, Camilla. You will not engage gentlemen in discussions that will render them uncomfortable, possibly insensible. You will be shy and modest. You will defer to me in all things. If I ask you to fetch something for me, you will do it immediately. Do you understand?"

Cam cocked her head at her sister. "Do you love Winstead?"

Eliza tossed her blond head. "Winnie attends me charmingly and he is rich enough. Because of who my father is, I know he'll treat me well. I will give him an heir and then, since he's a gentleman, he will leave me alone and go elsewhere with his male lust. I will have a fine life. His father, I have heard, isn't well, so perhaps I will be Viscountess Longham within the year. And there will be no mother I will have to deal with. Winnie told me she thoughtfully died a number of years ago. Naturally he didn't phrase it exactly like that. Yes, I will be the mistress with no one to gainsay me."

It sounded bloodless and actually perfect for her sister. Poor Winstead. To Cam it didn't sound perfect at all. But what else was there? Not only for ladies but also for gentlemen? Both had assigned roles in life and they were to obey the rules set down to fulfill their roles. But what if you didn't want the role? What if—Surely there was something else, something to strive for—she thought of Alex Ivanov. He was smart; he was actually inventing better ways for trains to run. He was going to earn his own way, not inherit a title and wealth. He was actually helping society to move forward. He was going to make his mark, a big mark.

And what was she doing? Nothing at all.

She looked at her sister and thought of what she'd said about the marriage bed. It sounded like Eliza didn't want to be intimate with her future husband, that it was simply a chore to be got through, a duty to perform, nothing more, or something else entirely—like Averil using the power of her bosom with her father to get what she wanted, namely, for Cam to be exiled to Bath. Did Averil enjoy the fleshly things with her father? Cam shuddered. She couldn't think about that, it was too uncomfortable, thinking of her father in bed with Averil and—no, no, don't think about that, but since this was a very murky subject, she wasn't sure at all.

Did Averil agree with Eliza?

Her sister turned to leave, her pale blue skirts swishing ever so gracefully as she moved. She said over her shoulder at the open door, "I remember Mother. She hadn't wanted to be what she was—an heiress married to a rich man, but she had no choice. She was nineteen, beautiful, her family leaders in society. She could have any gentleman and evidently she culled Father out of the crowd of suitors. I've heard the servants say Father worshipped her, that he was distraught when she died."

Cam said, "Is that true?"

Eliza shrugged. "Who knows? Actually, I can't imagine any gentleman caring that much for a wife. After all, they're not forced to be in mourning for an entire year like we are, particularly if they are still in need of an heir. They can remarry as soon as they like and society nods approval and life continues.

"I remember Mother said to me when I was just a little girl and didn't understand, that she didn't fit into the mold, that she didn't enjoy being with any of her peers, poseurs the lot of them, but she'd learned to hide herself, to smile, to say nothing of any importance at all, in short to say only what was pleasant and expected. Then she hugged me, whispered she wanted me to spread my wings, whatever that meant. Even at five years old, I realized Mother was an oddity, just like you. Listening to you, it's like Mother is speaking, all nonsense and naive dreams. I once heard her maid say Mother was like a little swan in an eagle's nest."

A little swan in an eagle's nest. Was she really like her mother? Cam felt her heart swell. "Thank you for telling me, Eliza."

Eliza shrugged again. "Who cares, really? She's been gone a very long time. Face it, Camilla, you will have to choose between Teddy and Pilcher. There are no wings to spread, you'll learn just as she did there is only as good a marriage as a lady can make and wrest as much pleasure as possible out of life.

"Now I'm going for a ride in the park with Winnie. I might even let him kiss me. I think you've destroyed your reputation in London what with attacking poor Teddy, so Bath it will be. Accept Pilcher, he's not a bad bargain. He's hunting mad and will leave you alone after you have a son." She gave her one long look. "Don't forget, at my wedding, you will keep your mouth shut and smile, nothing more. You will speak only when there is a civil inquiry. And, Camilla, if you say anything untoward, I will make your life a misery." The last look her sister gave her promised retribution.

Eliza whisked out of Cam's bedchamber. Cam heard the *tap, tap, tap* of her slippers on the polished-oak floor corridor. She raced after her. "Eliza, wait! How do you remember all of this? You were just a little girl. Tell me more of what you remember. What else did Mother tell you?"

But Eliza didn't turn, didn't answer. Cam heard her laughter.

She turned back into her bedchamber, sat again on the window seat. If it came down to Pilcher or Teddy, she'd escape to the Hebrides and live in a Viking hut.

CHAPTER 13

Cilly, shortened from Cillette by seven-year-old Cam, had been Cam's maid and companion since she'd been five years old. She said as she walked into Cam's room holding a basket of mending, "Word downstairs is you won't have to apologize to that overenthusiastic nitwit Teddy Jewel tonight because he isn't coming to dinner and isn't that a grand relief? Evidently he's coming on Friday night, so you have a reprieve. Evidently there are other guests tonight, friends of your father, according to Osbourne, there are no wives involved."

No Teddy Jewel. It was a huge relief. Cam said, "You always know everything before I do."

"You know as well as I do servants know everything, sometimes even before it happens."

Cam nodded. She'd learned when she was five years old there were no secrets in the household.

"Oh yes, I even heard that pinch-mouthed Elvira talking about it. Evidently your sister's fiancé will be here as well."

She sank into a chair, folded her hands beneath her chin. Cilly sat beside her, pulled out a lovely linen chemise and began mending a small tear, humming to herself.

She paused, looked up and said, "I remember when you were a little girl, you were as skinny as a townhouse porch railing. Ah, but I saw promise of beauty in you even then, Cam. You have your mother's glorious chestnut hair, your father's hazel eyes, lovely eyes, not as beautiful as mine"—this said on a grin—"but still very nice."

"Thank you, Cilly." It was true. Cilly's eyes were, in Cam's opinion, a gift from God above since her father and mother, now deceased, had mud-brown eyes so Cilly had told her. Cilly was now nearly thirty. She'd turned down at least three proposals of marriage Cam knew about. When she'd asked her why, Cilly had said calmly, "I want to marry a man who will love me for myself and not my glorious eyes." And, of course, she'd laughed.

Cilly looked down at the watch pinned to the belt on her waist, smoothed the mended chemise, and said, "It is time for you to get ready for dinner. I'll fix your hair in that special way that makes you look like a queen. First, let's give it a good wash."

After Cilly brushed Cam's hair dry she began to plait thick hanks to twist into a crown on top of her head. Then came the threading of a dark blue ribbon through the plaits. Still, she wasn't done. "Sit still." She carefully pulled down several little curls to lie against her cheek and neck. She then stood back to admire her handiwork. "I must say I've outdone myself. You look perfectly grand, Cam. Now, you're going to wear the matching blue evening gown."

It was a beautiful gown, a fitted speared waist, her shoulders quite bare, and the satin fell in smooth folds to her feet. It was a marvel and fit her perfectly. Cam stood in front of the Cheval mirror, Cilly behind her. She grinned at herself. "Well, I'm at least two inches taller." She kissed Cilly's cheek. "Thank you. If Teddy isn't coming tonight and I won't have to apologize to that idiot with his damp hands, why am I dressed fit for the queen? This gown is new, from Madame Giselle. All I can ever think about when speaking with her is a tumbril on its way with me to the guillotine. So do you know who is coming?"

"Mr. Slipper told Mrs. Willig who told Mr. Osbourne and Cook that his lordship had invited Mr. Sherbrooke and his ward Mr. Ivanov. Little Alice overheard that twitchy-nosed Elvira commiserating with her mistress, both of them bemoaning the wasted evening since it would be all that financial drivel. Evidently her ladyship was hissing like a snake she was so mad it wasn't Teddy Jewel who was coming because it meant you wouldn't be going to Bath tomorrow. But his lordship overrode her, which, I must say, is a surprise. She was yelling it was all your fault, somehow you made this happen." Cilly gave her a big grin. "His lordship told me you were to wear the new gown."

Cilly paused, gently tugged on another curl, became serious. "I believe her ladyship wants you gone because she's jealous of your relationship with your father. Perhaps too she's afraid of you."

Cam gaped at her. "Afraid? Of me? That makes no sense, Cilly. She holds the power in the household, she can do whatever she wants. Only my father can overrule her. Why would she care if I got along well with my father?"

"There's something else you should know. Little Alice was dusting in the hallway outside her ladyship's bedchamber and heard Elvira tell her ladyship the servants believed your mother knew things before they happened. She concocted medicines for servants who became ill, and the household was healthy. Evidently they believed your mother was magic and passed it on to you. Just maybe Averil is afraid you will give her a wart on the end of her nose or make her bosom disappear," and Cilly laughed.

"Papa once told me Mama learned medicinal recipes from

her own grandmother, nothing more nothing less. As to her knowing things . . ." Cam shrugged, sighed. "If only I could manufacture a wart."

Cilly said, "Henry told me when he accompanied you to Westminster Palace yesterday you actually sat on a bench with a young gentleman who was a perfect stranger and he didn't know if he could fight the gentleman off if he became forward. Then he said, in a shocked voice, mind you, that you laughed and the two of you had your heads together, all that before you met your father. Henry said at least fourteen minutes passed with the two of you stark alone."

Cam laughed. "Fourteen minutes? It seemed like no more than two minutes. I quite liked Mr. Ivanov, Cilly. And Henry stood near, ready to spring into action should the need arise. Oh yes, Henry puffed himself up, claimed he would allow no gentleman to besmirch the Whitsonby honor. But it was clear to all of us Henry was impressed with the young man."

Cam looked wicked. "Actually, I think if there was any forward behavior it would have been on my part. I have to say the young gentleman is beautiful. And those eyes of his—a shocking wild blue."

Cilly arched a perfect brow at this information. There was a good deal of interest in Cam's voice and wasn't that unexpected? "Now twirl around slowly, Cam, let me see you display yourself."

Cam dutifully shook out her skirts, did a slow pirouette.

"I must say the gown is perfect for you. The blue material shimmers, makes your skin glow."

"And it's so lightweight, Cilly, I feel like a feather. I'll wager I could raise the skirts and outrun a cutpurse. And don't you think it sparkles like stars in the candlelight?" She turned to look at herself again in the mirror.

"That image with you running like a hoyden with your knees showing burns my eyeballs. Now, the style suits you, thankfully no bows or flounces. You have lovely shoulders and they're on full display. I very much like the style with the fitted short sleeves and the bodice fitted at the waist—and the arrowing down a point, very elegant."

Cam thought so too. She particularly liked the gentle pleats flowing from her waist, and only two petticoats to give it a lovely bell shape. "You know Father took me to Madame Giselle, just the two of us. He chose the gown and the material, said I would look far more elegant than the queen because I was so much taller and my hair was more interesting. He then allowed it was perfect. Then again, he's my father."

Cilly twitched another pleat into place, stood back. "His lordship has an excellent eye."

Why did he want her to wear it tonight? That toad Teddy Jewel wasn't coming, but maybe—

"Oh yes, Henry also admitted, after a glass of Mr. Osbourne's ale, that even from a man's point of view, he recognized young Mr. Ivanov was a prime beaut."

Cam smiled. "He is, Cilly. He's quite the handsomest young man I've ever met here. But more important, he has a brain and wit and he made me laugh."

"A brain and wit are all well and good, but does he have money? Breeding? Does he have a sweet breath and no nasty habits?"

Cam laughed. "His breath is ambrosia and any bad habits he might have can't be all that nasty, he's too young for any unpleasant masculine habits to have embedded themselves in deep. And he's foreign, Cilly, his real name is Alexi and he's Ukrainian."

"Oh dear."

Cam laughed again, patted Cilly's arm and sailed out of her bedchamber. She was humming as she walked down the long hallway with its deep inset niches, each with a bust of a former Whitsonby viscount going back three hundred years, and only one viscountess from the last century wearing an incredible white wig towering nearly to the top of the niche and looked to weigh three stone.

She stood a moment at the top of the wide staircase and looked down to the large chessboard entryway. She remembered clearly sliding down the staircase to an appalled Osbourne who nonetheless caught her and set her on her feet. So many years ago, a lovely memory. She drew a deep breath. Soon she would see Alex Ivanov.

"Well, and don't you look as well as possible for a beanpole?" Eliza's frown quickly smoothed out because Claudine, her maid, had told her if a lady wrinkled her forehead it made a line that never left, even after you were put in the ground.

"Why are you wearing that gown? Averil wasn't happy our father took you shopping and selected it for you, but then she smiled, said he must have done it because you needed to look your best to encourage Teddy to propose, make him forget at least for a little while what you're really like.

"But alas, he's not coming tonight and surely the gown is much too fine for the gentlemen who are coming to dinner, financial men Averil told me, crashing bores, no doubt, and who cares what they think? At least Winnie will be here to amuse me. A pity you don't have time to change into a gown more fitting for you."

The flow of insults didn't make a dent in Cam's excitement. She only smiled at her sister, wondered what she'd think of Alex Ivanov.

CHAPTER 14

Wednesday night

Osbourne quite liked Ryder Sherbrooke and thus unbent and accorded him a toothful smile when he opened the front door to Whitsonby House.

"Good evening, sir. Allow me to say too much time has passed since you have dined with us. His lordship is quite pleased you could come." He eyed the handsome young man beside him and decided if he was with Mr. Sherbrooke he was worthy of a nod, which he executed with a king's condescension. "And this is Mr. Ivanov."

Ryder asked, "How are Mrs. Osbourne and your sons?"

"They are in excellent health, thank you for inquiring, sir. His lordship and ladyship are in the drawing room. Please follow me, Mr. Sherbrooke, Mr. Ivanov." He marched like a Prussian general to the white-painted double doors, back straight as a board, his full head of white hair glimmering in the candlelight. He knocked lightly, opened them, and announced in a deep, plummy voice, "Mr. Sherbrooke and Mr. Ivanov."

Whit set down his snifter of brandy on a lovely eighteenth-century marquetry table and came to them, his hand out-stretched. "Ryder, Alex, do come in. Welcome to my home."

Whit introduced Lady Whitsonby, his daughter Eliza and her betrothed, Mr. Winstead Towbridge. He added with a smile, "And of course you are already acquainted with my younger daughter, Camilla."

Gone was the young lady in her plain and proper gown, glasses perched on her nose, stout walking shoes on her narrow feet, and in her place—

Whit added, all good humor, "It must be said, she looks quite unlike the waif you met at Westminster."

Alex was amazed at her transformation. No glasses, her hair was plaited on top of her head with blue ribbons threaded through, the thick braids shimmering with blond and gold amongst the shades of brown in the candlelight. Lazy curls fell along the sides of her face, but no clusters of curls about her ears as was the current style. Her gown dazzled. She looked beautiful, but not in the common way—elegant, that was it, elegant and clever. Those eyes of hers were a soft hazel, more blue tonight to match the blue of her gown. If he wasn't mistaken, she looked excited.

To see him?

Alex was aware of something he'd never felt before, a deep warmth filling him, and even more odd, he felt a sort of recognition. He found himself smiling as he bent over her gloved hand and lightly kissed her fingers. When he straightened he said, "You're not wearing your glasses."

She grinned up at him. "If I'm not careful my soup might end up on my beautiful gown and since this is the gown's first outing, a stain might earn me a smack in the head. You're fairly clear, but beyond your right shoulder, everything is a pleasant blur."

He realized he wanted her to see him clearly. "Put on your glasses."

"Well, why not?" Cam knew why not. Averil had ordered her to take them off, they made her look a perfect dowd and bookish, horror of horrors, and so she'd dutifully put them in the narrow pocket of her lovely gown. She settled them on her nose, blinked up at him. "Oh, this is much better. Goodness, look at you—if asked, I would say you're a visiting prince to compete with Albert. You look very fine indeed, Mr. Ivanov."

A visiting prince? He opened his mouth to tell her, no, he was far from a prince, but she—Lady Whitsonby said from across the drawing room, "Mr. Ivanov, I understand you are a foreigner to our shores." Her voice was cool, but there was interest as well.

He turned, gave her a slight bow. Alex recognized Lady Whitsonby was exquisite, perfectly presenting herself in an apricot silk gown that pushed up her lovely white breasts. Was she really a wicked stepmother? "Yes, my lady. I am exceedingly foreign."

"But you do not sound at all foreign," Averil said. "Perhaps your guardian is jesting with us?"

Alex caught Ryder's eye. "No jest, my lady."

Whit said, "Alex, come with me, I wish you to speak to Winstead. Like his father, he is always on the lookout for ways to improve his farmers' lives and productivity, always installing new mechanical equipment."

Alex had asked Ryder about Winstead Towbridge on their carriage ride to Ormond Square and Whitsonby House. Ryder had known his father, Jameson, Lord Longham, for years, watched the son grow into a man. "He's three years your senior, Alex. Despite his being raised to have his every whim immediately satisfied, miraculously, it didn't ruin him. He's intelligent, cares for the lands he will someday inherit and there's no meanness in him. His marriage to Lord Whitsonby's eldest daughter is seen as advantageous to both families."

Now, Alex stood back as Ryder asked, "How is your father feeling, Winstead?"

"He does marvelously now, thank you, sir." Winstead grinned. "I have worried about him. He's been too much alone. I feared he was growing despondent, what with me spending so much time in London, but no longer." He smiled down at Eliza. "I haven't told anyone, but perhaps it's time. A very charming lady has recently moved into the neighborhood. She's the widow of Sir Thomas Levalle, who died of a chill that went to his lungs some four years ago. She was left with six children, the youngest only twelve. I must say when I visited Father last week he was overflowing with enthusiasm and vigor, eyes bright and perfectly well. I saw he quite enjoys the children and they him. He informed me I will shortly have a stepmother. Her name is Francis." He turned to add to Eliza, "He sent me a note only today, telling me, so forgive me for not telling you sooner. I know you'll be as happy for him as I am. I can't wait for you to meet Francis and all my future stepbrothers and sisters." He paused a moment, smiled. "Francis informed me with a laugh to please not call her mother, it makes her feel too old. There is once more laughter in the house and so much noise. It is amazing. Just imagine, Eliza, all the enlivening conversation around the dining table, for all the older children dine with the adults. Francis is very pretty and kind and very patient, a necessity I imagine for handling six children. She is anxious to meet you. All the staff at the hall are quite enjoying themselves."

Alex saw the shock on Eliza Rohman's face, quickly replaced with an attempt at a smile. She tapped her gloved fingers on Winstead's arm. "How naughty of you, Winnie. You should have told me much sooner. Of course I'm very pleased. Of course your father is all that is charming, but surely, isn't he too old to take up matrimony this late in life?"

It was a good thing Eliza didn't see her own father's reaction to her words. Would she have been sorry, would she have tried to retrench? Cam didn't know, but she'd seen his reaction. He was stiff as a board, his fingers clutching his brandy glass so tightly it was a wonder it didn't snap. She looked to see Winstead frowning, but he didn't have time to answer, a pity because Cam would dearly have loved to hear what he had to say to Eliza, because there was a loud clearing throat in the doorway. Everyone turned to see Osbourne announce, "Mr. Theodore Jewel."

CHAPTER 15

Teddy Jewel was dressed to the nines in perfectly tailored evening clothes, only a bit on the flamboyant side with the green and gray striped waistcoat, thanks to his valet.

"My lord, my lady. I thank you for the lovely invitation. I am so delighted to be with you." He looked at Cam, blinked rapidly, his mouth open. If a man could slaver, Alex had no doubt he was witnessing it. So this was the toad.

Cam leaned close. "Oh dear, what is he doing here? Wait, look at Papa, he's surprised and yes, he's not happy. He knows Averil has gone behind his back and he's not happy. Just look at her face, she can't hide her triumph, she's responsible for the toad's being here. Because Papa's a gentleman he can't very well blast her, at least not right here, not right now. And he has to be all that is welcoming to Teddy. He's probably worried about me, though, worried I'll hurl my fricasseed chicken at him, which he does richly deserve, but I won't. I look too splendid to be ill-mannered no matter what my stepmama has done."

And she remembered when she'd come into the drawing room, Averil had looked her up and down and slowly nodded. "Yes, you'll do."

Oh yes, Averil had known Teddy was coming because she had invited him. She wanted to offer up Cam to Teddy the toad.

Averil immediately stepped forward, her hands outstretched. "Theodore, how wonderful you could fit us into your very busy schedule. You are so popular I could only pray you would be able to come to dine with us tonight. Naturally I told Camilla of our treat for her and she was very pleased."

Teddy lightly pressed his lips to her wrist, lingered an extra moment, smiled down at her.

Averil said, "My lord, won't you bid Mr. Jewel welcome?"

Whit said easily, "Yes, indeed. How pleasant that you're here, and on such short notice too. Our delight in your unexpected presence must give us all pleasure, don't you agree, my dear?"

"Of course," Averil said, and she stared at Cam, a clear warning in her eyes.

Teddy shot a look at Cam. There was no way for her to miss he was expecting a fulsome apology from her after he explained himself. He probably wanted her to lie down in his path and let him trod on her. He said smoothly to Averil, his eyes on Cam, "Given the charming company, my lady, short notice is nothing."

"My lord, would you please introduce Theodore to Mr. Sherbrooke and Mr. Ivanov. Of course he already knows Winstead and Eliza and dear Camilla."

Introductions were made, pleasantries performed, and Teddy knew to his gut this Ivanov fellow was a dangerous interloper. Evidently Averil did too because she called out, "Mr. Ivanov, do attend me."

Alex had no choice. He saw from the corner of his eye Teddy Jewel walking quickly to Cam. She'd moved to stand behind a high-backed chair, not much of a fortress, but it was something. He saw Teddy's eyes were alight with purpose and confidence. He had no doubt Lady Whitsonby had told him Cam would welcome him and was eager to apologize for the punch in the nose. He wondered, smiling at her fisted hands at her sides, if she'd clout the toad again tonight. He looked toward Lord Whitsonby, saw this very polished lord knew well if he didn't do something fast his daughter might well blow like steam pressure building up beyond its limit in a water-tube boiler, the result a huge explosion, massive damage and casualties.

Alex saw Lord Whitsonby look at his wife again. Cam was right, even her besotted husband could tell she was all but rubbing her hands together, so very pleased she was with herself.

Alex wasn't surprised when Lord Whitsonby, a gentleman who very likely knew his way around any social situation no matter how fraught with danger, smiled at everyone, and called out just as Teddy Jewel had nearly reached Cam, "Teddy, do come and chat with Alex Ivanov and her ladyship. I believe you two have a lot in common. Alex was at Oxford, albeit many years after you attended."

Many years? It made him sound like a graybeard. Surely he wasn't more than five years older than this Ivanov fellow. No matter, Teddy only wanted to get to Camilla, cozy right up to her, make certain she was no longer angry with him. The bruise under his eye had finally faded away, and without it to remind him, he was finally able to admit he'd moved too quickly. She'd struck out in fear, maidenly fear and only accidentally connecting with his face. She was innocent of men and their needs and thus he would move more slowly, prove to her he knew what was what. He was ready and willing to show restraint.

He couldn't look away from Camilla's lovely self in the incredible elegant gown and pictured very clearly his wedding night. The very first thing he would do was to remove her glasses. They made her look like a bluestocking, and he knew from his father there was nothing more repellent. Yes, off with the glasses. He would teach her how to please him. Lust coursed through him. It was all he could do not to moan and cross his eyes, but he couldn't forget—success was at hand. Lady Whitsonby had assured him in the note she'd written to him that tonight would be his night with her, and his lordship would look favorably on his suit. Teddy didn't want to speak to Ivanov, who looked like a bloody god, curse him, or to Mr. Sherbrooke, who was more well liked than he probably deserved. He wanted to stay with her, but he realized he had no choice. Lord Whitsonby would be his father-in-law. He had no well-bred choice but to obey him.

When Teddy had first come into the drawing room, all his attention had been on Camilla and thus he hadn't seen Ivanov clearly. But Teddy fully realized now this young man was a clear threat, yes, like a god with the cursed fine figure that bespoke a sportsman. He turned, saw Camilla wasn't looking at him, her soon-to-be betrothed, but at this dangerous interloper, and Teddy wanted to clout his pretty face, surely dangerous to the ladies both wed and unwed, and ask who his tailor was.

Lord Whitsonby wasn't about to allow his wife to try to embarrass him in front of Teddy Jewel. He called out, "Osbourne, I believe everyone is famished. We'll have dinner now."

If Osbourne was surprised by this unexpected announcement, he gave no sign, his voice unperturbed. "Yes, my lord."

Lord Whitsonby said, "Ryder, if you would please escort Camilla into dinner. Teddy, Alex, I fear you are to escort each other. My dear?"

Cam was seated between Teddy and Mr. Sherbrooke. Alex was seated across the table, his dark hair shining beneath the candle chandelier, his blue eyes clear and dazzling in the soft candlelight. She looked beneath her lashes at him, saw he was listening attentively to Winstead. "Do call me Win," she heard him say to Alex, which certainly sounded better than Winnie.

Teddy, following his hopefully future mother-in-law's advice, wasted no time. He leaned close as the spring soup was being served and said in what he hoped was a winning voice, his eyes on her face and those wretched glasses, not her beautifully displayed bosom, "I must apologize to you for my overexuberance, Lady Camilla. You are a young lady of impeccable breeding and gentle upbringing and I shocked you. I was not a gentleman. In my defense it was only that you excited powerful feelings in me and alas, I was unable to help myself. Please forgive me. Tell me how I can come back into your good graces."

You were never in my good graces, you idiot.

She wondered if Averil had coached him on this artful opening. Cam smiled at him. "Actually, Mr. Jewel, I wasn't shocked, I was offended at your ill-breeding. You excited powerful feelings in me as well, thus my retaliation."

Teddy wasn't cast down by this seeming rejection since Lady Whitsonby had assured him he would have her and her magnificent dowry, he just had to bend down far enough and be fluent in his apologies, he just had to persevere. He patted her hand, which made Cam want to smack him then. But because this was a formal dinner and her father's eyes were on her, she said smooth as glass, "Perhaps a lady is prone to overreaction. Perhaps many times a lady is unable to explain herself cogently and with logic, she can only strike out in confusion and fear, but the truth of the matter is—" Her voice fell off a cliff because the look in her father's eyes was a clear warning. She took a bite of her carrot soup.

Teddy leaned close, said gently, "My dear, I know this is difficult for you, so let me say I accept your apology."

Cam said low, hoping no one could hear her, "Mr. Jewel, let me be perfectly clear—"

Cam broke off when she heard Averil say in a too-loud voice, "Pray tell us what you are speaking about, Camilla."

Cam smiled at her mother-in-law. "Ah, nothing much really, we were just speaking of a lady's lack of logic and her confusion. I was telling Mr. Jewel it is a constant cross to bear. A lady could easily become confused trying to decide, for example, which shoes to wear, which comb to put in my hair, which muffin in the basket to eat for breakfast. I daresay the list is as endless as a lady's confusion."

She smiled at the table at large, picked up her spoon and dipped up another bite of soup.

After an agonized moment, Teddy said, "Ah, your wit pleases me, Lady Camilla. May I call you Camilla?"

She met Alex's eyes across the table and his message was clear. *Do not stab him with your spoon.*

"No, Mr. Jewel, you may not."

When the boiled turbot and lobster were served in Cook's famous sauce that made your tongue tingle, Eliza said to Cam in a carrying voice, "I was telling my dear Winnie about how excited you were to learn Teddy was coming to dine with us." Up went a lovely arched eyebrow and her voice had more steel than a building girder. "Who knows what will come of this lovely evening?"

This sledgehammer made even Osbourne twitch and the two footmen exchange hooded glances. Of course everyone in this house knew what Teddy Jewel had done to the daughter of the house. Just as everyone knew the youngest daughter didn't wish to ever share her larded sweetbreads with Mr. Jewel despite his future honors as Viscount Dawes.

Cam smiled. "Yes, who knows what will come?"

CHAPTER 16

Ryder sighed in blessed relief when he and Alex were finally in the carriage on the way back to Portman Square. "That was an evening to give a man a gray hair. I must say I'm relieved Teddy Jewel didn't try to carry Camilla—Cam—off given the encouragement heaped on his head by her sister and Lady Whitsonby."

Alex grinned. "If he tried I'd have to feel sorry for him. Cam would lay him flat. She's a strong girl. Actually, she didn't need to clout him, her wit felled him quite nicely."

Ryder cocked a dark brow. There was laughter in his voice. "You mean despite her innate lady's confusion and lack of logic?"

Alex laughed. "She laid him out just as if she'd been taught by Jayne and Aunt Sophie."

Was that humor mixed with a good deal of pride he heard in his ward's voice? Ryder said, "I do wonder if Whit will burn his wife's ears over her mischief tonight."

"Ah, so you realize what she did."

"I'm sure even the footmen knew. I've never seen such a pained look on Whit's face in all the years I've known him. I daresay their bedtime won't be pleasant unless Lady Whitsonby is very talented indeed."

"I wouldn't be surprised."

Ryder could make out Alex's smile in the shaft of pale moonlight coming through the carriage window. He said slowly, "The two of you must have enjoyed a far-ranging conversation at Westminster."

"You don't know the half of it. As for this evening, it's a pity we had no opportunity to talk about our project plans what with Teddy hanging about until Lord Whitsonby kicked him out."

Ryder laughed. "I daresay this evening turned out to be far more amusing. You know Teddy Jewel will keep trying, but only because Lady Whitsonby pushes him to. It wasn't hard to see the lady and Cam do not get along. And there's her sister. I wonder what is going on in that house?"

Alex said, "Lady Whitsonby has the power. And the sister sided with her. Do you know I think Lady Whitsonby is jealous of Cam, wants her married off or shipped off to Bath, out of her sight, out of her husband's sight and thoughts. Impossible not to see how much Whit loves his younger daughter, and admires her."

Ryder said, "She has to remind him of Tansia, his first wife, a lovely woman and not in the common way, just like Cam. There is a great physical resemblance. In Whit's study, over the fireplace, is a portrait of Tansia. See if you agree with me when next we are visiting." He paused. "At least Whit had the sense to move his dead wife's portrait from the drawing room upon his marriage, but still, if I were the present Lady Whitsonby I'd probably be offended since he insisted on keeping it, but what can she say? Now, enough of the Rohman family drama. What do you think of Winstead?"

Alex laughed. "I like Win Towbridge. He'd just left Oxford when I arrived. He's smart and interested in everything that would improve his lands and his farmers' lives. He told me he and his father worked together to ensure their tenant farmers have the most modern farming equipment available." What he didn't say aloud was it was a pity why such a smart man couldn't see the character of the lady who would be his wife.

"I knew you'd approve of him. As for his fiancée, Lady Eliza, she is certainly cut from a different cloth from her sister. It was obvious she was appalled at the thought of a stepmother taking what she assumed would be her place at Lansdowne Hall. And imagine six children—not hers—running about and there's nothing she can do about it. But Win didn't see her face in that instant, he was too pleased for his father and his own excitement. Since he was an only child, having six new stepsiblings around, probably worshipping him, is an amazing gift. It sounds like a match with excellent prospects for success. I do hope Eliza doesn't try to poison her."

Alex said, "It wouldn't matter if she did, there'd still be the six children filling her house."

A pause, then Alex asked, "How can you know if the lady you think you love loves you in return, or if she simply wants what is yours?"

Ryder gave him an arrested look. Alex was always surprising him. "Now that's a question for the ages. You know as well as I do, Alex, many men don't expect or especially want love in their marriages; they want land, an heir, money, pleasure is something they take outside their marriage.

"If you're thinking of Lady Whitsonby, perhaps she was in dire straits and needed a husband for protection and to provide her with a nice home. Or perhaps she simply set her sights on him for his money and status. Perhaps she's in love with him. Who knows?

"Marriage is always a risk for both the man and the lady, but let me say, Sherbrooke men have all been lucky in their wives—well, your uncle Tysen did marry a perfectly dreadful girl, but she died and he found a splendid lady in Scotland who loves him sincerely. I've never seen a happier man." Ryder patted Alex's sleeve. "And I always think of you as a Sherbrooke extension, so I predict you will enjoy the same luck. Wake me up when we get home. I shouldn't have downed that third brandy."

A Sherbrooke extension. Alex liked the sound of that. He was no one and nobody, a man with no memory of his first fourteen years and yet this amazing man had made him his ward. Yes, he was a Sherbrooke extension. When would he be able to offer a lady a comfortable life? What would happen with Lord Whitsonby and Lord Carberry? Would the factory in Manchester come to fruition? Would it be successful?

And if it was successful, then what would happen? He closed his eyes and saw Cam Rohman.

That fine spring night Alex dreamed he and Cam Rohman were riding a train barreling through a dark forest, lurching from side to side, the train wheels barely keeping to the tracks. Cam wasn't in a seat, she was sitting on top of a shrieking boiler he knew was going to blow any minute. He begged her to come down, they would jump off the train, but she smiled at him, told him not to worry and she sang out Edward Lear's limerick, "'*It is just as I feared. Two owls and a hen, four larks and a wren, have all built their nests in my beard.*'"

The boiler fell silent and cooled. The train moved quietly and smoothly through the forest.

Alex jerked awake to the sound of a wren singing brilliantly outside his open bedchamber window. Echoes of Cam's singing the limerick flitted through his brain.

He lay in bed on his back, his arms behind his head, and smiled.

CHAPTER 17

Sherbrooke townhouse
Portman Square
Thursday morning

In the lovely Sherbrooke family dining room, Ryder took a drink of his coffee and began sorting through his mail. So many invitations. Didn't anyone ever want to simply sit by his own fireplace and drink brandy and read one of his son Grayson's terrifying otherworldly novels? He picked up a letter from Lord Carberry, addressed to him, not to Alex. He unfolded a fine sheet of stationery and read the strong black script. Now this was unexpected. He looked at Alex, who was staring at the eggs on his plate as if he were thinking deep and profound thoughts. "Alex, we're invited to luncheon at White's with Lord Carberry and his brother-in-law, Vicar Piercebridge. If Carberry wants to talk about the project and his investment, why ever would he drag along his vicar brother-in-law?"

For a moment, Alex looked perfectly blank.

Ryder said patiently, "Lord Carberry, Elijah Hallou, rich, wants to invest, lots of whiskers, six sons, silent wife, brother-in-law, Vicar Piercebridge, who, apparently, will be accompanying him." He paused. "You've been deep in thought, Alex. Have you figured out how to get the rats out of Buckingham Palace?"

"What? Rats? What rats?"

"Your uncle Douglas attended Victoria's nineteenth birthday banquet. He saw a rat run over a footman's shoe, said the poor lad couldn't move a whisker, had to stand there trying to pretend it hadn't happened. Evidently another enterprising rat wanted a nibble of the queen's birthday cake and ran under her skirts to hide when spotted." Ryder laughed, couldn't help it. "Can you imagine? The queen screamed her head off, all the palace servants were running around trying to chase down the rat and then another appeared and another. Ah, how I wish I could have seen that. Your uncle laughed himself silly telling me about it, said he wondered if the little queen had ordered the rat's head cut off."

Alex said, "Imagine rats in the queen's residence. That's appalling. Has anyone figured out how to get rid of them?"

Ryder said, "Douglas told me he'd heard Prince Albert had fixed the problem. Come now, Alex, what has you thinking so hard?"

Alex said slowly, "I think I might have a new idea for a better way to distribute air in a manifold."

"You'd rather think about a manifold than concentrate your attention on Cook's nutty buns? And the creamiest scrambled eggs in all Christendom? You must not tell her, Alex, she might lock herself in the butler's pantry, or put a curse on you."

Alex took a big bite of his still-warm nutty bun, sat back and chewed. "Now there are no more manifold improvements in my head, the nutty bun knocked them out. Do you remember Edward Lear's limerick Uncle Douglas recited to us last month, 'The Old Man with the Beard'?"

"Yes, very clever. I hope Lear gathers all his poems and publishes them in one book. What made you think of that?"

Was that a flush on his ward's face? Now this was very interesting indeed.

Alex said, "Oh, nothing really, it just came to mind. Evidently Teddy Jewel was looking down Cam's gown last night."

"I wonder why she didn't clout him again?"

Alex smiled. "Even better. She told him he had low manners and if he didn't elevate his low manners, she would gut him like a fish. It routed him. He left soon after if you will recall. Lady Whitsonby blames Cam of course, and I have wondered what happened if she got her stepdaughter alone, probably threatened to send her to Bath."

Ryder said, his voice all indifferent, but one eye on Alex's face, "Perhaps that is for the best. I understand there is a suitor in Bath who wishes to marry her as well, strange name, Goose or Gay or Geese, something like that. Ah, Gayson, that's it. As for his first name, I do not wish to let it pass my lips." He paused. "Of course then Lady Whitsonby will have her stepdaughter out of her house."

Alex drew tight as a bow string, the nutty bun forgotten in his hand. He said only, "The man in Bath is the second son of Baron Riggs and he's hunting mad, chews his nails and dances like an ostrich. His older brother lives in London, is part of a rabid liberal group that wants to kill every Tory living. He has no chin and his hair is receding fast. The older brother, not the one whose name shall not be spoken."

Ryder spurted out a laugh, coughed, drank some water, wiped his mouth. "All right, I will force his name out of my mouth—Pilcher. He dances like an ostrich?"

"That's what Cam told me. She doesn't want to go to Bath, said it was easier to evade Teddy here in London than Pilcher in Bath. Do you know her aunt Deveraux told her Napoleon put his hand under her skirt? The aunt's skirt, not Cam's."

Ryder laughed again, cocked his head. "It appears you became well acquainted with Camilla Rohman, very quickly. As to Pilcher's brother's wish to do away with all Tories, I daresay that's the wish of each side or each tribe, if you will. What one tribe says the other screams treason and idiocy. I doubt it will stop until the end of time."

Alex shrugged. "Uncle Douglas isn't a rabid Tory."

"You've never seen him tug at his hair when the liberals come up with a new—according to him—harebrained scheme." He paused, said, "I wish I'd been near enough to that bench at Westminster Palace Tuesday to overhear you and Camilla talking. Your conversation sounds quite amusing."

Alex seemed to collect himself, nodded, but kept quiet.

Ryder said, "Now, back to our invitation for luncheon at White's. As I said, Vicar Piercebridge is accompanying Carberry. He does not state the purpose of this meeting, but I cannot imagine it being a financial discussion since the vicar will be present. Are you free?"

Alex agreed. "Oh yes, of course." He added, "Perhaps it's possible the vicar has funds he wishes to invest."

Ryder said, "The only rich vicar I know is your uncle Tysen. Your uncle Douglas has invested his funds over the years. Tysen said he is embarrassingly rich but allows it enables him to keep his Scottish home, Kildrummy Castle, in fine shape, so he allows he will bear it. And he grins."

CHAPTER 18

White's Gentleman's Club
Leman Street
Thursday

At precisely one o'clock that fine sunny Thursday afternoon, umbrellas in hand since a single dark cloud was spotted over Heathfield not five miles to the east, Ryder and Alex entered White's to see Albert, a White's mainstay for thirty years, step forward to greet them. "Mr. Sherbrooke and Mr. Ivanov, welcome. Lord Carberry and his guest are in the coffee room."

Ryder smiled, inquired after Henry's far-flung family. Alex marveled at how his guardian never slighted anyone, be it a chimney boy or the majordomo at this prestigious club.

Henry took their hats and gloves and umbrellas. "Do follow me, gentlemen."

Ryder had always enjoyed White's, so clearly he remembered his father bringing him here when he'd been up from Oxford so many years before. To the very young man, White's had seemed a fantastical place filled with gentlemen who drank and gambled and owned the world. Now, he saw it as settled and elegant, so very certain of its place in the upper echelons of society, still a gentleman's refuge and a stalwart building, a place that had seen so many lose their fortunes on the turn of a card. His father had taught him a man who gambled more than he could afford deserved to rot in a ditch. A lesson well learned.

They walked up the lovely winding stairs with the score of portraits on the walls, the vague but always present smell of cigarettes and cigars, the constant low hum of men's conversations. They walked into the coffee room, sedate, welcoming, where gentlemen dined and didn't smoke, the only room in White's where it wasn't allowed. The room gave off an air of intimacy and calm, the promise of an excellent meal. The walls were painted a rich dark hunter green, the floor covered in a thick Aubusson carpet. The tables were covered with pristine white cloths, the cutlery as fine as the place settings. There were again the low sounds of gentlemen speaking, the whisper of fine china being set down or picked up, the quiet voices of the gold and blue garbed waiters speaking to members, the occasional clearing of a throat, a cough muted by a hand.

As Henry led them to the table where Lord Carberry and Vicar Piercebridge sat, Ryder glanced at Alex, wondered what he was thinking on their carriage ride here. Plans for mechanical improvements? He'd scarce spoken, stared off into space as the carriage clomped through the London streets. To Ryder's eye, Alex had the abstracted look of a man thinking about a woman, and the woman had to be Camilla Rohman. Rapier-sharp wit, that one, and Ryder really liked her glasses.

Alex was indeed thinking of Cam, wondering what she would make of this revered male bastion, austere and quiet this time of day, rustling newspapers the only sound coming from the Reading Room, the wafting smell of tobacco as one climbed the stairs. He smiled. Cam would probably remark that the table knives looked so sharp they'd make a perfect murder weapon.

Lord Carberry and Mr. Piercebridge both rose at their approach. The men shook hands and seated themselves again. The ever-present waiters were there in a flash.

They ordered their lunch after the requisite niceties, Alex his favorite lobster cutlets and Ryder boiled turbot. Wine was served by the silent, very efficient waiters. The four gentlemen clicked their glasses. Then, without preamble, Vicar Piercebridge said, "You may well wonder why I am here, gentlemen, but I believe it to be important. Mr. Ivanov, do you remember I mentioned you looked familiar to me at dinner Tuesday night?"

Alex cocked his head, nodded. "Yes, of course."

"As you might also remember, I live near Dover in the town of St. Lucy Head. Just outside the town is the great house in the neighborhood called King's Head. It's set amid incredible parklands and very prosperous farms. It's been called King's Head since Malcolm Hepburn bought it from a bankrupt friend in the middle of the sixteenth century.

"A few years later, Malcolm Hepburn was elevated to Viscount Whitestone by Queen Elizabeth for loaning her a great deal of money that was, as one would expect, never repaid. I suppose the title was his payment. The queen even offered him a very rich lady he duly married.

"The Hepburn line has endured, father to son, for nearly three hundred years. George II raised Malverne Hepburn to Earl St. Lucy in his early years, the reason for his elevation, I do not know." Piercebridge paused, searched Alex's face. "I gave you this background, sir, because it's important you know the players."

Alex tried, but could find no memory of a town called St. Lucy Head or King's Head or a Hepburn family or a St. Lucy earldom. He leaned forward, wanting to pull the words out of Piercebridge's mouth, but at that moment a friend of Ryder's came by to say hello and conversation turned to Prince Albert and his efforts to improve the unsanitary conditions in Buckingham Palace. "The place smells," Lord Ealam said, shaking his head. "Hard to get down the vermicelli soup when chamber pot smells waft into your nose. Er, sorry, you're about to dine." And he laughed.

Lord Carberry said, "The prince is a smart young man, Ealam, I don't doubt he will fix the problem."

When Lord Ealam returned to his own table, two waiters brought their macaroni soup. After the soup was removed Alex couldn't contain himself. "Sir, why do you tell us about the St. Lucy earldom and the Hepburn family?"

Vicar Piercebridge studied Alex's face and nodded to himself. "Carberry tells me you are the son of a Ukrainian count, sent to Mr. Sherbrooke when you were a boy to keep you safe. Alas, your parents lost their lives and their fortune. Mr. Sherbrooke made you his ward. But you see, it is all very curious. Your purported antecedents confuse me."

Alex didn't say a word, merely stared at the vicar. He felt Ryder stiffen, lean forward. He said, "Please explain your confusion, Vicar."

Piercebridge said, "In this generation there is only one younger brother who is the present earl's nominal heir. There is a daughter, Eugenie, thirty years old, quite lovely, I might add, married to Donner Oxbridge, the son of Viscount Morley.

"The current earl is an admirable man, a generous man, a man of outstanding moral character. His lady wife died many years ago, but he has not remarried in order to produce an heir of his body, and he has had many opportunities, presented with many young ladies."

The vicar paused, tapped his fingers on his napkin. "Here is the source of my confusion, Mr. Sherbrooke. There were two Hepburn sons, both sent abroad in their youth with their tutor. Neither they nor the tutor ever returned. Of course this happened before my appointment to St. Lucy Head, but many remember that dreadful time. Were the boys taken for ransom? Then murdered? Whatever happened, they were never heard from again. I was told the earl sent his own agents to search throughout Europe for any word of his sons, but nothing was ever learned. It's been eleven years now since the sons, Graham and Simon—Graham the elder by fourteen months and thus the earl's heir—simply disappeared.

"Earl St. Lucy, Vereker Hepburn, has never spoken of this tragedy to me, nor has he spoken of it to anyone else of my acquaintance in a very long time. I never knew Countess St. Lucy, she died before I came to St. Lucy Head. I did, however, see her portrait many times hung in a place of honor over the mantel in the grand drawing room. She was a striking woman, her features blending into a perfect balance. In her portrait, she looks out at you, as if ready to share a secret, a half smile on her mouth."

Vicar Piercebridge sat forward. "You, Mr. Ivanov, have her eyes, the same vivid, quite startling blue I've never seen before except on her face, and her smile. And, if I'm not mistaken, you have your father's stubborn chin and his dark hair, an unexpected combination, fascinating, actually. You, sir, have their combined features.

"In short, I believe you to be the long-lost son of Earl St. Lucy. But I do not understand how this could be since you are Ukrainian."

CHAPTER 19

Whitsonby House
Ormond Square
Thursday

It was cold in her mother's music room, untouched since Averil had moved in six months before and ordered all her mother's private rooms locked. Cilly had told her Mrs. Willig had asked Mr. Osbourne if he knew what her current ladyship was planning to do with the lovely room, and her bedchamber as well. Cam knew when Averil decided to unlock her predecessor's room she wouldn't keep it a music room, no, she'd obliterate her mother's memory. Cam didn't doubt she'd discard her mother's harp draped with a white Holland cover near the front window and her small pianoforte. She opened the draperies to bring in the morning sun. Now she could see. She pulled the covers from a small elegant writing desk done in the old Egyptian style decorated with women wearing Egyptian headdresses, carved scarabs and obelisks. She knew the furniture of the Regency time had tended toward clean lines and simplicity until Lord Elgin had rescued the incredible marble statues from Greece in 1812 before they could be destroyed and brought them to London. Almost overnight the Egyptian style became popular, a dramatic contrast indeed.

She always came here when she wanted to be alone, when Eliza or Averil was particularly bothersome. She sat down at the small desk, opened the top drawer in the small elegant desk. There were her pens, her elegant stationary, a gift from her father three years before, and her dark brown leather book. She opened the first page, smiled as she read the date, 1832. She'd been nine years old. She read: *Cilly told me Lady Trillow came to dinner and she'd heard the old besom had sniffed out the veal cutlets from the drawing room and demanded dinner be served immediately.* She smiled as she thumbed through to an empty page. There were still at least a dozen pages left in the bound diary since her tutor had always preached brevity in all things. She wondered if her mother had kept a diary. If so, she'd never seen it and her father didn't know. She wished she could remember her mother, but she'd been too young. And now she'd been replaced by Averil with her bountiful upper works her father couldn't resist. She wondered if her mother had kept a diary what she would have written about Averil.

Did her father ever think about her mother now he was married to Averil? In the second drawer of the small desk were old letters tied in a faded red ribbon. She'd gone through the letters many times, all written by her mother from her home in Sussex to her father before their wedding in 1811. Would he remember the letters? Would he want to see them? Would he cherish the memories they rekindled? She didn't know. She hadn't ever told him about them. Why, she didn't know.

At least Averil would never see them because if she did, Cam knew she'd destroy them, no question at all. And that was why just after her father had married Averil six months before she'd locked the door.

She started to write but couldn't find the right words to describe Alex Ivanov. And why was that? Well, she had to write something. *Shocking blue eyes and a brain.* Very well, those were her few words for the day.

Cam rose, dusted her hands on her skirts and looked at the three paintings on the far wall, all covered with white Holland covers. She pulled off the covers and stared at the long-ago paintings of her grandparents, dead these eight years. They were young, elaborately dressed, white wigs elaborately coiffed. Another painting of her uncle Nimrod, her father's older brother, killed in Poland in one of the interminable battles with Napoleon. Her father resembled him.

She covered the paintings again, and left the room, closed and locked the door behind her.

She was thinking about the letters in her pocket when Averil came out of her bedchamber. She looked at Cam, disapproval radiating off her like a noxious cloud. "I've been looking everywhere for you, Camilla. Elvira told me she inquired very nicely of your maid, Cilly, if she'd finished her packing for you since you are leaving today for Bath. Your maid was very rude to her, told her to see to her own affairs. Your maid, Cilly—a ridiculous nickname—is an abomination, her rudeness upset poor Elvira. I shall ask your father to dismiss her."

Cam looked at the beautiful woman she'd like to throttle and said in a low, mean voice, "Just try it."

That put Averil back on her heels, but only for a moment. "What have you been doing? Why aren't you ready to leave?"

Cam felt dislike swell to bursting, but she said only, "Mind to your own affairs."

"Don't you dare speak to me in that ill-bred, snippy voice. This house is my affair. Go see to your packing. You're leaving."

Cam said nothing more to Averil, turned on her heel and skipped down the great front staircase. She turned to the back of the house to her father's study.

She couldn't leave, just couldn't—she didn't want to go anywhere, she'd never see Alex Ivanov again. She hadn't known he existed two days ago and yet here he was firmly embedded in her mind—so filled with life and joy and ideas to change the world. Not to mention his eyes, the wild blue, and his laugh, his smile, his wit, ah, and his brain. She loved his brain. Somehow she had to convince her father to let her stay. She knocked lightly, opened the door. Her father was alone, bending over his desk and studying what looked to be an architect's plans. For the changes needed to make the plant fit his proposed manufacture of train parts? His venture with Alex Ivanov and Lord Carberry? He looked up, looked alarmed. "Cammie, what's the matter?"

It had been so long since he'd called her by her childhood name. Cam knew she couldn't tell him the truth. Her brain scrambled about. What to say to convince him to let her stay? She said, "Papa, please don't send me to Bath." She saw refusal in his eyes, wanted to cry and scream, and then inspiration struck.

Cilly had told her years before when she'd been caught in a lie, *If you're going to lie the trick is to look directly into the person's eyes and try for bedrock sincerity.*

It was worth a try. "Papa, Aunt Deveraux whispered to me she can't wait to tell me how she lost her virginity, and not, she whispered, on her wedding night. She told me I would be old enough on my next visit. She said she'd tell me about all her lovers and how her husband never knew, how she pulled the blinders over his eyes, the stupid old fish-breath. On my last visit she told me Pilcher Gayson is eager to teach me things so I don't go to our marriage bed an ignorant twit. She said most of the young gentlemen in Bath have reputations and knowledge, Papa, they are eager and willing to show young ladies."

Whit stared at his daughter, appalled. He couldn't believe his ears, but oh yes, he could. He well knew his much older sister, Marguerite, fifteen years his senior and old now, but her wickedness from decades before always fresh in her mind. She was deaf as a post, yelling at the top of her lungs since she couldn't hear, forcing people to shout in her old-fashioned horn. She lived comfortably in this world and a world fifty years in the past.

He believed every word out of his innocent daughter's mouth. He remembered his promise to Averil as he'd lain on his back, breathing like a bellows after she'd stroked him, taken him in her mouth and bought his agreement.

What to do? Surely Averil wouldn't want Cam to be exposed to such appalling young men, to possibly be corrupted. He remembered how his no-nonsense daughter had smashed Teddy Jewel, but surely this was different. Teddy was harmless, withal, and something of a buffoon. There was no real wickedness in him, only a man's lust he couldn't seem to control around his daughter, not like these slavering men in Bath. He couldn't help but wonder if Marguerite had taken many of their grandfathers as lovers. He shuddered.

What could he do? He said, "I will speak to Averil."

Cam felt no guilt at all as she flung her arms around his neck and manufactured grateful tears.

Her father hugged her close and wondered what his life would be like if he didn't keep his promise, a promise made under amazing, utterly breathtaking duress.

CHAPTER 20

Sherbrooke townhouse
Portman Square

Alex stood stiff-shouldered at the sparkling bow windows in the drawing room, staring out at the Portman Square garden surrounded by large plane trees planted five years before to enclose the garden, staunch sentinels Alex had always thought, protecting the myriad daffodils, roses and chrysanthemums beginning their colorful journey into summer, not to mention protecting the smaller oaks and chestnuts that gave them enough sunlight to thrive.

He knew he had to face it, accept it. Thanks to Vicar Piercebridge it seemed certain he was indeed one of the long-lost sons of Earl St. Lucy. He was Graham Hepburn, a notable although not ancient name with a rich, sometimes violent ancestry dating back to Elizabeth I, according to Ryder, who'd read the Hepburn history in DeBrett's. His own father, Vereker Hepburn, was the fourth Earl St. Lucy and he—Graham Hepburn—would be Viscount Whitestone. His younger brother, Simon, if he was still alive, an honorable, his older sister Lady Eugenie. Was Simon alive somewhere, in

France? Italy? Or was he dead as Alex was supposed to have been?

Questions, endless questions swirled round and round in Alex's mind. All right, so he and Simon had left on a tour of Europe with their tutor—and who was he and was he dead too?—if this account was true, then why had he been in London and hit on the head and thrown into the Thames, dead if Ryder Sherbrooke, by sheer happenstance, hadn't by chance been walking by the Thames at that particular spot at that particular time of day to see him being pulled from the water. The fishermen had believed him drowned, but Ryder had blown his breath into him, sat him up and sent his fist against his back over and over until he'd vomited up water, so much water. And if Ryder hadn't taken care of him, the following fever would have carried him off.

Alex remembered when he'd finally awakened he'd stared up at a face he didn't know, a strong, handsome face. He'd asked in a slurred, hoarse voice, "Are you God?"

And the handsome man had laughed, hugged him close and he'd felt calm warmth filling him.

Ryder said now to Alex's still-stiff back, his voice gentle, calm, "I can't imagine how you've dealt all these years with not knowing who you were, all your memories gone as if they never existed, no memories of those who loved you, no memory of all the joys and pleasures of a young boy's life.

"I've always admired you, Alex, the boy God gave to me, and I continually marvel at the excellent man you've become. You've shown me courage and determination, both a tribute to your character."

Alex turned from the windows to look at Ryder Sherbrooke's beloved face. This man had not only saved his life but kept him close, taught him, encouraged him endlessly, gave him a large, unwieldly family of children, abandoned or lost, like him, a man who'd loved him unconditionally.

Alex's voice was hoarse. "If not for you I would be long

dead. You not only saved me, Ryder, you've given me a wonderful life." He paused, felt tears sting his eyes, swallowed. "You've been my father and my best friend."

Ryder knew he was the lucky one to have found this amazing boy. He said, "Do you know Grayson considers you a younger brother?"

Alex stared at him, laughed. "I remember when I was leaving to go to Oxford Grayson told me to be careful of Mr. Phelps, my don in Christ Church. He told me even though he was very old he still managed to bend his ancient knees and check under boys' beds for bottles of gin." He paused, laughed again. "I never got caught."

Ryder grinned. "I didn't either. Mr. Phelps was young when I was at Oxford. I remember he crawled all the way under boys' beds, only his feet sticking out. Ah, I gave that same advice to Grayson." He continued, again, keeping his voice calm, gentle, "It's been eleven years, Alex, and at last we know who you are. I promise you that you will remember—something or someone at King's Head, an object from your childhood, something you hear your father say—yes, your father—whatever it is it will trigger a memory and your brain will right itself, everything will fall into place. You will be complete again and settle into yourself. It will happen." He smiled then. "Just think, Alex, you'll also have all the memories of eleven years you've spent with me and your family at Brandon House."

Alex nodded, but Ryder knew he was afraid to hold out hope for he'd lived so many years without a single odd memory. Trying to remember always gave him a headache, and that was because Ryder's wife, his aunt Sophie, had told him his brain simply wasn't ready. He said now, "I can't imagine really being this Graham Hepburn."

Ryder said, "I understand you're afraid to believe you are now a peer's son, but, Alex, think about how you have your mother's smile, how you have her eyes, and their color is unusual, very unusual. Now, think about how you came to me with a young gentleman's manners and speech. I knew something bad had happened to you and I wanted to protect you and thus you became a young gentleman from Ukraine, your noble parents friends of mine. And with the name Alex Ivanov you were as safe as I could make you."

Ryder gave him a big smile. "And you have an older sister." He paused, cocked his head at Alex. "Surely you're not thinking the story is a farrago spun out of Vicar Piercebridge's fanciful brain?"

Alex cocked his head to the side. Did his father or brother do the same thing? He shook his head at the strange stray thought. "The vicar is a serious man. I doubt he has a fanciful thought in his head."

"Then can you accept both in your brain and in your heart you're indeed Lord Graham, Viscount Whitestone and your father is Earl St. Lucy?"

Alex sliced his hand through the air. "What if the earl looks at me and tells me I'm not his son, yells I'm an imposter, a fraud, I look nothing like his dead wife, my supposed mother, Madeline. What if he accuses you of being my accomplice?"

Ryder's voice was as calm and easy as his wife Sophie's. He even shrugged. "Then we will bid him good day and come back to London. But this isn't going to happen. You will meet your father, Alex. *Your father.*" He paused, arched an arrogant brow. "Do you honestly believe anyone could accuse me of being a dishonest sharp? A coney catture? Really, my boy, *me*?"

Alex couldn't help it, he laughed. "Well, no. You and Uncle Douglas look like two kings."

Ryder walked to him, took him in his arms. He felt a moment of shock. Alex was taller than he was. He felt such love for this young man he'd raised for the past eleven years. He wondered fleetingly if he hoped it wasn't true, if the vicar was mistaken. But he knew in his heart it was no mistake. He wouldn't lose Alex when he became Graham Hepburn. He would present a fine young man to Earl St. Lucy and watch him take the place he was meant to have since birth.

Ryder hugged him closer. "I love you, Alex. I promise you everything will be all right. I will send Geoffrey to King's Head with a letter to the earl telling him we'll arrive, let's say Sunday, to meet with him on a matter of great importance. I will give him no particulars. And Vicar Piercebridge assured us he wouldn't say anything to Earl St. Lucy.

"I know we will be welcomed because the earl is doubtless acquainted with my brother, the Earl of Northcliffe. And then, Alex, we will face the truth, you and I together. And then we will deal with it. Together."

Alex took a deep breath, nodded to the man he loved and trusted above all others.

"Stop all those doomsday voices running through your brain. We will leave early Saturday." Ryder paused, knew he had to talk about it, no choice. "Is the person who tried to kill you eleven years ago still there? If so, we will unmask him. Together. Ah, I hope your father has a good cook."

When Alex was alone again, he turned again to stare out at the square, his thoughts still squirreling about. *Graham Hepburn, a name I don't know, a name that doesn't feel at all familiar. Who wanted to kill me as a boy? Is this supposed brother of mine also dead, murdered? Stop it. Step back, think of this as a mechanical experiment, consider adding another binding to the main valve to lower the chances of overheating in a boiler.*

What happened to the tutor?

He wanted to smack himself. He left the drawing room, told Mr. Plume who, like all the staff, knew exactly what was happening. Mr. Plume stood by the front door, nodded when Alex said he was going for a walk, and left the Sherbrooke townhouse. He walked and walked, not overly surprised when he found himself in Ormond Square, staring up at Whitsonby House. He wanted to speak to Cam, but when he walked up the broad steps to the dark blue front door, he stopped. What could he say? *I'm really not Ukrainian but probably an earl's long-lost son, and someone tried to kill me eleven years ago and still might try.*

Slowly, Alex turned and walked back to Portman Square. His brain didn't stop racing back and forth from an unremembered past to the person he'd been told he was now, in the present. *If this is real and I am Graham Hepburn, why hasn't my memory come rushing back? Maybe none of it's true, Piercebridge was wrong, only a similarity. It all seems made up, just as I was made up, created anew to be Alex Ivanov. I've said my real name over and over but this Graham Hepburn is only a name. Why don't I have any memory of this name, of this boy? Why can't I now remember King's Head, my home until I was thirteen, fourteen? How old am I exactly? All I know for certain is I'm no longer Alex Ivanov.*

Where is Simon? Was he meant to die as I was? Is he dead as I was supposed to be, or was he as lucky as I was? Was he saved as I was and given a home filled with endless love and so many children, all ages and all eager to play and fight and learn and become my younger brothers and sisters? I was lonely those first nights in a strange place and scared to my soul, especially in the middle of the night, but soon, always, Ryder's strong arms were around me, telling me over and over everything would be all right. I was safe and welcomed, he would protect me forever.

And Ryder was right. He smiled now, remembering how Ryder had slept with him those first nights, and when he awoke from nightmares, it was to hear Ryder's deep voice quiet in his ear, reassuring him. *Eleven years ago.* And now, he was thinking of all the Christmas presents he would buy, all the excited faces of the children on Christmas morning, the shouts, the laughter from those precious small beings who'd had no hope before Ryder Sherbrooke had found them and given them a home. Yes, he'd become one with all of them, a big brother to teach, to break up fights and read stories to before bedtime. He would never forget one of the first nights he'd slept alone, young Teddy, five years old, found by Ryder abandoned in an alley in Manchester, had slid in beside him in bed, patted his arm, and whispered he would make sure he got enough oatmeal for breakfast. And he remembered, he'd thanked Teddy, smiled. And slept deeply, no nightmares.

No matter what happened in the past or what could come in the future, I have to be one of the luckiest men on earth.

What will happen now?

CHAPTER 21

Sherbrooke townhouse
Portman Square

A vase filled with fresh tulips and lilies picked that morning from Mr. Turlip's renowned garden filled the air with a sweet fragrance. A light scent touched Camilla Rohman's letter to Mr. Alex Ivanov laying in amongst other letters neatly stacked in Mr. Osbourne's black lacquer tray on the entrance hall table, awaiting the return of the master and Mr. Ivanov.

More letters were delivered and stacked in the lacquer tray. The tulips and lilies were changed to roses, bringing a new scent to perfume the air.

CHAPTER 22

Aunt Deveraux's townhouse
Royal Crescent
Bath

Cam pressed her nose against the rain-streaked window in her bedchamber, felt the cold of the glass. Sighed.

The bosom had won. There was a very clear message in that, but alas, Cam doubted she would ever have Averil's awesome upper works in her weapon arsenal since she was nineteen years old and full grown. These awesome upper works could not only feed a babe but also manipulate a husband or any man with eyes and sufficient vigor. Did a man her grandfather's age still have sufficient vigor? Did a man have to be dead to lose this vigor?

She knew her father hadn't wanted to send her away, but Averil wanted her gone. She didn't want her on a train, she might sneak off, and so she'd been nicely ensconced in her father's newly refurbished carriage and sent on the two-and-a-half-day drive to her aunt Deveraux's, Cilly with her, of course, serving as both her maid and her chaperone. Cilly remarked as they ate grapes and apple tarts Cook had prepared for them, "Do not forget, Cam, I am your chaperone, an order directly from Her Highness, your stepmama. She ordered me to smack your hand—with my knuckles—if you don't stay in my shadow and keep your mouth shut."

Cam wanted to laugh, but couldn't. She chewed on a sweet grape.

Both her sister and Averil had stood on the top steps of Whitsonby House, each smiling, waving vigorous good-byes, looking so pleased it surprised Cam they didn't burst into merry song and dance a jig.

Cam sighed again. What was done was done and she was now here in Bath until the day before her sister's wedding at St. Paul's in the fall. She opened Mr. Ainsworth's *The Miser's Daughter* again, but she found she really didn't care about poor Hilda and if she managed to get away from her dreadful father. She laid the book on her lap and pressed her nose again against the glass, colder now with the heavy rain slashing down. She knew of course she was being an ungrateful wretch. She wasn't living in a dungeon or in a back alley; her bedchamber was lovely with its wide window looking out over her aunt Deveraux's well-tended back garden. The walls were a light blue silk paper. The lovely soft bed was set on a dais and covered with a darker blue satin quilt, made by Aunt Deveraux's mother, her grandmother, a grand old lady Cam remembered smelled of violets. The dresser and armoire dated from Louis XVI and looked very stylish sitting on the blue and cream Aubusson carpet. The oak logs in the Carrera marble fireplace burned brightly, keeping out the chill from the heavy rain.

And everyone was kind to her.

She was an ungrateful wretch, but she couldn't help feeling her life was on hold. She was marking time, doing nothing at all to count for anything, and wasn't that pathetic? But marking time for what? Of course Alex's face immediately flashed in her mind. *I'm marking time before I can see him again.* But *why didn't he at least acknowledge my letter?* She'd only known him a week, no, less than a week, and he'd already managed to park his lovely self in the center of her brain or her heart or her liver, who knew? Or all of them. She missed him, no way around it. Talking to him, laughing with him, goodness, maybe even feeding him one of the sweet grapes she and Cilly had shared in the carriage, if only he would but present himself or write to her, acknowledging her letter. But he hadn't. She had to accept it, accept he obviously didn't care enough. He had more important things to do, things that would change the future of train travel while she sat on a window seat looking out at the rain, acting like a lachrymose heroine in one of Radcliffe's romances, daydreaming about him, her prince. She was a useless wretch, that's all she was, wearing lovely gowns because she'd been born of a wealthy father.

She disgusted herself. But what could she do to make any difference to anything in this world?

A knock on the door. Cam called out, "Enter."

It was Finch, Aunt Deveraux's butler of nearly a year, a handsome young man of twenty-five who was basically more Aunt Deveraux's companion than her butler. Cam hadn't met him on her last trip to Bath, he'd been away, attending to an elderly uncle in Bodmin. She knew he would protect her aunt with his life. Cam quite liked him and agreed with all the female staff he looked very fine indeed in his black suit and white linen, proudly washed and ironed for him by Libby, the parlor maid, whose job it wasn't, and it burned Marigold whose job it was.

Finch said in his lovely deep voice, "Lady Cam, Lady Deveraux requests your presence at tea. She told me to inform you she will advise you on how to use your assets to attract the most reluctant of gentlemen since you were too young and ignorant to know anything."

She'd rather have lessons on repelling the species. Well, all except for one, who hadn't bothered to even acknowledge her letter. "Thank you, Finch."

"She also instructed me to emphasize that tea is now, not ten minutes from now and therefore in the future. Ah, her voice is in fine fettle today. Of course as you know I always close the parlor door when Lady Deveraux gives me instructions since many of our people have sensitive ears and are not necessarily wearing their cotton earpads."

"I shall be down in a moment, no longer than a bare minute. Finch?"

He turned at the door, gave her a lovely white-toothed smile, arched a thick brow. "Yes, Lady Cam?"

"Mrs. Tartle told me you're proficient at sign language. It occurred to me perhaps you could teach both me and my aunt. She is very smart, she could be proficient by Christmas. It would spare not only the unpadded ears in our house, but in the rest of the Royal Crescent as well."

"Alas, my lady won't hear of it."

"Was that a joke, Finch?"

He looked surprised, then smiled. "I suppose when one is gifted, one doesn't necessarily recognize when one makes a clever remark."

"I understand. I occasionally don't recognize when I've made a clever remark either. We will persevere. How do you come to know sign language?"

Finch said, "A much-loved cousin is deaf, and so I learned with the rest of his family. When I visit, there is silence throughout the house but fingers are flying. It is a pity, but it seems the Old Ones prefer their ear trumpets. Of course because they can't hear, they do not realize they are shouting, as you well know." He smiled again. "But there is progress. I quickly learned whenever I talk to Lady Deveraux I get close to her face and speak slowly, exaggerate each word. I will say she is becoming adept at reading my lips. Perhaps you can also try it."

Cam nodded. "I will, but I've always tried to stay at least twelve feet away from her. If she answers me and I'm that close to her face, my ear drums will burst."

He nodded, said philosophically. "That is always a possibility even with the cotton balls. Try never to forget them." He added with a smile, "I am relieved to say my hearing is still fine. Did you know Mrs. Tartle made them herself? Oh dear, at least a minute has passed. If you are ready I shall escort you."

Mrs. Tartle, called Mrs. Turtle by Aunt Deveraux, was her aunt's cook. She hadn't discovered the efficacy of earpads for two decades and thus she also spoke loudly herself from dealing with her mistress so many years.

Cam stuffed the earpads in her ears and shouted, "Onward, Finch."

CHAPTER 23

Cam held up her skirts, skipped behind Finch down the stairs and hurried into the lovely parlor, a perfect example of her aunt's excellent, if a bit outdated, taste. Soft and soothing pale yellow and cream were the dominant colors, perfect to calm the nerves. The draperies were a darker yellow brocade, closed now to keep out the damp from the chill rain. Aunt Deveraux had two obsessions Cam knew of, the major one concerning any and all activities of an intimate nature, and shepherdesses. Every surface of the stylish chestnut and rosewood furniture showcased shepherdesses, different sizes, poses, most garbed in flowing white dresses, beautifully sculpted. There were no accompanying sheep. When she'd been young, Cam had counted twenty-three. If she wasn't mistaken, there was a new quite lovely alabaster shepherdess in the standard flowing white gown on the mantel, holding a staff nearly as tall as she was.

When she'd been younger Cam had wondered if her gown could be so clean dealing with dozens of sheep.

"It's about time! Come here, girl. Pull back your shoulders and smile. A vacant face won't gain you gentlemen admirers."

Cam smiled, pulled back her shoulders, and laughed.

"*THAT'S EXCELLENT. YOU WILL WEAR YOUR LOVELY GOLDEN GOWN TONIGHT. DEAR PILCHER GAYSON—AN UNEXCEPTIONABLE AND POSSIBLE FUTURE HUSBAND—IS ESCORTING US TO THE ASSEMBLY ROOMS FOR A LOVELY EVENING OF DANCING AND FLIRTING FOR YOU AND GAMING FOR ME. I WILL PARTNER GENERAL HAMISH IN WHIST. WE ALWAYS WIN. AH, WHAT A ROGUE HE IS. OR WAS. THE SPORT WE ENJOYED DURING GEORGE'S REIGN, VERY DIFFERENT FROM THE STAID COURT OF THE LITTLE QUEEN WITH HER CLEVER GERMAN PRINCE. A ROYAL STALLION IS ALBERT, ALREADY TWO BABES—LITTLE VICTORIA AND PRINCE EDWARD—NOT MUCH ORIGINALITY TO THOSE NAMES—TO DANDLE ON HIS KNEE. I HEAR THE ROYALS SNEAK OFF DURING THE AFTERNOON TO ENJOY FLESHLY DESIRES. IT IS A PITY BUT DEAR GENERAL HAMISH NOW COMPLAINS ABOUT HIS DEMNED GOUT AND ISN'T THAT JUST LIKE A MAN, ALWAYS COMPLAINING WHEN THEY'RE NOT FILLED WITH LUST.*" A pause, frown, then, "*IT IS RATHER ODD BUT I FORGET HIS FIRST NAME.*"

And so it began. Wherever had her aunt heard about the queen's marital inclinations? Evidently Albert was blessed with sufficient vigor. On the other hand, he was only twenty-two years old.

It was interesting Aunt Deveraux no longer kept her silver ear trumpet on her lap, but it was well within hand reach on a shepherdess-covered table beside her. Finch walked to his mistress, smiled at her and gently laid an exquisite silk scarf around her shoulders. Now, where had he gotten it? He leaned close and said clearly and slowly, "For your exquisite shoulders, my lady. I do not wish you to catch a chill in this nasty weather."

"THE WEATHER IS ALWAYS NASTY IN ENGLAND, FINCH. IT SETTLES OVER BATH AND HUNKERS DOWN ON OUR HEADS KEEPING PEOPLE INSIDE THEIR HOUSES AND THAT GIVES PERMISSION TO INDULGE IN SIN AND WICKEDNESSES, ALL GOOD SPORT, OF COURSE, SO GOD BLESS THE RAIN."

Aunt Deveraux laughed at her own wit and took a big bite of her scone, clotted cream dripping off the sides. She chewed slowly, swallowed and announced, "*MY DEAR CAMILLA, IT IS MY DUTY TO ENCOURAGE THOUGHTS OF SIN AND WICKEDNESS AMONGST THE GENTLEMEN TOWARD YOU, OF COURSE THESE NAUGHTY AND DETAILED THOUGHTS ARE TO REMAIN IN THEIR BRAINS UNTIL YOU ARE MORE SEASONED. AS FOR DEAR PILCHER—A LOVELY YOUNG MAN AND QUITE ELIGIBLE—TRUST ME, CAMILLA, I HAVE MADE IT PARTICULARLY CLEAR TO HIM THAT HE IS TO KEEP MOST WICKED PLANS UNSPOKEN AND HIS HANDS IN HIS POCKETS. TO MAKE CERTAIN HE WELL UNDERSTOOD, I TOLD HIM WHAT YOU DID TO TEDDY JEWEL FOR HIS PREMATURE FORWARDNESS. I DO BELIEVE DEAR PILCHER WAS IMPRESSED AND TOOK HEED.*"

Cam, well used to hearing in great exhaustive detail her aunt's fleshly concerns, merely smiled and walked to her, she leaned down, kissed her powdery cheek. She always smelled of violets, her breath of almonds. She was the queen of martinets, her will as strong as her speaking voice, and she ruled Bath Society. No one crossed her aunt unless they wanted to be gutted, loudly, with detailed particulars.

Cam said, enunciating each word carefully and slowly, "Thank you, Aunt Deveraux. I do enjoy dancing in the Assembly Rooms. It is a pity a lady isn't allowed to dance alone or with another lady. But I promise you I will not smack too many of the gentlemen, only if they grossly misbehave." She smiled down at the still-lovely face, skin as smooth as her childhood German doll Yvette, her eyes the same soft hazel as Cam's father's eyes. She always found it amazing her father and Aunt Deveraux were brother and sister. They couldn't be more different. Her father had been a very welcome accident, born some fifteen or so years after Aunt Deveraux, and had survived hale and hardy to assume his father's title many years before. But were they really all that different? Hadn't her father succumbed to Averil's powerful weapon, her abundant bosom? Surely there were other weapons as well, but Cam had no idea what they could be. Whatever else there was, didn't he and Averil, just like Victoria and Albert, disappear into their bedchamber in the afternoons? It was a blessed relief her father didn't talk about his trysts like Aunt Deveraux.

"IF A GENTLEMAN TRIES A GROSS LEWDNESS, I EXPECT YOU TO MAKE A GRAND SCENE WITH STUNNING DRAMA, GIVE ALL THE OLD CRONES SOMETHING TO SLAVER OVER ALL SUMMER. FINCH, TELL TURTLE I WANT MORE WARM SCONES. NOW, MY LITTLE BEAUTY, LET ME TELL YOU ABOUT LORD OGLETHORPE, THE ROGUE, WHO NEVER LEFT MY BED FOR A WEEK THAT LOVELY EXHAUSTING TIME IN PARIS. IT WILL GIVE YOU STIMULATING THOUGHTS ABOUT WHAT AWAITS YOU."

Both Cam and Finch smiled and looked interested. Cam drank her delicious tea, nibbled on a cherry tart, crunchy and quite delicious, and let her ears ring. Mrs. Tartle, Turtle she'd been for well-nigh twenty years, delivered another covered plate stacked with warm scones, gave her mistress a sweet smile, and left quickly before she could be thanked loudly enough to make her ears ring for she'd neglected to put in her earpads.

Cam sat smiling under the amusing and deafening barrage of more amorous tales from her aunt's past and let her mind wander. She thought about what she could do to be more than a lazy twit, spoiled near to rottenness by her father. But her first thought was a question—Had Alex read her letter? No, no, not important in the long scheme of things. Perhaps Osbourne had forgotten to give it to him, perhaps he had and Alex had read it but he had more important things on his mind, he was far too busy inventing better ways to improve train engines or planning out the factory in Manchester with her father, or—her heart stumbled—perhaps he was too busy dancing with charming young girls who didn't wear glasses to even remember her.

Cam wanted to kick herself. What was wrong with her? She was being a twit, all her brain focused on a man she wanted to love her to her long but narrow feet, forever. It was all her friends in London had talked about as they navigated their first Seasons, their parents on the lookout for the perfect mate for their perfect daughter. Of course Cam had looked about as well at all the young gentlemen offered up to debutantes in the 1841 Season, but not a single gentleman she'd met made her heart quicken, even a little bit.

Were gentlemen different? Did they have two parts to their brains, one looking and dreaming about a young lady who'd be their wife, the other for doing important things, things to change the world, no thought to a petticoat? She didn't know. Whatever was true, thinking and doing important things certainly left out nitwits like Teddy Jewel. Did Pilcher Gayson think about anything other than hunting?

"OF COURSE, MY DEAR CAMILLA, YOU WILL BE EXPECTED TO BEAR YOUR HUSBAND'S CHILD—A MALE IS MUCH PERFERRED, NATURALLY, GIVEN THE AGGRAVATING RULE THAT ONLY A MALE MAY INHERIT A TITLE. SO BIRTH ONE OF THEM RIGHT AWAY SO YOU DO NOT HAVE TO GO THROUGH CHILDBIRTH AGAIN AND AGAIN AND POSSIBLY DIE. BUT AFTER YOU PRESENT THE HEIR, MY DEAR, YOU WILL BE FREE TO INDULGE YOURSELF AS I HAVE—FIFTY YEARS A WIDOW, A BLESSING THAT MY ONLY CHILD WAS A SON AND HE ISN'T A ROTTER, GIVES ME APPROPRIATE ATTENTION, PRESENTS HIMSELF ON CHRISTMAS WITH EXCELLENT GIFTS. YOU MAY BE SURE I WILL GIVE YOU INSTRUCTIONS ON HOW NOT TO CONCEIVE."

She'd just been given the condensed story of her future. It was unutterably depressing, but Cam nodded her head and ate her own scone with Cook's special clotted cream dripping off the sides. Had her mother shared herself with other men while married to her father? Had he sought out these bodily pleasures? Would Averil follow this advice? Was it the accepted thing? All she knew was she didn't want that, didn't want it at all. But what did she want? Her future seemed a mishmash of shadows and curtained windows, but one thing was very clear to her, one face—Alex Ivanov. Deep down, she simply knew he would become the most important person in her life. And then what? She rose, shook out her skirts, and smiled. She realized she was very content to wait, to have life unfurl its surprises, and in its center was him.

CHAPTER 24

King's Head
Home of Vereker Hepburn, Earl St. Lucy
Near St. Lucy Head
Sunday evening

It was a balmy evening for late March, the sunset vivid in the east. The Channel, only a mile distant, smelled fresh, no pungent fish overlay. And the very best? The train from London to Dover had been on time. Noisy, dirty, but on time. Nor was it raining. These miracles portended a full measure of good luck.

Before they hailed a coach to take them to King's Head, Ryder wanted to visit the pub in St. Lucy Head, a charming town with houses marching up and down the town's hills. There was a pond in the center with at least six ducks, squawking loudly as a young girl threw them bread.

While Ryder spoke to the locals, after buying the patrons a round of ale, Alex sat quietly, thinking, trying to remember, worrying. Had he and his brother, Simon, ever snuck into the Hare and Hound Inn?

After an hour, Ryder waved to all the denizens, and he and

Alex walked back to the station to climb aboard their coach to take them to King's Head.

Alex said, "You charmed all the locals. Did you wring them dry of information?"

"Of course. Never forget, Alex, a pub is where you learn everything you wanted and didn't want to know."

The coach rolled along a fairly smooth road, houses giving way to land and trees and hedgerows, larger houses.

Ryder was looking out the window. He drew in his breath and quickly poked his cane on the roof of the carriage. The coachman obligingly pulled the matched grays to a halt. Alex stepped out of the coach after Ryder. They stood together and looked toward the splendid Palladian manor in the distance.

"King's Head," Ryder said. "Mr. Kurtz, the local cooper, told me it was built in the mid-1700s by Robert Adam himself. It's not massive, not a dominating presence like your uncle Douglas's Northcliffe Hall. Look at the lush hill behind it, so many thick trees, trees everywhere, actually."

Nothing. Alex felt absolutely nothing, no memory at all. He thought King's Head looked confident, quite sure of itself, and wasn't that an odd thing to think about a house?

Ryder admired the requisite classical Ionic columns in the front of the manor, proclaiming its adherence to Palladio's classical theme. And of course the graceful arched windows all along the front on the mellow pink stone front, now deepening to red in the setting sun. In front of the house was a wide drive where two carriages could stop abreast. But what set King's Head apart, Ryder had been told by Mr. McGrout, a local farmer, was the large meadow dotted with pine trees that stretched from the wide drive in front of King's Head toward them. Several dozen sheep were roaming freely, grazing even to the edge of a stream that flowed toward the Channel. Ryder said, "One of the men at the pub told me it's called the Green Stream because of all the algae and water reeds. He said it was also considered cursed, but he didn't tell me why."

Alex was impressed, couldn't help himself. This was really his home until he'd been taken?

Ryder said, "It looks like a perfect gem in an ideal setting, like a painting, tranquil, charming, invites you to lie down and take a catnap. I imagine everyone who sees it for the first time thinks this."

Alex said, "It's more than that, it's magic."

Ryder said slowly, "Magic? Well, perhaps so."

Alex said, "Look how the sun shines on the Green Stream. There are twenty-three sheep, I counted them, and look. One of them is sort of strolling toward the water. To drink, I suppose, but the water looks vile. I wonder what it tastes like. What else did you learn?

"King's Head was built on the site of an Augustinian abbey, seized by Henry VIII and sold to one of his barons, this from Mrs. Janes, the serving woman. She said there are even some Augustinian monks' cells. It's said their spirits abound and roam the land."

I would have played in those ancient monks' cells.

Ryder said matter-of-factly, "Does anything seem familiar to you?"

Alex slowly shook his head. He didn't say it aloud, but he did feel a pull, but maybe that was only the result of the potent ale he'd drunk at the Hare and Hound in St. Lucy Head while Ryder was charming the locals and gleaning information.

Ryder only shrugged. "No matter, don't worry about it. Memory is a tricky thing. Look at the hills behind the manor—elm, ash, oak, so many different species." He paused. "I can picture you climbing those trees, exploring the forests, riding your pony through the parkland, avoiding the sheep, of course. I was told there are rich farmlands to the east all owned by Vereker Hepburn, Earl St. Lucy—your father, a popular man, fair and keeps his people prosperous and up to date with all the modern machinery, just like Winstead's father, Lord Longham. I wonder if the two men know each other."

His father. Alex looked again at the idyllic setting. It was perfect. It did calm the soul. Maybe that pull he'd felt portended a still-hidden memory? But try as he would, the pull he'd felt was now gone. He felt nothing at all. Alex suddenly felt like the boy Ryder Sherbrooke had saved—no one, nobody.

When the coach emerged from the thick copse of oak and maple, drove onto the wide drive and pulled up in front of King's Head, Alex leaned out the open coach window. "Look, sir, many of the windows have gas lamps."

"Yes, you're right. It's amazing, given how new an invention they are."

Since Vereker Hepburn had installed gas lamps, it made sense he was a modern man who embraced change and new inventions. He knew his father was fifty-six years old, according to Vicar Piercebridge, a fit man for his age, and still strong enough to lift heavy tree branches, this said with a touch of envy.

He would know soon. Alex felt his guts cramp.

Ryder hated the sudden bleak look on Alex's face, gripped his arm. "Stop your worrying. Everything will be all right. Now, I do wonder why the name King's Head. I mean, no king ever laid his head on one of the beds, not to Vicar Piercebridge's knowledge or any of the folk in the pub. But, a Mr. Bourne, the town butcher, did whisper to me about the ghost of one of the long-ago monks sleeping beneath one of the manor's beds."

A brief smile, but it fell away. Alex was still looking pale, tense. Ryder punched him in the arm. "Come, my boy, take a deep breath, call yourself Viscount Whitestone a few times and practice looking haughty. Good. Chin up. Come, let's meet the inmates of King's Head."

Ryder and Alex walked up the dozen deep stone steps, between the Ionic columns rising two stories, to the wide front door, painted, charmingly, a rich dark blue with a large lion's head knocker.

The door was immediately opened by a short, rotund man with a tonsure of white hair circling his head and a look of polite interest on his round face. He had shrewd dark eyes, took in Ryder's well-tailored clothes in a flash. "May I assist you, sir?"

Ryder nodded, smiled. "I am Ryder Sherbrooke and this is my ward, Alex Ivanov. We are here to see Earl St. Lucy."

The butler looked beyond Ryder's left shoulder at Alex. He blinked once, twice, grew perfectly still. Then he sucked in his breath, stared, paled. He stumbled to the side, caught himself on the doorframe. He whispered, "Oh my, it is you, Lord Graham! Oh my precious boy, it's really you? You're alive, you're home!" He touched Alex's shoulder as if to prove he was really flesh and blood, threw his arms around Alex, hugged him tightly. "By all heaven's divine blessings, you're here, you're really here. Home, at last you're home." He drew back, still clutched Alex's arms in his hands. He was crying. "Oh, my dear boy, your father will be astounded, he'd given up hope, all of us had given up hope, but here you are—oh, he'll be so happy, he'll—" He swallowed, swiped his plump hand over his eyes and stepped back. "Forgive me, Lord Graham, but we've believed you dead for so many years, so many—yet here you are on our doorstep, home at last. Oh my, do come in. I'll take you to your father immediately. His lordship is in the drawing room with Lady Eugenie—ah, your sister, of course, your older sister, but of course you know that."

He stopped, cleared his throat, searched Alex's face. "Lord Graham? What is wrong? Do you not remember me? I'm Blakeney, I put you on your first pony, watched you play with the sheep, swim in that nasty Green Stream with Master Simon trying to drown each other, laughing like loons—"

Ryder said, "Lord Graham is overcome, Blakeney. If you would please take us to see his lordship."

"Yes, yes, of course. I know he was expecting you, sir, but he told me he had no idea why you were coming.

"Ah, you're home. How handsome you are, Lord Graham—you are the image of your parents, ah, and your precious mother's glorious blue eyes, your father's stubborn jawline and your hair as dark as his. Oh yes, follow me, please."

Heart pounding, so afraid he might puke, Alex forced himself to step into a magnificent long narrow room, a large chandelier hanging down from three stories above his head. A waiting room with high ceilings painted with classical scenes and so many portraits covering its dark green walls. Chairs and sofas sat in groupings around the room.

Lord Graham? It sounded ridiculous, not him at all. Lord?

Blakeney didn't pause. Alex was aware of Ryder beside him, a rock, there for him, supporting him, he knew, as he'd always had. They walked from the receiving room down a long hallway covered with massive black and white tiles, more portraits hung on a single deep green painted wall. Hepburn ancestors? He looked at the magnificent stairs flowing upward, admired it, but his mind was in chaos, thoughts bouncing off one another, without form or meaning and beneath it all was blank fear, of who he was or who he wasn't. All he was doing was walking, walking, following this Blakeney who'd put him on his first pony and watched him play with the sheep.

Blakeney stopped, searched their faces. "Mr. Sherbrooke, Lord Graham, should you prefer to see his lordship alone?"

Ryder said, "Yes, Blakeney, I think that is an excellent idea."

Blakeney nodded, led them down a wide hallway and opened a rich mahogany door into a large library, three walls covered with books, a gallery overhead, a ladder to the gallery, warm and dark—and the smell—for an instant Alex remembered the scent of leather and tobacco, mixed together for years on end, soothing, pleasant, then it was gone. Gas lamps burned bright, lighting even the corners of the vast room.

Blakeney gave a searching look at Alex. "Please wait here, I'll fetch his lordship. I shan't tell him you're here."

CHAPTER 25

Alex stood motionless. He hadn't wanted to walk into that room, walk into that unknown. He felt apart from the man who wasn't really him, couldn't be him, could it? There was no spit in his mouth. Then he felt Ryder's hand lightly squeeze his shoulder. He said quietly, "I know you feel like you've been knocked sideways, but it will be all right. You are Graham Hepburn, you're finally home and that's a wonderful thing, a miracle really. Don't question yourself, don't doubt—don't question this miracle. Now, take a deep breath and look around at this splendid library. I do believe it rivals your uncle Douglas's library at Northcliffe, and that means your father—yes, your father—loves books just as you do. Take another deep breath, that's it, and look around."

Alex nodded numbly and stared around at the walls of books. Ryder was right. This magnificent library did indeed rival Uncle Douglas's. He walked to one of the bookshelves and stood looking at the books at eye level. He didn't see Cicero or Plutarch, but rather Brunton's *A Compendium of Mechanics*, Lardner's *The Steam Engine,* and there were well-worn copies of *Practical Farming and Grazing* and Stephens's *Book of the Farm*. And then, to his immense pleasure, he saw Kater's *A Treatise on Mechanics*. Alex felt some of his gut-wrenching anxiety fall away as he continued to read the titles. So many more treatises on agriculture, mathematics, even building a kitchen . . . Higher on the shelf he saw Shakespeare, John Milton, John Locke, Adam Smith, so many more, pages cut showing they'd all been read, probably many times.

My father is a modern man, a man of many interests. Alex reached for a treatise on modern mechanical designs for farm equipment but left it where it was. He grinned hugely, grabbed up a black leather-bound book and turned to Ryder standing beside a large mahogany desk, watching him. "Sir, here are Grayson's novels, this one's really terrifying—*The Demon in the Wall.* Here are all of them I believe."

"Obviously he's a man of excellent taste," Ryder said, grateful for the momentary distraction.

Alex heard voices outside the door and quickly pushed Grayson's novel back with its brothers. A man's deep voice and Blakeney's, low and smooth, a touch of excitement. He felt frozen to the spot.

The door slowly opened. Alex watched a tall man stride into the room, Blakeney at his heels. Alex's first thought was, *He looks powerful, he looks like a man who knows who and what he is.*

He wore fashionable black trousers, a white waistcoat, white neck tie and a white shirt. His thick dark hair was threaded with silver and brushed back from a high forehead, but unlike Alex's, his eyes were a pale gray. He looked fit, strong, formidable in body and spirit, this man who was his father. He recognized the stubborn chin, his own chin, the dark complexion, the high cheekbones.

Vereker Hepburn looked at Ryder. "You are Mr. Sherbrooke? Welcome to my home. I had expected Blakeney to show you into the drawing room when you arrived."

"Thank you, my lord. You must wonder why I am here."

Vereker Hepburn didn't answer. He was looking beyond Ryder to stare at a young man standing in front of the bookshelf. There was something, something—

Blakeney couldn't hold it in, he said, trembling, his voice nearly breaking with emotion and excitement, "My lord, it is Lord Graham. He is home again."

Vereker didn't move. "Wh-what?"

"Your son is returned to us, Lord Graham is home. Please come forward, my boy, come forward."

Vereker stood stock-still, unable to believe what Blakeney had said, unable to accept what he saw, unable to take in the magnificent young man who now stood not six feet from him, his hair mahogany dark, his lean face slashed with high cheekbones—no, no, it couldn't be possible—and then he stared at the vibrant blue eyes, vivid, startling, his precious Madeline's eyes. He was tall and fit and so very beautiful, so very perfect—no, how could it be possible? No, it simply couldn't be. Vereker swallowed, swallowed again, words beyond him. Eleven years spooled through his mind, eleven long years and no word of Graham or Simon. And he'd given up finally. His life had continued, but the hole in his heart remained jagged and deep, filled with distant grief. He stared at the young man, into those amazing blue eyes, wild eyes, and said, his voice hoarse, "Graham?"

He couldn't help himself, Vereker walked swiftly to him, grabbed his shoulders in big hands. He closed his eyes trying to take it in. Then he whooped loud and pulled him close, just as Blakeney had. Vereker pushed back, but only a bit, never looked away from his face and whispered over and over, "Is it really you, my son? Really you, Graham? I cannot believe it—so many men I sent out to find you and your brother, Simon, so many prayers and finally I knew you were gone forever. I gave up—eleven years!" Still Vereker was afraid to believe it even though he saw the stamp of his features and Madeline's on this young man's face, more refined than his or his mother's, so very perfect, pure, beautiful. Vereker was swamped with feelings deep and wild—and gratitude, heaps of sheer gratitude, and such happiness—he clasped this precious young man in his arms—*his son*—and wept.

Alex had had no more doubts this man crying and hugging him hard was his father. But Alex didn't recognize him, not even a glimmer of a memory—but wait, the smell of vanilla, a light scent teased his memory, only to disappear into the warm air. He felt his father's strength and that strength felt somehow familiar. Slowly, Vereker raised his face, tears sheening his eyes, and stared into his son's face. He realized they were of a size. "Graham," he said softly, so much love and pleasure in his deep voice. Slowly, Alex—no, Graham—felt the power of him, his strength, and felt this amazing man shudder and the realization of who and what he was slammed into him and he accepted it completely and utterly. *I am no longer Alex Ivanov, I'm Graham Hepburn and this man is my father. My father.*

Vereker couldn't look away from his son. He thought yet again, *You and I are both stamped on his face, Madeline.* He wondered at fate, remembered the pain, the grief, a part of him—but now, right this moment, everything was perfect, his son was with him once again. Graham, his son.

He whispered, "I knew you would have my height. Such long legs you had as a boy—" Vereker raised his hand and lightly touched his son's face and words burst from his mouth. "When I last saw you, you were no taller than my shoulder, but you were as brave and eager and wild as my stallion Brutus, always in trouble, always ready to fight and laugh and you loved anything mechanical. You were always fixing farming equipment, Mrs. Sample's store that gushed smoke, fixing the leaks in the bathing room—it didn't matter. The tenants loved you because you always spotted something wrong before they did and alerted me or fixed the problem on the spot, you, a young boy. You wanted to know how everything worked from your earliest years."

While Ryder looked on, beyond pleased, Vereker's words continued to flow, no rhyme nor reason, "I remember you and I together read and discussed Lagrange's *Reflections on the Algebraic Solution of Equations*. And I watched you struggle to understand and when you did there was such joy and excitement on your face.

"You loved Gyllenborg's *A Natural and Chemical Treatise on Agriculture*. And I remember how you wanted Odel, our chief lad in the stables, to teach you to shoe your own pony. And you did it well. Odel was so impressed with you." Vereker stopped talking, swallowed. He ran his fingers over his son's face. "You are just as I imagined you would be as a man. No, you're more, you're much more. You're a miracle."

He and his father had done all these things together? Alex looked at the tear tracks on his father's face, his still brimming eyes, so filled with pleasure and love. He said, "You really recognize me, sir?"

His father blinked. "Recognize you? Of course, you're my son, you're Graham. Your mother selected your name." *But what of Simon? Do you know where he is?* Questions for later, but not now, now he had Graham and he would be grateful for the rest of his life. Graham—ah, the taste of his son's name in his mind, it was exhilarating. He never released his son as he said to Ryder, "Sir, how come you to be with my son? Where has he been? What happened?"

Ryder smiled. "It is a remarkable tale of happenstance, my lord. Alex—no, Graham—has lived with me for eleven years now. He is my legal ward. In this instance the Lord did indeed work in a mysterious way. As I said, we found you quite by happenstance."

Vereker stared at him. "You said you have kept my son safe

for eleven years? I do not understand, why happenstance? Why didn't you bring him home to me immediately?"

Alex—Graham—said slowly, "Sir, I fear when my guardian saved me, I was nearly dead, drowned in the Thames, in London. When I mended, I had no memory of who I was." He searched his father's face. "I still don't know. I'm very sorry, sir, but I do not recognize you."

The earl stared from his son to Ryder and back again. "You were nearly drowned? You recovered with no memory? You have amnesia? But how is this? What do you mean you were in London? You and your brother and tutor were supposed to be in Paris. What happened?"

Before either Graham or Ryder could answer, the door opened and a very pretty woman marched into the room, lovely pearl gray skirts swishing.

CHAPTER 26

"Papa? What is this? Blakeney told me not to disturb you and tried to keep me out, said you had urgent business, but—is this Mr. Sherbrooke? Is he your urgent business? And this other gentleman?" She stopped. "Is everything all right? Did Mr. Sherbrooke bring you bad news?" She saw the young man was staring at her. She cocked her head to the side. "I do not understand, I—" Her voice fell off the cliff. She stared from Ryder to Alex. "What is going on here?"

Alex, no Graham—he had to accustom himself now to thinking of himself as Graham, not a bad name, just not his, not really, but it was. It was. He was Graham Hepburn now. He stared at his sister, Eugenie, older, thirty, Vicar Piercebridge had said. She was tall, statuesque, beautifully gowned in elegant silver showcasing pale soft shoulders, diamonds at her throat and in her ears. Her thick black hair was swept back from a center part, thick bunches of curls falling against her face. She had the look of him, yes, her eyes, not blue, but light gray like his father's. She was his sister, *his sister*. He said, barely above a whisper, "Eugenie?"

She frowned at him. "I do not know you, sir. You may address me as Lady Eugenie. And just who are you?"

Graham studied her face closely as he said, some humor in his voice, "Evidently I am your brother Graham."

"*My what? My brother?* Come, don't be ridiculous, that is impossible!" She waved her fist at him. "Graham and Simon are dead, eleven years dead, do you hear me, nothing heard from either of them. So many men my father sent out to search for them, but nothing. They are dead, do you hear me?

"Father, you cannot believe this young man to be Graham?" She didn't wait for her father to speak, whirled back to Graham. "You look nothing like Graham. You are an abomination, a fraud, an imposter, you are despicable, do you hear me? You're here to convince my father you're a long-lost son, but you're really here to try to take what is mine—"

"Eugenie." Vereker's voice was whip sharp.

She heaved a breath, stared at Ryder, and couldn't help herself. "You, sir, I knew my father expected you, all of it a mystery, but obviously you are in on this swindle, are you not? Look at you, dressed like your betters, but you don't fool me, you're in on this fraud with him, pushing this ridiculous person off on my father—"

"Eugenie! That will be enough. You will be quiet."

Eugenie gulped an angry breath, took a step toward Graham. Vereker grabbed her arm, gave her a shake. "You will attend me, Eugenie. Now, look at the young man—it is your brother, Graham. No, do not shake your head, look at his eyes. LOOK AT HIS EYES."

It seemed like an hourglass had emptied before she whispered, shaking her head, "His eyes? They're just eyes. No, he looks nothing like Graham, nothing. It can't be Graham, he disappeared, he and Simon were gone, eleven years gone. They're trying to deceive you, Father."

"Yes," Graham said slowly, "I was gone, but thankfully

not dead. I was living with Mr. Ryder Sherbrooke, who is not a sharp or a fraud. He is my guardian, for eleven years now. He came with me to support me. Believe me, he is not here to convince your father to recognize me."

Eugenie shook off her father's hand and walked slowly to Graham. She stopped directly in front of him, stared up at him. "You are a stranger. You look nothing like the Graham I remember."

He smiled down at his older sister, but not all that far down for she was tall, deep-bosomed, quite lovely, really, her father's gray eyes. "Well, evidently I am Graham," he said slowly, taking in her face, so many hints and whispers of his own. "Actually, Vicar Piercebridge said I have our mother's blue eyes. You're beautiful." He raised his hand, touched his fingers to her white cheek.

Eugenie hiccupped, and fainted dead away. Graham caught her.

Vereker said without ever taking his eyes off his son, "She has always fainted when alarmed or shocked. It began when she was a little girl and a garden snake tried to slither under her dress. She will revive quickly. If she isn't too heavy, just hold her and she will be herself again in but a moment."

Vereker rubbed his large, graceful hands together. "If you would not mind, my son"—ah, how he relished the sound of that—"now that we've had our Drury Lane drama and once your sister has revived, we will dine. You will meet your sister's husband, Donner Oxbridge, Viscount Morley's son. Graham, Mrs. Sample, our cook, is still here and she will be flying from the kitchen to hug you until your ribs crack." He looked over at Ryder. "I owe you everything, sir. I am in your debt forever."

Ryder merely smiled. "I was the fortunate one. Graham has been mine for eleven years. There is a great deal to tell you."

Vereker nodded. "After dinner, we will talk." He threw back his head and laughed, a full-bodied, joyful laugh that filled the room.

Blakeney said from the doorway, "Ah, a perfect day, my lord, beyond perfect—a wondrous miracle. When Lady Eugenie revives, you will dine on Cook's splendid boiled knuckle of ham."

A man's curious voice came from the doorway. "What is this? Why are you holding Eugenie in your arms? My lord, what happened?"

Vereker said, "Donner, Eugenie naturally fainted at the sight of her brother Graham, newly returned to us."

He turned to Ryder and Graham. "Donner Oxbridge, this is my son Graham and his guardian, Mr. Ryder Sherbrooke."

Donner cocked his head to one side and said in an admiring voice, "I knew you were arriving this evening, sir, and I wondered why. I was eager to meet you, for you are famous; anyone who is anyone knows your name. You are a man who has more illegitimate children than is proper by any measure and you managed to convince your wife to live next to them as you continue to procreate more, year in and year out, without pause. It is quite astounding, sir. A pleasure," and Donner Oxbridge hastened to shake Ryder's hand.

Ryder smiled at the pleasant-faced man. "I have not heard that particular explanation of all my children in a very long time. At my age, I will take it as an accolade and bask in my immense virility."

"Sir, you mock me. It is a serious matter, producing child after child with such ease and facility when many men, through no fault of their own, are unable—" He stopped, grinned.

Vereker said, "That was well done, Donner." He added with a smile to Ryder, "Donner is our resident jokester. Blakeney, I see you rubbing your hands together. Fetch my finest champagne for the dinner table for our celebration. Graham, give your sister into Donner's care."

Donner grabbed a fast-recovering Eugenie from Graham, stumbled, then straightened. "Looking at you closely, I see your eyes are those of Lady Madeline's. I have admired her portrait. You have finally come home. Welcome." And Donner extended a hand, nearly dropping Eugenie. "She is an armful, and isn't that wonderful?"

"It is indeed," said Vereker.

He gave Graham a bow. "My lord, I am pleased to have a brother-in-law, equally eager to know what happened to you all those years ago. Don't worry about your sister. When she is startled or taken off guard, down she goes. Ah, my love, I see you're recovering so I will plant your lovely feet on the floor, all right? I'm holding you steady. Can you stand?"

Eugenie nodded, stood tall. She drew a deep, steadying breath, shook out her skirts. She looked from her father back to her brother and back again. "Very well, you are Graham. Your eyes are indeed our mother's eyes—there has never been a blue color so vivid, so startling, all remarked upon it when you were born. So, it appears I am no longer an only child." And she laughed. "Dinner awaits. We mustn't be late or Mrs. Sample will punish us with dried scrambled eggs for breakfast. Come." She took Donner's arm and marched out of the library.

Graham smiled at the slender man in his formal evening finery, his brother-in-law, gave him a bow, and marveled he'd been able to hold his wife in his arms. He was fine-looking, his face narrow, a full mouth of teeth. His hair was so blond it was nearly white. He supposed he was in his early thirties. He looked a bit bemused. Well, who wouldn't be at the unexpected return of the prodigal son who had no memory of anything at all?"

"We are having champagne to celebrate Graham's return?"

"Yes, indeed, Donner. This is the best day of my life."

Donner said without hesitation, "I would have thought Eugenie accepting my marriage proposal would be the best day."

Vereker laughed, clapped his hands he was so excited, shouted. "Blakeney, alert the household, Viscount Whitestone is home!"

CHAPTER 27

Royal Crescent
Bath

Cam knew her aunt expected her to be perfectly presented. She was, after all, Lady Camilla Rohman, daughter of the Earl of Whitsonby, sufficiently toothsome and splendidly dowered, and thus it was her responsibility to be admired by all, including the gaggle of watchful older ladies who perennially lined the perimeter of the room eager to condemn whenever possible.

Cam could always count on Cilly to see she had as perfect a presentation as possible. She stood back when Cilly had coaxed the last curl into place, looking at Cam in the mirror. "Well now, aren't you ever a toothsome sight. You look like a princess, thanks in large part to my genius."

Princess of what country or city or neighborhood? Well, Cam did look better than she had an hour before. "Thank you, Cilly. You've done marvels."

"Well, of course." Cilly bent close. "There's this one dratted curl, why won't it lay still like its sisters?"

Cam didn't think the curl looked any different from its well-behaved sisters, but she kept her mouth shut and Cilly tugged and combed until she was satisfied. Cam rose and looked at herself in the long Cheval mirror. Her gown was pale blue silk satin with the requisite tight downward arrowed waist, her shoulders were bare except for her mother's lovely sapphire necklace, the sleeves little tight puffs. She quite liked the lovely fitted narrow pleats from neckline to the waist. She wore only two petticoats beneath the shimmering skirts. The toes of her matching blue slippers showed when she walked.

She might not look like a queen in wedding white, but she looked well enough for Aunt Deveraux's approval.

Cilly said in a pronouncement reminiscent of a voice from On High, "Lady Deveraux will applaud my efforts as well as your fine looks." She twitched the same soft curl over Cam's left ear, frowned, sighed. She handed Cam a matching shawl, gave her a light kiss on her cheek and smiled. "You will make all the old bats sigh and remember when they were young and ever so proud of their looks. Of course they will compliment you on your looks and secretly hate your lovely guts."

Aunt Deveraux always enjoyed jaunts to the Assembly Rooms, where she could flirt endlessly with any and every gentleman over fifty, and win at whist. She was ready, now tapping her foot. She wore her favored yellow, her white hair piled high on her head. She wore diamonds, a lot of diamonds, wherever there was uncovered space. She carried her evening hearing trumpet carved of fine antler horn, which didn't much help with her hearing, but it was splendid to look at. Cam had always admired it, knew she could use it as well for a weapon.

Finch gently draped a lovely shawl over her bony shoulders when they heard Pilcher Gayson's arrival in his father's ancient carriage, black and ponderous but very comfortable.

He complimented Cam, but was fulsome in his praise of Lady Deveraux.

Cam bore up well when Pilcher kissed her gloved hand. Like her, he wore white gloves, so she didn't know if he still chewed his fingernails. She had to admit he looked handsome in his evening garb. He was smart enough to treat her aunt like the queen. Before he was allowed to lay Cam's lovely cashmere shawl around her shoulders, he looked at her and slavered. It wasn't a good look for him. Did Alex ever slaver? Then again, Cam didn't think she'd mind his slavering as much as he wanted.

After he laid the shawl around her shoulders, Cam thanked him even though his fingers caressed her arm. She knew she had to be on her best behavior so she couldn't very well break his fingers or smack him, not in front of her aunt. He was taller and better formed than Teddy Jewel, but she didn't doubt she could give him a black eye.

When they walked into the Assembly Rooms, Cam looked around, smiled. She'd admired the long grand high ceilings since she was a child, marveled at the splendid chandeliers. It was painted a lovely pale blue above the wooden surrounds, the ceiling a sparkling white, just as they'd been for half a century. Musicians sat on a small dais at the far end, their instruments at the ready. The room was airy, not too warm even in high summer.

She knew all the unspoken rules and regulations, namely, all those with either mounds of money or a lovely long pedigree, preferably both, were welcome. Others could attend but they were ignored by their betters. Still, she'd always thought even if she was a miller's daughter, she'd be dancing to the same music, enjoying the lovely tea.

Unlike the snobbery of the Assembly Rooms, the formal gardens around the buildings were open to those even without money or pedigree. The Bath elite felt quite good about themselves for allowing this bit of democracy.

Lady Camilla Rohman was welcomed with open arms and effusive greetings because Aunt Deveraux was bosom beaus with most of the grand dames of Bath. Cam knew she disliked many of them and wondered if the dislike was reciprocated, probably so. But of course here under the bright lights of the glorious chandeliers, envy and dislike were kept behind hands and only whispered. Older gentlemen and ladies played cards while young people danced to the musicians' lively waltzes and country dances.

When Cam walked in on the arm of Pilcher, Lady Hornacker, renowned for her quivering chins, sharp eye and razor tongue, called to her. "Lady Camilla, how delightful to see you again in Bath. Your lovely sister is well? And your father?"

"My sister is well, excited about her wedding. My father is very busy with his new wife, my lady."

"Ah," a word that carried a wealth of meaning. She said, a leer in her hard voice, "A gentleman, I suppose, must be applauded at any age when he weds a young wife if he wishes another son."

If they continued as they'd begun, there would be a dozen children. Cam merely nodded. "Indeed, my lady."

"I was driving by the Royal Crescent yesterday and heard quite clearly your dear aunt Deveraux demand her early-afternoon restorative."

Most of Bath probably heard her. Again, Cam only nodded.

"Your aunt Mildred—ah, no, Marguerite, such a clever affectation your aunt chose when she wed with Raoul so long ago. And even now she insists upon it. Even at her age, she draws masculine attention." And the old bat scowled.

Cam said, "Marguerite is a lovely name, don't you agree, my lady?"

Evidently not, for Lady Hornacker said without pause, "There she is with Colonel Everhard, off to the game room. Not her usual choice, hmm. Ah, Pilcher, dear boy, how are your mother and father? Of course I had tea only two days ago with Aleria, but one never knows. Health can fail at any moment."

Pilcher knew he had to be polite to the old besom, his mother always warned him not only was she rich from two dead husbands, she was the third daughter of a viscount. You never knew when she would pop up. He gave her another grand bow. "My mother and father send their best wishes, my lady, and yes, my mother continues well."

She gave him a royal nod. "Pilcher, you may now lead Lady Camilla in a waltz."

"As if we need her permission," Pilcher said under his breath as he led Cam to the dance floor. "But Mother told me if she wishes to grant me permission to smoke a cigar, which I find quite nasty, I am to smile and bow and politely excuse myself."

Cam was surprised at that bit of unexpected jocularity. Perhaps she'd misjudged Pilcher, but then she quickly discovered he still waltzed like a lame ostrich. He had to apologize three times for assaulting her slippered toes. When he asked her if she wished to take a lovely walk in the gardens, she smiled and shook her head, knowing he wanted to get her alone. A lovely old gentleman she'd seen many times here at the Assembly Rooms asked her to dance. He was reputed to have been intimate with her aunt Deveraux many decades before. He waltzed like a dream. She smiled up at him and let him flirt with her.

And always in the back of her mind was—where was Alex? What was he doing, thinking? Why in heaven's name hadn't he answered her letter?

Did he waltz well?

Thankfully, Pilcher was forced to relinquish her to a lovely line of other young gentlemen and she danced and danced until, for minutes at a time, she forgot she'd like to shoot

Alex for not at least replying with a simple note. *Nothing from the lout.*

Pilcher tried his best to get her alone, but she knew his every ploy and was nimble. She was aware of his simmering frustration on their carriage ride back to the Royal Crescent, but with her aunt speaking nonstop in a voice loud enough to make the carriage horses snort and try to break their harnesses, there was nothing he could do about it. Lady Deveraux had won fifty pounds at whist and bragged without pause.

Cam bid him a chipper good night before he could invite her to go riding with him or invite her to luncheon with his parents, please, anything but that—and she used Aunt Deveraux as a shield. Her aunt kindly acknowledged Pilcher's escort in a voice loud enough to wake the neighborhood.

Even though Cam had told Cilly not to wait up for her, there she was, sitting in a chair, lightly snoring. Cam smiled, undressed herself and gently woke her and sent her to bed.

Once covered from head to toe in her favorite flannel nightgown and stretched out in her feather-soft bed, she lay there, staring at the high ceiling. She'd enjoyed herself. She loved to dance, even with the lame ostrich when he wasn't assaulting her toes. But she knew Pilcher was going to be a problem. She lay there listening to the oak tree branch lightly hit against the window. *I'm a female and until I'm married, I'm only a little pawn on a chessboard. I do as I'm ordered, go where I'm ordered. What can I do to be different? What can I do to distinguish myself, make myself—more?*

CHAPTER 28

King's Head

Vereker assumed they would stay the night, maybe two or three, maybe a week, maybe never leave. Ryder and Alex/Graham had each brought a portmanteau with changes of clothing for two days, but Vereker assured them it would not be a problem. After all, both men were similar to size as him. He would provide them with all the clothes they'd need. Even nightshirts. Ryder had expected this, but realized Alex—Graham—had not. He'd told his own valet, Flaubert, before they'd left for King's Head he would be away for several nights and thus he could have a congé, perhaps travel to Brighton to see his sister. His news was received with a quivering lip and a pronouncement of doom for his master's future appearance without his fine hand to guide the ship, so to speak.

It was Vereker's valet, Terrance, who would see to both Graham and Ryder. Terrance had been with his lordship only ten years, he confided to Graham, ever since the retirement of his former far-too-old-fashioned valet. "Nice enough was Mr. Marriot, and surely he could prepare and fashion a lovely white wig in his younger years, but now, in modern times, he was sadly ill-equipped to cut a gentleman's hair and style it appropriately." Terrance went on to tell a fascinated Graham he was married to a lovely round-cheeked wife and father of four exceptional sons, living in one of the houses on King's Head property, a lovely big cottage that could house future offspring, since he was a man of great vigor and his wife a woman of great fortitude.

Graham hadn't really wanted anyone to take care of him, but he let Terrance do as he wished since he was brimming with enthusiasm and excitement and amazing stories to regale the long-lost son who was finally home, at last. No sooner was Graham allowed to step into the high tester bed, no nightshirt much to Terrance's disapproval, the sheets warmed, naturally, than Terrance told him about his sharp-brained son Peter, who could catch any duck in the village pond. Graham was relieved to hear Peter was only four and not fourteen, and wondered if he and Simon had ever tried to catch the village ducks.

When finally Terrance bid him a pleasant good night and blew out the gas lamp, Graham found sleep was a long time coming. He stared up at the dark ceiling—were there fat cavorting cherubs lurking in clouds overhead? Maybe a young lady wearing a white flowing robe playing the lute?

As he finally dozed off, he thought yet again how his life had changed so utterly in such a short period of time. How long would it take him to come to grips with his new self? His family, his actual family. He repeated it to himself. *I am Graham Hepburn. I am now Viscount Whitestone. I have a father and a sister and a brother-in-law. I had a brother, Simon—and was he dead as I was supposed to be?* He had to be dead. Graham felt pain over his brother's death even though he had no memory of him. Graham—it was a good name and now it was his. He wondered what his middle names were.

He lay there, trying desperately to remember—anything—but there was nothing at all, not even a whisper of anything at all familiar. His last thought before he fell asleep was Alex Ivanov no longer existed and wasn't it odd what life could do to a young man?

He saw himself naked, sheep all around him in the large open park in front of King's Head, and he was readying to dive in the wide ribbon of green water, called the Green Stream. But he wasn't an adult, he was young, only a boy, and he was wildly happy, the sun high, bright and hot on his skin. When he cut cleanly through the water, he hit the bottom and prepared to kick off but suddenly he couldn't move his arms or his legs. He was suspended helpless, felt horrible pressure building in his chest. He saw bubbles from his breath and then there weren't any.

Graham jerked away, gasping for breath, his heart pounding. The dream faded away like fingers of fog in the sun, and all he could remember was pressure on his chest. But somehow it seemed now that he hadn't been the one to drown, another had been there, another who drowned, but that made no sense at all.

When Terrance awakened him the next morning for his bath, he felt again a phantom pain in his chest, or perhaps not his chest, but another's. He shook his head, looked at the ormolu clock on the mantel. It was early, but as Terrance said on a stifled yawn behind his hand, "I told his lordship you were young and needed invigorating sleep, but he is so very anxious to see you, thus this too-early hour. It must be said, I am a bit on the tired side myself since my precious wife did not wish to release me from her arms even though baby Kincaid wanted his milk."

Graham didn't take in all the words, but he felt the boundless enthusiasm and couldn't complain. He bathed, shaved himself much to Terrance's disapproval and tucked a white shirt into his britches. Terrance had told him his lordship really wanted his son to wear one of his own shirts since they were of a size and so Graham had complied, thinking again how strange it was to suddenly have a real father and to be someone else entirely.

There was a knock on his bedchamber door. Graham called out, "Come."

And there stood his father in the doorway, his heart in his eyes.

Vereker could only stare at his magnificent son, tall, straight, so finally made, such a beautiful face, and his mother's vivid blue eyes, miraculously returned to him. He was really here, wearing one of his own shirts. He was so filled with pleasure and gratitude he had to keep himself from shouting to the rafters. He'd decided during the long night he would donate a new stained-glass window to Vicar Piercebridge's church in St. Lucy Head. He would renovate the vicarage. He would increase his yearly stipend. He would bless this man for all his days. But for the vicar, his son would have been lost to him forever. Not unhappy, no—raised with love by Mr. Sherbrooke, but not his. Would he ever have remembered his own father?

Vereker had to force himself not to run to his son and pull him close, feel the strong heartbeat, the strength of him.

Terrance paused, felt a lump in his throat when he saw the incredible happiness in his master's eyes. He blinked, swallowed. "My lord," he said, "Lord Graham is nearly finished dressing. As you can see, your shirt fits him quite nicely. I saw to Mr. Sherbrooke first because I knew you'd want his young lordship to get much-needed sleep."

Graham looked at his father, strong and graceful, so very

perfect, and somehow it felt natural to smile at him. "Good morning, sir. Thank you for the shirt. Terrance is right, it fits me well."

The words burst out. "It fits you well now, but then, you were just a boy, tall, skinny as your fishing pole, always on the move if you weren't studying steam engines and trains, playing with all the farmers' children, not like Simon who was—" He shook his head at himself. "Look at you now, Graham, a man, full grown and your mother's brilliant blue eyes—" He stopped, smiled. "Forgive me, I probably am repeating myself." He watched Terrance ease his son into one of Graham's own morning coats. His smile bloomed again as he stared at this young god. "You look perfect."

Terrance said, "He does indeed. My lord, Blakeney told me Lord Graham is the picture of you at his age, with, naturally, his mother's unforgettable eyes. I polished his boots."

"Blakeney is correct. Thank you, Terrance, even his boots look perfect. Graham"—oh, how he savored saying his name—"it is time for us to meet Mr. Sherbrooke in the breakfast room. Blakeney has already escorted your guardian downstairs."

CHAPTER 29

Monday morning

Both Eugenie and her husband weren't ever up this early, the earl told Ryder and Graham as their coffee cups were filled by a smiling Blakeney who nearly danced around the small family dining room—the table seated only twelve people—so happy was he.

As for the earl, Vereker couldn't help staring at his son, a miracle, so perfect, even his boots. "I hope you will like Cook's scrambled eggs. They're always a marvel."

Once their plates were full, Vereker said, "Please, Graham, tell me about yourself."

Ryder saw Graham didn't know what to say, so he told the earl he'd found him, just pulled out of the Thames. He smiled toward the young man he'd loved for over ten years, mentioned how he'd fit in with all the children. It opened the floodgates and Graham found himself talking about the little girl Angela who sang like an angel, and Oliver who was married to his sister—well, Ryder's daughter—and how he managed Kildrummy Castle in Scotland and had four children. Then he spoke of his tutor, then on to his years at Oxford and his studies. He stopped, looked at Ryder, and said quietly, "It was at dinner at Lord Carberry's house we met your vicar Piercebridge. The next day he told me I had my mother's eyes." There was more, so much more, and with Vereker's urging Graham continued to talk—about their planned factory in Manchester, how he was designing new parts for the boilers.

Vereker said, "I've read about that, and wondered because I knew there had to be better ways. It is worrisome."

Graham looked excited and the earl's heart filled to near bursting. "Yes, sir, it is worrisome since boilers produce steam at very high pressures—" Graham stopped talking when Eugenie and Donner came into the dining room. The three gentlemen rose.

When Eugenie was gently seated by Blakeney, Graham smiled at the lovely woman who was his sister with her hair drawn back in a bun at the back of her head, curls touching her cheeks. Her morning gown was a soft gray, and she wore only a diamond-encrusted ring on her fourth finger. She looked tired, but no surprise since he'd suddenly appeared in her life. As for Donner, he yawned, smiled at everyone at the table indiscriminately. He paused, stared at Graham. "It is astounding. It is like looking at your mother."

Eugenie looked at her long-lost brother, managed a smile. "I trust you slept well?"

"I did, thank you. And you as well?"

Eugenie blushed, shot a glance at her husband, cleared her throat. "Yes, thank you, very well."

And what was all that about?

Eugenie said, "I studied Mother's portrait. You do have her eyes. It is quite amazing, all of it."

Donner nodded to Graham and Ryder, said to his father-in-law, "Good morning, sir, Mr. Sherbrooke, Graham, and how odd that sounds—my long-lost brother-in-law." He picked up a warm bun from the covered basket, buttered it, spooned on some strawberry jam and took a big bite, smiling around the table as he chewed.

Graham said, "Terrance was telling me about his four sons."

Vereker laughed, waved his newly filled coffee cup at him. "If half the things Terrance attributes to his brood is true, I doubt not one day they will rule the world."

Ryder said, "I have asked myself that question after seeing some of the pranks my children get up to. Currently I am blessed with fourteen children, aged from three to seventeen. My wife would doubtless say our current brood, indeed all past broods, could rival Terrance and his four boys. They might not rule the world, but I pray they will make it a better place."

Eugenie said, "Donner told me of your children, Mr. Sherbrooke. You have fourteen adopted children?"

Ryder, a charming storyteller just as was his own son, Grayson, regaled the listeners with tales of his Beloved Ones, Graham adding more stories of his own. As always in life, there was sadness and tragedy, laughter and tears and endless mayhem.

By the time Vereker took Ryder and his son—his son!—to the stables, he was wrapped in optimism. Eugenie appeared to have accepted her younger brother. There was still so much to learn about his son's missing years, years spent with a collection of children whose backgrounds and breeding were so vastly different, but listening to his son and Ryder talk about the Beloved Ones, he realized how very lucky Graham had been. Even with no memory, he'd been surrounded by love, endless encouragement, sent to Oxford, even made Ryder Sherbrooke's ward. He had a superb brain, always inquiring, ah, a mathematician, an inventor, Vereker marveled at life and what it dished up on your plate. His son, home at last.

Even as he showed Ryder and Graham the stables, spoke

of his farms, he was already planning a grand celebration party to reintroduce his son to the local gentry.

The three men had no sooner appeared back to King's Head for luncheon when Vicar Piercebridge appeared at his front door, a huge question mark in his dark eyes. And then seeing Graham standing next to his father, he smiled hugely. It seemed Graham Hepburn's arrival was already well-known and well discussed in every household in St. Lucy Head.

Over luncheon, Vereker told him what he planned. The vicar could only laugh, joyously, and rub his hands together. He blessed the Lord for the amazing gift. He confided how he hadn't intended to go to London to see his brother-in-law and his sister but something had pushed him, set his feet right on the train. And yet at what he'd believed would be a tedious evening with men talking of business, he was presented with Lord Vereker's precious son.

After luncheon and Vicar Piercebridge had taken his leave, Vereker believed he would expire with pleasure when his son asked him to explain his modern farming techniques to him.

Graham was dressing for dinner in one of his father's exquisitely sewn vests, a light gray wool perfectly complementing his evening coat, when he met Terrance's eyes in the mirror. "Why so formal, Terrance?"

"Ah, how splendid you look, my lord. His lordship will be so pleased to see you in one of his favorite vests—do remark upon the exquisite embroidery in a darker gray—did not his lordship tell you he's invited several local families to dinner to reintroduce you to old families of these parts? Mr. Sherbrooke is wearing a dark blue vest, also one of his lordship's favorites. Allow me to say, my lord, your guardian, Mr. Sherbrooke, is a fine gentleman, knows what's what, knows what he's about—he has exquisite taste as befits the brother of the Earl of Northcliffe and thus he approved the dark blue vest."

Graham realized of course neither Ryder nor his father had told him ahead of time, they were obviously concerned he might be overwhelmed. How like Ryder to protect him, he always had. And now his father. He said without thought, "My guardian uncle, the Earl of Northcliffe, would be pleased his peerage is a sign of good taste."

The light touch of sarcasm flowed right over Terrance's head. He was too busy admiring his handiwork. Dressing a young, strong man of perfect proportions was a delight.

That evening Lord Graham, Viscount Whitestone, met the most important local families. The gentlemen marveled at the serendipitous return of Vereker's son, the older married ladies appreciated the pleasing attention and wit of the young gentleman, and the younger ladies, unmarried or married, slavered. All in all, both Vereker and Ryder believed it was a very successful evening. Brantley nearly popped his lovely waistcoat buttons smiling so widely when he returned to the drawing room after showing out the last of their guests.

When Graham finally lay in his bed, he was exhausted, more from nerves and expectations than genuine fatigue. But he couldn't sleep. Because suddenly, after the house was quiet, a light breeze sent droplets of rain against the bedchamber window; he saw Cam clearly in his mind, heard her voice, her laughter, saw her glasses sliding down her nose. He'd thought of her off and on all day, realized with a start that he'd missed her. A lot. It was a new experience for him, and unsettling. Was she in Bath? If he addressed a letter to her aunt Deveraux, would it reach her?

CHAPTER 30

Royal Crescent
Bath

Pilcher came upon her in the back garden cutting daffodils, nearly ready to unfurl in all their glory, both yellow and white.

He walked directly to her, leaned down and kissed her neck.

Cam thought it was a bee and slapped her neck.

Pilcher said behind her, "So very sweet, my dear, so very invigorating."

She whirled around to see Pilcher standing not even an arm's length away, looking what? Determined? He'd kissed her neck? It was nearly as bad as Teddy The Toad. How had he found her? Had Finch let him roam free? No, more likely, Pilcher had snuck in through the garden gate.

Before she could smack him, Pilcher grabbed her shoulders, jerked her against him. "Camilla, at last I have found you away from watchful eyes. *At last*. I have admired you for so very long, courted you, given you all my attention. I have discovered my heart aches for you when you are not here. You must say you are mine, you must show me your regard. Lady Camilla, I want you to be my wife. Let me kiss you, show you my limitless regard."

Be calm, be calm. She slowly pulled away from him. It was close, but she didn't yell at him, she was frankly too surprised. What was this all about? He wanted to marry her? Just like Teddy. She said to the smashed daffodils she was still holding in her fist, "Not again. Bloody hell, am I cursed?"

A lady shouldn't say bloody hell, it grated on the ear, but Pilcher said, "You're blessed, not cursed."

Cam pushed up her glasses, stared at him. She was blessed? In that world did he live? "Your heart aches? You are in need of a physician, not me." She backed up, holding the daffodils out in front of her. How odd—he looked like a polished gentleman in riding britches and lovely black boots, but she saw the now fierce determination in his eyes, she'd heard it in his voice. She rubbed the back of her neck where he'd kissed her, slowly backed away. Use *reason, continue to be calm, don't knock him to the ground just yet.* She said with great restraint, "Let me be honest, Pilcher. I do not wish to marry you. You may leave now."

His smile never faltered. "I spoke too quickly. You must let me explain, Lady Camilla—no, give me leave to call you Camilla. After last night, I realized I simply could not let us continue with such intense feelings between us without acting. I had to finally tell you of my feelings, my deepest regard for you. And you, Camilla, the sweet looks you've been giving me and such shy smiles, full of pleasure in my company. I knew, my heart knew, it was time for me to speak. Marry me. Be my wife. I will give you all that I have."

She could but stare at him. Sweet looks? Pleasure in his company? She said, calm as could be, "Listen to me, Pilcher, I have not given you any sweet looks, any shy smiles. You must believe me, I do not find particular pleasure in your company—"

He grabbed her, the daffodils went flying, and kissed her, hard, grinding his mouth against hers, trying to open her lips. When he didn't succeed, he shook her shoulders. "No more teasing, no more flirting with other gentlemen to make me jealous. I am here to tell you I will take you to wife. So there is no more need for you to be coy, no more need to drive me to lustful thoughts."

She was all set to bring him low, all set to yell and so her mouth was open. He stuck his tongue deep into her mouth and without hesitation, she bit him, hard.

He yelled, jerked back, grabbed his tongue. Cam shoved at his chest hard with her fists. It didn't move him. He was much stronger than Teddy Jewel.

They stood staring at each other, Pilcher still rubbing his tongue, making him look ridiculous, and the look he gave her wasn't amorous. Cam wanted to kick him, mentally measuring how high she'd have to bring up her leg. Would her wretched petticoat let her leg go up that high?

He dropped his hand from his tongue. "Why did you bite my tongue? Do you believe I've moved too quickly? But you wanted me to kiss you, you've encouraged me, inflamed me! Listen to me, Camilla, you know what I feel about you. Seeing you here, with the flowers, looking so womanly and soft, I couldn't help myself. You didn't have to bite my tongue, it hurts, you could have chewed it in half."

By the end of his speech, he sounded like a bewildered little boy and it settled her, calmed her, but wait. Was he that accomplished an actor? She said, sarcasm thick, "Really, Pilcher? Was I to allow you to shove your tongue down my throat?"

"No, no, I wouldn't have done that, only a bit, a man likes to be inside a woman's mouth, it's like—no, no, never mind that. You know how I feel about you. You've encouraged me, given me your sloe-eyed looks. I am ready to come up to the mark. Listen, you are precious to me, you must know that—"

Since she'd practiced, she managed a credible eyebrow arch. "Really? I am so precious you felt you had to attack me?" She paused. "I guess you didn't hear about what I did to Teddy Jewel in London."

He flushed, stammered, "Well, yes, I heard, but I didn't believe it. You are so gentle, so innocent. I asked you to marry me, to be my wife. I wouldn't lie. You needn't fear returning my physical regard, you will be my wife."

She could but stare at him. "Pilcher, listen to me, I have not been teasing you. I have not been coy. I do not wish your regard or your wet kiss on my neck or your tongue in my mouth. Actually, I wish you would leave and I would never have to see you again."

That drew him up short. He stared down at her, not that far down because Cam was tall. She watched his Adam's apple stutter about in his neck. "I know you do not mean that, you are still teasing me, tempting me. You must believe I am not deceiving you, no, I am a man in love, Camilla, with you. I lost my head, admittedly, in my enthusiasm, but you should not have bitten my tongue. It wasn't the act of a lady. You shouldn't wear glasses either."

"You would have preferred I fainted?"

Her sarcasm floated over his head. He said with great sincerity, "Well, yes, of course that would be expected, the appropriate thing, and I would be pleased to soothe your maidenly sensibilities, convince you of my love and my promise to wed you."

Did he live inside the pages of a bad novel? Cam could but stare at him. "You really mean that? Honestly?"

"Of course. Any gentleman would agree with me."

"It's horrifying."

"Ah, here you are jesting again. But it's time to attend me, Camilla, it's time to tell me you will marry me, smile at me and tell me you want to bear my children. I will provide handsomely for you, you'll see, my father will adore you, you will be happy, content."

Bear his children? The thought curdled her innards. Was he an idiot? She pressed her palm against his chest to keep him back. "Pilcher, listen to me. I am not jesting. I am not the lady for you. I know you adore riding to hounds. Not only am I not an ardent rider, I abhor riding to hounds. I much prefer"—what did she much prefer?—"I much prefer studying mathematics and geometry and I am even developing my own theorems, my own applications for my own theorems. I also plan to be an architect, mayhap build another Royal Crescent here in Bath." She stopped, no place to go from here. Her brain stalled.

He stared at her, nonplussed, genuinely flummoxed. "But you're a female. Everyone knows a female cannot begin to comprehend such matters as mathematics and science. Develop theorems? Why that's ridiculous, a theorem is—that's—" Pilcher stopped cold. He had no idea what a theorem was. But it didn't matter, she didn't either. He got on his hobby horse and rode hard. "Come now, an architect? That is far beyond a well-bred lady. Such matters are far beyond them. Come, admit such pursuits are meant only for a man's brain, a man's intellect." There was clear dismissal in his voice, contempt in his eyes, a lovely infuriating broth. On the other hand, Pilcher was right. She was a lady, a female, worth little besides marrying and bearing children. The only difference between her and Cilly or a washerwoman was she had nicer clothes and didn't have to worry about her next meal. She was unutterably depressed.

He took a step toward her and Cam took another step back. "Listen to me, my love, I do not claim to be a man of science, but of course I could be if I wished to. But I think such things should be left for men with tedious brains and nothing else. They are not men of action like I am. If there were but a war, I would be riding my stallion into battle, my sword cutting down the enemy. But even in times of peace, I am still a man of action, a strong man, and that is what you need, Camilla, a real man to help you understand your place.

"I have courted you. I have given you all my attention. I have worn those white gloves that make my skin itch.

"You are nineteen years of age. It is time you wed, very nearly past time, time you birthed a child, my child, my heir. Now enough of your coyness. Both you and I know this is all a lady's game to bring gentlemen up to the mark so he may have you—make you a woman in all ways."

Cam said, "You are a terrible dancer."

He shrugged. "Once we are wed there will be no need to waste time twirling around a room. I will keep you content without dancing. Now, no more of your teasing games."

And he lunged.

CHAPTER 31

Cam wasn't ready, that's what she'd tell herself later when she tried to excuse herself from acting immediately—flattening Pilcher, sending her knee in his groin as Cilly had taught her or smack him like she had Teddy Jewel. He took her to the ground. He was heavy, lying flat on top of her, and his fists were wrapped around her braids to hold her head still.

She caught her breath and began hitting him on the back, but she had little leverage, and knew it. "Pilcher, stop it! Get off me."

When she opened her mouth he stuck his tongue in, realized what could happen and withdrew fast.

His hot breath on her face, he whispered, "Hold still, no need to tease me, Camilla. We'll wed, I've promised you that. Let me show you what a magnificent husband I'll be, just hold still and let me—"

If only she could get her arms free, she could slap her palms against his ears, but she couldn't budge him. She had to try reason. He was looking down at her breasts. She yelled in his face, his eyes glazed. "Look at me, Pilcher. Listen to me. I do not love you. I will not marry you in this lifetime.

Do you understand me? Now let me go!" And she jerked and heaved, but he was strong, determined on his course.

"You don't mean that, a lady never means that and besides it doesn't matter. I will have you and then you'll accept me, you will have to, but you will not regret it. But in any case, it will not matter." He released one hand so he could grab her breast and squeeze. Her freed arm shot up and she slapped her palm against his ear. He yelped but he didn't stop. She slapped his ear again, yelled right in his face, "Don't you do that, you ass, or I'll slap what few brains you have right out of your head!"

He was grinding himself against her, groaning, an occasional grunt, nearly beside him, her smacks against his ears not making a dent. He panted against her closed mouth, "Camilla, please, accept me, I must have you, I will have you, don't you see? I must, I have no choice, you have no choice." He ground his mouth against hers, forcing hers open and his tongue was in her mouth.

She tried to bite him, but he was fast. Suddenly, he yelled. Aunt Deveraux was standing over him hitting him with her griffin-head walking stick. *Whap, whap*—She wasn't going to smack him in the head, she wasn't stupid, she couldn't kill him, but the temptation was great. She shouted even louder than her normal speaking voice, "YOU YOUNG LOUT! MISCREANT! YOU HAVE NO FINESSE, NOTHING TO RECOMMEND YOU AS A LOVER! YOU ARE A DISGRACE, PILCHER GAYSON. YOU NEVER TAKE A YOUNG LADY AGAINST HER WILL, ESPECIALLY ON THE GRASS WHEN IT WOULD RUIN HER GOWN, YOU BLOODY NITBRAIN, REMOVE YOURSELF NOW! GET OFF HER NOW!"

Whap, whap on his arms and back, excellent cane cracks to his buttocks. He groaned, rolled off Cam onto his side, curled up, covered his head. "Please, please, stop. You're killing me! I didn't do anything. I only wanted to convince her to marry me, I—"

"HA! STOP YOUR WHINING, YOU PATHETIC LITTLE WORM! AT-

TACK MY PRECIOUS NIECE, WOULD YOU! I BELIEVED YOU A GENTLEMAN, MORE FOOL I."

Pilcher tried to get to his hands and knees to crawl away, but Finch struck a poker against his back. "Don't you try to creep away, you blank-brained knave, or I'll lay my lovely poker again on your back and next time, with greater vigor."

Pilcher stopped cold, fell again onto his side, moaned. He wasn't about to move.

Finch walked to Lady Deveraux, said slowly right in her face, admiration clear in his voice, "My brave lady, I see you do not need my assistance, but would you like me to thwack him again with the poker?"

"MAYHAP IN A MOMENT, FINCH, LET US SEE WHAT THE LITTLE WORM DOES. HA, NOT ALTOGETHER STUPID, THE LITTLE WORM. HE ISN'T GOING TO MOVE."

Cam looked up at her aunt, her lovely powdered face red with rage. She rolled up to her feet, gave her aunt a bow. "Aunt, you are magnificent."

"SPEAK UP, GIRL, DON'T WHISPER! EVEN THOUGH YOU ARE STANDING AND YOU GAVE ME A LOVELY BOW—I AM MAGNIFICENT, YOU SAY? WELL, THIS SCOUNDREL MUST THINK SO. FINCH! YOU MAY REMOVE THIS ARSE-BRAIN. WAIT, FIRST HE WILL PROMISE NOT EVER TO COME NEAR MY PRECIOUS CAMILLA OR I WILL SEE HE'S GOT TWO BROKEN LEGS. DO YOU UNDERSTAND, YOU BUGGERING LITTLE TURNIP? NOW YOU MAY RISE."

Pilcher staggered to his feet. His back hurt, his butt hurt, he was humiliated, but at least he was still alive. "My lady, I swear I'll never come near her again, not that I ever wanted to in the first place."

Finch nudged Pilcher in the ribs with the poker. "See you keep your word or her ladyship will break your legs and I will break your head. Now, get you gone, you gutless nettle, else I will hit you again with the poker for attacking my helpless young lady, well, not quite so helpless. You are no longer welcome in our peace-loving household."

Pilcher tried to pull forth a bit of his beleaguered manhood and shook his fist at them. "You are vicious, both of you!" He yelled at Finch, "And you are a mere servant, and you dare to have the gall to strike me?"

Finch grinned. "I am granted gall by birth and by her ladyship."

Pilcher looked at Cam, standing, her hand against an oak tree, her hair out of its braids, straggling around her shoulders, staring at him from behind crooked glasses. He actually hissed, like a snake. "As for you, Camilla Rohman, you're not a lady, and just look at her, wearing glasses. I don't care how great your dowry is, I will not marry you even if you beg me. I never wanted to marry you." He waved his fist at her, turned, tried to walk straight down the path leading to the garden gate but couldn't hide a limp.

"I'M GOING TO TELL YOUR FATHER WHAT YOU'VE DONE, YOU YOUNG LOUT!"

Pilcher paused, one hand on the gate, looked back at them over his shoulder. "It was my father's bloody idea. He ordered me to do whatever was necessary to get her to accept me. He said I could lock you away and forget about you once we were wedded. But I didn't want to marry you, you're too mouthy, you never appreciated me, deferred to me, you never gave me respect. I didn't care about your bloody groats, but he did. Told me my brother needed funds for his lifestyle in London, to impress all those idiots in government, to make all the Society ladies flock to his side and he could have his pick and marry a rich one, like you.

"Curse him, my brother, not my poor father who needs money." He waved his fist at Aunt Deveraux. "And you're nothing but a crazy deaf vicious old bat!"

The gate slammed behind him.

CHAPTER 32

Aunt Deveraux looked after him, said in a thoughtful voice, "I MUST SAY PILCHER DID LEAVE WITH A GOOD PARTING LINE. I RATHER THINK HIS FATHER MIGHT TAKE ANOTHER POKER TO HIM FOR FAILING TO NAB YOU AND YOUR GROATS, MY DEAR, FOR HIS FATUOUS BROTHER."

Finch patted Cam's arm. "Are you all right?"

"My mouth is a bit bruised. Pilcher has sharp teeth. My scalp hurts from him yanking on my braids, but otherwise—" She gave them a huge smile. "I feel perfectly splendid." She pushed her hair out of her face, hugged her aunt, pulled back, kissed her, grinned, and like Finch, said slowly right in her face, "You are a mighty warrior, my lady. Would you marry me since Pilcher has left me and my groats in the dirt?"

Her aunt patted her cheek. "ALAS, DEAREST ONE, IT WOULD NOT BE THE DONE THING. ONE CANNOT LIVE BY LIVELY WIT ALONE. FINCH! LOVELY BLOWS WITH THE POKER, MADE HIM VASTLY SORRY. BUT I WONDER WHY DID HE ACT SO SUDDENLY? I'VE KNOWN HIS FATHER FOR YEARS, HE'S A PALTRY SORT, ALWAYS WHINING. HE WILL DOUBTLESS CLAIM PILCHER IS INCOMPETENT. AS FOR THE MONEY BEING FOR HIS SON SYDNEY, FOR HIS POLITICAL CAREER AND IMPRESSING THE RIGHT PEOPLE, THAT LIE

WON'T FLOAT. AH, I SEE NOW—OLD NICKLEBY HAS FINALLY LOST ALL HIS POOR WIFE'S MONEY AND HE WANTS YOURS AND THUS PILCHER TRIED TO FORCE YOU TO WED HIM. HMM, I SHALL HAVE TO CONSIDER WHAT PUNISHMENT TO METE OUT. I MAY HAVE HIM BANISHED FROM THE TEA ROOM, THAT WOULD BURN HIS FATHER'S SELFISH BRAIN.

"NOW, CHILDREN, WE WILL RESTORE OURSELVES WITH A LOVELY CUP OF TEA. FINCH, DO TELL TURTLE TO BRING FRESH-BAKED SCONES WITH THE TEA TO CALM OUR JANGLED NERVES. AND DEAR BOY, BRING YOUR POKER, KEEP IT CLOSE. YOU NEVER KNOW WHEN ANOTHER MISCREANT WILL TRY TO TRIFLE WITH POOR LITTLE CAMILLA."

The old lady patted her skirts, threw her head back and marched through the gardens to the back door, swinging her cane. Was she whistling? No, impossible, if she were whistling the whole neighborhood would hear her.

Cam said in a meditative voice to Finch, "I wonder if she's done this before, say fifty years ago, when an unwanted suiter tried to force himself on her."

Finch pondered this. "I wouldn't be at all surprised," he said, looking after her, and added with a smile, "She is such a precious old relic, stout of heart, always ready to protect the ones she loves."

Cam rotated her shoulders, stretched, looked at the grass stains on her skirts. "Finch, I did do something to Pilcher. I bit his tongue but good."

"It appears so, my lady, and not a bad thing either. He'll suffer for another several days, an excellent lesson."

"How did you and Aunt Deveraux come out?"

"We were in the drawing room. She was telling me of a potion she used on a randy gentleman she did not wish to bed and it turned him, well, flaccid, but do not inquire into that, you wouldn't understand since you are an innocent. Then my lady was suddenly on her feet, amazingly fast, really, and she was out of the drawing room in a flash, waving her cane. How did she hear you when I didn't? It's amazing and I do not understand."

"I don't understand either, but I am very grateful to both of you. Thank you, Finch."

Cam started toward the drawing room to thank her aunt, kiss her powdered cheek and eat one of Mrs. Tartle's scones when the word *theorem* flashed in her mind. Where had that come from? Where had she heard that word? Yes, she remembered. She learned all about the Pythagorean theorem from the math tutor her father had finally sent to teach her after she'd begged him long and hard. But it wasn't Greek triangles she wanted to review, no, it was the word *theorem*—it was a wonderful word, a word with all sorts of possibilities, a word that sounded very scholarly and profound, like she was very smart when she said it aloud. But what exactly did it mean? She detoured to the small library, lovingly cleaned three days a week, all the tomes read according to Aunt Deveraux, all of the naughty ones many times, and she'd waggled her lovely plucked white eyebrows.

Cam pulled the dictionary from the shelf and looked up *theorem*. It came from the Greek in the sixteenth century. It seemed to Cam nearly everything she didn't understand came from the Greeks. She read through the definition and grinned—such a sophisticated word and yet its meaning was simple. All that was required to fashion a theorem was to look at something with your own eyes, observe it closely, record what it did, how it acted, and draw conclusions based on logic. And what was logic? It was nothing more than common sense. It was amazing. She'd just discovered that something she'd believed was beyond her ken, wasn't. She could see, she could observe, she could draw conclusions. She'd watched Averil manipulate her father by sticking her bosom in his face. Observation, logic—and the end product was always her father's capitulation. Her first theorem.

Cam closed the dictionary, shoved it back onto the shelf between a well-worn copy of *Fanny Hill* and Molière's plays, and returned to sit in her comfortable chair in front of the library fire. She straightened the stem on her glasses, and pictured Alex in her mind. She would speak to him of theorems and invite him to go observing with her. He would think she was very smart indeed.

On the other hand, Alex hadn't answered her note to him. Perhaps he was no longer interested in her. Perhaps he never had been interested in her, only very polite. He didn't care. He'd forgotten all about her.

No, that couldn't be. Cam rose, shook out her skirts, and up went her chin. No more pitiful helpless damsel. She was going to do something. She was going to read two scientific books in her father's library, then she was going to hunt Alex down like a fox. She was going to impress him, demonstrate how smart she was, maybe teach him how to observe properly, and she would kiss him.

Cam told her aunt Deveraux about Alex, how she admired him and how he hadn't answered her letter. Aunt Deveraux patted her cheeks and said at the top of her lungs, "*YOU ARE A SPLENDID, VERY SMART YOUNG LADY. THIS HANDSOME YOUNG BUCK HAS NO CHANCE. MAKE ME PROUD AND BRING HIM DOWN.*"

Six days later, Cam and Cilly left Bath.

CHAPTER 33

King's Head

Vereker announced to the table at large, "I'm glad all of us are here. I'm pleased to say after our second lovely gathering last night, the entire neighborhood nearly all the way to Canterbury has had its curiosity satisfied. All welcomed Graham warmly." He looked at his magnificent son, marveled at his mother's brilliant blue eyes.

Eugenie said, "Of course many remembered you, Graham, and they were so very pleased and surprised you survived, so happy to see you home again after so many years."

Vereker said, "Well, all except Marlin Cox. He's still a worthless little trout-wit. He was always jealous of you when you were boys."

"Marlin," Graham repeated. "The young man who was very solicitous and—"

Vereker merely shook his head. "When you were a boy, you always made excuses for him, Graham, but believe me, what I said is true and he never changed."

Donner said, "What I really appreciated was Cook's splendid boiled capon with oysters. I must say Lady Elsworth ate more than her fair share."

Vereker laughed, shook his head. "If there is an oyster hiding in the neighborhood, Lady Elsworth will find it and pop it right in her mouth, always has since I was a boy. Her poor husband is always on the lookout for stray oysters."

Strive as hard as he could, Graham couldn't picture Lady Elsworth in his mind, eating oysters or not. Last night when she'd seen him, she'd leaned onto her toes and given him a kiss on the cheek. She then allowed him to bend over nearly double and kiss her parchment cheek.

His father continued to wax eloquent, so pleased he was until Eugenie swallowed a bite of her scrambled eggs, and said, "Several guests asked me if we had word of Simon. I had to tell them no, Papa." Vereker felt a flash of numbing cold, felt that cold deep in his heart. He said only, "I am hopeful he will come home as did Graham. But for now, my heart is filled." He raised his coffee cup. "Welcome home, Graham."

Cups were raised, smiles radiated.

Eugenie set down her cup, cocked her head. "I wonder if Uncle Tally knows Graham is home."

Vereker said, "You know as well as I do, Eugenie, Tally knows everything that is going on everywhere. If he's interested, he will come. Otherwise we will see him for his monthly dinner, ah, it's only in two days."

Graham asked, "Who is Uncle Tally, sir?"

Eugenie sat forward. "His full name is Tallyrand Louis Xavier Hepburn, he's thirteen years younger than Father and he's quite eccentric since he got his head bashed on a rock as a young man fighting at Waterloo."

Suddenly, no warning, Graham saw a flash of white, a sort of filmy white, like fine curtains, pushed about by an unseen wind. No, wait, the filmy white was being pushed about as if by shadows trying to come through. He strained to see but then all were gone, the shadows, the filmy white. Graham would swear in that instant he heard a faraway man's voice calling out, but Graham didn't understand. He froze. He knew it a memory trying to come through, an actual memory. About this Uncle Tally?

Graham realized his father was staring at him, his fork raised, now motionless. "Are you all right, Graham?"

"What? Oh yes, sir, forgive my inattention." Graham cocked his head to the side exactly like his father, if he'd known it. "I'm sorry, but I have no memory of him."

Eugenie never looked away from Graham. "You remember nothing? About anything? Anyone? Even Uncle Tally?"

Graham shook his head.

CHAPTER 34

Vereker looked directly into his son's extraordinary eyes, his precious Madeline's eyes. He said, "Your uncle Tally. He was always very kind, very loving, but he always wanted adventure, wanted to spread his wings. At Waterloo he fell from a French soldier's sword in his side and, as Eugenie said, he struck his head. He survived the sword thrust, barely, but his head, his thoughts—it's quite true. Tally came home finally, but he was never the same." Vereker paused, then, "I saw a strange look on your face, Graham. Did you have a memory of him? He spent a lot of time with you and Simon."

Graham shook his head.

Donner leaned forward. "You truly can't remember anything, Graham?"

"No."

Eugenie said, "If Vicar Piercebridge hadn't happened to visit his brother-in-law in London, if you and Mr. Sherbrooke just hadn't happened to be at dinner—the happenstance curdles the brain."

"It was more than happenstance," Ryder said. "I believe it was meant to be, and that sounds odd, but I know Graham was meant to come home."

Vereker felt tears and quickly said, "I agree with you, Ryder. Now, Graham, let me tell you of my plans today. This morning I would like to show you around our home farms, introduce you to our people. You will find them hardworking, honest folk, well, except for Old Clapper, who sits about and complains and suffers his daughter-in-law's sharp tongue, a punishment, believe me. They will welcome you, you were always well-liked. As a boy, you were always playing with the farmers' children. And Simon too, of course. I'm certain Mrs. Flock will fill you with her very fine lemonade, perhaps an almond biscuit. Be prepared to repeat your story, all of them have heard it, but they will want to hear it from you.

"This evening, we'll dine with a man I hold in great esteem, Sir Malcolm Hopson, a mathematician, a philosopher, a man of wit and learning. I'm sure he'll tell you about a brilliant young man he became friends with then he traveled to the Galapagos Islands some years ago."

Eugenie snorted, a charming sound Graham thought. "He is a crashing bore, Father, drones on and on. I've heard all about this young man Charles Darwin and his outlandish ideas. Who cares about these islands with their silly name? Donner and I will dine with the Willowbrooks, win at whist and enjoy their fine wit."

Vereker grinned at his daughter. He said to his son, "Unlike you, my boy, she has little interest in science and mathematics and all those wonderful things yet to be invented."

Graham nodded. "I shall be happy to regale Eugenie and Donner with my adventures, particularly about little Angie who loved to put overripe plums in my bed." But he was remembering that white veil, those shadows pushing against it, and he realized he wasn't himself, he was young, only a boy, and he was looking up, probably at Uncle Tally.

Graham would find out from Blakeney where Uncle Tally lived and visit him. Perhaps seeing his uncle would spark more memories. He felt hope. He looked up to see Ryder studying him. Ryder knew him so very well. He'd been his father and confidant and his friend for over ten years. Did he guess something as his father had? Probably. What had Ryder and his father seen on his face?

As for Ryder, he pondered as he walked around the estate, through the magnificent gardens, wending through the dozen or so sheep grazing in the wide park opposite the manor. He stood at the edge of the wide ribbon of water, known as the Green Stream. He couldn't see below the surface and wondered what was down there, out of sight. He wondered what his children would think. Ah, there were only fourteen now since Teddy had left to become a solicitor's assistant. It was time to find another abused child. So many different personalities, his Beloved Ones. He considered himself the most blessed of men. As he stood there, the green water rippled, stilled again. Maybe there was something beneath that green surface, something frightening, something with slimy scales. He saw more movement, waves building and falling in on themselves. He picked up a stick and threw it at a hump that seemed to rise straight up, not quite breaking the surface. The stick didn't float away, it sank. Was there something beneath the surface that grabbed it, to gnaw on it, to swallow it? He laughed at himself. Ryder shook his head, he was rivaling his son Grayson's imagination.

He looked around at the sheep placidly grazing all around him, heard the occasional *baa* because he was encroaching in their area. He looked at the mighty oak and elm trees surrounding the acres of green grass, rising up the hills, thick and lush. He thought about Eugenie. She'd been welcoming, finally, but he wondered. He'd seen her eyes resting on her newly returned brother, and there was something he didn't understand in that look of hers, something she was thinking, feeling, but what? Jealousy? When Graham and his brother, Simon, had disappeared she'd been the only child left. Had she been smothered in attention and indulged until she believed herself the princess of the castle? Was she really happy he was home? He was a shock, certainly, to all of them. No, no, all would be good. Graham was home, where he belonged.

Ryder walked back to the house, weaving his way through the tame sheep. Of course Vereker hadn't invited him along with Graham on their jaunt to the home farms. He wanted his son to himself, to show him off to all the tenant farmers, the young god, so perfect. Ryder remembered the time Graham had lied through his teeth to sneak away to a traveling bawdy show in Lower Slaughter. He'd been seventeen, full of a young man's lust. He'd snuck back into Brandon House, his young male's eyes still glazed with lust and of course he'd been found out.

Ryder decided he wanted to meet Uncle Tally. Before he left King's Head he wanted to be certain there was no possible danger to Graham because he knew very well the danger to Graham as a boy was still here or nearby, ready to strike again. Was the danger from this poor man wounded so severely at Waterloo? Did he have any ideas on who had tried to murder Graham and his brother so many years ago? Had he been behind it?

Ryder sighed. Life was always changing and shifting in unexpected ways, bringing in new people whose motives were many times hidden, and people who lied. He also planned to speak to Graham tonight once everyone had gone to bed.

CHAPTER 35

King's Head

Vereker felt infinitely blessed as he listened to Vicar Piercebridge wax eloquent on the miraculous return of his beloved son, Lord Graham, Viscount Whitestone. He pictured a new stained-glass window, perhaps showing the Last Supper in bright colors, installed directly behind the ancient pulpit. Light would flood in, rainbow colors, if, that is, it wasn't raining. It would be perfect. He would visit Canterbury himself, make inquires. Perhaps a lovely window could be made and installed by the end of the year.

He couldn't stop smiling, even now remembering every detail of his time with his son the previous day, meeting all his tenant farmers who, naturally, remembered the young boy, friends with all of their sons and daughters, and Graham had met those sons as young men now, many married with children. Even if they knew he had no memory of any of them, nothing was said.

Vereker encouraged Graham to speak of his time at Oxford, his plans to make English trains the very best in the world, talking of his ideas for water boilers, and he felt so blessed that he himself had the same interests, only he didn't believe he was as smart as his son. Well, Madeline had been brilliant, so many ideas she'd had, so many improvements she'd made on simple everyday tools, like a special knife to peel potatoes, simple really but Mrs. Sample had been thrilled. It was odd, though. He'd never before thought of her in that light until Graham spoke of ideas to lessen the lurching of a train and he would swear he heard her voice.

Graham sat beside his father in the family pew, dark green embroidered cushions for Hepburn bottoms for nearly two hundred years now.

He was mildly embarrassed when Vicar Piercebridge smiled continuously at him during his sermon about God's wondrous miracles, giving himself no credit. But of course everyone in St. Lucy Head knew of his amazing discovery by the vicar, that he was the one responsible for the return of the Long-Lost Heir, no need to belabor the point and be accused of self-aggrandizement. To Graham's pleasure, the vicar also spoke about Graham's blessed savior Mr. Ryder Sherbrooke, who'd actually saved his life and made him his ward. He further added that because of Mr. Sherbrooke's goodness, he, the vicar, was able to meet the young Viscount Whitestone and recognize him as the Hepburn heir and he'd come home to his beloved family. Graham watched Ryder's face. He knew him well enough to realize he was deeply embarrassed.

Of course Graham had already met nearly everyone in St. Lucy Head, shaking so many hands, accepting so many bows and curtsies when they'd arrived at the late Norman church with its ancient stone bell tower set on a lovely grassy hill, the Channel its backdrop. An impressive church and he'd had no memory of it at all.

He was grateful Ryder sat on his other side, close, a bulwark from his earliest memories, always there ready and willing to protect him, love him, give him every opportunity.

Then his father, seated on his other side, touched his arm, smiled at him.

His father.

After service, given more hands to shake and well wishes, Graham wondered how he could get himself alone after luncheon. He wanted to visit his Uncle Tally. But it seemed the only time his father wasn't beside him was when he had to relieve himself. But then his father, all regrets, told him and Ryder he had to attend to a problem with a tenant farm dispute. He prayed it wouldn't take long to resolve, and looked toward Graham. Graham knew he wanted him to accompany him, but also knew it wouldn't be the done thing.

Graham left Ryder discussing hunters with Donner. He got directions from Blakeney for his uncle Tally's cottage in the eastern forest. He quickly changed into breeches and a simple white linen shirt and boots. He himself saddled the velvet-nosed chestnut Stanley, gave him a carrot from Cook's garden he'd seen lying in a basket. He rode the short distance to the cliffs overlooking the English Channel. It was a splendid sight, the sun bright overhead, fanciful white clouds scattered over a blue bowl, a perfect day.

As he stood there, Stanley beside him, softly blowing, a stiff wind off the water tangling through his hair, he saw Cam again in his mind's eye, smiling, no, she was grinning like a bandit at something she'd said—or he'd said. He missed her. He was aware of a hollow feeling deep inside him, muting the very air around him. She should be standing here beside him, making a jest, admiring the bright, choppy water, the glorious view from this vantage point, giving him a look of awareness, and he knew to his soul she would want to be standing beside him as well, the wind blowing her skirts against her long legs. It was an ache, deep and abiding. What was he to do? Well, now Cam's father couldn't object to him. He was now a lord—how very odd that felt—Viscount Whitestone. He was a proper gentleman, not a waif saved by Ryder

Sherbrooke, well educated, well dressed, to be sure, but still a nobody of no account at all who didn't even know who he was. But now he was somebody worthy of her.

Graham knew he was blessed, but he also knew to the deepest part of him that his life had now flown apart and was pushing him into a new direction. He was both afraid and excited. He remembered overhearing Ryder say to his wife, Sophie, *He speaks like a young gentleman. Someone didn't want him to live.*

He was now a peer, Viscount Whitestone, and that someone who'd tried to kill him was probably still close.

He turned away from the cliff and rode Stanley back into the eastern forest, looking for the path Alrick, one of the stable lads, had told him about. *Aye, ye needn't worry, yer lordship, me fine boy Stanley knows how to find Master Tallyrand. He knows the trail like the back of 'is hoof. Master Tallyrand don't want a well-marked trail, likes his privacy, he do.*

Oaks and maples crowded in, tall, still winter bare, each tree striving to get the most sun. The forest was silent, only the sound of Stanley's hooves kicking up the occasional pebbles or a pile of leaves. It took him only ten minutes. Stanley never paused, never sniffed the air, went left then right and left again until they reached a small clearing and in its center stood a stone cottage, a stream of gray smoke coming out its chimney. Graham saw a garden to the side of the cottage, well planted, enclosed with low white-painted fencing. He patted Stanley's nose and looped his reins over a tethering post. He heard a whinny from a stable off to his left. Stanley answered, tapped his right front hoof. Probably a mare.

Graham paused a moment to admire the well-scythed lawn. He walked along a beautifully set stone walkway leading to a heavy wooden front door painted a whimsical bright red. It was a lovely setting, a lovely property, an exquisite cottage.

The front door opened and a tall man, handsome, clean

shaven, dressed in well-worn black breeches and white shirt, old boots on his feet, walked slowly outside, his eyes never leaving Graham's face.

Again, Graham saw a flash of white in his mind, a thin sort of veil, then it was gone.

Graham said, "Uncle Tally?"

The man simply continued to stare at Graham, then he said in beautiful English, "Yes. I heard you were back. I've often wondered over the years if somehow you and Simon were alive, but of course as the years passed, I had to accept you were dead. So long, so many years. How many? Eleven years? But here you are. I heard there was no sign of your brother, only you. Blakeney told me you were blanked-brained, had no memory of anything at all." He paused, studied Graham's face. "You do not remember me?"

Graham said, "No, I don't remember anyone or anything. I'm sorry."

Tally cocked his head to the side, grinned, showing white teeth, then a full-bodied laugh. "Ah, then you can't remember when I called you and your brother insolent whelps, the two of you dirty little monkeys, both of you always into everything, always bothering me with your endless mischief and pranks, your constant demands I tell you all about Waterloo. Simon even wanted to see the scar on my side from the sword thrust. As for you, you always wanted to know how I made my gardening tools, not satisfied until I showed you each step. I even taught you how to shoe a horse." He grinned. "Well, it was actually the stable lad Odel, but I was there, watching closely."

Graham couldn't help it, he smiled back. "Did you show Simon your wounded side?"

Tally shook his head. "A young boy didn't need to see an ugly puckered scar. So it is true, you have no memory of anything at all? Not even your father? King's Head?"

Graham shook his head, but there—a blurred image of himself, a horseshoe in his hand, then it was gone.

Tally said, and Graham thought he heard a catch in his voice, "And Simon, he wasn't with you. Then he's gone."

Graham felt a clutch to his heart even though he had no memory of his brother. "It seems so. I myself was thrown, probably unconscious, into the Thames, pulled out by wharfmen who declared me dead. But Mr. Sherbrooke saved me, raised me, became my guardian. Vicar Piercebridge saw me, recognized me. Both Mr. Sherbrooke and I came to King's Head."

Tally nodded because naturally, he'd already heard all of this. He said softly, "You have your beautiful mother's eyes. She was wicked, was Madeline, she was always playing tricks on your father, on everyone, really. I remember how she'd hide from him, leave clues, most of them mathematical, make him search her out. Their laughter, it filled King's Head. So long ago it was.

"Madeline helped me plant my garden, taught me how best to set the stone walkway given the diameter and thickness of each stone and how deeply it would sink into the soil. But she died." He sighed. "It was an awful time. Your father, my brother, he was so very proud of her, and her death destroyed him for a time. Well, Graham, come in and I'll make you a cup of tea. How odd it is—you're taller than I am."

He paused a moment, stepped forward and brought Graham against him and squeezed him hard. "A man grown, of my size. I doubt you're an insolent whelp now, my lord."

CHAPTER 36

Sherbrooke townhouse
Portman Square
London

"The hackney doesn't smell, but still, all sorts of people have ridden in this carriage, sat on these seats. What will people think if they see Lady Camilla Rohman riding in a rented hackney?"

Cam was almost too excited and scared to think, but finally, she managed, "You're a snob, Cilly." *Distract her, distract her.* And so she did. "Forget the hackney, think about how we traveled all the way from Bath to London in the magnificent steam train. I only wish we could have ridden in her maiden trip to Bath. Can you imagine? Cilly, can you believe it only took us eight hours to arrive in London and only four stops? And none at all after Reading."

Cilly said, "I know, I know, and now you're going to have to repeat to me we had to have the stops, more water and more coal and just look at all the people who want to go to London with us. I didn't like the hopper."

Cam laughed at her. "But it was a first-class hopper. All right, so the small compartment with a seat with a hole in the middle open over the tracks was a bit different, but better than stopping by the side of the road on a long carriage ride, don't you agree? And you could close and lock the door."

Cilly had to agree.

Keep going, keep her distracted. She gave Cilly her most winsome smile. "And the seats were wonderful, the cushions so thick and comfortable, well, at least in first class. We didn't have to eat their food either."

Cilly said, "All right. We had a lovely lunch packed for us by Mrs. Tartle, not that I am particularly fond of the goat cheese she adores and no one else does."

Who cared about cheese? Cam said again, enthusiasm bubbling, "Just imagine, Cilly, only eight hours from Bath to London. Finch saw us and our luggage on the train in Bath at nine o'clock this morning and now it's not quite six o'clock in the evening. It's amazing—we live in an age of miracles."

Cilly looked out the window. "Yes, yes, all that is true. It's going to be dark soon and here we are in a carriage with no escort. How much longer?"

"We have another half hour until it's full dark. It's only dusk."

Cilly stared out the window again, she frowned. "Now what is this? I don't think we're going in the right direction."

Cam said quickly, "Our driver is probably taking a different route. *Distract, distract.* "Remember just two years ago how long it took us to travel by carriage from London to Bath? The endless hours riding in a swaying carriage, the posting houses with so much noise and as for the bed, who knew what you would be sleeping on, a board or a spring sticking in your back? Ah, Cilly, we are so lucky to live now in such an incredible age." *How many ways could she say the same thing?* She started to say it was no wonder Alex was so excited about trains, so eager to make them better and better.

But she managed to keep her mouth shut. "Weren't you impressed with the new Paddington Station?"

"It was loud and dirty and a rabbit warren. Too many people, all scurrying about trying to find their trains and even the blessed porters didn't know.

"Wait, this is Paulson Street, I recognize the redbrick house on the corner—"

"We were lucky. Our three young porters took excellent care of us. We didn't have to do a thing and they did at least know what route to get outside."

"Come, Cam, you had to pretend to be helpless and lost, which you were, and they came running because you're so lovely, well, and so am I and—"

Cam said, "Oh no, the lads recognized the expensive cashmere jacket and knew there'd be coin in it for them. And your lovely eyes as well."

Cilly didn't shake her head. She knew the power of her eyes. She smiled. "The one young man—remember how he hastened to tell you his name—Jedediah Spring—and he called two other young men to carry out luggage, while he directed them."

"Jedediah even turned down three hackneys until one was clean enough to suit him—and us."

The hackney pulled to a stop.

Here at last.

Cilly leaned out the window. "Wait, this isn't Ormond Square. This isn't your father's house. Cam, I know where we are. It's the Sherbrooke townhouse." She whipped around. "WHAT ARE YOU DOING? You didn't tell me we were coming here. This is where Alex Ivanov lives, isn't it? You are chasing him down here in his own home? You little hussy! Are you mad?" She grabbed Cam's arm. "Listen to me, Cam. I know Alex Ivanov is, well, to be frank, a beautiful young man, I'll admit that, but you've lost your reason if you think it is at all acceptable to chase him down like a hare. It isn't done, particularly by a young lady who would lose everything—her reputation, her good name, not to mention ruining her family."

She smacked her own forehead. "I should have known all your talk about the trains—you just wouldn't stop—you drew me in too. You said the same things during our journey and then you repeated it all again and again. Your father will give me notice, he'll see I have no character reference, I'll starve in a ditch, and why? Because my dratted charge lost her head and all reason over a bloody handsome face. I should hold you down, swat you like I did when you were a little girl."

A burly fellow with a lovely black felt hat curled up on the sides opened their door and gave them a big gap-toothed grin. Cam pulled free of Cilly's arms and eased over her, quickly jumped down. She asked him to wait, please. This was only their first stop. Yes, she would make it worth his while. "Cilly, your swats never hurt me, too many petticoats. Now, don't worry! I do know what I'm doing, trust me."

"Like when you asked me to trust you when you were five years old and pulled a worm out of a crab apple and wanted to stuff it in your mouth."

"Oh dear, I think I just tasted worm. Don't worry, Cilly, I'll be back in ten minutes, I promise."

And she was off.

CHAPTER 37

Cilly watched Lady Camilla Rohman raise her skirts and take the stone front steps two at a time and closed her eyes. They were doomed. Both of them. She wasn't a little girl anymore and Cilly couldn't swat her bottom. She was a woman grown, and the woman grown was about to make a very big mistake. Cilly watched her march right up to the front door of the impressive Sherbrooke townhouse. Luckily she saw no one else in the square, a blessing, but there were windows, so many windows with possible eager eyes to track her unladylike run to the townhouse. *A single lady, a YOUNG single lady.* She groaned when she saw the front door open, saw Cam step inside. What would happen? She leaned her head back against the mostly clean squabs, closed her eyes and thought of the myriad ditches that could be her home in the near future.

Cam had told her every thought in her young head, until she'd met Alex Ivanov. She'd spoken of him at first. After the debacle with that goose-brained idiot Pilcher Gayson and how he'd attacked her, she'd grown quiet. It was impossible not to feel pride for Lady Deveraux attacking the hapless Pilcher with her cane and Finch with his trusty poker. All the household spoke of it with great relish and delight and no doubt also spoke to every servant in the neighborhood, so within three hours, give or take, all of Bath knew what had happened. Thank the powers above, Lady Deveraux had power in Society so Lady Camilla Rohman wouldn't be blamed and called a scandalous hussy, no, it would be Pilcher to be punished, at least for a little while since gentlemen rarely paid for their bad behavior. Bless Finch, who'd learned from Galson, Pilcher's father's valet, that he was in financial straits and badly needed money not for his heir, Sydney, but for himself, and thus Pilcher's orders to wed the heiress, by hook or by crook, namely, Camilla Rohman, the prize of the current crop. Cilly smiled briefly remembering how Lady Deveraux presented Finch with a bottle of her finest champagne, and together they'd laughed and toasted each other until they were both snoring on the sofa.

Bless Lady Deveraux, she'd also sent champagne to all the servants as well. When she'd met Finch the next morning, they'd commiserated about their aching heads. Before she'd left, Cilly was aware of Finch looking at her in just a certain questing way, and she'd blushed. Hmm.

But that was Bath, and this was London, a very different kettle of fish. Cam was chasing after a man and there wasn't a way Cilly could help her if she was caught. Oh dear.

As for Cam, she felt her heart pound loud, fast strokes as she slapped the lion's head knocker against the door. Then her heart leapt into her throat when the grand Sherbrooke front door opened and the estimable Mr. Plume stood in front of her.

He blinked, but no other emotion appeared on his pleasant face. "Lady Camilla?" Mr. Plume was very smart, but then again even Mr. Plume's idiot brother-in-law would recognize a young lady in love. Was she alone? What was going on here? Oh dear, he knew to his boots this lovely young lady was chasing down Alex, now actually Lord Graham, Viscount Whitestone. Mr. Sherbrooke had written to him, and he and the household had toasted Lord Graham—and didn't that sound splendid? He recalled three snifters of brandy he himself had downed in the celebration. Lady Camilla looked scared, bless her, and excited, her lovely eyes nearly dilated. She looked neat as a pin and really quite lovely in a pale green walking dress and the matching cashmere jacket, her lovely hair drawn back, plaited into thick braids stacked atop her head, little loose curls dangling around her face.

Cam cleared her throat so she wouldn't squeak, and silently repeated, *I understand theorems, I'm confident. I can do anything.* "Good afternoon, Mr. Plume. Is Mr. Ivanov here?"

Mr. Plume gave her a gracious smile, a lovely bow, and quickly stepped back, waved her in. Best to get her off the front stoop as quickly as possible. "Ah, do come in, Lady Camilla. I see it's beginning to sprinkle, a lovely Scottish mist, you know, but of course you do not have an umbrella, which I might add is very optimistic of you." He looked around, thankfully saw no one. Still there was Lady Marchand across the square who loved nothing better than to spy on her noble neighbors.

"Thank you, Mr. Plume. Ah, Mr. Ivanov, could you tell him I'm here?"

"I fear not. He's currently with Mr. Sherbrooke at King's Head in Kent." Should he tell her about the precious young gentleman's new honors? No, it was not his place.

Mr. Plume watched her face fall, saw her stiffen her spine.

"Ah, King's Head is on the coast, near Dover."

Mr. Plume nodded.

What is this? What the devil is King's Head? And why not Queen's Head? Dover isn't all that far from London. Is there a train there? Some tracks needing fixing and they'd called Alex? Cam cocked her head to the side. "But why, Mr. Plume? Did Alex—Mr. Ivanov—wish to go to this King's Head near Dover, on the coast? He perhaps wanted to see the white cliffs? Did he wish to visit Dover Castle? Isn't this very odd?"

Mr. Plume's face was closed.

He was like Osbourne, never said a word about the family. "Ah, I had written him a note, telling him of my rather hurried departure to Bath to my aunt Deveraux. I never received an answer from him and, well, I was concerned he could be ill, you know."

Mr. Plume knew very well. "No, Lady Camilla, neither he nor Mr. Sherbrooke is ill. I fear Mr. Ivanov never received your missive. Please come into the drawing room. I have a lovely fire set against the chill, which there usually is in London, even in our supposed summers. That's right, just follow me. You can have a nice cup of tea, perhaps a nutty bun, though I doubt Cook has made any since neither gentleman is in residence, but perhaps some tasty seed cakes. Come, Lady Camilla. I shall fetch your letter to Mr. Ivanov, if you like."

Cam realized she did want her letter back. It was too pathetic she'd even written to him. And he'd left without telling her. *What will you do next? Weep? Stiffen your spine.* "Mr. Plume, could you please send someone to tell the hackney carriage to wait for me? And ask the lady to come in?"

Mr. Plume gave her a fatherly smile. "I think it best that I dismiss the carriage and you and your companion"—thank heavens she wasn't alone—"will be taken to Ormond Square in the Sherbrooke carriage."

Five minutes later, Cilly sat beside Cam in the drawing room, each with a cup of tea in her hand. Cam smiled at Mr. Plume, said in her most imperious voice, "Please tell me the reason for Mr. Ivanov's and Mr. Sherbrooke's abrupt departure for this King's Head near Dover, on the coast."

Mr. Plume tried to stiffen his spine, be polite and tell her nothing at all, but he fell prey to the misery he saw in her very pretty eyes. He sighed and gave it up. "Mr. Ivanov is no longer a man without a memory, saved, as you know, as a young boy, by Mr. Sherbrooke, who, I'm sure you already know, made him his ward. We discovered quite by remarkable happenstance he is actually Graham Hepburn, Viscount Whitestone. He and Mr. Sherbrooke immediately left for Dover, to King's Head, the estate of Lord Graham's father, Vereker Hepburn, Earl St. Lucy."

Whatever it was Cam had expected wasn't this. This was in a different universe, or beyond. Lord Graham? Then it struck Cam with the force of a bolt of lightning. He was now a lord and she was a lady. She burst into the biggest smile Mr. Plume had ever seen. She raised her teacup, toasted him. "Mr. Plume, what is your first name?"

"Ah, it's Ellison, Lady Camilla."

"You have given me such wonderful news that if ever I have a child, his name will be Ellison. Thank you, thank you." She set down the teacup, grabbed Cilly's hand, and dragged her, nearly danced from the room. She called out over her shoulder, "King's Head, you say, Mr. Plume?"

"Wait, Lady Camilla! Let Jeffrey fetch a carriage!"

Now five minutes later, Cam and Cilly were on their way to Ormond Square. Cam wanted to dance, maybe shout out a ditty or two. Now she could tell her father she could be a viscountess, Viscountess Whitestone, and she would assist her husband with improving train boilers. She would observe train problems, she would learn mechanical theorems to make improvements. She would kiss his face off.

Cilly marveled, watching her excitement turn the air around her vibrant with happiness. Life was the strangest series of happenings. Who could predict a rainbow when a blizzard had threatened?

But what if Mr. Ivanov—no, Lord Graham, Viscount Whitestone—didn't love Cam? Cilly closed her eyes and prayed. Finch popped into her mind—Edward, lovely name. When would she see him again?

CHAPTER 38

Whitsonby House
Ormond Square

Osbourne met Cam and Cilly at the front door. He looked like the ark had sailed without him and the water was rising fast. There was a tic in his left eye.

The house was absolutely silent. Cam grabbed his arm. "Osbourne, what is wrong? What has happened? Is my father—"

"It's her ladyship, Lady Camilla. Her ladyship—she's—" He shut his mouth, the tic quickened. "You must see your father, he's in his study."

Something happened to Averil? Cam pulled herself together, nodded to Osbourne and said to Cilly, "Take care of our valises, Cilly. I'll be up as soon as I can to tell you what is happening." And she was running past Osbourne to her father's study. The door was locked. She knocked. "Papa, it's Cam, open the door. Please, Papa."

An endless time passed, though Cam knew it was only seconds until the door opened. Her father stood in front of her in his shirtsleeves, his hair standing on end, his handsome face pale. He looked at her as if he'd never seen her before.

She grabbed his arms, shook him. "Papa? What's wrong?"

"Cam, what are you doing here? You're in Bath."

She shook him again. "Papa, it doesn't matter. I came home. What's happened? What about Averil?"

He pulled away from her, sighed and turned to walk back to the fireplace. He leaned his arm on the mantel, stared down at the orange embers sparking, then settling again in the logs.

She came after him, laid her hand to his shoulder. Whatever it was, it was bad. "Papa? What happened to Averil?"

He turned slowly and gave her a ghastly smile. "She's gone, Cam, your stepmother is gone. She left while I was in a meeting with our architect about the factory in Manchester."

"But where did she go?"

He pointed to a sheet of paper on his desk. "She wrote she had to go to her mother in Leeds, that she must stay as long as her mother needs her."

"She's never spoken to me about her mother, but I thought that was simply because she didn't like me, didn't want to tell me anything. I don't understand why she would leave without talking to you, asking you to accompany her—"

He shook his head, gave a ghastly laugh. He looked again at that single sheet of paper. He picked it up, wadded it into a ball and tossed it onto the logs. There was a brief flare, then ashes. He gave a harsh laugh. "I wasn't a complete fool. Before I married her, I made inquiries into her background. She didn't speak to you of her mother because both her parents are long dead. She was raised by an aunt who died and left her enough funds to come to London. Her aunt had been close friends with Lady Pelicourt, and so Averil asked her to introduce her into Society. As you know, Lady Pelicourt is very old, her mental powers on the wane. After much prodding, she did remember the aunt. Averil was charming and beautiful and so she happily loosed her on Society." He paused, laughed again. "The fact is, Cam, Averil could have been a pauper, it didn't matter to me. I loved her, wanted her desperately and so I married her." Pause, then, "Do you know it's been exactly six months today? I went earlier to Rutledge's and bought her a diamond bracelet. For our six-month anniversary." He gave a bitter laugh.

He not only looked devastated, he looked like the life was draining out of him. She hated it. *Bring him back, bring him back*. Cam said matter-of-factly, "Do you know where she went, Papa?"

Whit shook his head, laughed yet again, at himself. "She took all her jewels as well as all the centuries-old family emeralds, really quite valuable, as well as the five thousand pounds I always kept in my safe. She doubtless watched me open the safe, memorized the combination. Her maid Elvira who came with her here to Whitsonby House is gone as well. It was all a sham, Averil was a sham."

Cam said, "But why would she leave? She was the wife of a powerful man, she had servants. She had standing. Why?"

He sighed, sat down in his favorite chair. "Cook told me she'd just come out to her herb garden to pick parsley when she saw the mistress slip through the garden gate. She said she knew it was coming on to rain and her ladyship didn't have her umbrella. She hurried after her." He paused, drew a deep breath. "She saw Averil kiss a young man who then helped her into a black carriage, then entered behind her. The carriage left. Cook told me there was luggage strapped on top of the carriage. She thought she saw Elvira's face, but she couldn't be sure." When he stopped, Cam was pleased to see a blaze of anger in his eyes. "I asked her if she could describe the horses and she remembered one of them—a white mare with a black star. I know who he is—Gerrod Bartsleigh, a young ne'er-do-well, handsome, of course, popular with hostesses, they loved his wit and charm. He was invited everywhere. He's the third son of an army captain, a hard man, I'm told. Not the son, the father. She ran off with him. Ah, Cam, I am a great fool."

Cam couldn't believe it. "Gerrod Bartsleigh? You're right, Papa, he's a scoundrel, too smooth, in my opinion, always wears too much pomade in his hair. I heard one lady say he was always on the hunt, but still he was very popular. Do you think they were just biding their time until Averil could get enough of your money before they left?"

"Yes, that's what I think. He will leave her too, Cam, once they've spent all my money. I heard he cheated at cards. Does he have any moral fiber? It doesn't matter now."

Cam felt fury on her father's behalf, trusting the wrong woman, giving her his love, his name—ah, but she felt utter joy she'd never have to deal with the dreadful woman again with her manipulating bosom. What to say? How to hide her joy when her father was shattered by Averil's betrayal?

She wanted to say the two of them deserved each other, but she was quiet, watching him. Was he still in too much pain, too newly betrayed that he hadn't yet realized what was going to happen?

But of course he'd realized the implications. He said, "You know the moment this story leaks out of these walls, and believe me, it most assuredly will, I will be a laughingstock. The two of them could not have executed a more humiliating plan."

He was right, of course. *No fool like an old fool*, she could hear the words said over and over, gentlemen in small groups, supposedly commiserating, but not-so-secretly pleased he'd been taken in by a beautiful young female all of them had lusted after but he'd been the winner for her hand. And she'd left him with her lover, all planned, perfectly accomplished. The ladies would do the same, whispering behind hands, embellishing, laughing at him.

He said, staring at the dying flames in the fireplace, "The

few real friends I do have will honestly care about what has happened, ah, but all the others? Society is merciless, Cam, something you have yet to learn. Society will find this tale of a stupid man delicious."

He sat down in his big chair, looked at her with deadened eyes. "My old man's foolishness will touch you as well, since your gullible father bragged so fatuously to all his friends. You, my sweet girl, will be tainted. As for Eliza, I know Winstead won't break their engagement. He's a good man, but he will take her immediately to the country and return only for their wedding." He gave her a twisted smile. "Eliza won't like that. She'll be under the thumb of a new stepmother-in-law and six children pulling on her skirts. I find myself feeling sorry for my future son-in-law. It shames me, Cam, but the picture of your sister not anointed the queen of her little kingdom warms my heart. Maybe she'll learn, maybe she'll become—" He stopped, sighed. "No, I'm fooling myself. Ah, but you, my dearest one, you do not deserve this—you're magic like your mother—" His voice hitched and he fell silent.

Cam came down on her knees beside his chair, lifted his fisted hand, smoothed it between hers. "Papa."

He slowly turned his head to look down at her. She gave him a blazing smile. "Papa, none of this is going to happen." She leaned up and hugged him. "I know what we're going to do."

CHAPTER 39

Whitsonby House
Ormond Square

"My lady, Mr. Ivanov is here."

Cam, who'd just left Eliza in her bedchamber, her maid Claudine hovering over her, patting her ineffectively, whispering over and over that everything would be all right now, blinked at Osbourne. Her heart began to hammer, fast, faster. Alex—Graham—was here? Oh goodness, it was too soon—there was still so much to be done. She hadn't even thought to tell her father about Alex, no, Graham and his amazing transformation into Viscount Whitestone. Later, she'd tell him later, but now, her heart leapt into her throat, she grinned like a fool. "Do show him in, Osbourne."

Graham walked through the door, his eyes immediately watching her walk gracefully down the grand staircase, never looking away, now he was striding toward her. He grabbed her, sank his hands into her hair, lifted her off her feet, kissed her until she was—

He stood handsome and windblown in the open doorway,

his hands at his sides. He smiled at her as she walked down the staircase. He took a step toward her, stopped. "I received a message from your father, Cam. I came as quickly as I could. Why aren't you in Bath?"

Osbourne cleared his throat. "My lady, Mr. Ivanov, let me show you to the drawing room."

Osbourne, not a blind ninny, said, "When his lordship arrives, I shall tell him you are in here." And left them alone and closed the door.

Her father. Right now he was at White's, the gentlemen's gossip center in Society, performing his part, finally admitting the truth to his friends when they saw him so melancholy, sitting silent and alone, showing all how very devastating it all was and yes, a brandy would be good. Perhaps heated? Yes, yes. Her father was a fine actor—they would see his pain because it was real enough, and they would believe what he told them. And the gossip mills would grind out what had happened to Lady Whitsonby and Society would shudder and be thankful they didn't have her blood.

"Alex—no, I must call you by your real name now—Graham Hepburn, Viscount Whitestone, son of Earl St. Lucy. Father will be home soon, or perhaps not so soon, we'll see.

"I, ah, happened to stop by to see you—I'd just arrived from Bath and wondered why I hadn't heard from you, no answer to my note—and Mr. Plume told me of your good fortune. I'm so happy for you, ah, Graham—it's a fine name indeed." She couldn't help herself, she ran to him, grabbed his arms. "My lord. Ah, that has a lovely ring to it, don't you think?" She said his name again, slowly, as if tasting it." She paused, searching his face. "You still don't remember anything at all?"

Graham looked down at a face he'd memorized in his mind, but his memories hadn't delivered this precious face in all its glorious detail. He even loved her lovely ears with the small pearl earrings she favored. He'd missed her so much he hurt.

You're beautiful, Cam. I've missed you like the very devil.

"I'm sorry but I never saw your letter to me. It's lovely to see you, Cam, it's really quite nice."

It was a start. She took him in, his face, saw his incredible eyes were steady on her face, only her, and her heart sang. Surely she would never feel happier in her life, like she could float to the ceiling and drift back down like a feather, so easy and light. She looked up at his face and whispered, "Graham," and kissed him.

The feel of her mouth, the hammering of his own heart in his ears, the instant craving—He had to control himself, her father could walk in at any moment and she was an innocent, he couldn't—He managed to step back, the hardest thing he'd ever done, dropped his arms to his sides. "Cam, when Osbourne opened the front door, he looked at me like I was a knight here to save the realm. What is going on?"

"Right this minute, right this very second, it's not important. There is so much to tell you, but not now. No, not now. It's so wonderful to see you—Graham, yes, Graham. Ah, how I like your real name." She kissed him again, this time her hand was on his neck, her fingers sifting through his hair. "Your eyelashes are longer than mine. However did you manage that?"

He grinned at her as he forced himself to step back again. He took her hands in his. He said the words that had filled his mind, "You're amazing, Cam, delightful. I've missed you like the very devil. I know I'm still not worthy of you, even with my newly discovered bloody title, but I love you. Will you marry me?"

She simply couldn't believe the sound, the feeling of those incredible words. The world shifted and settled in an unbelievable new way, now a world of promise, of kisses and whatever else was involved, it could only be wonderful. Cam smiled like a lunatic. "I will agree only if you kiss me back when I leap on you again."

"No, not yet, the good Lord must give me strength, but I cannot, not here in your father's house. Stop your lustful thoughts about my eyelashes. Come, tell me what has happened, Cam."

She didn't want to let go of all these splendid feelings, but reality came crashing back in. "You're right, something has happened. I will tell you everything, but not just yet." Telling him would blight her lovely world. "Ah, would you like a cup of tea?"

"No."

"When Father returns, yes, you must speak to him. I haven't yet told him of your change in station and any possible objections can no longer exist. Ah, but, Graham, even without your new distinctions, your new elevations, ah, yes, a peer of the realm, a future earl. You know he likes you, admires you, extols your abilities even more. But there is so much happening, like I said, but please, not just yet. Graham—such a lovely name. Please kiss me again, it will give me strength to face things."

Whatever had happened must be bad, but it couldn't be her father's health. Then what? Eliza had eloped with Winstead? She wasn't ready so he let it go for now.

During the train ride from Dover, Graham hadn't been able to stop thinking about the few actual days that had passed since they'd met that rainy afternoon on the Thames in front of Parliament. So few days and look what life had given him? So quickly she'd become part of him, her thoughts, the way she looked at him, spoke to him. She was so perfectly alive, so exuberant. And he recognized she was an innocent despite her wit, her laughter, her admiring cynicism of her young stepmother, Averil, and her talented bosom. He imagined discovering something new about her every single day, just the thought of seeing her across the breakfast table every morning was enough to make him sing. Fate, he thought, was a wondrous thing. Graham slowly put his arms around her. "Have I told you how witchy your eyes are? Just like your mother's—he nodded to the portrait over the mantel. "Tansia was her name?"

"Yes. Alas, though, I doubt she was a witch. If she had been, then maybe I would be a witch too and then I would keep you safe, Graham, blight your enemies. Even if I were angry with you, know I could not turn you into a toad even if I wanted to at that moment." She added, giving him a fat smile, "But what's really important—I'm learning new theorems." She was laughing as she moved closer, pressing against him, feeling the heat of him. "Even your eyebrows are perfect."

One of his perfect eyebrows arched as he pulled her close. "Theorems, Cam? You will leave me nothing to know that you do not?" He grabbed her up, laughing joyously, and had only begun to lower his head when the door opened behind him and there was a shocked father's voice. "*What the devil?*"

Cam said against Graham's mouth, "Well, I suppose you will have to speak to my father sooner rather than later, despite everything that's happening." She slowly eased back, gave her father a joyous smile. "Hello, Papa. Please come in and meet my fiancé, Lord Graham, Viscount Whitestone, heir to Earl St. Lucy."

CHAPTER 40

Whitsonby House
Ormond Square

Cam grabbed her sister's shoulders and shook her. "Stop it! Shut up, Eliza, and listen to me. You will not swoon again. Not one more word or shriek or foot stomping out of you, do you hear me? I'm bigger than you and I swear I will sit on you. Yes, Averil is gone, with a man, Gerrod Bartsleigh, you know the degenerate you flirted with before you met Winstead. Yes, she stole Father's money and all the jewels including the Whitsonby emeralds. It doesn't matter, she's gone. Like to like and good riddance."

Eliza held her sides, moaned, "No, no, you'll see, we are all ruined, there is nothing we can do, it's all over. Winstead will leave me, he—"

Cam shook her again. "Would you please stop moaning and think? You have a brain. I'm telling you we will not be mocked or laughed at, ostracized. Nothing bad will happen. If anyone says anything at all, it will be with great sympathy. But I'm wagering no one will say a word."

"Are you insane? Yes, I have a brain but obviously you don't. Everyone who counts will laugh at us, particularly Father. Sympathy? Society has never felt that sentiment, ever. Society wants only scandal and this is perfect." Pause. Eliza searched her sister's face. She said slowly, "What do you mean? Sympathy?"

"Good, now you are listening to me. At this exact moment at all the balls, the soirees and dining rooms there will be gossip all right, but said in lowered voices since it's so very sad, so very difficult to speak about—Averil, my poor father's new wife, succumbed to her family's strain of madness. She fell into deep melancholia and our physician—Father has already secured his cooperation, promising, I doubt not, countless recommendations, probably excessive remuneration as well. In any case, Mr. Wicks could do nothing for her. Indeed, he recommended she be sent back to Leeds, to her precious family. In her profound depression, after her fits of trying to pull out her hair and screaming, once even trying to harm herself, her family was all she could talk about, incessantly, how she loved the moors, the only place where she could find peace."

Eliza stared at her. "But that's ridiculous, Averil wasn't mad. She was a cheap harlot. I knew Father shouldn't wed with a lady so much younger than he, but—oh."

"Eliza, yes, good, you understand. Now, it doesn't matter what she was—is. What is important is the poor woman is on her way back to northern England to live in the bosom of her remaining family, and they will tend to her and keep her madness inside the family."

"Bu-but how?"

"Father spent the evening at White's, let his friends convince him to tell them what worried him so profoundly. Father finally gave in and told his closest friends at White's about his wife's madness, hidden from him while he courted her, but he saw her slowly change, saw the episodes of screaming, of deep melancholia." Cam gave her a huge grin. "Father told me he'd practiced before he went. Everyone believed him. He told me he was now an accomplished liar, and it felt very good."

Cam rose, studied her sister's face. "Now do you understand? All will commiserate with us because, as you know, there's been so much inbreeding in Society for so very long, many noble families have a relative who is quite mad. And what does one do with a mad relative? It's the attic or a small house with a caretaker somewhere in the country, or a family willing to take the relative, like dear Averil." Cam dusted her hands, gave her sister a big smile. "Be prepared to look sad if anyone in Society offers you sympathy for our family's dreadful travails, that is, if they're not too reticent to remark upon it. Do you now understand we'll be pitied, not laughed at? Our father will not be mocked. All will shake their heads. All will be well. Now, I expect you to order Claudine to keep her mouth shut on pain of dismissal or being sent to the guillotine."

Eliza said, eyes cold, "Oh yes, I'll order her to keep quiet, she'll obey me—oh dear, all the servants, you know they all gossip, it's—" And she wailed, actually wailed.

Be patient, be patient. "Eliza, none of our people will ever say a word. You know they are completely loyal to Father. Osbourne assures us they will guard this secret to their dying days. Now, it is up to you to make sure Claudine keeps her mouth shut." Pause. She watched her sister take in everything she'd said. She could practically see her mind working it all out, to her advantage. She slowly nodded. "I will tell Claudine if she ever says anything to anyone, even her mother, I will find out and I will see to it she never gets another post, I will hound her to the ends of England, I will—hmm, I wonder if I will ever tell Winstead the truth."

"Perhaps in ten years, you could tell him. All right, Eliza? Are you all right now? Set on an excellent new path?"

Eliza said slowly, "All was lost and then you came home when you weren't supposed to and everything changed. It was you, wasn't it, Cam? You told Father what we would do to escape being ostracized and laughed at. And you know Winstead would have left me, he—"

"No, he never would have left you. And now, Winstead will come, he will commiserate with you. He will vow eternal devotion to you if only you will smile at him, assure him Averil's madness has nothing to do with us. We do not share her blood.

"Now, I must change. It has been a very long day. Cilly and I very much enjoyed riding the train. It took only eight hours to get to London. It's magic, Eliza." She paused, her eyes narrowed. "Now, speak to Claudine." She walked to the door, turned. "Osbourne told me Winstead is coming to dinner tomorrow night. You will be downcast and will tell him of Averil's madness, which I'm sure he's already heard about from many sources. Perhaps you can embellish a bit, talk about how she would fall silent, or walk from room to room muttering to herself. You can do it. Who knows, perhaps he will bring it up. If he doesn't, then you will. You will sob, if you wish, produce some tears if you can. Winstead will commiserate. He will clasp you to his manly bosom and assure you he loves you and will always take care of you."

Eliza pondered this. "Yes, actually you're exactly right. He will be perfectly understanding of my pain and reassure me."

"Excellent, threaten Claudine with bread and water in the attic, and all is done. Oh yes, one more thing—I'm going to marry Alex Ivanov who is really Lord Graham, Viscount Whitestone, heir to Earl St. Lucy."

She left Eliza's bedroom, nearly dancing down the hallway when she heard Eliza shriek.

CHAPTER 41

Whitsonby House
Ormond Square
Two and a half weeks later

Lady Marguerite, Aunt Deveraux, said placidly to her bosom beau of many decades in the privacy of her bedchamber two hours before the wedding, "*ALL HAS WORKED OUT JUST AS I IMAGINED, LUCILLA. MY PRECIOUS LITTLE CAM IS WEDDING A VISCOUNT, WHO, WHEN HIS FATHER PASSES TO THE OTHER SIDE, WILL BECOME EARL ST. LUCY.*" And she preened, fingering the lovely Brussels lace at her bony wrists.

Lucilla Bentworth, Lady Hawson, who'd stuffed cotton balls in her ears beginning the decades before when in her friend's company, said in a loud, slow voice, right in her friend's face, "What an amazing surprise when I received your missive, Marguerite. Such a pleasure, our little Cam getting married here in her father's house with only the closest family and friends to attend. I am very pleased you invited me."

Lady Deveraux said, "*SINCE I'VE JUST ARRIVED FROM BATH,*

TELL ME WHAT IS SAID ABOUT THIS DISTRESSING SITUATION, LUCILLA."

Lucilla patted Marguerite's hand in its lovely white glove. "It is quite remarkable given Society's love of fresh meat, but everyone is solicitous, and all agree a wedding at St. Paul's this soon after the appalling situation of Lady Whitsonby's unfortunate madness wouldn't be the thing to do. Yes, and all agree it is wise for the young people to wed quickly and leave London." She paused a moment, sighed. "Poor Whit, he must be strongly affected."

"MY BROTHER IS MADE OF STERN STUFF, LUCILLA, BUT YES, OF A CERTAINTY HE IS SADDENED BY HIS YOUNG WIFE'S MADNESS AND HAVING NO RECOURSE BUT TO SEND HER BACK UP NORTH TO HER FAMILY. COME, TELL ME WHAT YOU HAVE HEARD SAID, LUCILLA."

"Everyone I have visited with has spoken of poor Averil's madness, all very privately, of course. All appear to feel very sorry for Whit and the family and bemoan the fact poor Camilla must wed privately, not present herself at St. Paul's in full regalia as would befit her station and that of her fiancé, Lord Graham, Viscount Whitestone. All agree the wedding is best done privately and quickly. I must say, though, most ladies were surprised at the sudden wedding as none had known about their close rapport, but given all the smiles, I have to say most found it vastly romantic. Many have actually seen Lord Graham, an incredibly splendid young man, so handsome he is—Lady Anson even remarked it was a case of unquenchable lust, er, love and her eyes shone with wickedness. Of course Lady Anson is still young enough to understand the power of lust. She then drank down two glasses of champagne, and none doubted she giggled her way back home to her husband.

"I did hear one old bat remark Averil's madness wasn't all a sad thing since she thought poor Whit was near to expiring what with all the intimate sport he was having to endure with such a much younger, lusty young wife."

Lady Deveraux laughed, a boom that rattled her teacup. *"INTIMATE SPORT—SO MANY DECADES HAVE PASSED SINCE I DISPORTED MYSELF INTIMATELY WITH A SUPERB SPECIMEN OF MANHOOD. BUT THANKFULLY ALL MY MEMORIES ARE CLEAR AND QUITE DETAILED. I AM ALWAYS TELLING DEAR FINCH—HE IS MY BUTLER AND CONFIDANTE, YOU KNOW—ALL ABOUT MY EARLIER EXPLOITS."*

Lucilla patted her hand, took a sip of tea and said slowly in her face, "Dear Finch, such a lovely young man and so very devoted to you." She didn't add Finch had suggested she also speak slowly and distinctly, right in her precious ladyship's powdered face. "Ah, Marguerite, I fear when I try to call up a pleasant intimate memory, all I hear is dear Fossen's grunts, like a foghorn on the Thames."

Marguerite remembered dear Fossen very clearly, a very rich, very pompous little man, who had demanded an heir, and fortunately for Lucilla, she'd birthed three sons.

Lucilla added, "Of course there was charming Armand, my very brief lover, but he was gone so very quickly, I only remember his breath." She shuddered. "Garlic, surely not conducive to passion in the morning."

"WELL, HE WAS FRENCH, LUCILLA, ONLY TO BE EXPECTED."

Lucilla said, thinking back over the decades, "I never allowed him to spend the night after that morning he breathed in my face. Now, enough of my long-ago history. Perhaps after we see Cam married to the most striking young man I've ever seen in my life—and after their departure for their honeymoon, you can tell me of your most pleasurable memories."

Marguerite agreed. The two old friends spoke of the latest titillating scandals, never a shortage of those, drank their tea, spoke of the queen's babies Victoria and Edward. Lucilla said, "Marguerite, I remember so clearly when little Cam visited me in Somerset I watched her wriggle out of her clothes and leap into the lily pond, Eliza shrieking at her from shore. I laughed and laughed. And now she is nineteen and shortly to be a wife. How life simply continues and you're just swept along, unless, of course, you die.

"Now, you told me when you arrived from Bath two days ago, you had nothing to do to assist her. Cam was a whirlwind, she arranged everything, including having poor mad Averil's own seamstress make her wedding gown, all the while ensuring her sister Eliza's maid of honor gown was exactly the right shade of lavender she insisted upon."

"Very true. Since Cam's wedding gown is a pale soft pink made in satin-silk, the colors complement each other. Cam did consider wearing white like Queen Victoria two years ago, but Eliza told her she'd look like a dead stick. Alas, Eliza's right. I think the pale pink is splendid on her. Do you know she also arranged all the bouquets of flowers, mainly roses, all the while humming and dancing about, she was so happy? And Cook, she was pleased to be asked to make Cam's wedding cake and feed two dozen guests, she was singing Italian arias at the top of her lungs. My dear Whit laughed when he told me how Cam and Cook were alternately laughing and singing and arguing over the wedding breakfast menu." She paused. *"Dear Whit, he's holding up so well, a stiff upper lip, bless his stout heart."*

Lucilla said, "Just imagine, Marguerite, our little Cam only met Viscount Whitestone a month ago. Where did you say? On a bench outside Parliament?" She sighed. "It quite makes me want to believe in fate. True love, it blazes bright, makes everyone and everything brighter, more exciting, more alive, every feeling deeper, every word heard and spoken by the other more profound. It never ceases to amaze." She frowned. "Isn't it odd Eliza and dear Winstead will still wed in the Fall, all the extravagance you would expect even though it's possible some will speak of poor Averil's madness. But by then, I predict no one will really care."

"ALL ARRANGEMENTS HAVE BEEN IN PLACE FOR SIX MONTHS, NO CHANGING THEM. NOW, I TOLD YOUNG GRAHAM HE WAS NEVER TO GAIN ANY FLESH AROUND HIS MIDDLE OR CAM WOULD SCORN HIM. DO YOU KNOW, HE GRINNED AT ME, PROMISED HE WOULD ADHERE ALL HIS LIVING DAYS TO A MODERATE DIET. I TOLD HIM IF HE DID STRAY HE COULD ADOPT LORD BYRON'S DIET—POTATOES AND VINEGAR. I FEAR HE LOOKED QUITE HORRIFIED.

"I AM VISITING CAM IN HER HOME AT KING'S HEAD, EARL ST. LUCY'S COUNTRY SEAT—NEAR DOVER—IN THREE MONTHS, AFTER THEY'VE HAD A BIT OF TIME TO INDULGE YOUNG LUST AND SETTLE IN TO THEIR NEW HOME. I REMEMBER MEETING GRAHAM'S GRANDFATHER IN THE OLD DAYS. WHAT A FINE SPECIMEN HE WAS, UNDERSTANDABLE SINCE DEAR GRAHAM IS SO SPLENDID. CAM TELLS ME EVERYONE LOOKS AT THE TWO OF THEM AND WHISPERS, BUT NOT LOW ENOUGH SHE CAN'T HEAR—GRAHAM IS THE MORE BEAUTIFUL." She gave a low, cackling laugh, not loud enough to dislodge her two novels off the marquetry table, thankfully, drank more tea, and set her delicate bone china cup back on its hand-painted saucer. She consulted the small watch in her pocket, and slowly rose. "FINCH!"

Finch came into the small second-floor family room, smiled at the two dear elderly ladies, both splendidly gowned, walked up to Lady Deveraux and said slowly, distinctly, not an inch from her face, "You are a vision, my lady. As are you, Lady Hawson. Allow me to escort you to the top of the stairs, where his lordship will accompany you to the drawing room. All are now gathered. The pianist is already playing quietly, but I fear I have heard some discordant notes since Cook was so happy she gave him a bottle of champagne to drink, which, frankly, he guzzled. But we will hope. His lordship is presenting a fine brave front given the very sad nature of her ladyship's condition and her departure to the north. From what I've heard, everyone admires his fortitude given what happened to his poor wife. It is of course appropriate the only guests are family and close friends, which shows immense discretion and intelligence.

"It appears Lord Graham's sister, Lady Eugenie, is becoming fast friends with Lady Eliza. I heard Cilly say Lady Cam was trying not to smack her sister who was telling her not to smile so much, it reeked of ill-breeding, and she needed to push up her bosom."

"*YES, YES, POOR AVERIL, SUCH A PITY. NOW, AS FOR ELIZA, SHE IS LOVELY TO LOOK AT AND HER WATERCOLORS DO NOT MAKE THE EYES BLEED, BUT ALAS, SHE HAS THE DISPOSITION OF A CRAPPED-UPON GOOSE.*

"*YOU KNOW SHE FULLY EXPECTED TO RULE HER FATHER-IN-LAW'S HOUSE WITH AN IRON FIST, HERS, OF COURSE, AFTER SHE MARRIED WINSTEAD, A VERY NICE YOUNG MAN IS WINSTEAD AS IS HIS FATHER. YES, SHE FULLY EXPECTED HER WISHES AND ORDERS TO BE THE ONLY ONES TO BE OBEYED.*" She grinned like a bandit. "*BUT NOW I HAVE HEARD WINSTEAD'S FATHER MARRIED A LOVELY WIDOW WITH SIX CHILDREN. IT'S DELICIOUS—DEAR ELIZA WITH A MOTHER-IN-LAW WHO WILL RULE OVER HER AND SIX CHILDREN SWARMING THE HOUSE. WHAT IS EVEN MORE DELICIOUS IS WINSTEAD IS QUITE PLEASED FOR HIS FATHER. AH, POOR LAD WILL BE BETWIXT AND BETWEEN. DID YOU KNOW ELIZA CALLS WINSTEAD WINNIE? LIKE A HORSE?*" And Lady Deveraux punched Finch's arm and laughed and laughed. She caught her breath, patted Finch's shoulder. "*AS FOR YOU, FINCH, I MUST SAY YOU ARE A HANDSOME FIGURE OF A MAN TODAY.*"

Finch thanked her, offered each precious old dear an arm. "Your kindness overwhelms, my lady. Now, I believe all bespeaks a lovely wedding on this very fine day."

CHAPTER 42

The Royal Hotel
Ventnor, Isle of Wight

At last they were alone in the amazing suite of rooms on the top floor of The Royal Hotel. Graham unfastened Cam's dark green pelisse and laid it carefully on a chair back. Together, they looked through the narrow front windows that gave onto a wide sandy beach and the English Channel, although since it was full-on dark and there was no moon to speak of, they saw nothing at all. They did hear the occasional squawks from ducks sitting beside the wooden fence next to a wide stone path leading down to the beach. This fence and the birds were mentioned to them by Mr. French, the extraordinarily voluble manager of The Royal Hotel who'd escorted them personally to their handsome accommodation. He congratulated them on their union, talked volubly about the short history of The Royal and didn't stop there—he continued to wax eloquent about the splendid views of the coastline that would greet their eyes in the morning. They dutifully admired the lavish drawing room and their large bedchamber with attached dressing rooms, pointed to the smaller bedchambers for Cilly and Nutworthy, Graham's new valet, a cousin of Earl St. Lucy's long-time valet Terrance.

And lastly, he proudly showed them the water closet and attached bathing room.

Two liveried young porters had brought up their luggage under Mr. French's eagle eye, as well as Cilly's and Nutworthy's.

Mr. French nodded to the two young porters, and said, "A storm is expected tonight, but tomorrow, so the sailors assure us, we will enjoy the return of our splendid warm weather, unlike England proper, raining at the drop of a hat, but here, yes here, we will enjoy bright sun, so healthy, you know. You will doubtless want to enjoy a lovely walk on the beach and of course a stroll through our renowned south-facing gardens." He smiled at them, gave a sharp bow, and left the suite, herding the two young porters.

Cam whirled about, so pleased, so happy, she couldn't stand still. She hugged her new husband close, kissed his chin, laughed, "Can you believe there is a water closet, Graham? Though mentioning it was a bit daring of Mr. French. Oh my, this is luxury indeed. At last Mr. French took himself off. We are alone, husband, for the very first time in absolutely forever we are really alone. Even on the train people were close by, porters hovered, but not now. Ah, husband—what an excellent word—a delicious sound to the ear. It's been an incredible day, Graham, most all of it perfect except for the few minutes Eliza drew me aside and told me Eugenie, yes, your older sister, believes I did not have enough modesty for this occasion, that I was too exuberant, too free with my smiles and Eliza said she agreed with her. Do you know what I did?"

Graham stared down at her, gently pushed up her glasses. "Tell me, what did you do?"

Cam laughed. "I gave her a big kiss, told her she was beautiful in lavender and asked her to wish me well. And do you know what? She was so taken aback, she did.

"Oh my, Graham, I nearly swallowed my tongue when I saw you standing next to the vicar when I came into the drawing room, our families and close friends sitting there, turning to stare at me. I believed you the most beautiful man I'd ever seen in my life. I didn't tell you earlier because you might have puffed up in conceit." She touched her fingertips to his beloved face. "But now, you may puff up all you please. You looked so splendid, my lord—ah, how I love the sound of that. When you told my father who you really were—the Earl St. Lucy's long-lost son—I thought he would pop his vest buttons, he was so pleased, and frankly, relieved, and perfectly willing to overlook your made-up name and background. And there was Mr. Sherbrooke standing next to you, proud as a peacock, grinning from ear to ear, nodding to his brother, to the Earl of Northcliffe, who's really very impressive.

"Goodness, when I realized I actually had to walk into the drawing room, I was afraid I would trip on my gown and fall on my face since I wasn't wearing my glasses, maybe break my nose or worse, vomit since my stomach was jumping about like beans in a shaking jar, and I knew when I had to speak my feelings to you, I would stutter, my knees would knock together loud as St. Paul's bell—" She came to an abrupt halt, cleared her throat. "Then you looked at me and smiled. Those glorious wild blue eyes of yours made me want to run and leap at you." A beautiful hank of hair had come loose from the braids wound atop her head and lay provocatively against her cheek. He gently lifted the hair, smoothed the silk between his fingers, and smiled down at her.

"I was lucky I didn't have to walk in those two-inch slippers of yours, all I had to do was stand there and try not to shudder myself into the floor. You're mine now, Cam, at last. It seems I've known you forever and now you're my wife, a miracle of fate, and yet such a short time ago I didn't know you existed." He wrapped the thick hank of hair around his hand, pulled her close. "You are amazing, and now you belong to me. You're my wife, amazing really, since before I met you I hadn't even thought of marrying. You're beautiful and remarkable and—best of all?"

She stared up at him. "And best of all?"

"And best of all you can speak a hundred words without pausing for breath or a period. You give me all the information I need in a minimum amount of time. If ever we argue in the future, you will doubtless win since I will be fascinated just listening to you."

She gave this some thought. "Do you know Father wanted to count my words once? He told me my mother spoke exactly the same way, everything came out of her mouth at once. Oh dear, do you really think we will argue? I can't imagine what we would have to argue about. You are rarely a dolt."

"Thank you. I shall try for a record. Cam, when I saw you standing in the doorway, then walk—no, you nearly skipped on those two-inch slippers—into the drawing room, I nearly keeled over at the sight of you. Ryder had to steady me up or I might have swooned right there in front of Vicar Piercebridge. But you want to know what really pleases me as your husband?"

His lovely words settled sweetly, deeply, into her, and she wanted to kiss him with all the breath she had. "What really pleases you?"

He leaned down and kissed her nose. "Shall I tell you?"

She lightly poked his arm. "Yes, now, tell me. I must know."

"What really pleases me is you are so smart. I cannot think of anything more a husband could possibly ask for in a modern wife."

She started to laugh and couldn't stop. Soon she was holding her sides, gasping for air.

"My lord, what is the matter? Can I assist you? I was pulled by her ladyship's extravagant laughter from my very nice bedchamber even though I had three more shirts to place in my own armoire." Nutworthy paused, looked back and forth between them. Cam hiccupped. "Ah, there appears to be a problem of excessive jocularity. Perhaps a cup of tea to soothe her ladyship's throat?"

Cam hiccupped again, grinned over at Graham's new valet, Norton Nutworthy, just Nutworthy, please, my lady. She found herself charmed by his wonderfully proper and convoluted English, so stiff and formal, still, it was obvious his concern was real. His admiration of her new husband was obvious for all to see. She realized Nutworthy thought of the two of them as his new family. According to Cilly, who'd whispered to her on the train that she'd heard him bragging to the other servants that his master, Lord Graham, was the most handsome, the most splendidly fashioned gentlemen he had ever seen in all his thirty-seven years. A young god not at all stiff in the collar, only when it was right and proper. And he boxed, took on all comers, sweated and dirtied himself up too with all his tinkering with his inventions, appropriate for a gentleman of his stature since he was so smart.

Graham said to his very concerned valet, "There is a bit of jocularity, you are right about that, but nothing to concern you. Her ladyship was laughing at one of my jests, a good thing for a new wife to do. Mr. French told me our dinners would be arriving"—he consulted the watch in his waistcoat pocket—"in about ten minutes from now." He and Cam had decided what they wanted to do, this their first married evening. He looked from Cam to Nutworthy and beyond to Cilly, standing in the drawing room doorway. "This is our first meal together. We would like to invite you to dine with us."

Nutworthy was so appalled he couldn't help himself. "But, my lord, that isn't at all proper, it is—" Words failed him. He cast a quick look at Cilly, an odd name but it suited her. And here she was nodding and smiling. What was he to do?

CHAPTER 43

Graham laughed. "Gird your loins, Nutworthy. You and Miss Quick are now a part of our family. It is what we wish. Oh, and Nutworthy, I believe I can promise you there will be laughter in your future. Her ladyship is a right proper wit. You will never be bored as I'm certain Miss Quick will tell you. Now, dinner will arrive shortly, so please finish folding your shirts and join us."

Nutworthy blinked rapidly, bowed himself out of the drawing room, mumbling to himself, followed by a grinning Cilly, who gave Cam a little wave.

Cam said, "I'm a right proper wit, am I?"

"Among other things. Poor Nutworthy doesn't have a chance. He will have to unbend, he will have no choice."

Cam chewed that over a moment, then, "How did you know Cilly's last name?"

He cocked his head at her. "She is a part of our household. Of course I would know her full name. Cillette is her full first name, but you call her Cilly."

"Well, yes, I changed her name when I was very young to Cilly. Ah, you met Finch, my aunt Deveraux's butler and companion?" She leaned up, whispered, "I believe he and Cilly might be interested in each other. We will see."

Graham could but smile.

And thus it was, closer to twenty minutes later, the master and mistress sat with her lady's maid and his new valet to dine on salmon pudding, boiled bacon-cheek, French beans and potatoes, and Cam's favorite, lobster salad, followed by a rich plum tart, all served by The Royal's head waiter, Monsieur Andre, who was quick to replenish their champagne, opened a second bottle, and removed dishes. If he was surprised servants were dining with the newly minted Lord and Lady Whitestone, he gave no sign. Both Cam and Graham knew this social breach would likely be the topic of conversation among The Royal's staff, and what would their verdict be?

Nutworthy did not unbend but remained disapproving at this laxity in his new master until he'd drunk a third glass of champagne, given a small burp, and giggled. As for Cilly, she couldn't help her smiles, thinking of what she would write to Mr. Finch. What was he doing? Perhaps he was thinking about her as well?

When, an hour later, Cam and Graham were alone in their lovely bedchamber, the rich gold draperies drawn closed for the night and a brightly burning fire in the Carrera marble fireplace, Cam stood looking at the large bed, turned down for the night, showing white linen sheets exquisitely embroidered along the edge and she thought, *I'm married. Married. To Graham, and he's my husband—but he's still a man. Oh dear.*

She was being an idiot. But still, a man was a foreign being, no getting around that. But then again, she was certain Graham was at least as magnificent as the *Statue of David* she'd never seen in person, but had studied a drawing of it in her father's library when she was twelve. *Did Graham have big flat feet like David?* She knew he had to have other things south of his middle, things just like David's? The drawing hadn't impressed her much, but she'd heard whispers that men changed that part of themselves upon seeing a female without clothes—they changed alarmingly.

She had to get ahold of herself, had to remind herself she could simply look at him for an hour—well, his face, and not move and be perfectly content. Maybe longer, maybe a week. As for the rest of him, he was always clothed in her imaginings.

His hands were on her arms, gently and slowly sliding up and down. "Where have you been? You haven't said a word since—"

He paused, understood. "Cam, would you like me to call Cilly to help you undress? Or shall I help you myself?"

He wanted to undress her? Oh dear. Words tumbled out of her mouth, "I hope there will be nutty buns for breakfast, but how will we order them? Send Nutworthy to the kitchens? They are Cilly's favorites. We can share with her and Nutworthy. I wonder how old Nutworthy is, not above forty, do you think? And why don't you call him by his first name. I mean—Nutworthy—it's a rather unusual, well, really rather silly—oh dear, my tongue is running off the rails again." She leaned up, kissed him, stopped, jumped back. "Do you know, Graham, kissing you is even better than a nutty bun, but if it's all right with you, I would prefer Cilly help me."

He took her arms in his hands, leaned down and kissed her. "What I would prefer, dearest one, is that you had no gown on at all." She went stiff as a chair leg, looked as appalled as Nutworthy. He straightened. "Ah, let me say that in another way. I will call Cilly." He kissed her again, fast and hard, and took himself off. He paused at the doorway to his dressing room. "Cam, please don't be afraid of me. I want you to think only of the fun we will have. And, you know, perhaps you and I together can even develop a proper marital theorem with enough observation and experimentation."

She gulped, stared at him. "Wh-what? A theorem? You mean marital sorts of things can be the basis of theorems? Oh, I see, you are making fun of me because I'm—well, best not to go into any more detail. I forgive you, Graham, but you know"—she gulped—"the fact is you are very different from me, that is, we are not at all alike and you do not wear a gown. I do not have whiskers. You have big feet and I have a lady's princess feet, well, not really, but still, not as big as yours. You see what I mean?"

"Yes, I see." And he did. Graham walked back to her, took her arms in his hands again, waited for her to look at him. "Cam, you are God's finest creation. Unlike you, I am a sturdy creature, meant to protect you and worship you. No man could possibly be luckier than I am." He tweaked the end of her nose. "You will see we are two halves of a whole, meant to come together." He gave her a hug, kissed her again and left their bedchamber.

When Nutworthy was assisting Graham to undress, he said, now sober as a judge, "It was unexpected you would ask Miss Quick and myself to dine with you and her new ladyship. Ah, thank you."

"It was our pleasure, Nutworthy."

Nutworthy looked agonized but determined. "I also pray you will forgive my immoderate consumption of the extraordinarily fine champagne, my lord."

What? Graham's thoughts, every single one of them, were on his bride not twenty feet away. *Nutworthy, champagne.* "Ah, I am pleased you enjoyed the champagne."

"I also consumed more of the amazing plum pudding than I should have. I daresay my consumption of that remarkable dish reached an excessive degree. My only defense is the pudding was nearly as excellent as my dear now-departed mother's whose plums were from her own small orchard. So purple they were."

Graham didn't remember the plum pudding. Had he eaten

any? He was trying to form a consummation plan when Nutworthy said, "Mr. French is correct in his weather prognostications, my lord. It appears a violent spring storm is very nearly upon us. I am informed we are to be bombarded by heavy rain, possibly high winds. I believe I should fasten all the windows here and in your bedchamber."

"Thank you, Nutworthy. Do not concern yourself with the windows in our bedchamber. I shall see they're tightly closed."

Nutworthy assisted Graham into his new bathrobe, soft wool and warm, given to him by his newly discovered brother-in-law, Donner. Under it he wore nothing at all. He'd considered a nightshirt, rejected it. *Begin as you mean to go on.* He couldn't remember where he'd heard that sage advice, but it seemed to apply here. He'd never worn a nightshirt since he'd been a boy of fifteen and realized his idol, Mr. Sherbrooke, slept naked with his wife, in bed, all night, every night. It was a heady bit of knowledge to stir a young boy's blood.

Nutworthy was clearly distressed. "But, my lord, surely a nightshirt is appropriate on this of all nights since—ah, forgive me, but I cannot continue." It was a good thing he realized where his sentence was proceeding and shut his mouth.

Graham fought back a grin. "Gird your loins, Nutworthy. Now, you may go to bed. Thank you for your assistance."

Nutworthy gave him a sharp bow, said nothing more and surely that was remarkable in itself.

Graham stood quietly for a moment listening, but he could only hear low female murmurs from the bedchamber. What were Cam and Cilly talking about? He thought of Cilly speaking to her as Nutworthy had to him. No, surely not. His new wife was innocent and nervous and he was naked beneath his bathrobe. He had to keep control. He'd told Nutworthy to gird his loins. Now he knew he had to keep his own loins well girded.

Please don't let me muck this up.

CHAPTER 44

Cilly helped Cam change into her silk nightgown with its matching pale peach peignoir, a wedding gift from her new aunt Sophie, Ryder's charming wife, who'd eyed her up and down and declared her worthy, and laughed, hugged her, whispered, "Lord Graham will most certainly appreciate you. You will see the peignoir is more for display than for actual use."

Cilly said now, "It's so sheer and soft and hints what's beneath, but not quite reveals. Lord Graham might fall over in a dead faint at the sight of you."

Cam stared at herself in the Cheval glass and thought, *That might be best if he were unconscious on the floor,* but of course she couldn't let Cilly know she was ready to bolt. Up went her chin. "I know he won't faint, he's made of stern stuff. Maybe one of his perfect eyebrows will elevate a bit, but no more." *And his eyes will be so wicked I'll be the one to faint.* She met Cilly's eyes in the mirror. "He spoke of our being two halves and coming together would make a perfect whole. Well, he didn't say perfect. It sounds quite wonderful but since I don't really know what that means, well, I have a general idea, given the outrageous stories Aunt Deveraux is always telling me. When she saw the nightgown, she shouted "DELICIOUS WITH SUCH PROMISE OF WICKEDNESS," and she fingered the material. I swear she was remembering, ah, youthful and, well, maybe not-so-youthful assignations. But alas, Cilly, she was never really all that specific, and how could I ask her what exactly happened on a wedding night?"

Cilly wondered how many dozen trysts were stored in Lady Deveraux's brain, all very detailed indeed, she'd wager. She knew Cam was concerned about her wedding night, but alas, she was nearly as ignorant as her mistress, not that she would ever admit it on pain of torture. She said, "The idea of two halves coming together is a perfect metaphor. I will say without hesitation Lord Graham knows what he's talking about and you should trust him completely." She saw Cam's mouth open and added quickly, "Ah, what an amazing series of events, all of them happening so quickly and Lord Graham is such a lovely young man. It is difficult to believe you're now a wife. Oh, Cam, I am so happy for you," and Cilly burst into tears.

They hugged, Cam rocking her. She realized two things at once. Neither she nor Cilly was tipsy any longer, a pity, and she was now taller than Cilly. She whispered against Cilly's temple, "Shall I give you Aunt Deveraux's address in Bath? Perhaps you could pen a lovely note to Mr. Finch."

Cilly laughed, wiped her eyes. "And here I thought I was so very discreet, a veritable closed book. Mr. Finch—his first name is Edward, a lovely name, a king's name—he is delightful, isn't he, Cam? There is such kindness in him and he is so very solicitous of your aunt. I quite admire him."

"You have excellent taste. Edward is a fine name, a very romantic name as well. He is also very pleasing to look at, which is like royal icing on the cake."

"Ah, perhaps giving me his address would be quite all right, if you don't think it would be too forward of me to write him a short, well-wishing note?"

"Not at all. I believe when we leave Ventnor we will be traveling to King's Head in St. Lucy. I will ask Graham the proper address."

Cilly gave a watery sniff, got herself together and it was all business. "Sit down now and let me brush out your hair."

Oddly enough, this mundane everyday act calmed her. She thought about Graham and the two halves and smiled to herself as Cilly brushed her hair. She said, "I am so pleased Graham's father appears to approve of me. Still, I believe he wanted Graham to himself for a while before he married. So much has happened very quickly. Earl St. Lucy tried his best this morning, smiling, accepting congratulations on his son's return, eyeing me like he wished I was in China, but then, he slowly eased, I guess you could say."

"Of course he approves of you. He'll come to love you, you will make him laugh and want to hug you all the time, just like Lord Graham, come to think of it. So many smiles, so much laughter already."

"I certainly hope so. It didn't hurt he and my father have known each other since Oxford, and like each other, so he couldn't dislike the fact our marriage joins our families. He just hoped it wouldn't be so very soon." She paused. "Of course my new father-in-law had heard about poor Averil's madness and her departure back to her family in the north." She grinned in the mirror at Cilly. "He was most sincerely sorry and relieved, of course, that I do not share her blood."

Cilly frowned down at a tangle, gently brushed through it. She said, "I'd be relieved too. I'm sure you've noticed how everyone at home is smiling more now Lady Averil is gone. A dreadful woman, your father is much better off without her. And don't you ever worry anyone will say anything, they won't. All love your father as much as they disliked her."

"I rather hope she rots, Cilly."

"A sentiment shared by all," Cilly said. "Do you know, your sister and Lord Graham's sister, Eugenie, appeared to get along very well—her husband seems like a nice gentleman. I wonder what he thinks of Lord Graham appearing so unexpectedly."

"I'll ask Graham."

Cilly started to braid Cam's hair, stopped. "We will leave your hair loose. It is appropriate, I think."

"Yes, I suppose. Graham has never seen it loose."

"Your hair is glorious, so many lovely shades and so thick. Then your nightgown, he will indeed swoon."

Cam felt a bolt of alarm, then calmed again.

Cilly said, "He still has no memories at all of King's Head? His father? His sister?"

"If he has, he hasn't told me. Imagine, I also have another new family. Mr. Sherbrooke, his wife and all his Beloved Ones, you remember, the children Mr. Sherbrooke finds abandoned or abused and takes to his home between Lower Slaughter and Mortimer Combe in the Cotswolds. The house has a name, but alas, I can't remember it.

"And Graham's adopted uncle and aunt the Earl and Countess of Northcliffe—such incredible red hair she has with only the occasional white showing through. The earl—I believed he was the perfect autocrat and then he smiled at me, changed him utterly. So tall and fit he is, and a full head of stark white hair. As for their twin sons and grandchildren, I'm sure we'll all meet soon enough." She stopped, realized she was prattling on and on. And on. She shut her mouth, sent a fast look toward Graham's dressing room. Would he come in soon?

Don't be a clabberhead. You're a half of the whole. She looked again at the shimmering peach silk-satin.

Oh dear.

CHAPTER 45

A single branch of candles atop the mantel gave off a warm, soft glow, not reaching the corners of the large bedchamber, leaving them in deep shadow. A fire burned sluggishly, the glowing embers adding to the intimacy. There was the occasional exploding orange spark to break the silence. Rain had begun to fall but the sound was muted by the thick golden velvet draperies covering the windows.

A perfect night. His wedding night.

Please grant me fortitude.

Was fortitude what he really needed? Graham didn't know. He walked to his bride who looked ready to bolt, understood perfectly, smiled at her. "Hello, Wife. I didn't tell you my brother-in-law, Donner, whispered to me that your lovely smile warmed his innards."

"You made that up. Your bathrobe looks very soft. Your feet are bare."

She'd taken in the whole of him in under a half second, amazing. Well, he supposed he'd done the same. He tried not to stare at her glorious hair, all loose and wavy, a thick tress over her shoulder, falling over her breast. And that nightgown. He swallowed, got hold of himself. "Oh no, I believe

Donner is smitten with you. My father is close to smitten, but not yet quite there yet. I will give you one week when we settle in at King's Head to have him so charmed he'll offer you his crisp bacon. As for Eugenie, she is nice enough to me, but I do wonder what she really thinks. Sometimes I see her staring at me when she doesn't think I noticed. As for you, she'll have to love you, you'll give her no choice at all."

Cam still looked ready to bolt. He didn't move, said easily, "We'll explore King's Head, a new adventure for both of us since I still have no memory of it. Thank you for the compliment, the bathrobe is a wedding gift. Do you also like my bare feet?"

"Yes." She leaned closer, maybe six inches closer, more at ease now since he was speaking and not attacking her like that moron Teddy Jewel, or that fortune-hunting pork-brained Pilcher Gayson.

She said as she considered kissing his ear, "Papa said he would come visit us in a couple of months. We will return for Eliza's wedding in October. Do you like her fiancée, Winstead?"

She nipped his earlobe, and he grinned down at her. "I like that. Now, Towbridge is a nice man. He told me about his father's recent marriage to a widow with six young children. He told me he'd worried about his father's health since his mother's death and now this miracle—he said his father wrote to tell him he's hale as a stoat. Winstead nearly bubbled over, so pleased he was rubbing his hands together. He said the children are loud and boisterous and the house is once again alive with noise and laughter. He knew Eliza would love the children, she was so giving and loving."

Cam couldn't hold it in, out spurted a laugh. "About Eliza loving all those children—it is something I would have to see for myself. As for her new mother-in-law, I doubt they'll become best friends. With six children, though, I'll wager her future mama-is-law is a strong, resolute woman." She leaned up, bit his other earlobe. "Oh dear, I suppose I'm a small person."

Cam was suddenly aware his hands were now on her waist, gently kneading her through her nightgown, pressing in. It felt quite nice, so long as they kept talking and his hands stayed where they were.

Even though Graham was in a bad way, he managed to say, "Perhaps marriage will make her kinder. Mayhap Winstead will make her glow and smile."

"Perhaps so." But she doubted it. So far his love hadn't changed her at all. His hands were moving lower.

She held her breath, waiting, scared, excited.

Graham knew if he pulled her against him, like two books on a shelf, she'd feel every bit of him. Did she know how men were fashioned? Did she know what her closeness did to him? Her little nips on his ears? He thought of his first time with Maggie. He'd been fifteen and she an ancient twenty. She was the local blacksmith's daughter, and she'd called him a stallion and kissed him all over. A stallion? He'd preened and strutted around all the children who had no idea what had happened, but Ryder always knew everything. Ryder had taken him into his study, closed and locked the door, and told him he was never again to be intimate with a local girl. Ever. And he'd explained the world to him and how it had to work to keep things in balance. And what did that mean? It meant, Ryder told him, that young men were idiots to assuage their lust on young women since pregnancy was always more than a possibility and then where would he be? Where would she be? Graham remembered he'd paled and continued pale until he was told she wasn't pregnant.

When he was sixteen Ryder had taken him to London twice a month to visit a very discreet lady who had taught him everything he could possibly imagine.

Time to put Jayne's lessons into practice.

Now things were different. He was married. Pregnancy

was something devoutly wished for. He leaned down, not far at all, nuzzled her neck, lightly ran his tongue over her skin, whispered against her temple, "Let's talk about how we're going to approach the establishment of our theorem."

She nodded. "I like talk, Graham, well, and I like to kiss you and feel your hands around my waist, except your hands are lower now and that concerns me."

"Please don't be concerned. I want only to give you pleasure and, Cam, there's so much more. Can you trust me?"

"Of course, well—yes, I must trust you or—well, I suppose I must if things are to proceed, sort of like trains running straight on tracks to reach their destination."

"Just so." He smiled at her, kissed the end of her nose and took her hand.

It wasn't long before she was lying on her back in bed, all warm as her breakfast toast. She watched Graham stir the embers, watched him turn and walk to her, saying nothing. He removed his bathrobe and stood silently, letting her look her fill at him. It was close, but he kept motionless, his arms at his sides. He didn't hold his breath.

Her voice came out of her mouth with a bit of a croak. "I love you, Graham, I truly do, but seeing you without your clothes, it's rather alarming. You are even more different from me than I could have imagined."

Her eyes had moved in less than a half second from his face downward. He knew what she was seeing and devoutly prayed she wouldn't run screaming from the bedchamber. Finally, after an eon it seemed to him, she said, licking her lips, which made him want to leap on her, "Oh goodness, Graham, you said we were two halves of a whole. I have to say your half is amazing but still, rather unexpected, and alarming." She licked her lips again and his jumping on her was close—except he wasn't a boy, he had fortitude, it was the key. He still didn't move, he waited, waited.

"In general," she said, her eyes still on his sex, "I know in a general sort of way what you will do with your half, which is amazing, as I said, but I have to say further that seeing the reality of it is alarming. That man part of you is quite large. I'm sorry, Graham, but I cannot see how it could possibly work," and he watched her again run her tongue over her lower lip for a third time and he nearly expired.

"Don't be alarmed, everything will work just fine. Perhaps I could show you, Cam." Was that his voice, all low and nearly a croak?

Still he didn't move, and again, waited, waited.

"All right, Graham. I suppose you actually showing me how this all works is the best way forward and I know we must move forward since we're married and all. But it's difficult, Graham, I mean, I'm looking at you and imagining, and it's very worrying."

But then in the next second she opened her arms to him. He nearly shouted with lust and relief, a heady brew.

When he pulled her nightgown over her head and tossed it to a chair, she gulped, crossed her arms over her chest. "Graham, I don't suppose we could simply kiss all night. I really like that. It's quite invigorating."

"Yes, we will kiss, then we will explore even more activities you'll find even more invigorating." He pulled her arms away and gathered her against him. The feel of her, her breasts, her flesh, so soft and warm, it would break a saint. She wanted kisses? He could do that. He remembered Jayne's advice: *Talk, Graham, be amusing, do not grunt, do not stick your tongue down her throat, never rush her on pain of death—yours.* And so he leaned down and said, "Dearest one, open your mouth, just a little bit."

She did and every flower in the world bloomed. "Oh my," she whispered into his mouth. "Your tongue—I never thought of that. It feels really quite lovely. I feel the strangest things."

"Strange? Where exactly, sweetheart?" He touched his tongue to hers again, stroked and kissed.

"My stomach, well, no, lower, and it's really quite delicious."

Jayne had taught him the importance of control, but he nearly went over the cliff. *Ladies first, Alex, always ladies first. Never be a pig.*

He kissed her breasts and when she moaned, he believed it the most beautiful sound he'd ever heard in his life. He continued down the beautiful length of her, rested his cheek against her belly. His hands kept going. She squeaked, tried to push him away. Then, from one moment to the next, she was pulling on his hair to bring him closer. "Graham, that is wonderful, truly, but there's more, I know there has to be. Please show me."

He was supposed to talk? Be amusing? How could he even speak when his heart was near pounding out of his chest? "Yes," he said, and went lower—the taste of her, the feel of her, he didn't know if he could bear it, but he knew he had to give her pleasure first because he would hurt her, no way around that. He whispered against her, "No, Cam, don't try to pull away from me. Trust me. This is the way things are done. It's very important to me that you enjoy this. It's all about your pleasure. That's right, just relax and let me—" She stilled. He felt her surprise then her eagerness and he gloried in it. When she stiffened and screamed, he quickly closed his hand over her mouth and came into her.

CHAPTER 46

Cam felt boneless yet full of energy at the same time. She wanted to burst into song and she wanted to curl up against him and breathe him in. Amazing what had just happened. She'd had no idea. "Goodness, what you did to me, what happened to me, it was something I never imagined."

Graham was sprawled on his back, and wondered vaguely how she could put two words together. He was sated, his brain mush, but then he finally managed two words of his own, through great effort. "I agree."

Cam came up on her elbow over him, energy thrumming through her. "But I didn't do anything to you, I mean you did everything. I mean I hugged you and kissed you and looked at you—oh goodness. But, Graham, it was so embarrassing and then it wasn't. I have to admit you were right, it was all very invigor-ating."

All right, he'd take that bloodless word for the moment. As for suggestions for what she could do would remain unspoken tonight.

"It's the oddest thing. Even though my bones have surely melted, I still feel so light I could fly to the ceiling and perhaps simply float above us and look down at you. I could dip and swirl about, maybe sing to you—wait, here you are, lying there like a felled log. Don't you want to dance, Graham?"

She saw his grin in the dim candlelight. "Perhaps soon, Cam. Give me a little while, say another four and a half minutes."

She leaned down, kissed him, studied his beautiful face, his eyes now vague, dreamy. She said slowly, "You've done this before, haven't you? I mean you seemed to know exactly what you were doing. You have, I know it."

"Yes," he said, "but this is different. You're my wife, the only woman in my life and in my bed forever."

She was silent, unaware she was lightly kneading his belly, then lightly stroking—but he was. He felt a bolt of lust. No, he couldn't, she'd been a virgin. She had to be sore. He had to control himself—ah, but in the morning, before they ordered their breakfast, perhaps while she was still sleeping he could wake her up with kisses, everywhere, and he suddenly saw the world through different eyes. She was his. His. She was quiet and he wondered if she was falling asleep.

Cam was thinking of Averil, how she'd broken her vows to her husband and run away with another man, all planned. For how long? She thought of her dead mother, knew to her heels Tansia would have been faithful to her father forever. She whispered against his neck, "I think I want to stay with you forever, Graham. I cannot imagine not wanting you in my life."

"Good, that's good. I promise you've got me until I fold up my tent and disappear into the ether."

Cam yawned. Graham settled her against his side, pressed her face against his neck.

She whispered, her voice sleep slurred, "This is surely the strangest night of my life. I'm now an official half of a whole and I'm sleeping with a man."

"Something even better, dearest one?" He kissed her ear. "I don't snore."

"How do you know if you're asleep?"

Because Jayne told me. "Ah, well, a man knows these things, trust me."

She was smiling when she fell into a lovely deep, satisfied sleep.

He woke her up with kisses and wicked hands just before dawn. And just before breakfast was delivered.

The next morning the grass was still springy and soft from the night's hard rain, but the sun shined brightly, clouds danced in the sky and they heard the Channel waves spill onto the rocks, soft and rhythmic, like music.

They saw only an old man sitting on a rock with a fishing pole. He nodded to them. When they smiled and wished him good day, he looked at them more closely, and his mouth split into a big, toothless smile. "Happy marriage to you young'uns."

An hour later, they walked through the back gardens of the hotel, past the trellised rose bushes not quite ready to bud, and along the east side where yew bushes grew thick and tall. They were swinging their clasped hands as they rounded the end of the hotel to come into the front entrance. They heard voices, laughter, saw several couples and children walking down the walkway toward the beach below. "Nearly there," Graham said in her ear. He leaned down, cupped her face in his hands and kissed her, and his eyes became an even more vivid blue, such wickedness and promise, and Cam whispered, "Oh yes." Graham grabbed her hand and pulled her forward, nearly running, laughing.

Suddenly, one of the marble statues that stood proudly atop The Royal Hotel came crashing down, three feet behind them, and shattered against the stone walkway, loud as a cannon. Shards flew outward striking the walkway like bullets. Graham shoved Cam to the grass, threw himself on top of her, his hands over her head.

There was frozen silence. Then there were screams and shouts and running feet.

Graham reared up over her, his voice hoarse with fear. "Cam, tell me you're all right."

All right? She was lying on her back, Graham on his elbows above her, his face perfectly white. She'd heard the crash, but hadn't realized—"I think so. What happened?"

"One of the roof statues fell and broke apart not far behind us."

Yes, yes, she'd heard the thunderclap when the statue had struck the walkway. "Are you all right? Did any of the pieces hit you?"

"My coat is heavy so no parts of the statue hurt me." He was still breathing hard, fear about what could have happened nearly stopped his heart. But they were all right and all because of sudden lust. If they hadn't suddenly started hurrying, the statue would have struck them. His blood turned cold. It was close, too close.

People surrounded them, shocked voices filled the air, hands on his arms, his shoulder. Someone helped him to rise. Graham took Cam's hand and pulled her up. He said a general thank you, but he was studying Cam's face. He wiped some dirt and leaves from her hair. She was fine and after she ran her hands all over him, she was ready to believe he was as well.

Hotel staff and guests rushed out to see what had happened. Voices, so many voices. Then everyone was looking up at the hotel roof, at the line of three statues. So many voices wondering why the statue had crashed down, how lucky they'd been, and on and on it went.

Graham and Cam stood with them, staring at the hunks of marble scattered everywhere, even up to a stone bench near a prized bed of orchids. The statue head of the ancient Greek or Roman, who knew, had rolled to fetch up against a birch tree, the eyes looking directly at them. Cam swallowed. "I don't understand. Why would the statue fall? It—it crashed right behind us." She swallowed. "If you hadn't grabbed my hand and we'd started running—"

"Yes, I know, but we're all right. The statue was hollow but still heavy enough." *To smash us dead,* but he didn't say it, he didn't have to.

Cam stared around at the wreckage and at all the people. It had been so close, too close. She heard a gentleman say, "How could the statue have fallen? Look at the others, they look like they wouldn't move if a cannon hit them."

Everyone agreed, but still, the statue had crashed down and nearly hit guests. Soon Mr. French joined the group.

Everyone watched as the resident repairman, burly, silent Mr. Woodrow, climbed to the roof.

It didn't take long before he called down. "Looks be the statue jest fell over far as I can tell, near impossible. None of the four statues were bolted down, all standing free."

Mr. French told them the statues made in Southampton by a very reputable firm and winched to the roof of the hotel had been built eight years before. Yes, it was deemed impossible for the heavy statues to fall even in the strongest hurricane winds sent to batter British shores from Europe.

But one statue did fall.

All the other statues were examined, all were firmly in place, but Graham knew, just as did everyone else, they would soon be bolted down.

Mr. French faced them once the crowd dispersed. He was wringing his hands, so appalled he couldn't speak for a full minute. He insisted their stay be free. They did, however, have to pay for their meals in The Royal's excellent restaurant.

There was endless questioning from both Nutworthy and Cilly, who, white-faced, kept hugging Cam close. She knew both of them knew if they hadn't suddenly starting running, if they'd simply continued their stroll, they'd be dead.

Cam dreamed that night the statue's eyes were staring at her and she saw malevolence.

"Wake up, Cam, you're having a nightmare." Graham stroked his hands up and down her back, keeping her close. "It was a bad accident. We survived." She shuddered against him. He loved her again and she fell into a dreamless sleep, sated.

CHAPTER 47

Whitsonby House
Ormond Square
London
One week and a half later

Cilly said, "You haven't stopped humming and grinning like a loon since—well, since the beginning of your official married life. I saw Eliza staring at you, her eyebrows nearly meeting over her eyes. Claudine told me her mood has been foul since you and Graham returned yesterday."

Cam couldn't help it, a ready smile bloomed. Cilly was right. A smile seemed to be her constant companion since her honeymoon in Ventnor and she'd learned the amazing virtuosity of a man who knew what was what, and loved her. The combination was enough to make her want to dance even with Averil if the witch were here, she was just that happy. She said, "If Winstead is as, well, talented as Graham, she'll have no more foul moods, and wouldn't that be something? But why is her mood foul now, Cilly? I have done absolutely nothing to upset her."

Cilly patted the plaited braids atop her head, then wove in a pale blue ribbon, a perfect match to her new silk morning gown. Graham particularly liked it. It was loose fitting, with no corset beneath, hallelujah, and his hands could mold her and knead her and open the buttons and pull the gown over her head in but a moment. She gave a little shudder.

Cilly stared at her, rolled her eyes. "Surely you've seen her mood is foul when you're happy and everyone around you is happy for you."

"But since Averil left, Eliza rules the house again. I don't. I'm simply a visitor."

"As I said, you're happy and the whole mood of the house is different now that you and his lordship have come home. There's joy, Cam, in every single corner. It drives her quite mad, makes her nasty to all the servants, but they only shrug because, simply, you and Lord Graham are here."

Cam shook her head. "That makes no sense. Who wants a black cloud when if one waits long enough in London, there'll be a bright sun." She sighed. "I've never understood why Eliza dislikes me. Well, she won't have to suffer my presence for a good long while since we're leaving for King's Head next week." She paused, "At least she's polite to Graham."

"Who wouldn't be? He's charming, full of bonhomie, smiling as much as you are." Cilly stepped back. "There, you are perfection. Now go down and have your breakfast. If Eliza is there, I wonder if her eggs will curdle when she sees the lovely glow on your face."

"Now there's a thought." Cam rose, put on her glasses and studied herself. As she smoothed the gown although it didn't need it, she thought of the previous night when she and Graham had nearly run from the drawing room at precisely ten o'clock to her bedchamber, trying not to laugh too loudly. They were still fatigued from their journey from the Isle of Wight, yes, it had been two days, but still—and Cam had yawned. Of course everyone knew, her father in particular, but he'd only nodded, saying nothing, for which Cam was profoundly grateful.

Cam passed the tweeny Alice on her way downstairs, smiled and asked her about her mother who'd sprained her wrist. Cam smiled and bid good day to Osbourne who smiled back at her, showing a gold tooth in the back of his mouth, and bowed.

Cam was surprised to see both her father and Eliza in the dining room. "Good morning, Papa, Eliza," she sang out as she seated herself. "What an amazing morning, don't you think?"

"It's raining," Eliza said.

Whit regarded his daughter as he chewed on a roll. "It's London, of course it's raining. My dear Cam, Graham and I will be leaving to have a meeting with two new investors for our factory in Manchester, even though we don't really need their funds, but word gets around, you know, everyone wants to be part of it." He consulted his watch. "I believe your husband is adjusting some of the plans in my study as we speak, said he got an improved scheme for the boiler from you, Cam."

She bloomed. "Oh yes, we discussed fire-tube boilers, which as you know are not only smaller, they're more compact and will be easily assembled in your factory. Graham was up early, well, not all that early, really, lots to accomplish before adjusting the fire-tube design. He was very excited."

Eliza continued placidly eating her single coddled egg. "Winnie will never leave my side once we're married, for at least a month, unless, of course, I want him to. You've only been married a week and a half and yet he's scribbling silly train designs, his mind clearly not on you. I daresay he can't wait to leave with Father." She took a bite of a small sausage, a bread roll with only a dollop of Cook's homemade preserves, strawberry this morning.

Her opening salvo was really quite good. Cam gave her father a slight head shake when she saw he was going to say something. "Well, Eliza, not exactly," and smiled.

Eliza frowned at her. "What do you mean, not exactly?"

Whit cleared his throat, "That's not important, my dear. Now, Cam, Graham told me he hoped the meeting wouldn't last overly long since he wants to take you riding. Mr. Sherbrooke sent over Graham's bay gelding, Stanley. He's magnificent, a good seventeen hands high. He's settled right into the stable. Mr. Lacy is quite impressed with his appetite. He wants to exercise Stanley himself." Whit consulted his watch, stood. "My dears, I will see you later."

Graham appeared in the doorway, his eyes immediately going to Cam. She met his eyes, swallowed too fast, choked, and grabbed her tea. He walked quickly to her, never looking away, rubbed his hand up and down her back until she had her breath back. "All right?"

"Oh yes."

He leaned down, kissed her forehead. "No, don't get up. I will see you later. Eliza," he added to her sister and was off with her father.

Eliza said, "A lady shouldn't drink so quickly and choke. It is displeasing to everyone."

"I imagine so," Cam said, "but the fact is if I happen to see my husband, it's difficult to do anything but—well, stare at him he is so beautiful." She gave a little shiver. "He looks at me and I lose every thought in my head. Don't you agree?"

"Of course I do not agree. He is nothing compared to Winnie. He is only an upstart who claims to be Earl St. Lucy's son and now his heir. It's such a pity his younger brother hasn't been heard of. I ask you, what happened to his brother?"

Cam wasn't deaf to the sting in those words, the barely veiled accusations, but everything was different now, she was different. Eliza was Eliza and who cared if she wanted to be a viper?

Eliza jumped on her hobbyhorse and rode. "No matter he's snagged a title, he's still not a gentleman. He's in trade. Imagine he's building train parts. Winnie wouldn't ever do such a thing. He only pretends to be interested when he asks Graham questions. No, he will do as he's supposed to do, learn from his father, and see to his lands, as a gentleman should."

Cam said, "You don't believe our father is a gentleman?"

That stumped Eliza, but only for a moment. "Father is unique, he is established, he is recognized. He is admired because he is able to give his attention not only to his lands but to other things as well."

"I daresay Graham will be like our father and his own father as well. He is also unique. Perhaps Winstead will also be interested in joining Father and Graham. I imagine what with the incredible building of railroads all over England, there will be unimaginable profits to be made."

Her sister took a tiny bite of sausage. Did she perhaps look thoughtful?

Cam said, "It is a pity we don't know what happened to Graham's brother, Simon. It is very sad particularly since Graham still has no memory of him, well, of anyone really. But he will. I'm going to help him once we're at King's Head."

"Perhaps there is no memory of King's Head because he doesn't belong there."

Cam laughed. "Alas, there's no question he does belong. Graham looks like his father and has his mother's blue eyes. I thought you knew that." She paused, chewed on a roll. "Can you imagine, Eliza, what it would feel like to have no memory of your childhood years, not to know your own name, if there is anyone who loved you and missed you, looked for you?"

"Have you considered Graham was a bad penny, both he and his brother, maybe even bastards? And don't forget he was raised by Ryder Sherbrooke, a man known to take in strays, low-class children better off in an orphanage."

Cam stilled. The meanness of what her sister said frankly shocked her. She wanted to grab Eliza and shake her until her teeth rattled. *No, calm, be calm.* "You are very young to be so forgetful. Mr. Sherbrooke saved Graham's life. Imagine you not remembering Mr. Sherbrooke is much admired, an impressive man, praised for his kindness?"

Eliza gave her a dismissive look and drank her tea.

Cam said, "As to what happened to Graham and his brother, Simon, why I plan to figure it all out once I'm at my new home, at King's Head."

"You think you are so smart?"

"Well, no, but I am a fresh eye, so to speak. The odd thing is I think it's nearly time for everything to be remembered." Cam laid her napkin beside her plate and smiled at her sister. "Now I shall go write thank-you notes. So many thoughtful gifts. Have a lovely day." She was whistling, her step light as she left the dining room.

When she was writing her thirtieth thank-you card on the lovely gold-edged cream cards Lady Fortenberry had given her, she wondered how much longer Graham would be away. She wanted to go riding with him, perhaps speak of marital theorems.

CHAPTER 48

Tremaine townhouse
Cavendish Square

Two nights later Cam and Graham attended one of the premier balls of the Season given by Lord and Lady Tremaine in their opulent mansion on Cavendish Square. When they were greeted enthusiastically by the high and mighty of London Society, Cam realized how very different life would be now she was married, and not just married to anyone, but to the heir of an old, important and very rich earldom. The fact that Graham Hepburn also looked like a young god was an added bonus.

Cam had slipped her glasses into her small velvet reticule, joined the receiving line, and received congratulations from her host and hostess. When she and Graham stepped into the grand ballroom, the three hundred guests slowly fell silent when the Tremaine butler introduced their party in a wonderful deep baritone that very likely reached the ladies' withdrawing room. Her dashing father stood on her left, Eliza and Winstead just behind. It was the first time Cam realized she now had precedence over her older sister, and always would since she would be a countess someday. Cam didn't lord it over her sister, but she was smiling inside.

Graham leaned down, but not very far, and said close to her ear with its sparkling diamond earring, "Put on your glasses so you can see how everyone is staring at you, my beautiful wife, resplendent in the green gown I selected for her." He paused, grinned down at her. "Not to put too fine a point on it, actually Ryder selected it since he has amazing taste. He does, however, believe I will perhaps reach his level if I am assiduous in my practice."

Cam hesitated so Graham took her reticule, lifted out her glasses and set them on her nose, carefully hooked them behind her ears. "There, now you look perfect." He paused. "I shall ask my father if there are St. Lucy jewels for you to wear."

"Your father is still in something of a state of shock since his son is married, so let's wait until the queen invites us to dine at Buckingham Palace." She gave him a mad grin then blinked up at him. "Ah, this is splendid. Now I can see." She adjusted her glasses and looked out over the throng of beautiful gowned ladies, the men in their stark black with shirts so white they were nearly blinding. She didn't realize many were studying her, didn't realize her nervous stillness was taken by all to be a sign of proper arrogance. Graham leaned down, whispered against her ear, "They are all here to pay you homage. Do not forget that. Ah, Cam, should I tell you what we will do when we are finally back to your father's house, in our bedchamber? Should I whisper to you how I plan to lower your lovely gown, lick your beautiful white shoulders? And then slowly, very slowly, lick and kiss down your beautiful self all the way to your toes?"

She gulped, couldn't help staring into his eyes, so filled with wickedness and promise, she gulped again.

And she was no longer nervous. Her chin went up, her

beautiful white shoulders straightened. It didn't matter she was wearing her glasses. She was no longer a young girl at the mercy of her older sister and that witch Averil. Now, she was quite ready to take on the world. She saw her father had blended in with a group of his friends, she heard him laugh at something a gentleman said.

Lady Tremaine, mother of three healthy boys, her hair so blond it appeared nearly white, appeared at their side. Lady Tremaine followed Cam's eyes and said, "Poor sweet man, how my husband and I have always admired him, counted him a good friend, and now, to be saddled with a mad wife, such a dreadful thing to have happen. A pity her madness wasn't recognized before he married her. Everyone feels deeply for him. Everyone believes it proper that dear Averil is where she should be, with her family and kept safe." Was that a bit of malice Cam heard in Lady Tremaine's voice?

"I imagine both you and your sister were saddened at this tragic turn of events as well, ah, but life, it sometimes gives us sorrow, sometimes joy."

Cam nodded solemnly, said nothing at all. She towered over Lady Tremaine, who was as short as Queen Victoria. It was fortunate all three sons had their father's excellent height. Lady Tremaine was near fifty, but she didn't look it. Her incredible white-blond hair was twisted about at the back of her head and curls fell alongside her face. Her eyes were a lovely green-blue, and kind. As for her jewels—diamonds at her throat, ears, wrists sparkled under the soft candle chandeliers.

Lady Tremaine studied Cam a moment. "My dear, I first saw you when you were perhaps ten years old. You were clutching your maid's hand, your hair in thick braids down your back, glasses on your small nose. I remember you were laughing, nearly dancing with excitement when you saw a swan on the Serpentine. I knew looking at you that you would become quite beautiful. And do you know what I realize now? Your glasses with the stark black frames give you a wonderful distinction." She looked over at Graham. "As for your husband, well, I don't wish to be indelicate but let me say I cannot wait to see your children." And she trilled out a charming laugh.

She heard Graham thank Lady Tremaine, saying he only hoped their children would have his wife's face and his excellent eyesight, which made her laugh more, and caress his arm.

"My dears, allow me to introduce you to my friends. Ah, Lord Graham, my son Elias very much wants to meet you. And here he is, nearly crowding me away." Graham laughed, squeezed Cam's hand and joined a group of young men.

Cam greeted guests she'd met before, of course, but now they treated her differently. She was no longer a girl with a nice dowry whose father would ensure she wasn't nabbed by a fortune hunter. No, she was a future countess, not only a countess, but an important countess, a very rich countess. She was now *Somebody.*

As for Graham, his story had been the topic throughout Society for several weeks. He was soon surrounded by both men and women, the women to flirt, many of the men to discuss investing in his train projects. He was a man of the future. He was a man who would change the future.

When the first waltz filled the ballroom from the orchestra on a dais at the far end, Cam watched Graham weave his way in and out of the guests, not pausing, until he was with her. "Come," he said, took her in his arms. "Have no concerns about my stepping on your toes, my aunt Sophie taught me to waltz two years ago when I confessed I didn't know how. She worked me like a horse until finally she patted my cheek and said I was now proficient enough to dance with our new little queen." To prove it, Graham twirled her in a lovely circle.

Cam felt like she was floating, round and round they went, guests stepping aside to watch them. She laughed and glided and swayed and once he even lifted her off her feet to swing her around. When he slowed, laughing with her, Cam panting, she gave him a blazing smile. "That was splendid. Goodness, Graham, let me catch my breath and let's do it again. Mr. Petty taught me to waltz. He said I was as graceful as a swan's neck. He should have waltzed with you, he would have swooned. It was a pity he had such wet hands."

"Wet hands? I shall keep on my gloves, just in case."

Cam danced with a half dozen other gentlemen, Graham with an equal number of ladies, but when a waltz was played, they were again the focus, so smooth and elegant they were. Cam couldn't remember ever being happier than she was at this moment—sparkling candlelight, a room full of beautiful people, laughing, dancing, her wedding night, and that was a night she would remember when she was departing this earth. She saw Eliza waltzing with Winstead, saw her laugh at something he said, really a delightful laugh. She wished she could say something to make her sister laugh. Then again, at this perfect moment in time, she didn't care.

They didn't arrive back at Ormond Square until two o'clock in the morning. Six minutes later Graham was kissing her neck, her shoulders, her breasts, and she was clutching him to her, moaning, biting his ear, her hands rubbing up and down his back, and lower. His touch, his mouth, were amazing and all the while he whispered wicked things to her, many of them she still didn't understand, but it didn't matter. She knew she would understand everything by Christmas, and what a glorious thought that was. Wait, she was being shortsighted. She just might understand everything by next week.

CHAPTER 49

London

Lady Tremaine became Cam's mentor. She planned Cam's wardrobe for King's Head and gowns for her social life in London when she visited her father's house. Summer clothes, fall clothes, riding habits, gloves, hats, the most wicked underclothes since, Lady Tremaine said, she had to spoil her husband, and on and on it went. "When you return to London, we will shop for your gown for your sister's wedding. This is so pleasurable, Cam. I always wanted a daughter, but God sent me nothing but dirty little boys, who, thankfully, have grown up to be fine young gentlemen. So, I suppose I have adopted you."

And Cam didn't mind at all.

Because Lady Tremaine was sought after by every modiste in London, her custom was spread out amongst the most renowned three. Cam's wardrobe was completed in two weeks. Since all the bills were sent to Graham, Cam never saw them or she would have fallen over in a dead faint. Since Graham never said a word, just complimented her endlessly, kissed her whenever he found her alone or could pull her behind a curtain or a door, she never gave it a thought until Cilly said one evening as she fastened the exquisite silk-covered buttons down the back of Cam's delicate gold silk dinner gown, "Mrs. Willig told me Lord Graham was a very generous husband, given all your clothes were designed and made by the finest dressmakers in London, no expense spared."

Cam hadn't realized, hadn't thought, only nodded whenever Lady Tremaine had told her a particular item of clothing was going to be perfect on her—did he have sufficient funds? "Oh dear," Cam said. She planned to apologize to Graham, swear she would economize, but when Graham entered their bedchamber and she was ready to tell him she would never again buy a gown, he looked at her, leaned down and kissed her, told her she looked so beautiful every time he saw her he nearly swallowed his tongue. Finally, she managed to draw back and clasp his face between her hands. "I know I am close to losing my brain so I must get this out before I do. Thank you, Graham. You are the most generous husband. All my new clothes are lovely. But the cost, will my dowry cover it?"

He grinned down at her, like a bandit. "Please do not kiss your father as you just did me. He insisted on paying half and it wasn't out of your dowry."

When she thanked her father, she gave him a chaste kiss on his cheek, hugged him close. He'd moved from numb shock at his wife's betrayal to anger and now, thankfully, more to blessing his luck she was gone. He was, she realized, once again looking to the future and that meant excitement. He and Graham spent many hours not only with investors, but traveling by train to and from Manchester to meet with their local managers, both men with excellent experience that they'd managed to lure away with very fine wages indeed. To Cam's surprise and joy, Graham asked her to write out exact steps workers were to follow when building his designs or adapting existing machinery. So many questions, answers, simplifying each instruction until finally both of them were pleased with the results. As an experiment Graham gave the steps to building a steel cube of a specific size to hold a fire-boiler part to Whit's valet. He understood and managed, for the most part. When thanked for his excellent understanding, Terrance said, "I have to admit, my lord, even though this was of vague interest, all in all, I still much prefer the steps in producing my special pomade for his lordship."

And most days a letter arrived from Graham's father, always filled with news—the spring planting of beans, corn and squash, the bean seeds grown indoors until there was no more chance of frost. He gave Graham news of their neighbors with the hope he could perhaps remember them, remember something. But there was no memory. His father always signed his letters, *Your loving father who misses you.*

"A very smart man is my father. As you know from his letters, he and Ryder communicate often. They discussed how to improve this and that piece of equipment or a task that's been performed for the past five hundred years to make his farmers' methods more efficient and less backbreaking. Ryder and my aunt Sophie have visited King's Head, and my father, in turn, has visited Ryder's home in Upper Slaughter in the Cotswolds." He paused, kissed her, couldn't help himself. "I can just see him surrounded by a dozen children. They'd all bow and curtsey to him, all proper, but stay back because, after all, even though he appears to be Ryder's friend, they don't know him. Then my father would pull candies out of his pockets and spread them around with compliments to each child. Believe me, to a child, that means a friend for all time. As you know from his letters, they performed for him, singing, acted out plays written by the older children, and brought him into games of charades. You and I will travel there in the summer. I know Aunt Sophie wants to introduce you to the children. Now—" Graham pulled out from the envelope a folded sheet of paper, spread it out. "I wanted to show you this. Father wants to build a private train line from Dover with a terminus at King's Head because Dover is still too distant. This is a drawing of the topography of the land he considers most appropriate for rail lines and the best location for a terminus. He would like my opinion." Graham raised glowing eyes to her face. "Imagine, Cam, we would ride in our own train from Dover to King's Head and it would leave when we wanted it to." He paused a moment, frowning. "That would mean of course a separate set of tracks for the fifteen-mile trek to King's Head—ah, the cost, I can't begin to imagine what it would cost. And who would invest if it is only for us? And why would they since the train would only go to King's Head? Hmm, I need to speak to your father, see what he thinks." He grinned. "It is a marvelous idea."

There'd been so much change in her life. Cam realized with something of a shock that she now accepted such a grandiose plan with equanimity. Cam wanted to hug him, but she said matter-of-factly, "Of course he wants your opinion. Imagine, Graham, people could travel from London to King's Head in a single day. It is amazing."

Graham's voice was thoughtful. "Father wrote he'd first considered a private line from London to King's Head but realized soon enough the cost would be the size of a small nation's yearly budget. Imagine, Cam, a train car would remain at Dover and be only for our use. Ah, the cost of the connecting track, the labor, the materials—well, no matter, when you and I are home—" His voice fell off a cliff. He swallowed, stared at her out of wild blue eyes, and he paled.

She said matter-of-factly, "Yes, when we arrive home—?"

He shook his head at himself. "It is still all so foreign to me. For half my life Ryder's Chadwyck House was my home. Now, well, I suppose King's Head is indeed my home and yours as well—even though I have no memories. Not a single bloody one."

Cam hugged him close. "Our home, Graham. Listen to me

and believe me for I'm not lying to you. All your memories will come when they're meant to, you'll see." She pulled back, cupped his face in her hands, kissed him, smoothed her fingertips over his brows, smiled. "Imagine, our very own rail car all the way from Dover Station to our own private terminus at King's Head. You know our family and friends will drink champagne and eat the oysters prepared the French way."

He said slowly, "I'm picturing a train car with many wide windows to see the passing scenery, and leather seats, more comfortable than the usual ones even in first class." He paused a moment, shook his head. "Perhaps a private train car can't happen now, but in the future? Cam, I read about so many new ideas every day." He frowned. "I really don't like oysters." He kissed her again, walked away, whistling, his father's letter in his hand.

Cam looked after him, smiling, her heart full to bursting.

CHAPTER 50

Whitsonby House
Ormond Square

The next afternoon over tea, Lady Tremaine pointed out to Cam how many ladies were now wearing glasses, identical like hers. At the bewildered look on Cam's face, Lady Tremaine laughed, patted her face. "My dear, albeit you were well dowered, you were still a debutante, not all that important except for a few men who admired your wit and lovely face and of course those on the lookout for an heiress.

"But now you are married to a lovely young man who, through violence, lost his memory and his heritage until very recently, and now, all is returned to him."

She lightly laid her palm against Cam's cheek. "You are the diamond in your husband's crown, not entirely an apt metaphor, since he himself is such a superior young gentleman, but no matter. Yours is a vastly romantic story and will keep polite Society talking and speculating for several months."

"My what—my glasses?"

"Cam, don't you understand? You are now a lady of influence, a lady of great importance in Society. Your gowns will be admired and copied. Your clever turns of phrase will be copied as well, and yes, next time you are out, do regard the number of spectacles you see on young ladies' noses."

Cam set down her lovely Meissen teacup. "But that makes no sense. I'm still just me, well, new gowns and such, but still I'm the same as I was before I married. And many times what I say is absurd. My glasses tend to slide down my nose."

Lady Tremaine laughed. "Do not change, Cam, you are delightful. Simply accept your new position and remain yourself." And she saluted her with her teacup.

Her new position. Graham's new position. And suddenly she remembered what Earl St. Lucy had written to Graham.

You wrote of a heavy marble statue falling from the roof of The Royal Hotel, nearly striking you and Cam. Graham, you consider it only an unfortunate accident, but you cannot be certain the statue wasn't heaved off the roof by the same individual who tried to kill you when you were a boy. If this is true and I am inclined to think it very possible, there is no reason to assume he will not try to kill you again. I have finally accepted this individual did indeed succeed in killing your brother. You must always be on your guard until we can figure out who is behind this. By now, knowing Society, everyone knows your history and they will ask questions. Do let everyone find out about that very unlikely accident on your honeymoon, the more people who know, the more likely it is you will be safe, at least in London.

Eugenie informs me a friend of hers in London wrote that your story obviously titillates Society and has made you a hero for surviving so well. She also wrote Society thinks your wife is both charming and smart and she will see to it you remain on the hero pedestal for at least this Season. Please speak to your father-in-law, trust him to make inquiries. I am worried for you, my son.

Cam smoothed away her frown. She looked now at Lady Tremaine's perfect aristocrat's face, her straight, narrow nose, her high cheekbones, her perfect arched brows. And the spray of glorious white-blond ringlets touching her cheeks. Her eyes, Cam thought, hinted at secrets and worldly knowledge and good sense. Cam nodded slowly. "Yes, I understand. I know you have heard about the falling statue in Ventnor on our honeymoon. Let me tell you all of it."

As she spoke Cam felt gooseflesh rise on her arms, she felt sheer terror choke her as it had when she'd been thrown to the ground, Graham coming over her, his arms around her head. She swallowed again, the sound of the statue striking the walkway, shattering, spewing out shards, some large enough to kill. She remembered the smell of the earth, people screaming, running.

Lady Tremaine listened closely. When she'd finished, she took Cam's hand, squeezed. "Lord Vereker is right; Graham won't be safe until the person responsible is identified and dealt with. I will ensure everyone knows more details of this. If anyone knows anything, it will come out. You must promise me to always be alert, Cam, you and Graham."

Cam said, "I've wondered if the person responsible for taking both Graham and his brother and tried his best to murder Graham was the same man who shoved the statue off the roof of the hotel. It was more than ten years ago. Is his rage still so great? But why? I think it's very possible this person is afraid Graham will soon recover his memory and know."

Lady Tremaine said slowly, "If this person is close enough to the Hepburn family he would quickly know about your honeymoon in Ventnor. He also must have known Graham had lost his memory, a great relief to him, I imagine. Did he wait for his chance?

"It seems to me he wants very much to make Graham's death appear an accident." She laid her hand over Cam's. "I will tell everyone the added details, and we will see. Speculation is always good, perhaps it will clear the air, people will pay attention."

But perhaps it had been an accident. No, Cam would never believe that, ever.

Lady Tremaine said, "Now, back to you, my dear. You must not forget to come to London every month, with your husband, to keep your reputation on everyone's mind. Finally, and this is important. The more popular you become, the more admired you are, it redounds on your husband and his plans with your father and their investors." She placed a soft white hand on Cam's arm. "Do not forget this, Cam. It is a fine thing to have power in Society. It makes for a very nice life and paves the way for your children." She paused, frowned. "We will hope the miscreant who is behind this misery is uncovered quickly. Believe me, now. As I said everyone will be discussing it."

Osbourne cleared his throat in the drawing room door. "My lady, your coachman wishes me to remind you of your appointment."

"Thank you, Osbourne. Yes, I must be off." Lady Tremaine rose, shook out her lovely pale gray skirts that seemed to shimmer when she walked.

Cam said, "My lady, what would you think of my having a gold chain designed to fasten to my glasses? Then I could simply take them off and let them hang around my neck."

Lady Tremaine cocked her head to the side. "I've never seen such a thing. Do you know I think it is a splendid idea." She added with a chuckle, "I daresay it will be copied within a matter of days."

Cam shook her head at the absurdity of it all. Both she and Osbourne showed Lady Tremaine to the front door. Lady

Tremaine said, "I believe it is now appropriate for you to call me Madeline."

"Oh my, that is Graham's mother's name."

"Yes, I know," she said, and patted her face. "I knew her, of course, a lovely lady, such a pity she fell into the Green Stream. Such a strange name for such a nasty stretch of water. I still miss her. Be alert, Cam, both you and Graham. We will try to discover the person behind this."

Cam and Osbourne both gave her into the tender care of her coachman and Cam went back in the drawing room, humming. She already had a lovely gold chain with a locket attached. She left immediately to go to Hancock, the premier jeweler in London. An hour later, her glasses were dangling on the chain when she left the magnificent store. She saw several ladies staring at her glasses and smiled.

She'd no sooner arrived home than Eliza came into the drawing room, pulling off her lovely York tan gloves, humming. She hummed until she saw Cam sitting in front of the fireplace, her chin in her hands. She stopped, put her hands on the hips of her very fine green wool riding habit. "Winnie is seeing to our horses. He will be here in but a moment for tea. I had not expected you to be here. What are you doing here? And what is that around your neck?"

CHAPTER 51

Cam smiled, said, "This is how I will wear my glasses from now on. What do you think?"

To her great surprise, Eliza didn't tell her she looked like an idiot, rather she looked thoughtful, said, "It is a good solution. Who gave you the idea?"

"Actually it was my idea."

Eliza looked disbelieving, but she didn't say anything and wasn't that a shock? Cam watched her remove her lovely riding hat, a military style that looked quite well on her. She smiled. "You asked what I'm doing here. I live here for the next three days. Did you have a pleasant ride?"

"It wasn't particularly pleasant, no."

"Why ever not?"

"Everyone stopped us, not to inquire about our wedding in the fall, which is what they should have done, but no. Everyone wanted to know everything about your new husband's history, and how he came to discover his identity. And who tried to kill him so many years ago. And constant talk of the falling statue in Ventnor. No one would speak of anything else." She shrugged. "It was provoking. Even Winnie can talk of nothing else.

"Since you're closer, ring the bell and tell Osbourne to order tea. You may also greet Winnie when he comes in, offer him brandy. He likes Father's. I'm going upstairs to change. Oh yes, I believe friends of Father's are dining with us this evening."

"Yes," she said to Eliza's retreating back.

Eliza turned in at the door. "I saw Ellie Otis. She was wearing glasses just like yours. She looked ridiculous, just like you do. The chain does, however, lessen your look of a governess or a companion."

Only three more days.

But what would happen at King's Head? So many new people, and Eugenie—would she be a friend or a possible Eliza?

When Osbourne showed a windblown Winstead into the drawing room a few moments later, Cam walked to him, took his hands. "It is so good to see you, Win. Do come in and let me pour you some of Father's French brandy."

Winstead said as Cam walked to the small sideboard, "You are all the talk, Cam, you and Graham. This statue falling—it scares me to my toes. Most want to believe it an accident, but no one really does."

Cam said, "We wanted to believe it was too, but no, it very likely wasn't an accident." She handed him the brandy, watched him take a sip, set the snifter on the small French table beside the sofa.

He sat forward, clasped his hands between his knees. "No, I do not believe it was an accident either. I'd hoped to speak to you alone. I am very concerned, my dear. Someone tried to murder Graham when he was a boy. Not only is Graham alive and well, it means this someone is trying again. Of course you are aware of all this, as is Graham, and you are both being vigilant. I'm trying to think of what I can do, but as of yet, there's nothing except reiterate to you that you must be careful."

Cam said slowly, "This person who tried to kill Graham when he was a boy, who did murder his brother, Simon, and their tutor, he didn't know he'd failed with Graham until Graham discovered who he really was and appeared at King's Head. I imagine he was relieved Graham had no memory of who he was, but of course he couldn't take the chance he'd remember at any time and so he knocked the statue off the roof of the hotel in Ventnor. Of course he will try again, he must. It has to be someone close, Win, someone very close."

Winstead nodded. He found himself studying her face, a face he always thought very pretty, distinctive, and he'd always liked her glasses and now what was there? Her glasses were dangling on a lovely gold chain. He watched her put them on her nose. It was distinctive, really quite an excellent idea.

Yes, Cam was always lively, always moving, smiling, eager for life, yes, that was it. He knew Eliza didn't like her sister and he'd wondered why, but when he'd asked her once after overhearing her say to Cam her gown was common and the color made her look like oatmeal, she'd stared at him a moment, then laughed. "Oh, Winnie, it was all a jest." And she'd patted his hand.

But it hadn't been a jest. He now watched Eliza's sister pace in front of him in her long-legged stride, her glasses sliding down her nose. She pushed them back up without thinking. She stopped, looked at him, and whispered, "Win, I am so afraid. If only Graham could remember, he would know. We would know and we could hunt this person down and I could smack him with a rock. Maybe a boulder, or my fist, that would make me feel better." She sighed. "He's always there, this black shadow, hovering in the back of our minds. Graham doesn't say much, but I know it drives him crazy that he can't remember." She paused, felt tears well up, swallowed. "He's afraid, for me."

Winstead said, keeping his voice matter-of-fact, "This person is now desperate, Cam, since he knows once Graham is living at King's Head surrounded with his past, he will remember, remember everything. He will take more risks and that makes him more dangerous."

Winstead rose, took her restless hands in his. "I will say it again, you and Graham must take care, which is a stupid thing to say since of course you will. Keep family around you as much as possible." He smiled. "Fact is, I am looking forward to our children growing up together." And he leaned down, only a bit, and kissed her cheek.

Cam heard a movement, looked up to see Eliza standing in the doorway, staring at them.

She smiled, thankful Eliza didn't have a pistol or she'd shoot Cam on the spot.

In a voice dripping with sarcasm, she said, "I trust that is a brotherly kiss?"

Win slowly released Cam, patted her arm, smiled at Eliza. "I was just telling your sister I very much like her glasses. They make her look distinctive and really quite clever, don't you think?"

"No, I think she looks—" Eliza paused, shot a look at Cam, then smiled, drawled, "Yes, she looks as distinctive as a governess we had as children."

"Ah," Cam said with as much humor as she could dredge up even though she wanted to sink into the floor, "Miss Millstone. She was really clever as well."

Eliza shrugged. "Well, you are distinctive, I'll say that for you."

Win looked from his fiancée to his future sister-in-law, saw her expression hadn't changed, knew she was quite used to this. Win's brow furrowed. He said, his voice deep, slow, "Eliza, I have watched you charm everyone in your orbit, everyone except your sister. I have watched you belittle her and wondered why you have this animosity toward her, your own flesh and blood. I think your sister is really quite beautiful, not to mention kind. She is your sister, Eliza. You should cherish her, laugh with her, shop with her, and yes, compliment her."

He raised his hand when she would speak. "No, I do not wish to hear any excuses. I want to be very clear about this, Eliza. You will cease this unkindness toward your sister. And there is my new family, a surprise, I know. I also know you had assumed you would be mistress. But you will not. My new stepmother will be mistress. You will not treat her or any of the children with anything but kindness and smiles and gaiety. They will be your family, every one of them."

He paused, studied her set face, softened his voice, just a bit. "I love you, Eliza, and I expect your love and respect in return, not just for me but also for my new family. I will not allow any other behavior from you. I also hope your respect, maybe even a modicum of caring, will extend to your sister." Again, he paused a moment, then, "Do you understand me? Clearly? Do you agree?"

Eliza took a step back, searched his face, saw this man she'd accepted to marry wasn't as malleable as she'd believed. No, he was another man entirely. There was iron at his core. She felt her insides twist and turn, turmoil showing on her face. But then she really looked at this man who would be her husband. She saw a man to admire, a man to respect, a man who would protect her and hold her close for all their lives. The pliable man she'd expected to wed and rule disappeared into the wainscoting. She looked at Cam, saw she hadn't moved a muscle, her face down. She didn't wish her ill, she didn't. She was just—Eliza said slowly, "But why have you changed, Win? You have never spoken to me like this before."

Win smiled at her. "I have not changed. I daresay I've been too easy, too acquiescent. But, Eliza, I'm not blind. I know you. And finally I knew it was enough, it was time for me to act. If I am to marry you, if I am to agree to accept you as my wife, you will obey me in this. I ask you again, do you understand and accept what I demand from you?"

For the first time in her life, Cam saw her sister back down, saw her look at Win with new eyes. Still, Cam wished fortitude for Win and a sea change for her sister. Would it happen?"

Cam watched her sister slowly nod, hold out her hand. "Yes, Win, I understand."

"Do you agree, Eliza?"

Eliza said, her voice strong, "Yes, Win, I agree."

CHAPTER 52

King's Head

Cam watched Graham speak to the engine driver when they arrived in Dover on the Southeastern train, doubtless questioning him about all the problems he saw with the steam engine and any ideas he had about improving them. Her beautiful husband was leaning slightly forward, all his attention on what the elderly, whiskered man in his soot-covered black wool clothing and his ancient square-toed black boots was telling him. She was content to sit on a bench outside the small station and chat to Cilly.

Cilly said, "It still amazes me Mr. Towbridge laid down the law to your sister. I really wish I could have been there to witness it. I always believed he was too kind, too patient, no match for your sister. He's shown great strength."

Cam said, "I've been thinking about it and I believe Win will keep the reins firmly in his hands at least with his family. I have no doubt he will keep her on the straight and righteous path. But when Eliza and I are alone? I don't think she'll be able to help herself, her treatment of me has lasted such a long time—"

"I think you should smack her a couple of times," Cilly said.

Cam laughed, then fell silent. Perhaps she should, remind her of the promise she'd made.

It was a pleasant day, the wind bringing only a slight chill to the air from the English Channel. The sun was trying its best to give them some shine. Cam sat back, felt what sun there was on her face. Graham's valet, Nutworthy, walked to and fro, stopping to repeat instructions he'd already given to the single porter, a gangly lad with a thatch of coal-black hair and a space between his teeth. He looked to Cam like he wanted to throw Nutworthy onto the tracks with a train coming.

Luckily, a pony cart arrived not three minutes later and the lad stacked their luggage in the back and strapped it down. Cilly smiled at the boy, gave him half a guinea, which made him smile from ear to ear and do a little dance.

Nutworthy gave Cilly a nasty look. "That was unnecessary and much more than he deserved; he was a rude boy. I knew he wasn't listening to my careful instructions. Just look at his lordship's valise, I see a black smudge, possibly grease from the little lout's dirty hands." But then Nutworthy fell suddenly silent; he appeared to look inward. He sighed. "His lordship is always telling me to be kind, to be tolerant, but it is sometimes difficult when all I want is for things to be done properly. Ah, I must try harder."

And both Cam and Cilly were disarmed.

The Hepburn coach with its coach-door insignia of a great golden eagle pulled up during the luggage transfer and Riker the coachman jumped down and strode toward them. The two horses, beautiful matching grays, stood placidly. Riker gave Cam a sharp bow and a wide smile.

Graham called out, "I'll be just a moment, Mr. Riker," to which Mr. Riker shook a fatherly head and said with the freedom granted a forever retainer, "I see Lord Graham is a copy of his father and his poor dead mother, interested in anything that has a moving part. I'm told by Terrance, his lordship's valet, not this young lordship's valet, but his Lord Vereker's valet, that this drives Lady Eugenie quite mad. Mr. Blakeney remarks she's a muttering pacer.

"As for Master Tallyrand, he just grunts, but all see smiles with those grunts. Then he swings his rifle over his shoulder and walks back to that charming little cottage he built himself in the eastern woods, and very fine it is indeed. Mr. Blakeney visits Master Tallyrand, you know, takes sweet buns from Mrs. Sample, she's the cook, you know, the moment she takes them out of the oven and wraps them lovingly in soft wool cloths to keep them hot. I visit Master Tallyrand to see his horse, Galahad, is well, and I always find he is properly shoed and healthy. Master Tallyrand is just that good."

Cam was enthralled with this outpouring. He'd taken only two breaths. She would have to ask Graham if Riker was as efficient as she was in his explanations. She grinned up at him. "Thank you, Mr. Riker. You've provided me excellent information very economically. Are you married?"

"Oh aye, eleven years now to my precious helpmate, Mathilde, and we were blessed with two strapping boys."

"I look forward to meeting your family, and well, everyone's family."

He gave her a wide grin showing beautiful white teeth. "Welcome home, my lady. You will find King's Head is a special place, full of beauty and mystery and sheep."

Cam laughed, introduced him to Cilly.

"Ah, here comes his lordship, doubtless the train driver has made his brain buzz with new ideas, better ideas, just ideas in general, but alas, these sorts of ideas shouldn't be encouraged in a young man's brain given he's a brand-new husband." And his white teeth gleamed with humor. Cam hoped Mr. Riker was going to be an excellent ally at her new home. Then he added, all seriousness, "I want you to know, my lady, everyone, from Cook to the new stable lad, is on the lookout for anyone who wants to do Lord Graham harm. All are stout-hearted."

Cam felt a lump in her throat, managed to say, "Thank you, Mr. Riker. Needless to say Lord Graham and I are very concerned."

Mr. Riker said, "Mrs. Mince and Mr. Blakeney will speak to Miss Cilly here, and Lord Graham's valet. Everyone will be alert."

A royal homecoming could not be more splendid than theirs at King's Head, replete with a celebratory feast prepared by Mrs. Sample over a period of two days, the marinade, French, you know, taking the longest with constant attendance to ensure perfection.

There was a graceful curtsey from Mrs. Mince, the housekeeper, who made introduction of all the female staff, lined up in a straight line, frank curiosity on all their faces, and Blakeney introduced the porters and footmen. Cam repeated each name and smiled at each curtsey. And so many new faces, and behind those faces Cam knew they would do their best to protect the Lord Vereker's long-lost son now returned to the bosom of his family. What struck her most was the joy on her father-in-law's face at the sight of his son. He held him and everyone looked on, smiles on every face.

Once Blakeney showed them to their very fine bedchamber with its attached dressing and bathing room and yes, even a water closet, he lightly touched his hand to Graham's shoulder, smiled, bowed, and left them.

The moment the door closed behind him, Cam threw her arms around Graham, whispered in his ear. "King's Head is huge, larger than my father's country home, Bryne Hill."

"Ryder told me Bryne Hill is a lovely manor house near

Loddenwell in Devon. He also told me he'd heard your older brother is a fine master, though he's rarely in London, preferring to live in Boston." He stroked his fingertips over her eyebrows, slid her glasses off her nose and slipped both glasses and gold chain into his vest pocket. He said, all conversational, as he unfastened the long row of beautifully sewn buttons on the back of her traveling gown, "King's Head is old, built way back in the time of Queen Elizabeth on the ruins of an Augustinian abbey. You and I will explore the ruins, the monks' cells, picnic with the dozens of sheep under an ancient oak tree. No, we will not swim in the Green Stream as it's called. It's far too terrifying. Everyone believes there is something lurking beneath those green waters, something from another time, something dangerous." He didn't add he always carried a small pistol in his coat pocket, a knife strapped to his ankle.

She blinked up into his vivid blue eyes, saw there was even something more, and it was passion. She said, "It is close, but perhaps Mr. Riker is even more informative than you were."

He laughed as he slipped the gown off her shoulders. "Now." Graham kissed her, nuzzled her neck. Her finally sewn linen chemise and the light corset, the three petticoats were familiar to him now so it didn't take him long to strip her down to her lovely bare flesh. He couldn't stop kissing her, telling her what he was going to do, quite graphic he was—thanks to Jayne and several hell-raising young men at Oxford—and if she wondered where he'd learned such immensely delicious phases and words, she was too beside herself to ask.

When Graham was down to his skin, she couldn't help but stare at him. He was so splendid, so very perfect. She stroked her hands down his back, over his flanks, as far as she could reach. She bit his earlobe, kissed his neck, whispered, "Do you think the servants know what we're doing?"

He reared up, smiled down at her. "My father tells me they're a smart bunch, and, of course, all-knowing when it comes to the family, like all your people at Whitsonby House."

"But, Graham, we were so discreet on our trek to our bedchamber perhaps they believe we are in here behind a closed door pondering the mysteries of the steam engine or maybe examining the bedchamber furnishings and the wallpaper, or perhaps napping due to fatigue from our long journey from London. Don't you think?" Cam leaned up, bit his shoulder, licked where she'd bitten. "Or perhaps all the males are talking about how strong and manly you are, that you could easily demolish the heavyweight champion Ben Counts."

"However do you know about Ben Counts?"

She grinned. "I heard two stable lads had won bets on him. Now, where was I? Oh yes, I know all the females are whispering how very beautiful you are and wondering if I've fainted dead on the floor at the sight of you."

"Am I as bare as you are, dearest, or am I modeling my new vest and trousers?"

"Surely that is indelicate. Well, yes, your vest is probably under the bed." Cam pulled him down on top of her.

CHAPTER 53

The bedchamber was bathed in late-afternoon shadows when Graham, heart still pounding, managed to come up on his elbow and look down at Cam's beloved face. She was still breathing hard enough to please him greatly. Jayne would have approved. He wasn't a clod. He marveled that this lovely creature with her shining hair tousled across the white pillowcase was his. His wife. It was amazing. He found himself wondering if he hadn't been the long-lost heir to Earl St. Lucy, if he'd merely been a business partner of sorts, would her father have considered him a fortune hunter, certainly not worthy of her, and kicked him to the curb? Very probably so.

From one day to the next, he, Alex Ivanov, with a blank brain, had become Viscount Whitestone, his earl father's only heir.

And someone wanted to kill him because of it.

Graham sighed, banished the ever-present fear, and lightly smoothed a fingertip over her eyebrows.

Cam opened her eyes, dreamy, still glowing with pleasure, her cheeks still a bit flushed. He kissed her, felt the tip of her tongue glide over his mouth, and of course he stirred. He said nearly touching her mouth, "No matter our wondrous subtlety in excusing ourselves, you know as well as I do every single staff member knows exactly what we're doing and that is why we haven't been disturbed. I doubt if we didn't emerge from this bedchamber for two days, trays would be left outside with only a discreet knock on the door.

"However, my father is a different matter. He could well be pacing outside the door right now, so alas, dear one, we cannot remain in bed for much longer." And he grinned, kissed her eyebrows, the tip of her nose.

Cam sifted her fingers through his hair. "Silk, your hair, glorious silk."

He picked up a thick, heavy tress currently fallen over her forehead. He brought it to his cheek. "I'd like to wrap myself in your hair."

Cam blinked up at him, grinned like a bandit. "I shall have to grow it for ten more years because my hair could be a blanket. Then perhaps to earn an extra groat or two, you could let me play Lady Godiva."

"The thought of you wearing only your hair atop a horse with dozens of men staring at you makes my blood clot in my veins. So I'll be content to rub your hair on my face. Now, about my father just outside, possibly listening for snores or conversation, I think it best we rouse ourselves."

"It's marvelous—your father is so happy to see you, so happy to have you home, at last. And now that you are here to live, under his roof, he just might come to approve of my snagging you so quickly after he'd finally gotten you back. Wait. Graham, maybe I do hear someone just outside, maybe walking up and down in the corridor, maybe muttering."

He laughed and kissed her, oh how he loved her mouth, and laughed some more. "Maybe both my father and Nutworthy are pacing together." He forced himself to pull away from her and sit up. He said nothing for several moments, looked thoughtful. "Wife, do you think perhaps now we have conducted sufficient observations to draw conclusions and posit a marital theorem?"

Cam said, "An excellent question. I read one cannot conduct too many experiments, consider too many results before forming a theorem. One must be committed, regardless of the hour. But I suppose I am nearing starvation, so our next experiment will have to wait. Well, for a little while. Maybe three hours. Do you agree, my lord?"

He didn't agree, not at all, but there was duty and expectation and his father, an excellent man he prayed he'd soon remember. The love Graham felt from him, the absolute joy, it moved him unutterably. He wanted his father again, wanted him in his heart, where he belonged.

It turned out only Nutworthy was walking up and down the hallway. Graham's father was pacing in his own study, looking at the very old ormolu clock on the mantel every other minute, waiting, waiting, close to wearing holes in the Aubusson carpet, Blakeney observed later to Mrs. Mince.

Nutworthy said while assisting his lordship, "When Mr. Blakeney asked me about your absence, my lord, I replied in very proper English obfuscation. I told him since you and Lady Camilla were newly wedded, your union sanctioned by God and the English government, it was to be expected there would be the very frequent exercise of vigorous young blood. Ah, did you notice my wit, my lord?"

Graham grinned at Nutworthy's face in his mirror. "Yes, your wit is noted, Nutworthy. I could not have explained in a more proper manner or disagreed with anything you said."

Cam's first evening at King's Head was a rich tapestry of faces, of voices slowly becoming familiar to her and delicious boiled capon and oysters. She was happy and content and eager, all at once.

If dinner was at first somewhat stilted, her father-in-law so pleased he couldn't stop smiling at Graham and talking of what they would do, she soon relaxed, answered his questions, trying for humor, not difficult when she told him a story of her aunt Deveraux and the Duke of Wellington, both dancing far into the night at a ball in Brussels three days before Waterloo. Cam wondered aloud if the duke, near her aunt's age, remembered that special night drawn from her aunt's prodigious memory. Even Eugenie smiled and Donner guffawed.

But always, always, Vereker turned to his son, asked him endless questions, hanging on to every word out of Graham's mouth. And he told his son how together they would visit the farms, not quick visits like his first time at King's Head, but lovely long visits, and they would speak of needed new farming equipment, and he and Graham would design them and oversee their being made. What did Graham think of a new water wheel set above the flowing Green Stream, and on and on it went. Graham, she saw, was nearly as excited as his father.

Eugenie managed to ask them questions about the Isle of Wight and Ventnor, a place she wanted to visit. Both she and Donner were astute enough not to mar the joy of the evening by mentioning the statue toppling off the hotel roof.

Cam was near to falling asleep when Cilly finally left her to retire to her own bedroom down the hall, selected for her by Cam. But because she hadn't felt she had any firm footing yet at King's Head, she'd asked Graham to inform Mrs. Mince of her selection, but he'd shaken his head, tweaked her nose. "No, you are the mistress, you have the reins. Ride, Cam, ride."

If Mrs. Mince was surprised at the bedchamber Cam had assigned to Cilly, she'd merely nodded, said it would be done. As Cam was walking away, she heard Mrs. Mince mutter,

"London ways, such strangeness, but if her new ladyship even wanted her maid in her bed with his lordship, who am I to say?"

Graham had laughed when she'd told him, and lightly buffeted her shoulder. "Apparently you ride very well right out of the gate."

CHAPTER 54

A cheerful fire burned in the fireplace, the corners were in shadows from a single lit lamp, a light rain glistened on the windows and the draperies were still hooked open by their splendid ancient gold tassels. It was a perfect night when at last Graham walked quietly through the connecting dressing room into their bedchamber wearing his old dark blue velvet bathrobe, his big feet bare. He stretched, yawned. Only three hours has passed, yet all he had to do was look at her and he wanted her, powerfully. When she'd spoken at dinner, he'd wanted to make love to her, when she'd drunk a cup of tea after dinner in the drawing room, he'd wanted to throw up her skirts behind the sofa and kiss her until she was shouting with pleasure.

Finally.

She was seated upright in the big bed, reading a copy of *The Pickwick Papers* he'd bought her in London and slipped unseen into her valise.

Cam knew he was there, she'd sensed him, and wasn't that amazing? She looked at him, smiled.

Graham felt that smile all the way to his feet but he wasn't about to simply leap on her, which was exactly what he wanted to do. He eyed her nightgown, all gorgeous cream silk that made her skin glow. He could make out the curve of her breasts through the tresses of thick hair. It was difficult, but he didn't move. Not yet. He said, his voice all offhand, "Are you enjoying *The Pickwick Papers*?"

"Oh yes, Cilly told me it was Dickens's first novel. It's very amusing. Thank you for buying it for me, Graham, it's a wonderful surprise." She watched him stretch again and the tie on his dressing gown loosened. Cam never took her eyes off the tie as she placed a leather strip in the book and closed it.

"You did very well your first night at King's Head. Everyone enjoyed the Wellington story. Nutworthy told me the staff, so far at least, are hopeful you're charming and I'm a lucky man." He paused, "Well, to be perfectly honest here, they believe you're also a lucky lady. There was apparently a good deal of relief, Nutworthy added. Evidently there was some concern you would be more stiff-lipped like my sister. Eugenie's maid—she's called Trumpet by staff because of her piercing voice—evidently she could compete with Aunt Deveraux—my sister insists her name is Marie because she tries to pass her off as French from a small town in Normandy, which amuses staff no end when she mangles a French phrase. Of course they only laugh after she leaves the room."

Cam said, "I am impressed. You are becoming like me, Graham, all that information in one tidy monologue, said with scarce a single pause. I like that because it means I can kiss you and caress you all over and not have to wait."

"Thank you. Of course they are careful around my sister. I must say, though, she turned over the household reins to you with grace."

"I told her she would have to teach me. And she gave me a long look and nodded. I added that I would already be excellent at overseeing the stables and she gave me a small smile. There is so much for me to learn, Graham."

"My father told me when we adjourned to the drawing room for tea that Donner wants to be master of his own household, and believes he's found a home not too far distant from King's Head. Donner said he and Eugenie have many friends in the neighborhood. But evidently the main reason they're not moving back closer to his family is because Donner cannot tolerate his brother and thus has no desire to be within a hundred miles of him." Graham paused. "Father also admitted he wished my sister were more, ah, impressed with me, and you, by extension, something I really don't understand. It's as if she blames me for not bringing Simon and his tutor back, only myself."

Cam said calmly, "I daresay she is still in shock at your return. You, and I by extension, will simply give her time to come around. I think Eugenie will be very happy as mistress in her own home, not her father's house.

"Now, husband, come here and I'll kiss you all over and then perhaps we can discuss Donner's new home. Do you know anything about it?"

Graham thought he'd expire on the spot. He jerked back the covers and gathered her to him. He had to get hold of himself or he'd be a pig and that would never do. He drew a deep breath, tried to ignore the heat, her heat and her mouth, right there, her mouth. He said, "Now, wife, before I seduce you, tell me what do you think of King's Head?"

The last thing Cam wanted to do was discuss King's Head. She slowly licked her upper lip, something she'd heard another young lady say one did to enthrall a gentleman. She really couldn't believe it actually worked. Graham didn't wait for her to say anything, merely stared at her tongue then he began kissing her, his tongue running over her lips until she opened her mouth and nearly expired at the touch of his tongue and all the while his hands tangled in her loose hair. He kissed her throat, tugged at her nightgown, and it seemed in the next instant he tossed it to the floor to land next to his bathrobe.

Cam whispered into his mouth, "I really hope you do not wish me to read from *The Pickwick Papers* to you precisely at this minute."

Graham laughed, moaned, nipped her earlobe. "If you become bored, tell me, and I'll read to you." Neither of them read to each other. When Cam pushed him onto his back and proceeded to kiss him down his belly, as he had her, Graham knew if he didn't stop her it would be all over for him and he wasn't about to leave her unsatisfied, not because of Jayne's imperative from so many years before, but because he wanted her pleasure, he reveled in it, wanted to hear her scream his name, feel her become one with him. It made him feel like a god.

When Graham could once again form words, he managed to come up onto his elbow and whisper against her soft mouth, "I knew I had to get through this intimacy business before I could ask you to read to me or you'd believe me an inattentive husband, selfish, a clod, in short." He smiled down into her dazed eyes. "Oh yes, dearest one, we mustn't forget there is also the matter of exploring the results of our just-concluded experiment to decide if finally we have enough information to posit our theorem."

She managed in a croak, "No, I am certain it is not enough. Perhaps by next year or the end of the next decade or the next decade after that we'll have gathered enough observations to perhaps begin to posit anything at all."

CHAPTER 55

King's Head

The wind was sharp off the Channel, dark clouds roiled over the water and everyone knew there would soon be heavy rains. But it was England and it was Sunday, so no one paid much attention.

Cam had said to her father-in-law when he remarked upon the coming rain, "I have never doubted umbrellas were invented in England, sir. Surely we must have the stoutest in the world."

Vereker laughed even as he tucked his umbrella under one arm and Cam's hand in the crook of the other. Blakeney had told her the earl himself had designed new stronger shafts and ribs to keep them from furling up in high winds, and Riker had seen the improvements done to every umbrella in King's Head. They were heavier to carry, but no one cared. When their neighbors and St. Lucy Head villagers heard about the new improved umbrellas, there were so many requests Vereker hired three local lads, set them up, and put them to work, no charge to the villagers for the new and improved umbrellas. Only one reason, Blakeney had told her, everyone loved the earl. And now it appeared his precious son, Graham, had his father's talents. Cam agreed, naturally. She wondered if Simon had lived if he'd have the same interests as his older brother and father. Had Simon also had his mother's incredible wild blue eyes, Graham's kindness, his wit? She thought of herself and Eliza. Had Simon been as different from Graham as Cam was from Eliza?

The Hepburns filed into the magnificent eleventh-century church, nodding to villagers and neighbors as they walked briskly from the nave down the long aisle to the altar to the sound of Mrs. Finch's beautifully performed processional song "Jerusalem." Cam heard whispered conversations, knew she was being studied and would wager they deemed Graham the magnificent peacock, not her. She was the passable little peahen.

They seated themselves in the family pew. The old, hard oak bench was covered with thick goose-down cushions for their exalted bottoms dating from the late seventeenth century and replaced every ten years or so when they were sufficiently flattened by said exalted bottoms, paid for by the current Earl St. Lucy.

King's Head servants filed into the pew behind them, all dressed in their Sunday best. She felt Cilly's light hand gently tug on a curl over her ear, and raised a hand to give her a little wave of thanks.

Tallyrand sat next to Cam, Graham on her other side, her gloved hand tucked into his, resting on his thigh. Tallyrand was a handsome man, tall, muscular and surely very strong since he chopped his own logs and had built his own cottage. There were only a few gray strands threading through his dark brown hair. His eyes were a vibrant green, an odd color, sort of the shade of the Green Stream bordering the sheep's field in front of King's Head. If his beautifully tailored morning coat was out of date, no one remarked upon it since Master Tallyrand had no wife to see to him. All knew he chose to live by himself in the middle of the eastern woods because he'd been severely mentally afflicted by the long-ago Battle of Waterloo and the death of so many soldiers, many his friends. Even though he kept to himself, he readily offered his help to any who asked him. He was well liked, the men giving him respectful bows, the ladies smiling and nodding. She wondered if he was aware that many of the ladies were attempting to gain his attention.

When her father-in-law had introduced them in the entry hall of King's Head that morning, Tallyrand had smiled at her, lightly kissed her wrist. "Please call me Uncle Tally since you are now my niece." Did she see a faint resemblance between Graham and his uncle? She wasn't sure. Tallyrand had arrived at King's Head to ride with the family the three miles to church. He'd remarked to Cam in the carriage, "I usually walk, but I feared it will rain today and indeed it has, and wet wool tends to smell, not a pleasant thing in church. Even one of my brother's sturdy umbrellas wouldn't spare me from mud puddles."

Vereker had mentioned to Cam that perhaps Tally would now have dinner with the family more than once a month since her arrival at King's Head.

Tally leaned close, whispered to her, "Riker sang your praises."

Cam wondered what Riker could have said since he'd been the one doing all the talking. She whispered back, "Mr. Riker met us at the station yesterday, told me about the people I would meet at King's Head. It made everything easier for me. And now it appears I'm on parade for all the local populace."

Tally nodded. "I doubt not they'll believe you a fine wife for Graham. And your glasses chain, quite innovative, my brother pointed them out to me, told me how smart you were. As for Riker, he brings me his wife's stews, a very fine dish indeed, and Blakeney brings me fresh scones right out of Cook's oven. I believe Riker wants to speak to my brother about starting an umbrella business in Canterbury." He laughed quietly. "If I know my brother, he'll think it an excellent idea and provide everything Riker needs to make it happen."

Graham leaned over and whispered in her ear, "You're hearing about the great Umbrella Project?"

"I think it's grand."

Graham had told her he'd only visited his uncle Tally once, and he admitted he'd prayed he'd recognize him, but Tally had been a perfect stranger, like everyone and everything else.

Cam was very aware of her husband, felt ripples of remembered pleasure and wasn't that a fine thing? Seated next to Graham was his father, of course, then Eugenie and Donner next to him, the two of them whispering. About purchasing their own house, perhaps?

Vereker said quietly to Graham, "I've never seen the church so packed, some people I've never seen before, and some are even leaning against the walls. It appears everyone has heard you'd brought home a bride and wanted to see both of you." He paused, added, "My valet, Terrance, told me Mrs. Mince couldn't stop smiling after meeting your wife. Camilla—no, Cam—a lighthearted nickname and it suits her—has already impressed our people. Blakeney remarked that all stopped and listened when you laughed. I myself have noticed a lighter tone in the house, and Cam's been here only a day."

The organist laid down an impressive last chord, the echo rippling through the church. Whispered conversations faded away. There were a few stray coughs and clearing throats as the congregation settled in.

Vicar Piercebridge, in a knee-length white robe over black trousers and white shirt, stepped up the six well-worn steps to the dark mahogany pulpit, replaced in the last decade of the sixteenth century and embellished with elaborate carvings of saints and Christ. He nodded to Vereker, gave a big smile to Cam and Graham. He looked out over the gathered congregation. When he spoke, his deep baritone rang out to the farthest corner of the church. "On this blessed day in our Lord's house, let us give praise not only for Graham Hepburn's blessed return but also the wonderful addition of his new bride, Lady Camilla." He raised his arms. "Everyone rise. We will raise our voices in thanks to our loving God and sing 'Rock of Ages.'"

Vicar Piercebridge turned to nod to the organist when there was suddenly a huge crack of thunder, a white streak of lightning speared through the windows. The vicar smiled, again nodded to the organist, who played through a verse of "Rock of Ages," then a multitude of deep, rich voices soared above the successive claps of thunder, filling the ancient stone church. It was much loved, this old hymn, well known to the smallest child. Cam felt the familiar warmth and sense of rightness as she sang. Then, suddenly, she felt something else, something just out of her vision, something dark, frightening, blacker now and thick, and it was coming closer. She thought of the statue at Ventnor and wanted to grab Graham and run, maybe to Scotland or Boston, to her brother. What she felt, was it a portent? Was danger just on the horizon? No, no, she was being dramatic. It was Sunday, she was singing one of her favorite hymns. Everything was fine. But deep inside, she knew it wasn't.

She concentrated on Graham's rich baritone. It warmed her to her bones, but the chill remained deep inside her.

After a lovely homily extolling the goodness and love of the Lord, Vicar Piercebridge blessed the congregation and the organist played a solemn hymn unfamiliar to Cam. The Hepburns followed the vicar down the nave, umbrellas at the ready, out of the church and stood stock-still. There was no frigid rain beating down, no black clouds anywhere in the sky. There was only bright sunlight, the once-sharp wind had mellowed into a gentle warm breeze off the Channel. White billowy clouds lazed across a blue sky.

People were openmouthed, they left the church to walk outside and bask in this unforeseen miracle.

Mr. Kurtz, the local cooper, announced loudly, "Behold a Sunday miracle, no need for Lord Vereker's umbrellas!"

Given it was England, all agreed it was indeed a miracle. All looked toward Cam and Graham as they relished the incredible day and there were whispers behind hands. Graham said to Cam, "I think many in the congregation believe you and I are the cause of the now glorious weather."

Cam said in all seriousness, "How could you think differently?" and she poked him in the side with her furled umbrella.

Vicar Piercebridge introduced Cam and reintroduced Graham to every man, woman and child standing in a long line. She shook hands and nodded, smiling all the while, as did Graham. So many names, so many well wishes, so many welcome homes to Graham. And to her. It was gratifying. Well, they'd brought the sun, hadn't they?

Everyone was surprised when Uncle Tally accompanied them back to King's Head for luncheon, the first time in many years. Vereker felt blessed beyond measure. He couldn't stop smiling.

CHAPTER 56

King's Head

Cam wanted nothing more than to nab Graham, currently drinking coffee with his father in the library, grab his hand and pull him outdoors on this beautiful sunny morning. She wanted her promised tour of King's Head, especially the eastern forest where Uncle Tally lived. Then there were the old Augustinian ruins some one hundred yards behind King's Head to explore. She wanted to pet the sheep always grazing in the large front swatch of land bordering the Green Stream. She wanted to look deep, see what she could see. Graham had laughed at her, said you couldn't see below the green surface of the water and one of the rams, King Henry by name, might try to shove her into the water. She especially wanted to meet all their farmers, maybe drink some of their particularly powerful ale and then—She had to be patient. First she had to eat her breakfast. She was wearing a new riding habit, a lovely dark green wool jacket cinched at the waist and a form-fitting skirt and her favorite black boots picked out for her by Lady Tremaine. Her high crown riding hat had a jaunty narrow brim and a narrow blue ribbon. She wore her hair in a thick braid down her back, something Cilly deemed unusual but clever, maybe Cam would bring in a new style.

She was eager, not only for the promised tour but to see her husband. It had, after all, been two hours since he'd left their bedchamber to meet with his father. She met Eugenie at the door of the small breakfast room, a lovely room she'd seen briefly, more feminine than not with its pale green walls and dainty Louis XVI furnishings. Eugenie was dressed in a lovely pale gray morning gown, a small book in her white hand.

Eugenie said, "I have never seen a lady wear her hair braided like that to go riding, to go anywhere, for that matter. It is quite charming."

Cam smiled. "That's what Cilly said. Do you think it might become a new fashion?"

Eugenie stared at her a moment, shrugged and waved the book at her. "This is a book of menus, and dishes are marked that I've found Mrs. Sample excels at. You will want to meet with her this morning." She handed Cam the book, her smile never wavering.

Cam eyed her sister-in-law. She seemed quite content with the change. Still, Cam started to tell Eugenie she was certain Eugenie would do a better job than she with the menus when she suddenly heard Aunt Deveraux's voice ringing in her ear: *Begin as you mean to go on. I forgot that rule with my second lover and he took gross advantage until I got him under control.* She realized in that moment whenever she'd demurred to Eliza to keep the peace it had only made Eliza more strident and dismissive, as if Cam had no importance at all in the household. She realized she'd always been a rug to be tread upon by her sister. She'd been a pathetic nod-cock. She didn't want her relationship with Eugenie to be like Aunt Deveraux's second lover. And so Cam said matter-of-factly as she took the dark brown leather book,

"Yes, thank you, Eugenie." She added on a clean lie, "It was my responsibility at home, every Monday morning. You needn't worry I'll ask for anything out of season." She smiled.

Eugenie nodded, not really paying attention now, and walked gracefully into the breakfast room. She called out over her shoulder, "After breakfast, I'll show you my accounting room and review all the procedures I've set up."

Was Aunt Deveraux nodding and smiling? She'd made a good start. She had the menu book. She thought of Graham, but he would have to wait. She now had a responsibility and she wasn't about to shirk it. After breakfast, she walked downstairs to Mrs. Mince's small office next to the kitchen, where she met Mrs. Sample. She gave her a cup of her precious oolong tea and a warm raisin scone with Devon cream dripping over the edges. Together they reviewed the menus, adding chicken vol-au-vent and Charlotte Russe, two dishes Cam particularly liked. She would have to ask Graham his favorite dishes.

She saw Arthur, one of the very young footmen blessed with startling white-blond hair and eyelashes longer than a girl's, waiting for her outside Mrs. Mince's office to tell her Lord Whitestone was at the stables, waiting for her. She left Arthur, skipped down the deep stone stairs, picked up her riding skirts and ran to the stables. She arrived out of breath to see her lovely husband rubbing a brush over the neck of a magnificent chestnut whose head rested on his shoulder. Did she look as happy as the horse did? Cam would swear she felt her heart fall to her toes as she paused a moment simply to watch him. She wanted to jump him and take him to the ground, but there was a great deal of activity, three grooms leading out horses, cleaning saddles, so she had to show restraint.

Graham looked up to see her standing very still, looking at him. Her glasses sparkled in the sun. He saw wickedness in those eyes of hers and grinned. "What is this? What are you planning?"

CHAPTER 57

She said, all demure, "I can't tell you, husband, there are too many people about to hear my rather indelicate ideas."

His eyes nearly crossed, he took a step toward her, got hold of himself. He introduced her to Stanley. She'd petted him, of course, when Mr. Sherbrooke had sent him over to her father's house. Graham gave her a carrot to feed him. Cam praised him, a beautiful boy, so full of spirit, perfect for his equally perfect master. Stanley, obligingly, whinnied.

Riker brought out a cream-colored mare with a thick line of brown down the middle of her nose and brown withers, a lovely creature with liquid brown eyes.

"Lord Vereker believed you would deal well together. Her name's Glory and she will keep you on your toes." Riker handed her several carrots. "If she gets twitchy, feed her the carrots." He gave her a huge grin. "I was in church yesterday when you and Lord Graham stopped the big storm. God was smiling, he was." And he nodded, stepped back.

"Oh dear," Cam said to Graham as they cantered along the wide graveled driveway. "Do you think folk really believe we controlled the weather? Could this mean all believe we're magic?"

Graham said, "Maybe so, at least until it rains after church next Sunday."

The path into the eastern forest wasn't particularly well marked, but Stanley knew his way. He shared the trail with Glory. The day was cool, the sun in and out of gray clouds and who knew when those clouds could turn black as sin?

Graham said, his voice thoughtful, "Blakeney told me Simon and I knew these woods better than anyone else, perhaps even better than my father when he was a boy. He talked about how we fought with wooden swords, shot bows and arrows from the branches of oak trees, raced each other from Uncle Tally's cottage back to King's Head. Blakeney said we were always laughing like loons no matter who won. He told me about the time Simon and I tried to herd the sheep into the Green Stream—I asked and no one knows who first named it that, not even my father—but when the sheep got to the edge, they'd drink but they wouldn't step a hoof into the water. Froze they did, he said, wouldn't move no matter how much Simon and I shoved their hindquarters." Graham paused a moment. "My father added stories of our adventures at the Augustinian ruins, how we were convinced there was buried treasure, namely, church relics and naturally stacks of gold coins. As you know, the abbey was closed by Henry VIII in 1537 and the monks had to flee." He paused, looked through Stanley's ears. "I know my father and Blakeney are telling me stories to spur my memory."

"It's an excellent idea. I only wish I knew stories to tell you as well. They both love you, they want you to remember how much they've always loved you."

Her words snapped him back from feeling sorry for himself. His first fourteen years were gone, but forever? He prayed not. Since he'd come home, he'd had the occasional glimpse of something or someone blurred behind a sort of white veil or curtain, nothing solid, only a tease. He was afraid to hope but maybe, just maybe, it could be a beginning. He smiled at his wife and knew to his boots if he had to choose between a childhood forever lost to him or a lifetime with her, there would be no contest.

They came out into Tally's meadow, nearly a perfect circle, oak and Dutch elm trees surrounding it. Grass was turning a lovely spring green and was perfectly scythed. A wide stone walkway cut through the middle of the big circle and led from three tethering posts to the front door of the cottage. A stream of gray smoke spiraled out of the single stone chimney scenting the air with sweet maple.

Cam couldn't help but stare. "Goodness, I really hadn't expected this. It's lovely." She pointed. "Oh my, Graham, look at the garden. Tally's built a white fence around it. To keep out the varmints, I suppose."

Graham dismounted, petted Stanley's nose and looped his reins over one of the tethering posts. He lifted Cam down off Glory's back before she could jump down. Glory tossed her head, tried to pull free, her tail swishing. "Twitchy, are you? Let's see if Riker's right." Cam gave her a carrot. She chuffed, quieted and if Cam wasn't mistaken, she moved a bit closer to Stanley, unfortunately for her a gelding.

"The miracle of food," Cam said, stroked her gloved hand down her glossy neck. "Look, the door is bright red. Your uncle has a touch of whimsy." She turned in a slow circle. "I don't know what I expected, but this? Everything looks perfect."

Uncle Tally met them at the red front door, showed them into a small, quite charming parlor, and if Cam wasn't mistaken, there was a Carrera marble fireplace with a lovely stone mantel. Burning embers sent up the occasional spark, keeping the room cozy. There were paintings on the cream-painted walls, most of ocean scenes with tall ships in full sail. Tally waved them to a lovely dark blue velvet sofa. After serving them tea and some scones sent that morning from Mrs. Sample and brought to him by Blakeney, he said, "There are raisins in the scones. I'll admit I was leery at first but I've discovered they're quite good."

Graham laughed. "I hear her ladyship had only a single slice of toast. Mrs. Sample was disappointed since she'd made them for her as a welcoming surprise."

Her ladyship. And didn't that have a fine sound to it?

Tally said, "I knew staff would like you, Cam. You're cleaning out the shadows, and will add much-needed laughter and, well, lightness, to the house. My poor brother has lived in these shadows for far too long."

Cam knew it was Graham's presence, not hers, that had lightened King's Head.

After laughing at Riker's comments on Cam and Graham being responsible for diverting the after-church storm, Tally, like Blakeney and Lord Vereker, began telling them stories about Graham's youth. Cam would wager they'd all gotten together and decided this was the way to spur Graham's memory.

"—once two sheep got into a fight, all the other sheep were baaing, probably placing bets. I believe one of the fighters was King Henry, ready to take on the dominant role. King Henry finally managed to butt the other ram into the Green Stream. The baaing changed immediately. The sheep began bleating their heads off, raised such a ruckus, you, Graham, and Simon, your father in the lead, of course, came running. The three of you managed to pull the ram out. I remember you and Simon and all the stable lads poured bucket after bucket of water provided by Riker on the sheep to clean off the green slime. Your father laughed himself silly and asked the next buckets be thrown over the lot of you since all of you smelled as bad as McCulty's rotted mushrooms. If I remember aright, Blakeney formed a bucket brigade."

Odd, but at that moment, Graham smelled something vile in the air. Was it a memory of the sheep before they'd cleaned him, or of him and his brother and father? But then the smell was gone and Graham wondered if he'd imagined it since Uncle Tally was such a good storyteller.

When they took their leave half an hour later, Tally said, "Wait a moment." He went through the small gate into his garden and pulled up two carrots and fed one to each horse. He hugged Graham, smiled at Cam and wished them good explorations. "Graham, be sure to show her the monk's cell with the writing on the stone wall. Oh yes, I'll be dining with the family tonight." And he turned, whistling, and walked back into his cottage.

CHAPTER 58

King's Head

"Which king, I wonder?" Cam asked as she snuggled against Graham's side.

Graham, still panting like a bellows, marveled she could even speak. "Which king? What king?"

"I was thinking about how there had to be a king who spent some time here, maybe camped out right on this spot in olden times or hid from bandits in the bushes and that's why your house got its name—King's Head."

"Huh."

Cam laughed, came up on her elbow, and kissed his throat, laid her cheek against his heart. She whispered against his warm flesh, "We will ask Blakeney; if anyone knows, he will. Do you think it's possible to expire from too much love-making?"

"No. Absolutely not."

She nuzzled his neck. "That is very good to hear. Do you know I heard your sister laugh when I passed their closed bedroom door? I know Donner was inside. Do you think—?"

"That's nice."

Cam leaned over and picked up her glasses, slid them up her nose, blinked down at him. "There, I can see your splendid self quite clearly now. Do you know what I want to do? I want to kiss every single inch of you."

His heart stuttered; he licked his lips. "Do you really mean every single inch?"

"Just a moment," and Cam shoved the covers down to his feet. "Oh yes, particularly your lovely hard belly." He felt her fingers splay over him and nearly expired.

"I love you, Graham. I love you all the way to my own toes, even the one that's a bit crooked from when I smashed it against a rock in the park when I was seven."

His lovely hard belly? He felt warmth all the way to his own toes. He looked up into her eyes, saw endless caring meant for only him. He said, "I've kissed that toe, admired the slight bend, makes it more interesting than your other perfect toes."

"Ha, so you're back to being yourself, that is, you're ready to seduce me again to the wicked side. Yes, with my glasses firmly in place I can now even see every lustful thought coursing through your man's brain."

"I hope those lustful thoughts are in great detail." He pushed her onto her back and came over her. He stroked his fingers through her tousled hair, thick lovely stuff, smoothed it over the pillow. He pulled a thick, waving curl to his face and rubbed it over his cheek. "You delight me, Cam. The first time I saw you I wondered, Who is this tall, mouthy girl with no chaperone who walked right up to me, a stranger, and treated me to a wonderful monologue?" He paused, kissed the tip of her nose.

Cam said, "When I got a good look at you and saw your amazing wicked eyes, I swear the cobblestones shifted beneath my slippers. Did you mind my glasses?"

"No. A mouthy girl needs to wear glasses to add to her mystery."

"Averil and Eliza never wanted me to wear them, told me no gentleman would even want to get near me. They'd believe I read books, a horror."

He looked shocked. "Really? You can read?"

She bit his neck.

"I saved you from all those unworthy gentlemen. I believe you must owe me your gratitude for the rest of our years on this earth."

She grew thoughtful. "Do you think before we expire, our children and grandchildren and great grandchildren weeping on their knees beside our bed, we will see trains crisscross the world?"

She'd pointed him to his hobby horse and he jumped right on, passion and promise lighting his eyes. "Oh yes. And there'll be so much more, we will never stop moving forward, making our lives better, making the world larger. I believe nothing is impossible."

"It's hard to imagine what could be invented beyond our modern world, well, trains going everywhere is a fine idea and very useful. But what else could we possibly want? We even have a water closet and our own shower room. Even Mrs. Mince was telling me about the incredible efficiency of her new potbelly stove. Oh yes, I meant to ask you. At dinner your father told a story about how you and Simon were daring each other to stick a single leg into the Green Stream, each yelling the other was a coward—and then your father intervened, called you both nod-cocks and ordered you back to your tutor. You looked suddenly odd, Graham, then you blinked and shook your head. Did you remember something?"

He stilled, said slowly, "No, not really. Maybe the memory of Simon is in the back of my brain, nothing solid."

She searched his face. "Then he spoke of the two of you playing in the abbey ruins, climbing up on an ancient worm-eaten beam still holding up walls in a monk's cell. He said he yelled at the two of you, told me Simon was daring you to walk across the beam. How old were you, Graham?"

"I have no idea. But I suppose it makes sense I was about twelve, maybe thirteen, Simon a year younger. Wait, there's something teasing me, I can hear it, Simon is angry at me, calling me a coward, maybe—Why couldn't I have seen him laughing with me, shooting a bow and arrow, crowing when he hit the bull's-eye? But no, it was anger I heard."

"Maybe, just maybe, it's the strong emotion you felt that gave you the brief memory, at least the sound of a memory."

He hadn't thought of that. "I don't know."

She kissed his mouth. "Don't worry about it. It's a beginning, Graham. I promise you there will be more. It won't be long now before your childhood is returned to you. Did Simon resemble you?"

"From the painting of him as a young boy, I think he had more the look of our mother. No, not her eyes, but her light hair, maybe the shape of her face. I'll show it to you tomorrow."

"And you look more like your father except for your mother's wicked eyes. She was incredibly beautiful, Graham. How old were you when she died?"

"I don't know. We will ask my father." He added slowly, "If my memory does come back, will I remember who took Simon and me, who tried to kill me?" He swallowed. "And who obviously killed Simon and our poor tutor?"

She felt fear scald her throat, but she forced herself to say matter-of-factly, "The fact is whoever was responsible for taking you and your brother and tutor eleven years ago must still be here or close by, watching, waiting. He followed us to the Isle of Wight. He's afraid you will remember, Graham, and that's why he pushed the statue from the hotel roof on us.

"You know he followed us here. He's waiting, I know it, you know it. Your father hasn't said anything to me, but I know he is terrified for you. We will speak to him again, to everyone, to be on guard."

"Everyone is on guard, Cam. There's always someone close to me."

CHAPTER 59

When Graham and Cam breakfasted with his father the following morning, he assured them that before they'd arrived from Ventnor, he'd spoken to all staff both inside and outside King's Head so everyone was keeping watch for strangers. Graham hated it, but how could it be a stranger? Unless the stranger was hired by someone here. More likely it was someone closer, someone here, someone who'd always been here.

Vereker had set guards since they'd come back to King's Head. They were never alone when they left the house. Graham spotted Arlo, the most muscular stable lad, tough as an old Cornwall tin miner's boot, from the corner of his eye when they'd left King's Head to explore the Augustinian ruins some fifty feet behind the formal gardens and the orchard. He was grateful, more so because it meant keeping Cam safe.

They were both dressed in old clothes, Cam wearing an old gown, faded to gray after so many washings, and stout boots, her hair in a thick braid down her back. Even in simple black pants and an old loose white linen shirt, old scarred black boots to his knees, Graham still looked like a young god, well, in her eyes he did, and surely hers were the only important eyes.

As they walked through the orchard, Cam pointed out the Adams Pearmain apple trees. "It's a pity we can't enjoy them until August. Mrs. Tartle, Aunt Deveraux's cook, made the most delicious apple pies, always claimed Adams Pearmain apples were the very best."

Graham said, "When I first came, my father showed me Mr. Dickens's orchard. He said every year Mr. Dickens enters contests with other locals to judge the finest-tasting apples in the area. He said King's Head has won now five years in a row, claims Mr. Dickens sings marching ditties to the apple trees, some of them lewd enough to raise even soldiers' eyebrows. The contest will be in September."

They walked through a white gate from the orchard into the formal garden. Rhododendron and azaleas spread throughout. Cam said, "The bushes look like they are dying to burst open and bloom. It's a pity they have to wait a bit longer."

They wound their way through arbors and past stone benches along stone-covered paths, all beautifully maintained. Two fountains with naked Roman nymphs spewed water from their open mouths.

Graham pointed. "There, through the back stone wall, do you see the central section of the abbey?"

Cam had seen many ruins from Roman times in Bath and at Stonehenge, but this once-magnificent ruin made her mouth drop open. The Augustinian abbey had been huge, abutting thick Dutch elm trees, oaks and beaches that climbed up a steep hill behind the ruins.

They walked carefully over moss-covered dark stones or steps, nearly white from bird droppings. Several arches still stood over collapsed walls. The central core of the abbey still had standing walls, several rising up to at least thirty feet. The floors were covered with rocks of all sizes and black dirt.

Graham said, "When I was here with my father in the middle of this big central hall I swore I could hear monks chanting."

Cam tried, but she only heard the faint scurrying of rodents, a single bird song from a nearby Dutch elm.

"Here is the abbey scriptorium. My father read there were more than three hundred monks here working on illuminated manuscripts. I can imagine long benches lined up the length of this long room. See, there are still a couple of rotting wooden boards and the niches in that single standing wall."

Graham grabbed her arm. "Take care, Cam, these stones could slide and topple you over." She looked up into her new husband's blue eyes and felt her heart full to bursting. There was such concern for her. She smiled, gave him her arm despite the fact her boots were nearly as old as she was and had never let her slip.

"Come let me show you the monks' cells. My father, Donner and I went through them on my first visit here. Some walls are still standing and two still have a couple of ceiling beams. In several of them you can still make out Latin writing carved into the stone walls."

They walked into a very small room, the two remaining walls only waist high. Cam imagined all the loose rocks had been hauled away hundreds of years ago.

"Come, here's the one I really wanted to show you." In the second monk's cell, two walls still remained, and there were two rotting overhead beams. Cam couldn't tell if there'd ever been a window.

She stood in the middle of the small cell, tried to picture a man in a long robe, a belt or a rope around his waist, sandals on his feet. Was there a chair for him to sit on? There had to be a bed with thick ropes to hold a straw-stuffed sack. Did the monk have blankets in winter?

She whispered, "Their lives were so disciplined, so austere. I read so many of them died when their monasteries were destroyed because they didn't know how to survive in the outside world."

He nodded. "Evidently no one ever found the wealth from this abbey if indeed the abbot hid it here. My father told me stories of abbey treasure still abound. Simon and I were always—" He stopped cold. He looked white. He grabbed her hands. "I saw us, Cam, I saw two boys, it had to be us—we were pulling at rocks, hoping to uncover treasure behind them, even under them. We were filthy, our faces grimed. Then—it was gone."

CHAPTER 60

Cam pulled him against her, said against his throat, "What are you saying to your brother?"

Graham blinked. "Saying? I don't remember—wait, Simon was bragging he was going to find all the hidden gold and sell it to fat old George IV or better yet, he'd become the King of France and if I licked his boots he might make me his valet."

He stopped. Simon's face, the images, the words, the boy's bright bragging voice, so full of bravado, all were gone, blinked out, like a popped bubble. There was nothing more. But he would swear he heard the echo of the boy's crowing voice, a sound memory.

"How old was Simon?"

"Maybe eight, nine."

"Did you and Simon ever find anything?"

"I-I don't know. No, surely not or my father would have said something."

Cam kissed his cheek. "We've been at King's Head for only three days and already images and words are coming back to you. Now, you said there was some Latin here in this cell. How I hated studying it, but it was better than Italian. I remember conjugating Latin verbs for my father. I wonder if I still remember any words."

The carved Latin words were so faded they were difficult to make out, but she did make out a single word: *Beware—*

Graham spit on his handkerchief and rubbed at the line of words scored into the stone. He whispered, *"Beware the evil behind the stone."*

He sat back on his heels. "Evil behind the stone. Which stone?" And she pulled and prodded, but the stone didn't move. She sat back on her heels, stared at it, willing it to move and show treasure beyond belief.

She said, "This is highly disappointing. Graham, would you and Simon have brought your tutor here and asked him what the Latin meant? I mean, even if you could make out the words, you were young, you could have been wrong."

"That sounds logical. I don't remember. But, Cam, how many people do you think translated the Latin over the years and pushed at that stone and all those around it? And nothing."

"Maybe a hundred, a thousand." And she sighed. Together they studied more Latin words that were carved in other stones, but they were too worn to make out. Were there more warnings carved into the walls about evil? Was the evil Henry VIII? Graham doubted anyone would ever know. He said, "On the other hand, maybe someone did find treasure here but kept it quiet, became rich and lived like a lord for the rest of his life?"

Cam said, "I like that, but you know as well as I do a secret like that would never remain a secret. Ah, what a fascinating mystery, but you know, if there is some sort of curse involved, it's so very old it's long passed into oblivion."

Graham frowned. "Wait, there's something more, something strange. It's there, at the edge of my mind, but—now it's gone. I don't remember." He shrugged. "It was probably just more boys' foolishness. Come."

They walked into the great central area and stared at the vast room, three sides still standing, several wooden beams still overhead. How many thousands of stones had been used to build this central hall? The abbey? But there were no piles of loose stones on the dirt floor, again, very likely hauled away centuries ago for building.

"Let me show you the abbot's sanctuary, well, really his office, I suppose, where he kept records and studied and met with the workers and monks."

They walked into a good-sized square room off the central hall. This one had all its walls and three overhead beams. There was a small fireplace, really, only a square hole, in one of the walls, a single small window.

Like all the other rooms, this one was empty. Cam turned a slow circle in the middle of the room. "I wonder where the abbot sat? Was his desk close to the fireplace? What did he think when he knew the king's soldiers were coming to dispossess him and all his monks? There must have been relics, treasures gathered over the centuries. What did he do with it all?" She grabbed Graham's hand, tried to pull him toward the fireplace, but he wasn't moving, laughing at her. "Maybe there are treasures stuffed up in the chimney, maybe—"

There was a tearing sound from above, over Graham's head. Without thought, Cam leapt at him, smashing him back and fell on top of him. The beam crashed down, struck Cam's temple, splintered and fell to the dirt.

"No! Cam, wake up. Cam!"

As gently as he could, Graham lifted Cam off him and lay her on the dirt floor.

He yelled, "Arlo!"

Arlo came running into the room. "My Lord—Oh no, her ladyship—"

Graham heard himself say, "A beam fell, she pushed me out of the way and it struck her head." He fell to his knees beside her, saw a trickle of blood snake from above her left temple down her cheek. He pressed fingers against her throat. He felt nothing and his breath hitched. His world turned to chaos. No, no. He pressed again and there, and there it was, a faint pulse. He felt such relief he wanted to yell. He took his handkerchief out of his pocket and daubed at the blood, then pressed it against the open wound at her temple. And he prayed.

"She's alive. Arlo, run back to King's Head and see a doctor is fetched. I'll bring her back."

He vaguely heard Arlo racing away. He looked over at the beam, lying on the black earth, broken apart, sharp shards sticking up. He could see the rot, yet it had held together for centuries and only now it had come down? He looked up at the ceiling, but saw no one, heard no movement.

Graham kissed Cam's cheek, her slack mouth. He clutched her shoulders, gently shook her. "Cam, wake up, you can do it. Please, open your beautiful eyes." He said her name over and over, but there was no response. He lifted the handkerchief. It was covered with her blood. He pressed the handkerchief harder again at the wound. When he lifted it, the bleeding had nearly stopped. He whispered her name over and over, but she didn't open her eyes. He lightly slapped her face. Still she didn't move. Was she possibly injured internally? He couldn't stand it.

He gathered her against him and rose, pressed her head against his neck. He felt the wet of her blood against his flesh.

The walk back to King's Head was the longest in his life.

She didn't wake up.

She'd saved him, curse her.

CHAPTER 61

Dr. Edison Crutcher, newly moved to St. Lucy, wasn't old at all, but he walked slowly because he'd been struck with arthritis in his knees when he was only thirty years old. Thankfully that condition had nothing to do with his brain or his hands. He was riding his beloved mare Tamsyn not five minutes after Riker, white-faced and grim, had arrived in his surgery. He'd immediately called to his sister to clean and bandage Mr. Stave's neck boil.

When Edison walked into the bedchamber, he saw Lord Graham sitting beside his wife on the big bed holding her hand. He said the moment Edison appeared, "An ancient beam in the abbey ruins split apart and fell. It struck her on the temple. I staunched the wound but—she hasn't woken up, hasn't moved."

His new young lordship's voice was flat, emotionless. Edison didn't have to see his dilated eyes to know he was in shock. He was struck as he had been at church on Sunday by the young viscount's beauty, his startling blue eyes. He bowed briefly to Lord Vereker, who stood close on the other side of the bed, his face nearly as pale as his son's. There were two other men and a woman standing off to the side, all looking worried, actually, he realized, they looked afraid.

Edison said as he gently moved the viscount aside and sat down beside the unconscious young woman, placed his hand over her heart, "My lord, you said she has been unconscious since she was struck down?"

"Yes." He heard Lord Graham swallow. "I tried to wake her but she hasn't opened her eyes. Her head was bleeding. I did manage to stop the bleeding."

"You did well." Edison looked down at the young woman's pale lovely face, saw the bruising all along her cheek. "How long ago was she struck?"

Lord Vereker said, "Nearly an hour ago. As my son said, she hasn't moved."

Edison lifted a bloody tress of hair from the wound, leaned close, lightly probed with sensitive fingers. He said without looking away from the wound, "Thankfully, the gash isn't deep but still I will have to stitch it. My lord, please hand me my bag. I will get this done while she's still unconscious."

Cilly said, "Please don't shave off her hair. It's so beautiful."

Edison looked up at the striking woman, smiled. Her maid? "I promise, only a bit, only a very little bit."

Graham watched every move he made—shaving off only a small square of hair, cleaning the wound in alcohol, threading a needle. He couldn't help it, he flinched as the needle went into her flesh, the black thread in and out, pulling tight. It was obscene. He heard Cilly catch her breath but he never looked away from his wife's still face. He wanted to cry and kill. He felt buried in fear and deep, deep rage.

His wife. She lay so still, as if her life force were extinguished. Always, always, Cam was moving, so energetic, so filled with life, with the excitement of sheer living, and she'd given herself to him, all of herself, and the fullness of her big heart, yet now she lay motionless, her face deathly pale, and so still, she was so utterly still. He'd never been so afraid even when he'd been a boy and locked in the dim hold of a boat—*what, what*? Graham started, tried to grasp the thought, no, the memory, he knew in his gut it was a memory, but it fell away and there was nothing and he couldn't be sure of anything.

Cilly had removed her boots, straightened her gown. She should have looked like she was simply asleep except for the line of dried blood on her neck. He swallowed.

After Edison set six stitches and knotted off the thread, he took a small bottle of brandy out of his bag and patted it on the wound, then dusted with white basilicum powder and covered the small square with plaster. He washed the blood out of her hair with a wet towel Cilly handed him. Then he silently studied her face, listened again to her heart. Finally, he looked up and blinked. The bedchamber was filled with people, and when had they all come in? There was the earl, two strange men who looked to be valets and Riker stood by the bedchamber door.

Edison looked across the bed at Graham, a young man with no memory of his formative years, if all the village stories were to be believed. And now his new bride had been hurt. He said as he rose, "My lord, you told me there were overhead beams in a room at the abbey ruins. One was rotted through and fell, struck her ladyship."

"Yes," Graham said, his voice still flat. "Be honest with me, will she be all right?"

Edison knew stark fear when he heard it, but he knew he had to tell him the truth, tell the roomful of people the truth. He kept his voice calm, straightforward, "Even in this modern day, we still know very little about head injuries, about how the brain deals with injuries." He paused, looked at their faces and didn't say, *Will she wake up? I'm sorry but I do not know.* He said instead, his voice firm, "Her ladyship is young and healthy. Riker told me she's very active. I have every expectation she will wake up." *But if she does wake up*

I do not know if she will have all her wits. He added firmly, "She will be fine, perhaps headaches for a while, but she will recover." He slowly rose, wincing because his left knee pained him today.

He said, "Give her laudanum when she wakes up because as I said she will have a headache. Keep her awake for a while until she's solidly back. We do know it's possible if she falls back asleep"—*she might not wake up again*—"it may be more difficult for her to wake up again." He searched their faces and saw hope. He smiled. "Her ladyship has an excellent chance to recover. I'll be back tomorrow. If something happens to concern you, I shall come immediately."

After Riker escorted Dr. Crutcher from the bedchamber, Graham looked at everyone hovering around the bed. "Thank you all. Please leave now, Cilly and I must get her into her nightgown."

Lord Vereker placed his hands on his son's shoulders. His voice was as gentle as windless rain, yet as believable as a promise from God, "She will recover, Graham. I know your children and their children will lead the Hepburn family into the next century and beyond. Now, I'm taking a good dozen men to examine the abbey ruins. If there are signs of anyone tampering with the falling beam, we will find it.

"Graham, you remain here with your wife. It is not only for her protection but yours as well. Trust me to be thorough." Vereker drew him to his feet and hugged him tightly against him, patted his back and left the bedchamber.

Cilly knew she had to be calm. She couldn't show fear even though her belly was roiling with it, fear and rage and impotence. She wanted to strangle the person responsible, but who could it possibly be? She knew she had to hold herself together for Cam and Graham.

When she and Graham were alone in the bedchamber, they gently removed Cam's clothes, now torn and dirty, her ripped stockings. Graham saw a hole in one toe. It nearly broke his heart. Graham held her up while Cilly slipped a fresh nightgown over her head. It wasn't one of her wicked satin nightgowns, it was, he imagined, from her days before they'd wed, simple cotton, white, and finely stitched, covering her from head to toe. The white made her look so pale he wanted to cry. Dr. Crutcher had gently removed her glasses so they now dangled from her gold chain. He gently eased the chain over her head. He saw one earpiece was bent and automatically straightened it.

Her eyelids looked bruised, and why was that? He took one of her limp hands into his. Her flesh was warm, a relief. He said to Cilly, "It was like the falling statue in Ventnor. It had to be the same person, no doubt in my mind. I agree with my father. The falling beam had been weakened even more, by the same person in Ventnor. You're nodding, Cilly. It has to be. I know it was meant for me. Both Cam and I heard it break apart. As I said, she hurled herself at me, knocked me down, threw herself on top of me. The beam struck her head." He swallowed. "Cilly, she saved me." Just saying the words again made rage build in his belly, and god-awful fear. It nearly broke him. "She can't die, she can't. She has to get well so I can thrash her for what she did." He stopped cold, and his voice became deep and hard. "As God is my witness, I will kill who did this."

Cilly said, her voice just as hard, "Not if I can kill him first. Listen, you heard Dr. Crutcher, she won't die. She will survive this." Cilly lightly touched her hand to his shoulder, then turned and began pacing, smacking a fist against her palm. "But who is it? Who is this person? Who from your past still wants you dead?" She stopped short. "Oh dear, it just occurred to me. Should you send a message to Lord Whitsonby?"

Graham cursed softly, then shook his head. "No, not yet. She will wake up, she will be fine. No, not yet."

But what if she never woke up?

CHAPTER 62

Time passed. The first day, the second, and there was no change. People came and went, neighbors, their tenant farmers and many of the villagers, and, of course, Vicar Piercebridge. Of course the story of what had happened to Cam changed and evolved all around the neighborhood until Vereker said to Graham he wouldn't be surprised if the next iteration was an attack by a dragon.

Gifts arrived from neighbors—a finely embroidered French shawl so soft Cilly said it was like a spun dream to beautifully boxed chocolates from Belgium to soft delicious loaves of bread from Mr. Kirt the miller. There was a special lemonade from a local healer, which Graham dribbled down her throat.

Graham refused to leave her. He paced the bedchamber, glancing as he usually did when he passed by the small marquetry table with the single envelope holding the letter he'd written to Cam's father in the darkest hour of the previous night when he'd despaired. He knew it was everyone's objective to keep his spirits up, but when he was alone, now, at the end of the second day, he stared down at her in the candlelight, felt his heart hitch. She was so still as if she really weren't there any longer. No, he couldn't, wouldn't, think that.

He looked over at the letter to her father. No, he wasn't going to send Riker with the letter to Lord Whitsonby in London, not today, not tomorrow. It would be admitting to himself, even accepting, he believed she would never wake up, she would simply fade away and die. No, no. She would wake up, she had to.

She would not die.

As he had the previous night, Graham eased into bed with her, held her against him, prayed that somewhere deep inside her, she felt the strong rhythm of his heart. He talked endlessly to her, telling her how much he admired her enthusiasm with theorems, telling her stories from his years with Ryder Sherbrooke, stories about each of the children, ah, even wicked stories from his years at Oxford, imagining she would enjoy the one when he and two equally drunk friends had painted Cambridge's Blue all over his don's front door, and he smiled, briefly. So many stories and he spoke until he was hoarse. Yet he never stopped except when he kissed her cheek, her forehead, her mouth. When at last he slept, he held her hand all night, knowing, simply knowing he'd awaken if she did. He hated it because his fitful sleep was filled with nightmares, Cam calling to him, telling him she had to leave, she had to—he'd jerk awake, his heart pounding, cold sweat on his face.

And on the morning of the third day, when he awoke, her hand still lay slack in his.

After he'd forced more of the healer's lemonade down her throat, eaten his own toast and drunk his coffee, his father came in, lightly touched his palm to her forehead, kissed her cheek and sat down. He didn't say a word about his son's pallor, the fear he saw in his eyes. He merely sat there and spoke of local happenings to distract him. Cilly bathed Cam and brushed her hair, braided it, and returned to sit by the fireplace in a high-back winged chair, sewing. Graham and his father received Dr. Crutcher, who examined the wound, changed the bandage and tried to be optimistic, Graham would give him that. Keep the faith, he said. Words, naught but words that meant nothing really. Graham didn't tell him about the healer's special lemonade.

Graham and Cilly and Vereker kept vigil. Graham paced back and forth over the soft Aubusson carpet, half listening now to the steady, hard rain hitting against the windows. The maple logs in the fireplace burned steadily, the room was warm, too warm, but it didn't matter. Neither his father nor Cilly said a word.

Every few minutes Graham walked to her bed, studied her still face, kissed her, told her over and over to wake up, he wanted to burn her ears for saving him. He laid his palm on her forehead. Still no fever, thank heavens. He rubbed cream on her dry lips, dribbled water and lemonade into her mouth until he prayed she'd swallowed enough. He sat in his chair beside her and read to her, his father and Cilly a treatise on the advantages of a water-tube boiler. When he finished, he looked at his watch. Another day was coming to a close. His father left to speak briefly to another well-meaning neighbor. Blakeney himself brought their dinner and a bottle of claret. He always said, "She will recover, my lord, she will recover."

Graham and his father ate together, or his father ate, then Graham would give her more water and the healer's lemonade, a fresh batch always appeared as if by magic at the kitchen door every morning.

After dinner, Graham and Vereker quickly fell into the habit of each sitting in a chair on either side of her bed, speaking to her, taking turns, Vereker telling her stories of Graham and Simon as young boys. But mostly, they were quiet, knowing time was passing and if she remained unconscious, she'd starve to death.

Vereker said for perhaps the fourth time, "It was sheer

luck that Harley, one of the stable lads, found footprints just before it started raining. He said they were half a finger's length longer than his feet. We measured. They're still smaller than my feet.

"Riker believes the man used a pole with a heavy hammer at the end of it, struck the beam, weakening it even more. He must have been on the lookout for you and saw you come to the abbey. He waited until you and Cam came into the abbot's office, smashed the pole down on the beam and since it was nearly rotted through, it quickly broke in two. Riker showed me the splintered remains of the beam, much of it scattered on the floor. There was no sign of the pole, which means, of course, the man took it with him. You saw nothing?"

Graham shook his head. "I suppose he was lying on his belly on one of the remaining beams. Dangerous, but that must have been what he did."

Time continued to pass. Cilly bathed her, brushed her hair, braided it; Nutworthy sang "The Cuckoo Song" to her in a lovely baritone, and Eugenie read Chaucer's "The Miller's Tale" to her. It was in the early afternoon of the third day when Eugenie finished reading, looked up to see her brother pacing, always pacing when he wasn't beside her, holding her, speaking to her endlessly. "Graham, go eat, you look like paste and you've lost half a stone. I'll stay with her. I'll call you if she awakens."

Neatly three days had passed, minus five hours. Actually, Graham knew down to the second. In twelve minutes Graham would tilt her head back and dribble water and lemonade into her mouth. Most ended up running down her chin, but he didn't give up until he was convinced some of it went down her throat. He knew it couldn't go on, but every time the thought intruded he shut it off. She would wake up.

And the letter to her father still lay on the marquetry table.

The household kept vigil, everyone counted the hours, everyone knew if she didn't wake up she'd die for certain, but of course no one said anything. Dr. Crutcher visited three times, listened to her heart, peeled back her eyelids, but all knew there was nothing he could do.

They waited.

Was she even getting enough water? Was the lemonade helping at all?

Time trickled by. Graham would not give up hope. If he did, he knew it would be all over for him. She'd been in his care and now, only a month after she'd become his wife, she could die. Trying to save him. The pain of that nearly drove him to his knees.

CHAPTER 63

Mama? I heard the noise, a sort of cracking sound, and that beam came crashing down.

My brave girl, you acted so fast, you saved your husband.

Mama, who is doing this?

So much betrayal and hate and blame, and for what? So much tragedy. It is all of a piece, Camilla, and so close to home, but you and your husband both know that. There's Madeline, my dearest, ask Vereker about her.

Wake up now, come back into yourself and open your eyes. All want you well again. It is enough, Camilla. WAKE UP!

His father said suddenly, "Graham, did you see that?"

Graham was on his feet in an instant. "Wh-what?"

"Her eyelids moved."

The two men hovered over her, staring at her face, Cilly trying to shove in. She said, "Camilla Rohman, wake up! I have stitched you three new chemises!"

Vereker said, "She's a Hepburn now, Cilly. There, again. There, again—did you see?"

Graham lightly shook her shoulders, kissed her slack mouth, the tip of her nose, nuzzled her cheek. "Come on, sweetheart, open your eyes. Tell me I'm as much a rotter as

Teddy Jewel or Pilcher Gayson. Tell me I dance like an ostrich. Tell me you love me to distraction."

She opened her eyes, whispered, "You dance like a prince." She blinked, moaned. "Oh dear, my head, it hurts, Graham, it really hurts."

Cilly measured out drops into water and handed Graham the glass. He set the rim against her mouth. "Drink it down, Cam, it's laudanum. It will take away the pain."

Graham tilted her up, slowly fed her the water. She drank and drank, panting when the glass was empty.

He pressed her back down. "Lie still, sweetheart, no, don't talk, let the laudanum work. Everything will be all right now." He kissed her forehead. He felt such gratitude, such blessed relief he wanted to shout with it. He smiled hugely and kissed her again. Her lips were soft from the cream he'd rubbed in.

Since she was Cam, of course she talked. "Are you all right, Graham?"

"I'm better than I have any right to be, curse you, Cam, for knocking me down."

She smiled, a small smile, but it was real. "Mama said I acted fast. You're blurry."

She closed her eyes. Graham set her glasses back on. "Try again. Can you see me now?"

"Yes, but I don't want to. I want to take a little nap."

"I'm sorry, Cam, but you can't sleep yet. Cilly, come here and sing to your mistress."

For nearly an hour two men and a woman sang in lovely harmony to "Rock of Ages."

In between their various renditions, Graham studied her face, saw her eyes clear, saw her focus on his face.

She whispered, "You have your mother's eyes. I wish I could have known her." She didn't move, but turned her eyes to Vereker. "When did Madeline die, sir?"

There was a long moment of silence, then Vereker said,

everyone heard the anguish in his voice, "Madeline died when Graham and Simon were boys."

"Do you mean she was swimming? She drowned?"

There was silence for a long moment, then Vereker said, low, his voice pain-filled, "No, she took her own life."

Graham's head whipped up to his father's face. "I didn't know. I'm very sorry, sir. I assumed—But why? I don't understand."

Vereker swallowed, the devastating memories burning tears in his throat. "It was a long time ago, Graham, and the truth is I do not know why your mother killed herself. For several weeks before her death, I knew she was unhappy about something, but I don't know what. I pressed her again and again, but she wouldn't tell me what was bothering her. I blame myself for it must have been something I had done. You and Simon were so very young, both of you devastated. We were all devastated for your mother was much loved. No one knew why she would do such a thing."

His wife dead and then his two sons taken. Cam couldn't begin to imagine the pain, the absolute despair. She squeezed her father-in-law's hand, really only a slight movement of her hand over his, but it was enough.

There was deep silence in the bedchamber.

When Vereker spoke again, it was as if the words were being pulled out of his mouth. "We found her facedown in the Green Stream. Her glorious hair, it was fanned out about her head, laced with the hideous green algae."

CHAPTER 64

King's Head
One week later

Eugenie smiled as her husband, Donner, announced at dinner over Cook's delicious Charlotte Russe, "As you know, I've purchased a manor house near Canterbury, only twelve miles from King's Head. Eugenie and I have decided to name it Longfield. It has thirty acres and several tenant farmers. It isn't nearly the size of King's Head, but it will suit us." He took her hand. "And our growing family."

There was silence, then Vereker said, "Blakeney, champagne. I am to be a grandfather and all of us will be visiting Longfield."

Eugenie was grinning from ear to ear and Donner looked so proud he might pop his vest buttons.

When toasts were made and champagne drunk, Donner said, "I'm assured by our man the house will be ready for us to move in next week. We want you all to come for dinner to celebrate."

Cam remembered the laughter she'd heard from Donner

and Eugenie's bedchamber. Blakeney brought out more champagne and there the toasts continued through the second bottle.

Uncle Tally, who now ate at the house most nights, called out, "My beautiful Eugenie, may I come dine with you occasionally?"

And Eugenie laughed. "If you are not at our dining table once a week, I shall be sorely upset."

Cam studied their happy faces. Eugenie even smiled at her over a witty toast by Uncle Tally. She wondered how she could have ever believed, even for an instant, that Eugenie and Donner were behind this misery.

So close to home. Betrayal, hate, blame, her mother had said. No, not Donner or Eugenie. And, of course, she knew it could only be one person.

Graham hadn't asked her how she felt more than a dozen times today. Cam grinned up at him, laid her face against his shoulder. His bathrobe was velvet, smooth and so very soft beneath her cheek.

He kissed her hair, hugged her closer. Soon the stitches would be gone from above her temple, but now a constant reminder and whenever he thought of the beam hitting her, his heart seized.

She leaned back in his arms. "It's time, Graham, time we talked. Come, let's sit by the fire. And it's time I told you about my mother. She woke me up, you know."

He stared at her. "I don't understand."

She took his hand. "Come." They settled in side by side in the comfortable dark blue velvet chairs. The embers were orange, occasionally sparking up. The room was warm, the unremitting rain slid drops down the windows. The draperies were open, as both of them preferred.

He squeezed her hand. "Explain this to me. Your mother woke you up?"

"Yes, right before I opened my eyes I was speaking to her. She told me to wake up. She was rather insistent."

He said carefully, "You were dreaming of your mother?"

"Well, of course I was dreaming, in a way I guess, carrying on a dialogue between us, playing both her and myself, I suppose. But, Graham, when she yelled at me to wake up, I did. And isn't that curious? I've thought and thought, but I really can't explain it.

"But that's not what's important. I asked her why the attempts on your life and she told me it was all of a piece, betrayal, blame and hate, and then, of course, tragedy. She said it was close, Graham, so close." Cam drew in a deep breath. "It's time I said it aloud, time we brought it into the open. You know it's someone here, and you know as well as I do who it must be."

"Yes, it's time we brought everything out in the open. I didn't want to speak of it sooner, not with you still recovering." He drew a deep breath, stared at the embers in the fireplace, glowing red, occasional sparks flying up. He never looked away from the fire, and said, his voice emotionless, "It has to be Uncle Tally, there is simply no one else, certainly not pregnant Eugenie or Donner, who simply wants to be his own man, out of another man's house."

"Yes, there is no one else. But why, Graham, why would Uncle Tally try to kill you and Simon? What about the betrayal, the hate, the guilt, the tragedy? What does that mean?"

Graham said slowly, "Uncle Tally was my father's nominal heir until Simon and I were born." He pressed his palms against his head. "But to murder your own nephews, it smacks of something I can't bear to accept." He struck his fist against the arm of the chair, winced. "If only I could remember, then we'd know, Cam, we'd know." Even though he had no memory of Uncle Tally, it still hurt him, knew it would devastate his father. But had his father always realized there was simply no one else?

Cam said matter-of-factly, "He abducted you and your brother, he wanted you both dead. He killed Simon, but Ryder Sherbrooke saved your life. You survived.

"He wanted you dead, Graham. You told me Mr. Sherbrooke said you'd been struck on the head before you were thrown into the Thames to drown."

To hear the words said aloud—"Yes. As I told you, before Simon and me, Uncle Tally was my father's nominal heir. With both Simon and me dead he would be my father's only heir."

"But, Graham, would he also have murdered more children had your father remarried after your mother's death?"

"I don't know, but why not? Damnation, I like him, Cam, his dealings with me since I returned have been that of a loving uncle."

If Uncle Tally was the monster, she would kill him. Cam's voice was as cold as the ice in her belly. "I'd be loving too if I needed to be. I'd surely hide the evil inside." She paused, added, "And that is why he's now dining nearly every night here. He wants to find out our plans, what we're doing and when and how so he can make plans."

He drew a deep breath. "Yes. I think it's time to speak to my father."

"You know he has the same conclusion."

Graham nodded again. "Yes. I cannot imagine the pain it's causing him. As for Eugenie and Donner, I doubt they've given it much thought since she's with child and they're getting ready to move into Longfield."

CHAPTER 65

They found Vereker in the estate room finishing up his quarterly review of rents and expenditures with Mr. Spalding, King's Head estate manager for seventeen years. Graham had spent little time with him yet. He was a square man both face and body who'd reached his fiftieth year, and had, Blakeney had told them, a brain stuffed with so many facts he spewed them on anyone within hearing. "Many times I fear I've wanted to smack him, I mean, who wants to know how many children Queen Isabella of Spain produced? Of course he keeps his trap shut when he is with his lordship."

Vereker looked up, smiled at them, waved them in, thanked Mr. Spalding and sent him on his way. Mr. Spalding bowed to Cam and Graham, opened his mouth, thought better of it, and left them.

Vereker stopped smiling. He rose slowly and came around his desk. "Spalding shows restraint upon occasion. Come in. You're still feeling fit, Cam?"

"Yes, sir." She walked to her father-in-law, hugged him, kissed his cheek. "I am ready to waltz with you, sir. Blakeney assures me you are a better dancer than your son, who perhaps, when he's not concentrating on his steps, jumps around like an ostrich."

"Unfair and a lie," Graham said. "You told me I danced like a prince."

Vereker met his son's eyes, Madeline's eyes, and he thought, *If only you could see your son, Madeline. If he could only remember he would see himself in you—*

Graham took his father's arms in his hands. "Sir, it's time, past time, we faced this head-on. You know as well as we do the person who took Simon and me also tried to kill me again, here and in Ventnor. Cam and I know you've given this endless thought as have we. Who do you think it is?"

Vereker said slowly, "I can see it in your eyes, both of you." He sighed. "There can be no one else, I know that in my gut but still I don't want to accept it. I ask myself why? How is that possible?" He turned and walked to the fireplace, stood silently, staring down into the glowing embers. He said without turning, "But like you, I've examined this every way I can think of, I still cannot understand why. Tally loved you, Graham, both you and Simon. I remember so clearly how the only times he seemed really happy was when he was with you boys. He taught you archery, he took you fishing, he—" His voice fell off a cliff.

Cam saw the pain in his eyes but she didn't stop, she couldn't. "Sir, I'm very sorry, but Graham's life is in the balance. Since he cannot remember, it is you who must remember for him. You must face this head-on." She studied his face, stiff, his eyes pain filled. "Sir, do you believe Tally would kill two young boys—his nephews—to become your heir?" She paused, watching him shake his head. "Sir, would he kill any more boys if you had remarried? Would he kill you?"

Vereker looked as if she'd struck him. He started to shake his head, then he said slowly, "I've told you when Tally came back from fighting at Waterloo, he was changed, everyone saw it. He wanted to be alone. He built the cottage in the eastern woods. For years he only dined here once a month.

"But he loved both you and Simon, I know that to the deepest part of me. But now? After Ventnor and the falling beam at the abbey ruins that could have so easily killed you? If he did these things, and yes, I know I must accept there is simply no other choice, but listen, I would swear to you he simply never wanted my title, my birthright. That wasn't what Tally was ever about. He loved life, loved being a soldier, told me he was born for it—until he came back from Waterloo. And wouldn't that mean he'd abhor violence? That he would protect Graham and Simon with his life?"

Neither Graham nor Cam said a word, merely stood quietly watching him.

Vereker said finally, "So it makes no sense unless he is mad."

CHAPTER 66

Graham knocked on the bright blue door and waited, Cam beside him. He knew he had to accept it, as his father had, there was no choice. He only wished Cam didn't have to be part of it, but of course there was no way to keep Cam away and safe, short of tying her down. As for his father, Graham hadn't told him what they planned. Did his father guess he would face down Uncle Tally himself? Graham hoped he didn't. They'd left him in his study, staring out onto the east garden, and knew he was trying to figure out what to do. As they'd left the study, Graham looked back at this man who was his father, this man who'd accepted him without hesitation, who'd welcomed him, loved him immediately with his whole heart. It didn't matter Graham had no memory of this man, he would do anything to protect him as much as he could. Which wasn't much at all, really, but Graham knew he had to deal with this himself.

As they waited, Graham felt the burn of renewed fury because Cam could so easily have been killed, and all because of this man who was supposedly his loving uncle. Like his father, Graham had not a single memory of this man, no memories of his growing-up years with him. Was his father right? Was Uncle Tally mad? Or was it all a lie? For years this man had lied, believed his nephews were dead and he was indeed his father's heir? Biding his time, waiting, content that all would come to him? What was one more murder, namely Cam?

He knocked again. He felt Cam stiffen beside him at the sound of light bootfalls, a man's whistle. The door opened.

"Graham, Cam—oh my dear, are you well enough to walk all the way from the house here?" He paused, cocked his head to the side. "You both look very serious. Is something wrong?"

But he knew, Graham and Cam saw it in his eyes. He knew. Tally stepped back, said in a calm voice, "Do come in. I'll bring you some tea, just made and not too strong." He turned away.

Graham called after him. "Uncle Tally, we do not want tea. Come with us to the parlor."

Tally looked at them, slowly nodded. "I must turn off the kettle. Go into the parlor, I will join you in but a moment." And he walked away.

Cam said low, "What if he runs away?"

"No, he won't run. There's no place to run to. He cannot know we haven't told people we were coming here. No, Uncle Tally knows it's over. Come, let's sit down." He hugged her close, said gently against her temple where the beam had struck, "This must be done."

When Tally joined them a moment later, he said in a deep, calm voice, "I was waiting for someone to come but I believed it would be my brother, not you two." He sat opposite them. "Yes, my dear brother—he was more like another father to me growing up. He was always fussing over me, so careful he was—" Tally shrugged. "I believed he loved me but you see, he stood in my way, always. After our father died, I knew I should be Earl St. Lucy, not he. I thought about killing him but knew it would be too dangerous. And so I left to fight Napoleon. Years I was gone but finally I came home. At last your mother, Madeline, birthed you and Simon—little interlopers, that's how I always saw the two of you. Of course I pretended to love you, pretended to enjoy playing with you, teaching you, but I knew I had to, else what would my brother think? I knew I could do it and I did. I waited until I knew the time was right. The two of you disappeared." Tally paused, smiled. "Gone, just like that," and he snapped his fingers.

Graham looked at him emotionlessly for he felt no betrayal since this man was a stranger. "But you failed, you didn't manage to kill me. I am here and healthy and your reign of terror is over."

Tally tapped his fingertips together. "Yes, I failed with you. For the longest time I believed you drowned, that you'd probably floated dead and fish-eaten up to the shore of the Thames in London because I'd struck you down and simply tossed you overboard. There are always dead bodies floating in the Thames, what was one more?

"I had no idea you'd survived until you returned here and I heard the story. Imagine Ryder Sherbrooke saving your life and then he whisked you away to that orphanage of his and raised you. I knew of Sherbrooke, of course, he's a fool. Can you imagine taking in the worthless dregs from the gutters then foisting them on the world?"

Graham's hands fisted. He wanted to smash this man, but he held himself still. He had to hear it, hear it all.

"I will admit I was flummoxed. Why hadn't Sherbrooke brought you immediately back to King's Head? I was ready to leave England because you would accuse me before I could kill you. I will admit it, I was afraid. And then I learned you had no memory at all, you were nothing more than a blank slate, one of those worthless brats Sherbrooke took home.

"At first I believed it an amazing stroke of luck for me, but then I realized it was more, I realized my plans were blessed. But I also realized once surrounded by all you knew as a boy, you would remember and you'd know, so I had to act fast." He searched Graham's face. "I had to, now didn't I?"

Cam said, her voice vicious as the winds in January, "Yes, you acted fast but yet again, you failed, both in Ventnor and breaking that overhead beam hoping it would fall on Graham and kill him. Listen to me, you insane monster, you will never be Earl St. Lucy.

"You call Mr. Sherbrooke a fool. Well, you're a failure, so inept even given three times, you couldn't kill Graham. I would kill you myself if I could. But I will smile knowing you'll hang and your evil will die with you." She paused. "It is a pity but I doubt my father-in-law will agree. Unlike you, Vereker is good. Despite everything you've done, I know he could not bear to end your life. He will probably give you money and send you off to the Continent. Me? I would gladly see you exterminated, one less evil, twisted creature to prey on innocents."

Tally laughed. "Graham, I must say you married a hard young lady. Evil, am I? Twisted? Tell me, does she want your title or does she love you?"

"Of course I love him, you idiot." She stared at him. What was in his mind? What was he planning? She said easily, "What other reason could there be, you worthless excuse for a human being?"

"You mock me. Such a mouth on a young lady. You are silent, Graham."

Graham said, his voice remote, "My wife has been quite thorough in her assessment of you and what you are. What I do not understand, however, is if you wanted my father's title so desperately, why haven't you killed him? It's been years since you tried to kill me and Simon and I assume our tutor as well."

"Ah, he has come close several times, but it appears he's as lucky as you were. For how much longer? We'll see. There'll be mourning of course. As for you and your little bitch, your luck is at an end." Tally slipped his hand in his pocket and brought out a pistol, pointed it at Cam's head. "No, Graham, you will not move or I'll shoot her dead. If you but remembered, you'd know I never miss. The benefits of being trained as a soldier." He studied them a moment. "I knew time was fast running out, but now actually facing the two of you I can't decide which of you to shoot first. What do you think, Graham? Would you like to die first?"

"You are insane," Graham said, his eyes never leaving Tally's. "You will never be Earl St. Lucy. If you kill us or don't kill us, you will still have to flee. It's over, Tally. Rather than killing us I suggest you escape instead."

The gun quivered but a moment, then steadied. "I plan to bury you two deep, very deep. You will never be found. Will I run? We'll see. It will hardly matter to you."

CHAPTER 67

Cam felt bile rise in her throat, but she held steady. She lightly laid her hand on Graham's. She studied Tally from his face to his well-born boots. "You really are a paltry man, aren't you, Tally? Have you always been this way? Tell me, at Waterloo, you didn't fight honorably, did you? I'll wager you ran, didn't you? You killed one of your own soldiers because he saw you running? And then you set up this pretense, this lie, the brave soldier returning home from Waterloo. Did you intimate you were yourself responsible for bringing Napoleon low, did you—"

"No! Damn you, no! Shut up." He was breathing hard, focused on Cam. "You bitch, how I hoped you would never wake up. It was hard not to pray for your death whilst pretending I cared. You have caused me nothing but trouble. But now it is over." He steadied the pistol on her face, his attention on her.

Graham lifted his hand from the sofa and fired. The bullet went into his uncle's shoulder. Tally fired at nearly the same time, but the bullet went wide because he jerked. Tally yelled, dropped the gun. The gun skidded across the oak floor to fetch up against a chair leg. He was moaning, gasping with pain, pressing his ruined shoulder hard with his hand.

He was panting. "Damn you, you two planned this, you held the gun all the time, waiting, just waiting for me to act against you. You don't deserve to follow your father—you are no gentleman! Where did you learn to shoot?"

"My guardian, of course, Ryder Sherbrooke, who loves every abandoned and abused child he finds. But of course you would have no understanding of such a man."

Cam eyed the tears of pain still wet on Tally's face. "Comparing you to Ryder Sherbrooke is like comparing a snake to a stone, which doesn't make much sense, but you get the idea. Now, you miserable excuse for a human being, we will take you back to your brother who will decide your fate. I will cast my vote for the gallows."

Graham slowly rose, gave Cam his hand and pulled her to her feet. He continued to hold the gun on Tally. "Did you really want Simon and me dead so you could eventually inherit my father's title?"

"Of course, you stupid whelp. I was a good soldier, I would never desert. And like every other soldier, I knew life is fragile. Any of us can die of some disease or accident at any moment. My brother is so much older than I am, that after I failed to kill him, accidents, of course, I was content to wait and let disease befall him. There are so many ills can fell a man, an inflammation of the lung, an infection, so many things, but damn him, Vereker has always been blessed in his good health." He stopped, gasping with pain, and pressed his shoulder harder. Blood still seeped through his fingers, thick red.

Graham studied Tally's white pain-leached face. "You had to know there was no other who could possibly be behind our attempted murders. Why have you remained? Why haven't you left England?"

"Because my work wasn't done." He leapt at Graham. Blood flowed over his white shirt, but he was still strong. He pulled the pistol toward him and pulled the trigger.

Time froze. Tally didn't make a sound. Slowly, Graham released him and he fell to the floor.

Graham fell to his knees beside his uncle, lightly pressed his fingertips to the pulse in his throat. Tally opened his eyes, stared up at him.

"You never deserved to be your father's heir. Never. With any luck, you never will be." And they heard a death rattle, then nothing. Tally's eyes fixed on Graham's face.

Graham pulled Cam against him. He buried his face against her throat. "My uncle. He would so joyfully have killed both of us."

Cam felt the shock of death, the violence of it, but shoved it down. It was Graham who was important. She smoothed her hand over his hair, pressed her cheek to his. She said only, "He wanted to die. He deserves to be dead."

They held each other for a very long time.

CHAPTER 68

Unspoken pain filled the house and unspoken rage at what this man all had trusted had done and would have succeeded if not for Graham and Cam.

There was deadening silence at the dinner table that night. Cam knew there was silence at the staff kitchen table as well since most had known Tally Hepburn all their lives. She knew she'd never forget the tears in Blakeney's eyes, the awful pain on her father-in-law's face. Eugenie fought against the truth until she collapsed in tears against her husband's chest.

Vereker finally raised his head from the uneaten slice of thick ham on his plate. He said with all the firmness and conviction he could muster, "Tally was consumed with madness because of the damnable war. And Waterloo, it was so bloody, so many men lost. There can be no other reason for what he did to you and Simon, Graham, and tried to do to you and Cam. I believe he wanted to die when he realized he'd failed, and he realized there would be no future for him."

No one said anything. Did anyone believe it? Cam remembered clearly Tally's words and knew he wasn't mad, he was a vicious monster who'd coveted his brother's birthright. He'd killed Simon and their poor tutor and tried to kill Graham. He'd said it himself, his plans were blessed when he discovered Graham had no memory.

No one wanted to adjourn to the drawing room after dinner. Donner and Eugenie went upstairs. Vereker excused himself. Graham didn't want to leave his father, his pain and shock were too deep. He and Cam followed him into his study. They stopped in the doorway. His father and Blakeney were standing together, holding the other. There was no sound. Graham waited, then said quietly, "Father."

Vereker looked at them. And now Graham saw not pain, but rage. He saw the same expression on Blakeney's face.

"We will survive this, my lord," Blakeney said, nodded to Graham and Cam, and left the room.

Vereker said, his voice steady, "No more excuses for Tally. He would have killed both of you. He tried twice. When you went to his cottage, he was ready for you. You should have told me. We could all have gone."

Of course Graham hadn't wanted that, hadn't wanted his father to face his brother's treachery, but he didn't say it aloud.

Cam said, "Sir, please tell us what you believe Tally would have done if he had succeeded in killing Graham in the abbey ruins. Wouldn't he have realized there was no escape for him? Wouldn't he have known we were coming? But rather than run, he stayed. He was ready. He had the gun in his pocket. He would have shot us, both of us. Why, sir, why didn't he simply leave, escape to France?"

Vereker said. "I have asked myself the same question. I knew to my gut after the attack at the abbey ruins it had to be Tally. But I didn't act, I waited, hoping, praying there was someone else, someone—" He stopped, shook his head. "I was afraid to face the truth until both of you came to me."

Graham said, "I'm very sorry for all of it, Father. But again, why would he remain to face what he'd done? The statue falling in Ventnor, it could be explained as an accident, but the attack in the abbey ruins—it pointed right at him. If nothing else, it was very poor strategy."

"Yes, I agree. But he told you why he'd wanted you and Simon dead. He wanted what was mine. The thing is, I never saw this jealousy in him, this hatred of me in him, coveting what was mine by birth. But it had to be there and I didn't see it." His eyes filled with tears. "It meant killing both you and Simon and your tutor, Timmons, poor man."

Cam said, "Sir, you have said Tally was very smart, but again, the abbey ruins—what he did, it was so simplistic, so ill thought-out."

Graham slowly nodded. "It was like he was presenting himself to us on a platter."

Vereker said, "He saw an opportunity and took it. He admitted everything. He knew it was all over so he gave it up. But I don't understand why he would still want to kill you. It would gain him nothing and he'd be caught and hanged." Vereker paused, added, his voice low, furious, "Why did the pair of you go to his cottage by yourselves?" He strode to Graham, grabbed his shoulders in his big hands, tried to shake him. "Damn you, Graham, if he had succeeded—" Vereker shuddered, swallowed, jerked away. "I could not have borne it, Graham. Not a second time. I could not."

Graham walked to his father and pulled him into his arms. Father and son held each other. Cam waited, silent, and wondered what the consequences would be of this unspeakable day. She thought of Tallyrand Hepburn's body at Mr. Milly's funeral parlor, knew everyone hereabouts was speaking of his treachery. She was, she knew, glad to her soul the man, mad or not, was dead.

That night, Cam lay awake next to Graham listening to his even, deep breathing, thankful he was finally asleep. They hadn't spoken much, merely held each other. As for Cam, she couldn't sleep, too many questions roiled and bubbled in her brain. But there were no answers. She realized she had to accept it. Whatever was in Tally's twisted brain, it didn't matter now. He was dead. She had to stop worrying it like a dog with a bone. Everyone had to accept Tally's betrayal.

CHAPTER 69

Three days later

Tallyrand Hepburn, second son of the third Earl St. Lucy, wasn't buried at King's Head cemetery with his ancestors, but in the graveyard beside the St. Lucy church. Cam knew this decision broke Vereker's heart, but there was really no choice, Tally's betrayal was too great. There were many in attendance, for all had known Tally, and now the townspeople stood silent and still at the grave site, a solid wall of support for Vereker and his family. If gossip and speculation were rife, they didn't hear it that day. All King's Head staff and tenant farmers stood behind the family, all in somber black.

Graham pressed Cam closer to his side, protecting her against the stiff winds that blew in from the Channel. He whispered against her ear, "Despite our letters to your father and to Ryder, I know they will come. Actually, I expected them to be here sooner." He paused, said, "I hope Ryder is able to come. I-I need him."

She squeezed his gloved hand, leaned up and breathed in

the clean, sweet scent of her husband, and realized she too wanted her father to be here, knew she needed him. "They'll come, you'll see. Will we have to tell my father about my sleeping for three days?"

"He will hear all about that, count on it, so no choice." He paused. "I imagine he will want to see the wound over your temple, just to make sure you're all right again."

Toward the end of the service, both Lord Whitsonby and Ryder Sherbrooke arrived together and moved through the crowd to stand beside Cam and Graham. When her father's arm came around her, Cam leaned into him, felt his warmth, his love. She felt immense gratitude for him, always there for her. She saw Ryder Sherbrooke stood close to Graham, his hand on his shoulder. Both men were rocks. She saw Vereker nod to them.

And somehow, their presence lessened the bite of the bitter winds that blew through the graveyard. If Vicar Piercebridge's words didn't comfort, though he tried, they at least put an end to it.

Her father did indeed examine the wound over her temple.

CHAPTER 70

Four days later

Graham said to Cam as they stood on the wide stone steps of King's Head and waved as both her father and Ryder left in a carriage to the small train station in Dover, "Your father hugged you until I was afraid I'd hear your ribs crack."

Cam leaned into him as the train disappeared from view. "Ryder hugged you just as hard. They're both amazing men. You and I, Graham, are very lucky."

Vereker said from just behind them, "I've decided to build the train track from Dover here to King's Head so both fathers—yes, Graham, I do consider Ryder Sherbrooke to be your second father and he well knows I am forever in his debt—can travel to us more quickly and easily. I should also like to see all Ryder's children running about, Blakeney chasing after them, and Sophie perhaps making one of her amazing apple pies." He gave them both a hug and walked back into the manor.

Graham said, "Blakeney told me my father had to meet with two of our farmers to improve a particular drainage ditch. He said I was to take you to Sally's Cove and gave me directions when I looked at him blankly. He wants a return to normalcy, of course, he wants us to continue our lives, leave the past in the past where it belongs. He said now there is no more danger, it is time for us to enjoy ourselves. Evidently this particular cove was a place Simon and I spent a great deal of time in our small skiff, fishing, swimming or sparring about with wooden swords on the beach—or more likely fighting and throwing sand at each other."

For the first time in too long a time, Cam felt a leap of excitement. There was still too much silence in the great house, still shock and rage, and infinite sadness so clear on all the staff's faces. But there was less with each passing day. It was true her father and Ryder had lightened everyone's mood, both gentlemen popular with all the King's Head people, Terrance and Nutworthy in particular.

Cam gave her husband a smacking loud kiss. "Sally's Cove, yes, let's go. I should love that. I'll wager Blakeney's hoping it will spark your memory. But it doesn't matter, I should like to visit a place where you spent so much of your childhood with your brother. When can we leave? Do you know who Sally is or was?"

"Sorry, I don't, but we'll ask Blakeney when we return. Go put on some stout boots." Then he saw the question in her eyes and pulled her into his arms, kissed her hair, held her quietly a moment. He said against her temple, "It's over, Cam, finally over, there's no more need to wonder and constantly be on our guard. We will come to accept Uncle Tally was mad with jealousy, wanted what is my father's. It is time to get back to living and soon"—he kissed the tip of her nose—"I must resume work on my water-tube boiler. Ideas have begun to flood my brain, thankfully, and your father will expect me in London in a fortnight to meet with Lord Carberry to discuss financial matters including the status of our factory in Manchester, all the hiring we must see to, the machinery—I have other ideas, say how to make the train run more smoothly and—enough of that.

"I will tell you everything in detail later and you will ask me questions and together we will come up with a theorem or two. But now, we're going to go to this Sally's Cove."

Cam didn't think a theorem applied in this particular situation but she was too excited to care. She hoped soon there would be no more black worn in King's Head. It was time to bring light back into the house. She gave him a wonderful smile, a kiss and a nod, and ran upstairs to their bedchamber.

Blakeney stood by the front door as they came down the grand staircase, handed Graham a wicker basket bound in leather straps. "It is your lunch, my lord. Ah, there is a bottle of champagne wrapped in ice cloths." He searched Graham's face. "I hope you have a pleasant day."

The day was cool but the sun was high and the wind was thankfully more quiescent than not. They walked hand-in-hand the quarter mile to the coastline and with each step, the day seemed to grow brighter, the future more exciting. When they stood on the cliff edge, they shaded their eyes and looked toward France. The wind kicked up here, tugged at Cam's braids atop her head. Graham sheltered her against him, pointed. "And there it is, England's mortal enemy, probably extending back to the invention of writing. It's always amazed me, the constant desire to want what another has and be willing to fight and die to gain it."

Cam said, "I wonder how many men have died fighting, how many lives were destroyed, and for what? A piece of land? Making people your slaves?"

He nodded. "Lust for power and possessions, greed for what someone else has, it seems to be bred into a human's very bones. After Waterloo and Napoleon's banishment, all hoped there would be no more wars, at least with France, but I'll wager wars will continue throughout the world to the end of time." He thought of Uncle Tally, of the man he'd been told he'd been—young and exuberant, wanting adventure and excitement, wanting to make his own mark, and then when the man returned from the devastating three-day battle known as Waterloo, he was someone else entirely. Or was he? It didn't matter now, Tally was dead, his hatreds and resentments dead with him.

Graham felt profound gratitude he and Cam had found each other. He wondered what they would accomplish together. He kissed her, smoothed her hair in the wind. "Come, let's explore."

As for Cam, she was wondering how she could establish a theorem based on observations of his water-tube boiler, but that was for later, now was for them. She said, "Blakeney told me there's a cave somewhere along here. Do you think we could perhaps visit, perhaps—" Her voice trailed off as she ran her hand down his cheek, lower to his chest.

Graham felt a bolt of lust, always there since he'd first met her sitting on a bench waiting for Ryder to come out of Parliament. He stilled her hand, gave her a nipping kiss on the end of her nose, shoved up her glasses, fingered the gold chain, a very neat solution he wished he'd invented, not Lady Tremaine. "Blakeney told me of the cave as well, told me how to find it. He warned me the tides were extreme here so we have to be cautious. We'll explore the cave before the tide comes in."

They found the path that led some thirty feet down to Sally's Cove, a near-perfect circle, enclosed by two skinny arms stretching out into the Channel, all barren land and rock. The beach was strewn with driftwood and algae and small tidal pools. The sand was dark and the water looked frigid. Cam looked up at the chalk cliffs, as white as her new chemise, sewn for her by Cilly during the long wait for Cam to wake up.

They took off their shoes and stockings and ran along the gritty damp sand to stop at the face of the cliff with a spill of boulders on the sand nearly touching the wall.

"Blakeney said the cave is—ah, yes, here is the opening, right by the stacked rocks. I wonder, did Simon and I carry these rocks here to mark the entrance to the cave?"

"It makes sense since the opening looks hard to find. It disappears into the cliff."

There was no need for Graham to bend down as they walked into the cave. They stood in the middle of a small chamber, no more than twelve feet wide, perhaps ten feet deep. The ceiling was well above Graham's head. There were no rocks, only damp sand beneath their feet. Graham set down the wicker basket. "Blakeney said in the second chamber there are magnificent stalactites and stalagmites, some broken off when the tide surges strong during storms." He saw her shiver, and pulled her close. "I'll keep you warm, don't worry about that, Madam Wife."

Their laughter rang out, echoing back to them. They ran into the second chamber and stopped cold.

A man stood facing them, a gun in each hand. And he was smiling. He was wearing buckskins, scuffed black boots and a wrinkled white linen shirt, not the clothes of a working man, the clothes of a gentleman despite their condition. There was stubble on his face, and his hair was long, dark, nearly reaching his shoulders. He looked fit and strong. He was young.

Cam and Graham stared at him. Something deep stirred inside Graham, but he couldn't grasp it. "Who are you?"

The man said in a lovely deep voice, "What a surprise. The last thing I suspected was you two coming here. Luckily, I saw you riding here and imagined Blakeney told you about this cave, told you to visit. I beat you here. I've been waiting. And sure enough, here you are. I heard you two laughing." He eyed the two of them up and down. "My father always counseled me to be prepared for the unexpected because the unexpected was always nipping at a man's heels. Your coming, it's really quite excellent. Now I do not have to devise another way to kill the two of you."

CHAPTER 71

"Who are you?" Graham said again, but deep down, some part of Graham recognized him. He moved closer to Cam, took her hand, squeezed it. She was steady, staring as he was at the man.

The young man laughed. "I see you don't recognize me. How depressing that seeing me doesn't bring your memory snapping back."

"No, I don't know you." Graham studied the man, young, about his own age, tall, lean, dark coloring, a beard covering his cheeks, his gentleman's clothes wrinkled. His eyes were dark. Something elusive stirred again, faded away.

The gun he held never wavered. "Of course you don't remember the extreme tide here in Sally's Cove. It fills the cave twice a day, impossible to stay here because it's always damp. I was forced to stay in an empty crofter's cottage near my father. After you murdered him, I moved into his house."

He gave them a big smile, and that smile was vicious. "I never really doubted I would win out in the end. This time, though, I will admit it, I was lucky. As I said I hadn't yet decided how to proceed, but here you are and everything is now clear to me. This night I'll be returning to Brussels. Well, for a time."

He smiled at Cam, a sneering smile that made her go cold to her soul. "And you are the new wife. I daresay if I hadn't struck the beam so it split apart in the abbot's office, I would have seen the two of you mate right there on the stone floor. I admit I wanted to see you naked, you're really quite lovely." He paused, his eyes falling to her breasts. "It's a pity I can't ever have you and more a pity you didn't die when the beam struck your head."

Cam felt rage build. She sneered back at him. "Well now, I didn't die, did I, so you did a pitiful job, didn't you? All this braying—nothing you're saying makes any sense. Who are you?"

He laughed. "What a bitch you are, but I must admit, I was impressed when you saved him. You were fast, I'll give you that, throwing yourself on him to protect him. I didn't know a lady would do that." He looked at Graham and again he sneered. "Of course you know me, Graham Hepburn, regardless of how much I've changed since you last saw me. Of course I would know you anywhere, those eyes of yours that Madeline passed on to you. Yes, you have her distinctive eyes, but my father said I have some of her expressions. Of course I don't remember since she died when I was only four.

"I made fun of you when we were young, said you were too pretty to be a real boy and as I recall you'd pound me when I couldn't outrun you. Being older, of course, you always won. But now, both of us are men, both of nearly the same size, and you will no longer win.

"Look at you—such a hero you look—and such accomplishments, so impressive for one so young. I daresay I am smarter, though. My father told me this one had a fine dowry, but I, I outdid you in wives. I wedded a young lady far richer than this one here. Her poor father passed soon thereafter, with just a bit of help from me, and I now own a good deal of Brussels."

Cam stared at him, and now she knew all of it, and it was horrible and evil. Of course Graham knew as well. What was he thinking? Feeling? She couldn't imagine the depth of this betrayal.

Cam said, "I'll wager while Madeline lived she never had an ugly sneer on her mouth. You're Simon, you're Graham's younger brother."

He gave her a bow. "Just so, sister-in-law. Yes, I'm Simon Hepburn."

He turned to Graham. "What, nothing to say to your long-lost brother? Well, no matter." He turned back to Cam. "He's only my half brother, as I'm sure you've figured out."

Graham stared at this man, his brother, no, his half brother. Simon wanted him dead. It was hard to grasp, to make real, yet it made a horrible sense. His father was Uncle Tally, yet another man who'd wanted what his brother had. Graham knew he had to stop this madness, had to stop him. Time, he needed time. He lightly squeezed Cam's hand. She squeezed his back. He felt her calm, her focus and admired her greatly.

Graham said, "Tell me how this happened."

"Well, why not? I am lonely, truth be told, no one to talk to since you murdered my father. Yes, yes, I know you and this wife of yours swore he killed himself, and if indeed he did, it was to save me."

Graham nodded. "Yes, he killed himself to save you, though I can't see that you're worth saving at all."

The gun jerked in Simon's hand and Graham very nearly threw Cam to the floor of the cave.

"Shut up, damn you!" Simon waved the gun between the two of them, let it come back to rest on Cam's face. He drew a shuddering breath, then he smiled at them, a ghastly smile that terrified Cam.

Simon laughed. "Not worth saving, am I? I'm the one, not you, to make the St. Lucy line truly great and more importantly, powerful. I will bring wealth from Brussels and I will have limitless influence here. I will control lives, I will control the future. I am the true heir, not you, a worthless little inventor." Simon drew a deep breath. "So you want to know how all this came about. Why not tell you, we have time. When I was young I looked quite a bit like our mother, but then when I was no longer a child my father told me I began to resemble him until he knew our likeness would be too great to be ignored, and he feared for me, and for himself, of course. He told me when I was still a small child he began to devise a plan. What plan, you ask? He wanted me to be the Viscount Whitestone then Earl St. Lucy, not you, brother." Simon paused, shook his head. "He knew he had to act. My father convinced yours to send us to Paris with our tutor since he had many friends there and all wanted to meet his nephews. And so it happened just as he'd wished. After he believed you were dead, he killed the tutor, a pathetic little man, and he took me to Brussels."

Graham said slowly, "Yes, even with the beard, I see the resemblance between you and Tally."

"Ah, the irony of it all. You will finally go to your grave with no memory of either your father or your mother—our mother—or of me, your half brother. My father assured me he would arrange an accident for the earl and then I could come home and take what was mine. I would be Earl St. Lucy. There would be no questions for my father made certain I had all the papers to prove my identity as the long-lost son, Simon." Again, the ugly sneer marred his mouth. "But I couldn't come home because my father couldn't bring himself to kill his brother. He was weak, something I didn't realize until I was older. He told me he loved Vereker, you see, something I railed against. He kept telling me Vereker would die soon, he was so much older, now wasn't he? And I had to understand I couldn't come home sooner because Vereker would see not only Madeline in me but my father as well. And so I grew up with a rich banker in Brussels, a man whose life my father had saved at Waterloo. I was educated as a gentleman, just as you were. And I had to wait, I had no choice. My father visited me for two weeks every month, taught me who and what I was, what I would become, what was destined for me. As to the banker, he was a kind man, and he never questioned me why I wasn't at home at King's Head. Whatever my father told him must have been very moving. My father told me over and over to be patient, that all would come to me one day. He kept my dream alive, stoked it with promises of the power he knew I would someday wield and I would someday take my rightful place, but not yet, no, not yet."

Cam said, "It isn't your rightful place, it is Graham's."

Simon flicked his gun at her. "What you believe no longer matters."

Graham said, "Finish your tale."

"Very well, half brother. It was only three months ago my father discovered you still lived, but you had absolutely no memory. But he and I both lived in fear you would recover your memory any day and all would be lost. He knew he had to act."

CHAPTER 72

"Both my father and I found it amazing that Ryder Sherbrooke saved you, that he went so far as to make you his ward. But then that ridiculous Vicar Piercebridge chanced to meet you and tell you who you were, and thus you were reunited with the earl.

"My father was afraid once you came to King's Head you would remember, and all would be lost. He sent for me immediately, but before we could act, you married. An heir would be soon to follow given the amount of time you two spend in bed. There was no choice, no more time.

"Believe me, I've chafed at the waiting, nearly a week now since my father's funeral, and I will be honest, I've been unsure how to proceed. And during that week I mourned for the death of my father, and my rage at you grew, but as I said, you're here, all unexpected, a sure sign my luck has changed. Now I can avenge my father, and carry out his plans for me. Everything will be as it should have been. Are you content now with all the answers?"

Graham studied his face, this half brother of his, a stranger's face. "Did you ever love me?"

Simon laughed. "I suppose I must have, initially, but after my father finally told me the truth, the future changed for me. I saw everything in a different light. I would be the important one, not you. I would be Viscount Whitestone. I knew I wanted it, deserved it. So long now I've wanted nothing more than to come home and take my rightful place."

"Did you mourn my death at all?"

"I don't remember, but if I did, it did not last long. Now, enough. I've answered all your questions." He looked at his watch. "It is time. Both of you come in here and sit your backs against the cave wall. Yes, you may continue to hold hands, I find it touching."

Cam said, "You weren't a small child and yet you wanted *to kill your own brother?* You're vile, you're insane."

Simon stared at her, a brow arched and she recognized that arch—it was Uncle Tally's. Without the beard, the resemblance would be unmistakable. Cam was scared to her soul, but she wasn't about to let this monster see any fear.

Even as the words dug into him, even as he accepted the truth of them, the treachery didn't dig deep. Graham felt no particular pain. This man was a stranger, insane, evil, as Cam had said. He said, his voice calm and cold, as if he were discussing the merits of a certain grade of steel for more reliable train tracks, "Tell me, brother, no, half brother—was it your father's plan when you returned to King's Head after my father's death to tell a hair-raising story how you and I were kidnapped, and I was killed and you were taken? Where? France? Italy? You were kept prisoner? But there was no ransom letter? Come, what was your heartrending tale to be?"

"My father never told me what he planned to tell everyone, but I'm certain it would have made as much sense as you being raised by Ryder Sherbrooke and having no memory." He paused, then yelled, "Damn you, all you had to do was die! Why didn't you just drown?"

"Well, I didn't. Listen to me, Simon, it's over. Your father is dead. My father, the earl, is very healthy and will remain so for many years to come. You should leave and return to your life in Brussels. You know my father would not believe any tale you would tell him if you killed us and returned here to claim my place."

Cam said, never looking away from Simon, "He does not intend for your father to be alive when he returns, Graham. He plans to murder your father."

Simon gave her a short bow. "Just so, sister-in-law."

"But why? You're rich, you're wedded. Why do you still want what is mine?"

Simon stared at Graham as if he were witless. "Why? You are so stupid, so simple, to ask me why? I should have been Vereker's heir! I deserve to be Earl St. Lucy. My father believed it with all his being. It is what he wanted for me. It is why he murdered for me. It is why he died for me. He gave me everything. I honor him. I will always honor him and I will take what he wanted me to have. What should have always been mine.

"I stayed with my father until you showed up again, brother. And I learned everything since he began going to the house for dinner every night. Everyone thought he was coming again because of you." He gave a sharp laugh. "Of course it wasn't the reason. It was to learn about you and your precious father's plans."

Keep calm, keep calm, and so Cam said, her voice mocking, "It didn't work out for you, did it, Simon?"

His gun hand jerked. "Shut up if you don't want me to shoot you in the face. Everything will now work out as it was supposed to. When your bodies are found, there will be no questions, no doubts. The two of you will drown. A terrible accident. You misjudged the tides since you have no memory of them. Not long now." He looked at his watch again. "Soon I must leave."

Graham said, "Wait. Are you telling me my mother took

your father as a lover, her husband's own brother? No, I will never believe that. Your father, my precious Uncle Tally, raped her and she birthed you, passed you off as the second son. Your father threatened her, didn't he? Threatened her if she told anyone? I know it's believed she committed suicide. But that's not what happened, is it? Your father murdered her when she was going to confess to my father."

"Shut up, you know nothing. My father loved her, loved me. They were lovers until he told me she didn't have the heart for the subterfuge. She was eaten up by guilt, ready to confess all to her husband, but she knew if she did, I would be cast out and Tally too, of course. When she couldn't bear it any longer, to save me, to save my father, she killed herself. She threw herself in the Green Stream. She couldn't swim.

"My father was devastated, the earl was devastated, all the multitude of people at King's Head were devastated. I was, I suppose, for a while. My father did not kill her."

Cam said, "Suicide? I do not believe that for an instant. Graham is right, poor Madeline was murdered by your precious father. He was a monster, after all, just as you are—his son. And he did it because Vereker would know Tally was your father, not him."

"You bitch—shut up! You know nothing. My mother was weak, her guilt destroyed her. She killed herself to protect us."

She shook her head at him. "What an unbelievable lie. However did you manage to bring yourself to believe it?"

"Damn you, shut your mouth." He was panting with rage. He raised the gun.

CHAPTER 73

He got ahold of himself, slowly lowered the gun. He studied them a moment, shrugged. "No, I will not let you make me lose my temper. Oh yes, whilst you two are dying, think of your father, dead soon as well. Such a terrible accident."

"And what tale will you tell about where you have been for the past ten years?"

"I'm considering that after we were kidnapped, you, my poor brother, were killed, and I was sold into servitude. I selected Macau, ruled by the Portuguese. I even taught myself Portuguese so no one would doubt what I told them. Then I managed to make my way home. Everyone will comfort me, welcome me home, at last. Of course I will have all I need to prove I'm the long-missing heir.

"But none of this concerns you for you and the bitch will be dead. Can you hear the tide coming in?

"Since you have no memory of this, brother, let me tell you what will happen to you two. The tide is vicious. It will fill both the chambers quickly and the two of you will drown. You cannot remain with your heads above water until the tide goes out again. It will drag your bodies with it. And that will be the end to both of you. I rather wish you could remember the time you and I were nearly caught by the incoming tide and nearly drowned, then you would understand better what will happen to you." He frowned. "You saved my life. You were a strong swimmer, but now it doesn't matter.

"Don't even think about swimming out of here. I will be outside on a stack of boulders the tide doesn't cover and I will shoot both of you dead and bury your bodies deep. Ah, the tide is already covering my boots."

Simon laughed, saluted them, and splashed through the water back to the first chamber. Cam and Graham heard the sound of the relentless waves coming closer.

"Graham." Her voice was a thread of sound but he heard it over the crashing water. The water was to their shins, rising fast. Cam knew they'd drown if they stayed, but to be shot—He smiled down at her, hugged her close, said in a low, deep voice, "It's all right, Cam. I know exactly what to do." He grabbed her hand and led her toward the back of the cave chamber.

Even as the relentless tide crashed into the second chamber, everything was perfectly clear in his mind. Everything from the lost years was now in its place, his rough and tumble childhood, his boy's innocence and excitement at everything life had to offer. He remembered his experiments with his father, remembered thrashing wheat with the tenant farmers. And he remembered the blow to his head. He saw Ryder's face above his.

Graham pulled her to a stop at the back of the second chamber. Cam didn't understand. There was a wall there, damp, but solid and piles of rocks and boulders stacked up haphazardly in front of it, as if a giant had pushed them in with the tide and thrown them against the back cave wall. It was a dead end. There was no place to go. They were trapped. She felt fear and panic. She didn't want them to drown, she—

But there was no panic in Graham's voice. "I know what to do. We will be all right, Cam. Now, stay right there and be ready to grab my hand."

She watched him numbly find handholds and footholds on the rocks, and he climbed. He knew what to do? But how was that possible? When Graham reached the top, his head was only inches from the cave ceiling. She watched him steady himself, watched him begin to pull rocks out of the wall and hurl them out into the roaring water. An opening gradually appeared. He called down to her, "Cam, start climbing, put your hands and feet exactly where I put mine."

She didn't question him now, whatever had happened, she knew they would survive. She tucked her skirts into her drawers and started up, the water splashing her legs, the tug of the water strong but she managed to grab the next rock up and pull herself up. The water was closer, closer, another couple of minutes and the cave would be filled. She slipped, knew she was going to fall, but Graham leaned down, grabbed her hand, then her wrist. "Find your footing again, yes, that's good. Come to me." She was right below him now. The water was tugging at her skirts. He said again, a blazing smile on his face, "Trust me." And she did. Even though she knew the rocks would grow even more slippery when the water covered them, she felt calm and it filled her. She felt hope.

She stopped right below him. He said, "I didn't tell Simon I'd found a way out of the cave, I don't know why, but I guess I wanted it to be my secret."

"You remember, don't you, Graham?"

She saw a flash of a grin. "Yes, I remember, I remember everything." Graham dug out one more rock, hurled it out into the water. "Now this is as big as I can make the opening. Beyond is another chamber, very small, but it gives onto a higher part of the beach that doesn't flood completely because the tide runs back downhill. It's a very short passage and we're going to pull ourselves through. Cam, it's narrow. As a boy I could make it through that hole, but now—Listen to me, Cam. If I can't make it, well—"

Her heart was jiggering in her chest, the water tugging at her skirts, cold, numbing, but her voice was calm, "Graham, both of us are going to make it out of here. You go through first. I will follow. No, be quiet, you're wasting time. The water is halfway up the rocks. Go!"

"No, Cam, you must—"

She looked him square in the face. "If you don't go, we will drown together."

CHAPTER 74

Graham knew that voice—Cam's heels were not only dug in, she was digging in knowing her life was on the line. He put his arms over his head and stuck them in the passage, felt the opening to the next cave chamber with his fingertips. Not more than two feet long. He had only to work his body through two feet, but it was narrow, too narrow. He was a man, not a boy. He felt her hands pushing at his feet, his legs, his hips, as hard as she could, but there was no purchase, he wouldn't get his shoulders through, it was no good—he had to squirm out and push her through, he had to—

"Graham, you can do it! Go!"

And then his fingers closed around roots, nice dug-in roots. He didn't remember any roots. He didn't doubt for a minute it was a miracle. He grasped them with his fingers and began to pull himself through. Cam's hands were shoving him harder as she felt him move. He didn't think he would make it, he couldn't get through, they'd both drown—but then he gave a final tug on the roots, felt them pull free—no, no, too soon. But then his hips and legs slid through. He fell three feet, landed on the damp sand and rolled. He yelled, "Cam, stick your arms through, give me your hands."

He pulled her through the passage. When she dropped, he caught her, held her close for a moment. Water was flowing through the passage now. She whispered against his neck, "You remembered. Thank God you remembered."

"When I believed we would drown I suddenly saw Simon's face, saw the fear, and I remember yelling at him to swim. We did, as hard as we ever had. It was some weeks later I came back and it was pure luck I discovered this small chamber beneath an overhang. The opening was small, but not as small as that damned passage. I saw the small opening at the back, up high, and realized it connected to the flooding chambers. I found I could dig out the rocks at the very top and squeeze through."

"Why did you put the rocks back to cover the opening?"

"I stacked them up again because the next time Simon and I came to the cave I wanted to scare him when the tide came roaring in and then I would pull the rocks away and we'd go through the passage. I'd save him." He laughed aloud, hugged her, kissed her hard. "Cam, I'm whole again. It's amazing. Everything is in place, there are no more unknowns. I am Graham Desborough Hepburn, Viscount Whitestone and I will be twenty-five in November. Let's not get any wetter. We have to find Simon. We have to stop his madness."

The cave chamber was small, the opening narrow but not as narrow as the passage. They crawled out onto a rock-strewn beach thankfully on an upslope so the incoming tide reached only to their knees but still, the tide was vicious, powerful, and they had to slog their way up the beach over piles of rocks to even higher ground, Graham pulling her because her skirts were wet and heavy. They skirted more rocks and boulders. When they were finally above the high tide line, Graham stopped, both of them panting. He held her close against him to catch their breath. "Look just a bit to the south. The slope isn't great, but it is enough. You can see the incoming tide is so powerful it covers most of the rocks. Only a few of the boulders are tall enough to escape being beneath the water at high tide. It's called the Devil's Fist. Look at the larger boulders pressed together, like fingers. There are many more boulders and piles of rocks on top of the cliff."

Cam was shivering, but said, her voice vicious, "I'm ready. Let's hurry."

"There's a path maybe twenty yards ahead, Simon had to go that way. We will stop him, Cam, we must. There's no choice."

But what will you do when you catch him, Graham? But she said nothing. His own brother—his half brother—but what did that matter when you were children together, played together, battled together, believed you were sons of Earl St. Lucy and yet his half brother had wanted him dead.

Three times he and Tally had tried to kill him. Had Tally taught Simon to hate and covet what his half brother had, and the boy had sold his soul to the devil? Was Simon innocent until Tally twisted him? Cam didn't know, she didn't think they'd ever know. She didn't care.

They climbed the cliff trail to the top. Boulders were strewn everywhere, some close to the cliff edge as Graham had said. Why here, she wondered, and how long ago had the earth vomited them up?

Some twenty yards distant they saw Simon preparing to mount a chestnut stallion tethered to one of the boulders. He saw them. He stared at them, disbelieving, then raised his gun and fired. The bullet struck a boulder three feet in front of them.

Graham jerked Cam down behind a large boulder. He said, "That was a mistake. He shot without thinking and we're too far away. He's got only one more bullet." Before Cam could stop him, Graham stood, shouted, "Four times you've failed to kill me, Simon. You're nothing but a puling coward, afraid to come fight me, aren't you?"

Simon shouted, "Damn you, how did you two escape? You should be dead, drowned!"

"I remember everything now, Simon. I remember being struck down. I remember being tied in the hold of a boat and wondering where you were, if you were dead, if our tutor was dead. I remember a man coming in and striking me on the head again and then he threw me into the Thames. I remember all of it, Simon, all of it."

Hundreds of years of bone-deep pride rang out in his voice. "You will not win, Simon. You will not have what is mine."

CHAPTER 75

Cam rose to stand beside him. "He's right, Simon. You and your bloody father failed. The statue in Ventnor didn't kill us, nor did the ceiling beam in the abbey. Graham's right, you're a coward and a failure."

"Shut up, you bitch!"

"Why? Look at you, just listen to you. You are pathetic. I've never seen a more contemptible man. *To want your own brother dead.* How despicable you are. You are evil walking."

Simon was cursing her, running toward them, heaving with rage, his gun straight out, screaming, "I'll kill you this time, brother, and then I'll throw your bitch of a bride off the cliff."

When he was no more than six feet from them, panting hard, beyond himself with rage, his arm raised, his gun trained on his brother, Graham aimed the rock he held and threw it as hard as he could. The rock struck Simon hard square in the chest. Simon stumbled, went down on his knees. Graham was on him. He smashed his fist in his face, knocking him to the side. He grabbed Simon's wrist, bending it to make him drop the gun.

But Simon managed to jerk up the gun and strike Graham's head, knocking him onto his back.

Cam yelled, picked up a rock and ran at him. She raised the rock to bring it down onto his head when he lurched sideways and knocked her away with his fist.

She rolled over to see the two men fighting, fists striking flesh, blood spurting, and their grunts and curses filled the air. They were evenly matched until Graham stumbled over one of the loose rocks.

Simon reared back and kicked him in the belly. Cam screamed as Graham went backward over the cliff to the beach fifty feet below. She was beside herself. She was screaming as she ran at Simon. She struck his face with her fists, kicked him. He tried to grab her but she was beyond herself, so enraged he couldn't prevent her fist hitting him again in the face so hard his head whipped to the side and blood spurted out of his nose. He grabbed a rope of wet hair just as she punched her fist as hard as she could in his chest. At the same time she brought up her knee and slammed him in the groin. He yelled, hunched over, and she shoved him with all her strength backward toward the cliff edge. She kicked him again, hard in his belly. Simon flailed the air as he lost his balance. He went over. She heard his screams. She was breathing hard, numb with rage, with pain so deep it was unspeakable. She couldn't make herself look down at the beach below. She knew she'd see Graham there, dead. Cam fell to her knees, hugged her arms around herself, rocked. An unearthly moan filled the air. She couldn't bear it, couldn't—

"Cam! I'm here, I'm here! Hurry!"

She heard his voice, but it couldn't be, couldn't—

"Cam!"

She crawled to the edge of the cliff, saw only Simon speared on the sharp point of a giant boulder. She leaned forward over the edge and she saw Graham, saw his arms tightly holding a rock that stuck out from the cliff. He was alive, alive, his brilliant blue eyes fastened on her face.

"Don't move!"

Cam looked around but didn't see anything. Then she knew what to do. She ripped off her skirt, her petticoats, and began frantically knotting them together, but the material was wet and she pulled and tugged, her fingers numb and cramping, but she was strong and her bone-deep fear made her stronger. Finally, finally, she managed to tie the second petticoat to the skirt. She ran to the cliff edge, lay on her stomach, and scooted as close to the edge as she could. She threw over the cloth rope, praying it would reach him, praying it would stay knotted. She yelled, "Graham, grab the end. I'm going to run behind a boulder to brace myself and pull you up."

He stretched up his arms and managed to grab the end of a petticoat and gave it a tug. It pulled taut. How could she be strong enough to pull him up? The rock loosened. It wouldn't hold him much longer.

Cam yelled, "Now! Pull yourself up!"

As he pushed off and grabbed the petticoat with both hands the rock pulled free, crashed and broke apart. It sounded like bullets striking the cliff as it fell down to the beach.

Graham pulled. The knots held. He didn't want to die. He thought of Cam, thought of their life together, only begun. He kept his feet moving upward against the limestone, and prayed. The material was wet so his hands didn't slip. He pulled and climbed, and prayed.

He heard her yell, "You're doing it. I've got you! Climb!"

How could she keep pulling him up? How long could her knots last?

"Hurry, Graham!" The strain was immense, but she had her legs around the largest boulder, the end of a petticoat wrapped around her fists. She held fast against the incredible strain, she had to, had to. The knots would hold, she prayed harder than she ever had in her life.

Time crawled. Her arms, shoulders were screaming with the strain, with the grinding pain, and she would swear the wretched boulder was beginning to move.

She leaned to the side and finally, finally, nearly a lifetime later, she saw Graham's hands, his arms, and finally, his head clear the top of the cliff. She heard him grunt as he pulled himself over the cliff edge and rolled away.

Graham collapsed on his back, breathing hard, disbelieving he was alive, disbelieving that he'd landed on that narrow out-jutting rock ledge as he'd fallen. He saw the blue sky, then Cam was on him, feeling his heart, her hands all over him, feeling, pressing, then she was leaning down and kissing him, stroking him, kissing him more, her breath catching, tears streaming down her face.

Graham looked up at his wife, saw she was stripped down to her chemise, her hair straggling in wet ropes around her dirty face. He'd never believed her more beautiful. Amazingly her glasses sat crookedly on her nose.

They'd survived. He had his memory back. His wife had saved his hide, and—he was coming to accept it all the way to his soul—they were alive, yet again they'd survived. To his own astonishment as he stared up at her beloved face, he began to laugh. Cam stared down at him, kissed him again. He stopped laughing, brought his arms around her, squeezed. "We're all right. I'm all right, you're all right. Thank you for saving me."

"I couldn't have borne it, Graham, if—" She stopped, swallowed. He kissed her, settled her on top of him, kissed her throat, her chin, her cold mouth. He swallowed because he suddenly saw his brother flailing in the air, screaming, as he fell to his death. He swallowed tears and the dreadful pain. Memories, so many memories of the two boys, always together except for their lessons, the laughter, the fights—no, he had to place both Tally and Simon in the past. He saw his brother's body, knew it was all a dreadful waste. Was it all Tally's fault? Or had Simon—Graham cut it off. Simon was dead. Tally was dead. He didn't know how she'd managed to push Simon off the cliff, but it could wait.

He and Cam were alive. Graham pulled her over to her side, hugged her close. What if he hadn't remembered? What if he hadn't managed to pull himself through the passage. What if . . . He stilled. No more questions, most of which would never have answers. It was over. They'd survived.

Her arms tightened around him.

EPILOGUE

Nine months later

The Carberry-Hepburn Manufacturing Building
Manchester, England

Graham held Cam's gloved hand as they stared from the second-floor railing down into the vast work area. The noise on the floor was loud with the whirring and grinding sounds of machinery. There were seventy-five workers, cotton in their ears and heavier material over the cotton, tied by a strip of bright red cotton under their chins, a stylish touch, Cam told him and grinned hugely.

It was Carberry-Hepburn's three-month anniversary. The business was growing so quickly there were already plans to reconfigure a second warehouse they'd purchased just down the road. Hiring and training had already started. So many ideas filled Graham's brain, but he was still trying to improve the fire-tube boilers because the consortiums that controlled the growing network of trains in England were fast coming around to changing from water tubes to fire in large part due to Graham's speaking to so many of them—fewer maintenance problems, no more possible explosions. He spoke to groups on making the fire-tube boilers even smaller, more compact, shown them plans. He spoke of using clean water to avoid clogs and hot spots. To the gentlemen's collective astonishment, Graham gave credit to his wife who'd developed a theorem, based on countless observations, that proved the efficiency and safety of spring water.

Graham felt Ryder's hand on his shoulder. He turned briefly to smile at the man who'd saved his life, loved him, housed him, given him so many brothers and sisters, educated him. He had been his father in those long years when he had no idea who or what he was. He was his second father, though he never said this to Vereker. Sometimes he felt his heart would burst with love for this man, for both men.

It was as if Ryder understood the smile, the myriad expressions on his face. He nodded, squeezed his shoulder again. He leaned close to say over the noise, "I am so proud of you, Graham. You are a son of my heart."

Graham's father stood beside Cam. There was such pride and pleasure on his face as he gazed around at the vast manufacturing floor. Graham saw him look briefly at Cam's swelling belly. His second grandchild would be born in four months. Eugenie had birthed a son some months earlier.

Cam felt near to bursting with pride with Graham's accomplishments, enough pride to make her ignore her aching back, for the most part. She wondered if Eliza had backaches now she was pregnant. Cousins, Cam thought, cousins would abound, hopefully. Her backache disappeared when she saw her father, finally, climbing the stairs, a huge smile on his face. Doubtless his train had been late, something, alas, that happened all too often. She had thoughts about how to fix that.

Graham smiled down at his wife as she waved to her father. He leaned down, kissed her ear, prayed she and their son or daughter would be healthy. He knew well life was so very fragile, so fraught with unknown perils, not to mention simple ill fortune. You could only forge ahead into the future and hope for more sweetness than pain in the years you were given.

For now, in this moment, it was a very fine day.